THORNS OF LUST

To my daughters, husband, family, friends and my readers.

Please skip over the sex scenes and focus on the plot. You DA best!
Love ya!
To everyone else, thank you for reading my stories.

THORNS OF OMERTÀ SERIES

Each book in the Thorns of Omertà series can be read alone with the exception of Thorns of Lust and Thorns of Love, which is the story of Tatiana Nikolaev.

If you'd like the preview of the next standalone book in this series, Thorns of Death, keep reading after this duet ending.

EVA WINNERS

EVERLASTING ROMANCE FOR EVERY CENTURY

THORNS OF OMERTÀ PLAYLIST

https://spoti.fi/3mp6fBl

AUTHOR NOTE

Hello readers,

Thorns of Lust is the first book of a duet and is NOT a standalone. Tatiana Nikolaev's story completes in *Thorns of Love*.

Furthermore, please note that this book has some dark elements to it and disturbing scenes. Please proceed with caution. It is not for the faint of heart.

Don't forget to sign up to Eva Winners' Newsletter (www.evawinners.com) for news about future releases.

BLURB

My husband.

His secrets.

Our tragedy.

I thought I knew him. I didn't. I thought he was trustworthy. He wasn't.

But nothing in this world is as it seems.

I caught the attention of the most notorious man in the underworld.

Konstantin wasn't the type to be ignored. He commanded his criminal empire with an iron fist but he had secrets of his own.

But I was Tatiana Nikolaev. I'd never bend to a man's will or be used as a pawn. Not again.

The moment I tempted the fates and played with fire, life spiraled out of control.

My only way of survival was to trust again.

But could I?

PROLOGUE

TATIANA

Death smashed into the back of Adrian's slick Maserati, demanding our lives. My body jerked forward and the seat belt cut into my chest. My heart jumped, racing as fast as my husband's driving.

"What's going on?" I whimpered frantically as I glanced over my shoulder. The headlights of a black SUV filled the rear window. *Smash*.

My body jerked forward again. "Adrian!" I screamed. "Gun, get a gun."

He acted as if he hadn't heard me, just kept speeding down the dark road. My eyes darted to my husband as my ears buzzed with fear. Adrian looked scared. Terrified even. This wasn't good.

Not. At. All.

"Head back to New Orleans," I yelled. We were way outside the city limits, headed for Adrian's place. Dark roads highlighted only by the light of the moon. We hadn't seen a house or another car for miles.

"Head down," he barked. I obeyed at once, as I struggled against the seat belt.

If Adrian was worried, there was something terribly wrong.

"Adrian," I screeched, fear seeping into my bones. "Turn around.

and get us into the city. We'll be safer around others. My brothers have men everywhere."

He didn't react, just kept driving forward.

It was the only time I wished we had my brother's bodyguards with us. I hated them lingering behind me, always tailing me and reporting to my brother. Vasili had men following me before I was married, and he had bodyguards after Isabella and their kids at all times. Alexei did the same with his wife, Aurora.

They didn't mind it, but they didn't grow up suffocated by bodyguards that reported everything to your brothers. Even how many times I fucking went to the bathroom. It was annoying as fuck. Except now, I really wished they were here.

The bullets began flying, shots echoing around the car as they whizzed past us. A loud pop shattered the back windshield and shards of glass rained down on us.

A scream tore through the air. Mine. But I could barely hear it over the buzzing in my ears and adrenaline pumping through my veins. I clutched the seat, glass shimmering like diamonds over my red Valentino dress.

The tires screeched as more gunshots whistled through the air.

Bang. Bang. Bang.

Adrian was shooting, but from the sounds of it, he wasn't hitting anything because more bullets rained on us. More windows exploded. Pain erupted in my forearm and warm liquid trickled down my skin.

And amongst all that violence, the oddest thought crossed my mind. I shouldn't have worn a sleeveless dress. I could have protected my skin.

The throbbing pain pulsed through my body. Fear gripped my throat.

A sharp turn and my body slammed against the door.

"Fuck," Adrian snarled.

There was a moment of calm before the car began spinning wildly out of control. I wrapped my arms around myself as if to offer some sort of protection. My body jerked forward, then back. The air rushed out of me with each loud thud, pain slicing through me. I couldn't breathe. My heartbeat slowed. The echoing sound of metal screeching, folding in on itself as the car rolled. Once. Twice. Three times.

Our eyes connected for a fraction of a moment. The terror reflected on his beautiful face that usually had women swooning. The look in his eyes held secrets. Regret.

He'd started to mouth, *"Tatiana, I'm—"*

His lips moved. He said something else. I couldn't hear it.

Smash.

My head slammed into something hard and the world turned black.

Drip. Drip. Drip.

Screeching tires. Distorted voices. Throbbing headache.

"Kill him." A firm order. A deep voice void of emotions

I blinked. *What? Who?*

My brain was enveloped in a fog. My ears still rang. My pulse raced. My lungs squeezed, and I desperately tried to inhale a lungful of air. I blinked to get rid of the dots swimming in my vision.

I turned to the driver's side. Empty. As if I couldn't trust my vision in the eerie yellow glow from the headlights, dark, my hand reached out. Nothing. Just air. Adrian wasn't there. The silence lingered in the surrounding wooded and swampy area, even the crickets ceased their noise. As if they held their breaths in anticipation of what was to come.

The sizzling sound of liquid against the hot metal sounded from somewhere - too close or too far, I couldn't distinguish. The pungent scent of gasoline and oil seeped into my lungs, suffocating me. A warm liquid trickled down my temple. Slowly, I brought my fingers to it. Blood. My hair was wet and sticky, plastered against my forehead.

"They both have to die," the same voice commanded. The gruff sound of grunts and foreign words filled the air.

My heart stopped beating and panic slowly overwhelmed all my other senses. I had to get out of here. Whoever was after us wasn't our friend. Where was Adrian?

More screeching tires. Loud voices. Foreign language. I struggled to process. Was it Italian? French? My brain was too slow, the buzzing vibrating through it too loud and overwhelming.

All I knew was that I had to get away.

I jerked against the seat belt. Unsuccessfully. The unbearable scent of gas drifted into my nose, and smoke filled the small space. My eyes burned. Although it wasn't just the smoke. Tears stung the back of my lids.

"Wrong time," I whispered.

Sasha, the brother I was closest to, always said it was the wrong time to cry. I was almost twenty-seven and had yet to learn when it was a good time to cry.

My trembling fingers frantically jerked on the seat belt.

"Please, please, please." My voice was a soft whisper.

If I could get my phone, my brothers would come to our rescue. They always came to the rescue.

Where was Adrian? What if he was dead already? Who was out there?

The ache in my bones pulsed harder.

My fingers finally found the button and pressed it. The seat belt came undone, hitting the door with a loud bang. It sounded like a gong going off and instantly everyone stilled outside.

The popping of bullets being fired broke the silence.

Instinctively, I ducked down, although I was already crammed down, before placing both hands over my ears to block out the loud noises. It reminded me of the crescendo of a bad opera piece. The pitch became louder and harsher, piercing my brain. It felt like they went on for hours, when in fact it was just a few seconds.

It stopped. A deafening silence. I should be relieved, but it felt even more ominous than the sound of gunshots.

My heart squeezed in my throat, the pulse choking me slowly.

More voices speaking in a foreign language. Unrecognizable words. The voices were high-pitched, angry, and not holding back. Until I recognized one word.

"Moya." Mine. *Russian.*

At least one of those men was Russian. Did my brothers come already?

More words. It was hard to hear them over the buzzing in my ears, but I recognized it. I was certain it was Italian. *Russian and Italian.*

More bullets. More screeching tires. Until it suddenly stopped. It would have been one second or one hour, I couldn't distinguish.

"She dies. No loose ends," one of them demanded in English, and instinctively I shrank further back into the car, although it was burning, coming dangerously close to an explosion.

"No." A cold voice. A hard tone. But it wasn't Adrian's. Was he even alive?

My nails dug into my palms, squeezing so hard that pain exploded on my skin. More commotion. More words. I couldn't process a single word because my brain was still stuck on 'she dies' and terrified they meant me.

"Are you sure?" The deep masculine voice filled the air along with the sound of crunching glass. A pair of expensive, leather Italian shoes filled my vision.

I had to be in shock. Because I registered the brand. Santoni's men's shoes. My husband was in danger, and I stared at a pair of five grand Italian shoes.

"The woman doesn't know anything." The voice sounded vaguely familiar. I couldn't place it. "I'll take full responsibility for her."

"If I find out she had anything to do with her husband's games, I'm coming for her." A light Italian accent. Deep voice.

"She knows nothing. If she does, I'll handle it." Another pair of expensive shoes. Art. 504 shoes. Even more expensive. Dark suit pants. Perfectly fit in length. Expensive material.

I shook my head. I needed to get out of here, not identify their wardrobe.

Another pair of expensive shoes entered my vision. A pair of Prada shoes. *Adrian wore Prada shoes.*

Was that him? I should have called out to him, but instead I stayed frozen in my spot. Staring at the Prada shoes like the ones I'd bought my husband.

"D'accordo." Definitely Italian. What the fuck did that mean? "Don't make me regret it."

Bile rose in my throat and I inhaled deeply to stop myself from retching. One of the men left, a pair of expensive Italian leather. Two remained. My heart raced. My vision swam. My ears buzzed. My lungs burned as I waited.

Bu-bum. Bu-bum. Bu-bum.

Bang.

The last bullet. It felt like the final bullet before it was my turn.

A body hit the dirt with a loud thud. My eyes pulled from the shoes outside my window to the other side of the car. Adrian's dead eyes met mine. An expression I couldn't identify was still etched on his face. The last expression before he died. Staring back at me. A single bullet hole in his chest, blood seeping out.

A gasp left me, and my heart stopped beating.

"A-A-Adrian," I choked out, my voice broken. He didn't move. His stare blank, fixed on something I couldn't reach. His face bruised and bloodied, whether from the impact of the car crash or someone's fists, I couldn't tell.

With each heartbeat my life slowly faded, following him. Until something inside me snapped.

"Nooo!" I shrieked and my world as I'd known it ceased to exist.

ONE
TATIANA

Beep. Beep. Beep.

A steady beeping. The nauseous scent of disinfectant all around.

Blood. Bleach. Sterile coldness.

Adrian's scent cocooned me, citrus and sandalwood, but there was a spice in it too. Maybe it was just the hospital.

There were sounds of hushed voices.

"You better heal her if you want to live." The voice was hard. Cold. Russian accent. It wasn't my brother's voice. But who?

"Sir, we'll do our best."

"You will do everything," he roared. "Not your best."

More commotion. The sounds of a struggle and shouting. More voices.

Was Adrian here? Instantly images of his dead eyes flooded my brain. Blood trickled down the corner of the mouth I used to kiss. The taste of copper flooded my mouth.

Clammy, cold skin under my fingertips. The cold kiss of death.

"Breathe." A scream. Mine. Maybe? I wasn't sure. My mouth on Adrian's.

One. Two. Three. Air into his lungs. One. Two. Three.

7

An explosion. Loud. The earth shook.

Everything was fuzzy. My chest squeezed, a sob choking my throat. Yet, nothing came out.

But I heard the screams piercing my brain. I heard the cries. I tasted the blood.

I felt the loss.

No, Adrian wasn't here. He was gone. I knew it deep down in my soul. In my heart. And it fucking hurt like hell. It felt like a bullet lodged itself in my lungs and refused to ease up. It hurt to breathe. An ache swelling inside of me, until it drowned me.

"I'll find you again," I murmured.

Or maybe my brain whispered the words. I wasn't sure. I couldn't feel my mouth move. Every single inch of me was numb.

"She's awake." The same deep voice shouted. A pair of hands gripped my shoulders. "Tatiana, look at me." I followed the voice but my eyes couldn't focus. My head ached. Even my brain hurt. "Look at me, *moya luna.*"

Moya luna. I'd heard that before. The words were buried deep in the fog. Why can't I get my brain to work?

I turned my head in the direction of the voice. There was nobody there. I blinked, then blinked again. The light was too bright. I couldn't see anyone.

"A bad dream," I said as a sob erupted from my lips. I couldn't hear it, nor the words. But I felt them. In the marrow of my bones, right along with a fear that whispered of nightmares.

I licked my lips and tasted blood.

Eyes without any light in them stared at me. My husband's eyes. *He's gone*, the nightmare whispered. It sent a soul-shattering ache through every inch of me. I couldn't handle it. I needed more numbness.

More words shouted. I couldn't hear nor understand them. I was too far inside my head where despair consumed me. Adrian's dead eyes. Blood covering the lips that used to kiss me.

The lips that used to say kind words to me. The same lips that used to put bullies in their place. The same lips that called me 'pipsqueak' when I was a little girl.

"Adrian!" I screamed, my heart shattering, a nightmare consuming me.

My body started to shake. My teeth chattered. My soul split. The sound of glass breaking and metal clanking against the floor. Hands on me.

Then a prick in my flesh and the world ceased to exist again.

TWO
KONSTANTIN

Y*ou have to prepare for the worst.*
I couldn't process those words. I refused to accept them. I had lost my shit on the doctors more than once over the last twenty-four hours. I had paid them all off, but it was only a matter of time before her brothers learned of this accident.

Doctors here understood the risks if they slipped my name to them. I wouldn't hesitate to use their families to make them pay. And my wrath wasn't a nice thing to bear. But that wouldn't be necessary because they knew to keep this secret for me.

Now, they just had to save Tatiana and all would be well with the world.

Her forehead needed stitches, as well as her shoulder and forearm, but fortunately she didn't have any internal injuries. She endured a head injury that might have caused some brain damage. But she has been in and out of consciousness, and until she was fully conscious, the extent of the damage couldn't be determined.

The accident happened yesterday.

Twenty-four hours of anguish. A whole day of pacing the length of this hospital room over and over again. A whole day of watching her face, praying for the first time in my fucked up life. I couldn't endure not having her in my life, but the knowledge of her not walking this Earth would fucking end me.

Without her, there was nothing.

A sardonic breath left me. How fucking ironic? She didn't even know I existed, yet she was the reason for my being. And somehow, I had almost ended up in the same place as my father.

I sat down in the same chair I had occupied and took her cold hand into mine.

"I should have taken you all those years ago." My thumb glided over her faint blue veins. "It was you all along. Didn't you recognize that?"

Fury at Adrian mounted and heightened. He put her in this position. He started to fuck with the Omertà. Instead of being thankful I stopped my father from ending his life, he came back to fuck with us all.

Motherfucker.

That was the reason second chances weren't worth giving. Adrian was smart, too smart. And he hid behind the Nikolaev family. It was the reason it took us so long to figure out who kept hacking our system, copying our data, and then taunting us with the sins we'd committed.

Nobody in the underworld was innocent.

Some of us were worse than the others. Nonetheless, that chip could put all of us behind bars and get us executed. It would expose our world, but not only the Thorns of Omertà's world, but also all of the others. Kingpins. Billionaire Kings. Cosa Nostra. Cartels. Yakuza.

It was the Yakuza who grew the most impatient. It was the Yakuza who attacked them first tonight. Marchetti got a tip from Dante Leone that they'd attack in their attempt to snatch the chip from Adrian. The moment I learned about it from Bitter Prince, I came swiftly. Except, it was almost too late for Tatiana.

The door to the hospital room slid open and Nikita's heavy foot-steps echoed on the floor. I was surprised he insisted on staying. He hated hospitals with a passion. I figured he felt bad for the woman. It was the first time he witnessed a woman almost dying.

Boris had witnessed it once before - that night my father executed my mother. He came from the slums of Russia. No parents. No connections. No relatives. It was the reason my father pulled him into his world. Men like him made the best recruits. But it didn't take long for Boris to switch alliances from my father to me. I suspected it had something to do with Papa's cold blooded execution of my mother.

Nikita joined us much later, but he proved his loyalty many times over.

"How is she?" Nikita asked.

"No change."

"Her brothers learned of the accident and Adrian's death." Fuck, I had hoped for another day. Just until she was out of the woods. I needed to see her blue eyes one more time before I let her recover on her own. "Isabella Nikolaev has connections with medical staff everywhere due to her profession."

"Did the doctors talk?" I hissed, my breathing harsh.

"No. But they're on their way here. They've checked every other hospital in the area already."

I released a long breath, wishing things were different. But wishing was for fools. I had to act. "How much time do we have?"

"An hour."

I nodded, dismissing him without a word.

Tatiana's eyes opened and she blinked a few times.

Relief slammed into me, and I thought my eyes were burning. They better not be fucking tears. I brought my hand to her cheek and stroked it softly.

"You're going to be okay," I rasped, emotions thick in my voice. "Because our story has barely begun."

THREE
TATIANA

"Y**ou're** going to be okay." A deep, raspy voice spoke to me. The drug induced haze began to wane, and I could make out a pair of dark eyes watching me. "Because our story has barely begun."

Then his footsteps echoed in the room, taking him away from me.

Beep. Beep. Beep.

The hospital machines were too loud. The room was too cold. Too dark. The scent of disinfectant filled my lungs. A buzzing in my ears.

Yet, the only thing I could concentrate on was *him*. I could feel him. Lingering in the shadows. Watching me.

Shifting my head to the side, I zeroed in on the double glass doors on the other side of the hospital room. Lights sparked through the glass, a clear outline of a figure standing there. It had to be a man. A tall man.

"Adrian?" I croaked, my head dizzy from that small movement.

I should be afraid. Yet, I felt safe. Maybe there were still too many drugs in my bloodstream. The door opened, barely a foot. The shadow stepped through it. I couldn't see his face, the light behind him casting a shadow.

But it had to be him. The scent of citrus and sandalwood drifted over the antiseptic of the hospital. Goosebumps broke over my skin.

"Adrian?"

No answer. Only the beeping of the machine. But he was there. In the flesh. I couldn't get to him, but I could see him. He *was* there. Fog drifted around him. The buzzing of the machine was a constant noise. My hand reached for him, but he was too far away and my hand was too heavy. It refused to move, lying limp on the cold hospital sheets.

I blinked, my eyes burning and desperate to hold onto him.

"P-please." My voice cracked, bleeding with the truth I wasn't willing to admit. That maybe, just maybe, this man was a figment of my imagination. "Don't go."

Tears blurred my vision further. I could taste salt on my lips. It stung. It ached.

The man's jaw tightened. His eyes were like two deep black pools, yet tears continued to distort my vision. I couldn't see his face clearly.

I reached out for him again, using all my strength to keep my hand in the air. He moved closer to me. My strength was failing me. A soft string of Russian curses.

"We have to go," someone said.

He was close, so close that I could smell him. I opened my mouth to speak, but the increased buzzing of the machines drowned out my words.

"Go to sleep, Tatiana." The voice. I knew it, but then I didn't. Maybe my eardrums were damaged. He turned his back on me, those broad shoulders swallowing the doorframe.

"Please don't go! Don't leave me!" I screamed out at the gaping loss that swallowed me whole. "I love you!" Like a deep dark corner full of shadows, the nightmare threatened to swallow me whole. The unbearable pressure in my chest.

He paused. He didn't turn around. Gut-wrenching cries left my lips as tears flooded my cheeks. And all the while my heart bled all over the white crisp sheets of the hospital bed.

"I'll be back, moya luna." It sounded like a promise. "I'll be back when you're ready for me."

Then darkness pulled me under once again.

FOUR
TATIANA

There was a time before you.
    There was time with you.
    Now there's time after you.

I never counted on after you, I'd never be ready to deal with the time after you.

"There shouldn't have been an after you," I whispered as I stared at my reflection in the mirror. Two weeks without him seemed like an eternity. My fingers trembled as I reached for my phone sitting on a little nightstand.

I never got to say goodbye. I never got to say goodbye. I never got to say goodbye.

The words played on repeat. My heart thundered against my chest in a painful beat. I stared at my phone, the time staring back at me. Time was so important before. Now, it meant nothing. There was too much of it.

I set my phone down on the table, but my eyes never left it. I wanted to say goodbye. I needed to hear his voice. Just one more time. I picked up the phone again and I dialed his number. My fingers slowly traced the keyboard of my phone, pushing the digits that represented my husband's number.

His name appeared on the screen with the picture of our first event at The Den of Sin together. I must have lost my mind because I completely forgot I could have just pulled up Adrian's name to dial him.

The call went through and I held my breath at the first ring. Then second. On the third, he picked up.

"This is Adrian. I'm not around. Leave a message, and I'll call you back."

The same voice. The same light notes to his speech. *His voicemail doesn't know he's dead*, I thought with a strangled sob. If I started crying now, I'd break down. I had to keep it together.

No time to cry, my brothers' motto.

The voicemail ended. And like a glutton for punishment, I dialed his number again. I listened to the voicemail again and again. Each time I held my breath as the line rang, expecting Adrian to pick it up. Against all odds, I hoped he'd pick up the phone.

I didn't know how many times I'd listened to his voicemail when I finally put the phone down.

The psychologist at the hospital told me there were five stages of grief. I was still in denial. My brain couldn't process my husband's death. Numbness and pain was all I felt. But not even physical pain compared to the pain I felt deep inside my chest. A pain that made it hurt to breathe.

I stared at my reflection. My body seemed to be in better shape than my heart.

My forearm had a slash down it. My shoulder was slowly but surely healing. My cheek had a gash on it. My left eye was bruised purple. My clothes hid bruises and cuts all over my body.

Two weeks. A car accident. A life forever altered.

My brothers dug for information to figure out what exactly happened that day. They hacked into city surveillance but found nothing. They questioned the hospital staff to find out who brought me in. Who saved me? Yet, they kept running into roadblocks.

They learned nothing. Only that Adrian died in the explosion.

There was nothing left of him. An explosion. His body burned to ashes. Along with my life. My memories. How did I survive? I remembered the SUV smashing into the back of Adrian's car. I remembered our car flying through the air. Rolling. Rolling. Rolling.

Screams and pain. Then blank. Nothing. Just darkness.

Except for the nightmares that came when I slept, which wasn't very often. I hated the nightmares.

I swallowed the lump in my throat. *Focus on the good.* That was what the therapist said. *Focus on the good.* I survived. Maybe, just maybe, I could have what I'd been begging for. A baby of my own.

My trembling hand hovered over my flat belly. Maybe God would grant me this small mercy and not leave me alone. My period was late. A whole week late.

I was never late. It had to be it. I was pregnant; I was sure of it.

The timing was bad. But the blessing would be welcomed. Something of Adrian's to keep under my heart and with me. I'd love it enough for both of us. Our baby would want for nothing. A tremor rolled through me and pain squeezed my throat.

I swallowed a shuddering breath, trying to keep my shit together.

"Please," I whispered to the empty room. To my reflection. To anyone who was listening. "Just don't leave me alone."

My voice cracked, the empty penthouse daunting. Every little sound echoed through it. When Adrian was here, there was always noise around, even when he wasn't around. His gadgets and computers beeping. Now, it was nothing. Just deadly silence, echoing the death in my soul.

I wiped a stray tear from my cheek. If I started crying, it'd be hard to stop. *No time for tears*, Vasili's voice whispered when I was a little girl. *You're a Nikolaev.*

Was I? I'd taken Adrian's last name, so maybe that no longer counted.

The year-end approached and promised loneliness. Tears. Dull pain somewhere deep down where I didn't dare to go. The lump in my throat grew, bigger and bigger, until my airway clogged. The back of my eyes burned. My nose reddened. An ache swelled in my lungs until it suffocated.

I felt alone. I was alone.

The pain was fresh but something deep down inside me dulled. The sharp, stabbing agony in my chest became a constant companion.

A baby would ease it, I thought desperately. Surely if there was a God, he'd grant me that.

For the first time ever, I prayed. I closed my eyes and prayed. For a baby. For inner peace. For the pain to go away. And all the while hot tears pricked at my eyes.

"Tatiana." My brother's voice drifted through the air and my eyes snapped open to meet his eyes in the mirror. The coldest eyes. The most broken eyes. Until recently.

Alexei.

The most fractured one of us. Although his wife mended his wounds. He even cracked a smile occasionally. If he could heal, then so could I.

Right? Then why did I feel so hopeless?

"Are you ready?"

I raised a brow, my lips curving into a bitter smile. "Am I ready to bury my husband's non-existent body?" My lungs felt tight. My voice sounded acidic. I resented his happiness. I resented Vasili's happiness. I fucking resented everyone. "Sure, I was born ready for it. I am a Niko-laev after all."

I should have known in our world something always got fucked up. Someone always died. Father died. Alexei's life was hell because of my mother. Revenge was an ongoing theme in this life - mafia or not. Someone got to Adrian. It was the reason for the car chase. It had to be.

The question was why?

"You hate the world right now." Alexei's voice pulled me away from the fog of unknowns.

"I don't—" I cut myself off. There was no sense denying it. I did hate the world. I hated that I couldn't remember much from that night, leaving me with a million questions. I hated that the last words from Adrian that I remember were said in anger.

A bitter laugh slipped through my lips, sounding almost hysterical. My future died that night.

Alexei's gaze, pale blue like mine, was heavy and dark, pinning me to the spot as my heart shuddered.

"He wasn't as good for you as we hoped," he said in a cold voice, sending a shock wave through me. "Not anymore."

Our gazes met. My brows furrowed. Why would he say that?

Shadows in his eyes danced and threatened. He held my stare, as if he waited. Waited for what though?

"Alexei, you know something." It wasn't a question. My voice shook worse than my hands. The oxygen failed to make its way into my lungs. My blood started buzzing in my ears. Emotions circled like a tornado, threatening and dark. One wrong move and it'd swallow me whole. "Tell me," I rasped.

His jaw ticked and his gaze dropped to the ground. As if he was hiding something.

I opened my mouth, but before I could question him, Vasili and Sasha walked in.

"You ready?" Vasili asked and it took all of my self-restraint not to snap at him.

Instead, I closed my eyes and prayed.

My sunglasses hid most of my face. My black dress fluttered with the breeze.

Red roses covered the black shiny casket. An empty casket. There was nothing left of Adrian to bury. Another bouquet of red roses was thrown on the casket. The color was stark against the shiny black, reminding me of blood.

Blood spilled. Blood wasted.

I stared at the date carved into the fancy niche plaque.

The date of his death. It'd soon be turned into just another crypt. It'd be a cold stone, just like his memories.

The sky darkened and the large clouds moved, hovering above me. The first raindrop was only an opening. Another followed, then another, until it became a constant pitter-patter. People slowly dispersed, running for cover. Absent-mindedly, I noticed Vasili opening an umbrella to shelter his wife and children.

Sasha opened his umbrella and took two steps towards me, sheltering me from the rain. The pitter-patter became louder. Puddles began forming fast around me, and I watched the water surround me. Dampness seeped through my dress and into my bones.

Drowning.

This felt like drowning amongst the living.

Fourteen days since the accident. My brothers had questions too, and I had no answers for them. No idea how I got there. No idea how I survived the explosion that left no trace of him. It left me with nothing - no memory, no clues. Nothing.

Nothing felt real anymore.

Not the casket. Not the thorned roses wrapped around it. Not the people who stood surrounding the gravesite.

"We should go," Sasha murmured. The rites were read, the final blessings given, final goodbyes said. From all except me. I stood still, staring at the eternal resting place covered in flowers. "You need to rest."

Except, nightmares and voices came when I slept. Whispers. Ghosts.

I swallowed, watching the coffin disappear into the tomb until I could no longer see it. My hands shook. My temples throbbed. But it was nothing compared to the clenching of my heart. The suffocating pain, dragging me deeper and deeper into a dark abyss.

The lump in my throat grew bigger until it was impossible to breathe. Until I felt nothing. Just a numbness, which spread through my veins. The silence grew heavy, but I accepted it. It was better than those whispers I heard in my dreams. Tormenting me.

The cool breeze swept through the graveyard, soaking the rain into my dress, which clung to my legs. I felt like I was suffocating. There wasn't enough space. There wasn't enough oxygen.

There wasn't enough room for the living and the dead.

A shuddering breath left me as fear rolled down my spine. I had never been scared, knowing my brothers would always be there to save me. But now I feared these demons were unbeatable. And the secrets Adrian left behind were punishable.

"Tatiana, let's go," Sasha repeated. Another shuddering breath filled my lungs.

Black suits slowly drifted away, taking their black hearts with them. The sea of underworld men came to pay respects. Russian. Italian. American. Canadian. Colombian. A sea of black, which I'd always been a part of. No matter how much my brothers sheltered me.

My eyes flickered to my brother, seeing him through the fog of grief. It felt like I wasn't really here. But then I was.

"We have to go home, Sister," Sasha said softly. I didn't want to go back home. I didn't want to be alone. Yet, I felt so fucking alone no matter where I was or who I was with. Except for the damn ghosts haunting me. They were in my mind, thriving. Torturing me. And when I slept, my mind revolted. I couldn't understand my dreams… memories… or paranoia. "You'll stay with me."

I shook my head wordlessly. I couldn't let anyone hear my dreams. I couldn't let anyone know.

My mind immediately revolted, remembering last night's dream.

I smiled so much that my cheeks ached. But it was a good feeling.

"Look, Adrian. Our baby," I beamed, glancing up from the hospital bed to find my husband's eyes. Except, displeasure stared back at me. Instinctively, I shifted my body, shielding the baby.

"Adrian?" I asked, hesitantly. "What's the matter?"

"I told you," he hissed as he took a step forward. Then another. And a dark, looming shadow clouded over me, stealing my happiness. "I told you, Tatiana. No children."

"But it's a blessing," I rasped, my voice hoarse with emotions.

"No, it's a curse," he bellowed. "A poisonous thorn."

23

His face twisted. I didn't recognize him. His hand wrapped around my throat, squeezing. Harder and harsher. My lungs seized.

"P-P-Please." My body shook. I held my baby, but I could feel my strength leaving me. I didn't want to drop my newborn miracle. Shoving my elbow against my husband's ribs, I fought. I was a Nikolaev. We fight. We never give up.

Then Adrian's big hand wrapped around my baby's throat and terror, unlike any I'd ever felt before, shot through me.

But before he could take one squeeze.

Bang.

Dead eyes.

"Tatiana."

I startled, jumping in my spot. My body shook. My ears buzzed. Adrenaline swam through my veins, as if the nightmare was real. My oldest brother's hands came to my shoulders and squeezed as if he tried to pass me some of his own strength. It wasn't enough.

My mind was tormenting me. Maybe I was crazy like our mother.

"You have to say goodbye, Sestra." Vasili's voice came from behind me. It had been only two weeks. How did one say goodbye in two weeks? I needed more time. I needed answers.

"Tell us what you need." Sasha attempted a different tactic. I didn't bother turning around to see them. I was scared they'd see something in my eyes that would reveal my demons. "Whatever you need, it's yours."

I didn't answer. Instead, I let the pain and doubts fester inside me. The ache burned through my veins, leaving me empty and confused. And I was certain it had something to do with the accident.

Except, I couldn't fucking remember.

So I remained, standing in my spot.

"I'll be right there," I choked out. "Just wait for me in the car."

They shared a fleeting glance, then Vasili nodded and they left me. Their footsteps faded with each step they took against the century old stone of the St. Louis Cemetery, leaving me alone with the ghosts and the dead.

With *him.*

I stared at the word *husband* and *friend* for the longest time, searching for something. Something pricked my mind, but it refused to come forward.

My skin prickled. My gaze caught a movement to my side. A tall figure stood by a car, hands in his pockets and his gaze on me. It touched my skin and a shudder rolled down my spine.

My brows furrowed and I winced from pain. There was a familiarity about him. I'd seen him before. I was certain of it, but I couldn't remember where.

Who is he? I thought as I brought my hand to my cheek and gently massaged the fading bruise. His eyes followed my movement and darkened as a muscle ticked under his stubbled jaw.

Who was this man? He seemed familiar. Important.

Now I wished my brothers had remained behind so I could ask them. The man was tall. Taller than most men, including my brothers. Dressed in all black and a gray coat that reached to his knees. He looked elegant. Dark. Dangerous. *Familiar.*

The feeling of familiarity pulled on my consciousness.

The voice in my head. *Stay alive, Tatiana. For me. Stay alive, moya luna.*

It called to me - calling me his moon. His eyes were intense, even from this distance. There was something uncomfortable in his dark gaze - borderline aching. It was as if he demanded something from me, but I didn't know what.

A feeling I couldn't shake off consumed me. Except, I couldn't quite pinpoint it.

Moya luna. Russian. The voice was speaking Russian. Could it have been Adrian? Except, he hadn't called me that since that night in the gazebo. It was always pipsqueak and I had outgrown that nickname.

The intense stranger watched me, his thick brows drawing over his eyes and something about him kept dragging me into his savage darkness. His dark eyes reminded me of the harshness of Russian winters - merciless and bone chillingly cold.

I swallowed, then glanced around me. Everyone was gone. Just the stranger and I remained.

With a shake of my head, I returned my eyes to the crypt.

"Goodbye, Adrian," I muttered softly, then rushed in my brothers' direction. The stranger's eyes remained on me like a thorn in my skin.

Strangely enough, it was almost a pleasurable pain.

Maybe I had turned masochistic and sought pain to torture myself.

FIVE
KONSTANTIN

The smell of roses drifted through the air. For me, it represented the stench of death. I had hated them for most of my life. They reminded me of my mother. The mother who betrayed her vow and had been executed in front of my eyes. It was the first death I witnessed, but certainly not the last.

The last image I had of her was her casket covered in thorns and roses as she was lowered into the ground.

It all started that night my mother died. That fateful night that changed the course of our lives. Even Tatiana's, who hadn't even been born yet.

Somebody shook my body, but I was sleeping too heavily.

"Wake up." A hushed whisper. My mother's voice. The scent of roses. Mama always smelled of roses. My brain dazed, I blinked the sleep out of my eyes. It took me a while to take in my surroundings. I was in my bedroom. My eyes connected with my mother's green eyes, her messy blonde hair framing her face.

"We have to go, baby," she said in a hushed tone.

It was on the tip of my tongue to tell her I wasn't a baby. I was six. A big boy. At least that was what my father said all the time. My twin,

Maxim, was already awake and crying. It was nothing new; he always cried.

"It's okay, Maxim," I mumbled sleepily, accustomed to comforting him. "Don't cry. Everything will be okay."

Although I had no clue what was happening. Mother gently yanked me out of bed, then handed me my shoes.

"Mama... where are we going?"

Her gaze, the color of the deepest green forest, darted around, as if she feared someone would appear at any moment. "Somewhere safe." I gave her a confused look. We were safe here. Father was the Pakhan and protected us from everyone. I opened my mouth to argue but she stopped me. "Don't argue with me, Illias Konstantin. You are my sons, and I'm not leaving you behind."

I hurriedly put my shoes on and took Maxim's hand in mine as Mama led us outside. My younger brother, although only by a few minutes, stumbled behind me, still crying, his steps clumsy.

"It's okay, Maxim," I comforted him. "We're together."

Before I could say anything else, Mama pushed us gently into the back seat of the Range Rover that Papa gifted her only days before.

"Fasten your seatbelts," Mama ordered in a whisper, then rushed to the driver's side and got in. Just as I helped Maxim with his, the tires screeched as she took off, and I hurriedly put my own seatbelt on.

The streets of Moscow were empty as we left our city house. It was dark and freezing cold, this winter being particularly cold. Most of the city slept, no other vehicles or people for as far as I could see. I glanced at the dash and saw the red '3:30 a.m.' staring back at us.

"Mama, why are we leaving in the middle of the night?" I questioned her, staring at the back of her blonde head.

Mother's hand trembled, her knuckles white as she gripped the steering wheel. She was paler too; her expression was fearful. She kept glancing around as if she expected someone to appear and hurt her. But Papa wouldn't let anything happen to her. He loved her too much.

I heard Papa's friends say that he loved Mama so much that it made him blind. It was dangerous to be like that in our world. The Omertà vow was above all else and nobody survived violating it. Not even a family member. The thorns are poisonous, Papa's second-in-command muttered. The Black Rose means death.

Back then I struggled to understand what it meant.

"I don't want to go," Maxim whimpered. "I want my toys."

Mama paid him no mind. My brother cried a lot and got attached too quickly. At least that was what I heard Mama and Papa say.

"We'll get them," I said softly, just as mama took a sharp turn, and I reached out to steady Maxim before he'd hit the door as I held onto the seat with one hand. I glanced out the window and saw we were leaving the city behind.

"Mama? Where are we going?"

Her eyes flickered to the rearview mirror and she smiled. That special smile that always softened even the hardest hearts.

"We'll start a new life," she whispered roughly. "Somewhere away from all this." The answer made no sense. "A real family. You'll gain a brother. We'll be a happy family. Away from your father."

That answer made even less sense. Mama didn't have any more babies. Maxim and I were her babies. She always said that. And father said we would always be together.

"But Papa won't be happy," I said softly. "He'll be sad without us."

Her eyes lit up staring in the distance, but she didn't answer. Just as I thought maybe she realized the error of her ways, she turned into a dark, gravel lot. Then I saw it. Another car sat there, a beat up van. Our car came to a stop and the van flashed its lights. Once. Twice. Three times.

A soft squeal left Mother's lips. "Unbuckle your seatbelts," she said. "Our new life awaits."

She reached for the large bag on the passenger seat that I hadn't noticed and jumped out of the car, then opened the door for us.

"Hurry," she rushed us.

I assisted Maxim with his seatbelt and as he scooted out of the car, I followed behind him after unbuckling my own. Once outside, the other car switched to high beams and the doors opened.

Holding Maxim's hand, I sheltered my eyes with my other. The door slammed. A soft gasp came from my left. It was my mother's.

I barely had time to process it all when two of Papa's men grabbed Mama. She didn't fight, but her face paled even more. Maxim and I remained completely still, staring at our papa who wore a scowl and cold expression on his face. The coldest I'd ever seen.

He gripped a man by his throat. A man I had never seen before. He was choking him to death.

"Stop," Mama screamed. Papa ignored her.

"Please, Konstantin," Mama pleaded on a whimper. Lenosh, Papa's right hand man, kept her captive as she struggled against him. "Please." She kept fighting, her eyes on the man my papa gripped. A little boy stood behind him, shaking like a leaf. Was he supposed to be our brother? He looked nothing like us. He wasn't a Konstantin. "Please don't hurt him. It's my fault."

That seemed to infuriate Papa even more. The boy's high-pitched wail registered.

"He touched what was mine," Papa growled. "Took what was mine. He poisoned you against me. He'll die, my little black rose. For your betrayal and his own, he dies. So will his line."

Maxim started crying even louder, his hand gripping mine like it was his life raft. This wasn't a life for him. Mama said he was too sensitive. Too weak for it. But not me. When she looked at me, she saw my papa. I knew it. She even said it a few times.

For the first time in my life, I saw Mother fight him. She clawed at the guards, spit at them, and screamed. She screamed so loud, it pierced my ears, and I was fairly sure it matched the boy's high-pitched cries.

"I was his before I was ever yours," she screamed. The words were directed at Papa, but her eyes were teary on the man Papa was slowly killing. He was gasping for air. It almost looked like Papa gave him just enough air to inhale then resumed his torture. "I hate you! I hate your touch. Sleeping in the bed next to you. I hate when you fuck me. I hate that my sons are your sons."

The last sentence was Papa's undoing. In one forceful move, he snapped the man's neck and threw him onto the gravel. Mother finally freed herself from Papa's men and ran to the stranger. Her lover.

She fell down to her knees, uncaring of the rips on her dress nor stones digging into her knees. Papa's eyes turned black as the starless sky above us. Darker than the deepest depths of the oceans.

He retrieved his gun and pointed it at Mama.

My breaths felt heavy and my heart thundered violently. Maxim squeezed my hand so hard that he cut off my circulation. The cries of the boy, the whimpers of my brother... it all faded away, leaving only the harsh breaths of my mother with mine.

It all happened in slow motion. A gravel stone moved. A teardrop stained Mama's beautiful cheek, rolling down her chin. The scent of roses against the freezing temperatures.

Father didn't even hesitate. He pulled the trigger. A loud bang. Hot liquid splashed onto my face.

My mother's blood. Even that smelled like roses. It stained her blonde hair, ruining it forever.

Roses and death. It was all it represented.

It was the first time blood touched me. Since then, I'd been drenched in it.

My phone beeped, pulling me out of my thoughts. It was my confirmation that the surveillance cameras were installed in her penthouse. Putting my phone away, my eyes flickered to the simple stone next to Adrian's crypt.

My mother was buried here. A New Orleans native. I never understood why Papa brought her body here. Maybe he wanted her out of his country. Or maybe he felt guilty.

So yes, I fucking hated roses. There was only one person who had come close to eliminating my hatred for roses. Tatiana Nikolaev. My eyes flickered to her. The lone figure standing in front of the stone crypt.

Why did I save her? Maybe I didn't want to witness the life leaving her eyes. From the moment I first spotted her, she had captured me. Too effortlessly. It wasn't good to love a woman in our world. Just look at my father. Just look at Maxim.

Her brothers and the rest of her family stood only a few feet away. Their worried glances were on their baby sister. The sister they almost lost. The sister who married their best friend. The sister who didn't know she held the destiny to most leaders of the underworld in her hands. That fucking chip. Adrian loaded all those goddamn videos on that chip along with information that wasn't for public knowledge.

Her eyes stared at the niche plate. She hadn't been crying, although even from a distance, I could see that she was pale. Her face was still marred by the fading bruises, despite her attempt at hiding them with those dark sunglasses.

Just seeing that bruise was enough to make me want to snap Adrian's neck with my bare hands. He put her in that spot. He caused the underworld to go after her just by being his wife. As far as I was concerned, he got off easy. His death was too quick.

When she removed her glasses, those pale blue eyes hit me. The dark shadows under her eyes made them look even bluer than normal. It felt like peering into her soul while at the same time pulling all my darkest secrets from my own.

But the beautiful blue eyes that men had been falling all over themselves for years had lost their spark.

Her brothers strode away from her, leaving her alone. Tatiana stared at Adrian's grave, keeping her spine stiff. At five-foot-seven, she wasn't short, but in her state, she seemed petite. Fragile. Almost breakable.

As if she sensed my gaze, she shifted her head my way. Her pupils dilated, the black almost swallowing her blue. A visible tremble rolled down her body, and for a fraction of a second, I saw emotion pass through those pale blues.

Raw, unfiltered emotion. As if she remembered. Did she?

But then she blinked and returned her gaze to the tomb. As if walls were coming around her, she wrapped her arms around her small waist. She was alone, someplace else where nobody else belonged.

Somewhere where she'd feel nothing but numbness. She'd sealed her heart and her soul. She thought it was the end.

It was only the beginning.

SIX
TATIANA

Five stages of grief.

I might still be stuck on the first stage. I didn't know. All I could feel was pain. The kind that shredded your soul into pieces. Although there was a glimmer of hope. *Before*.

The red stain extinguished that hope.

And here I thought I was on my way to recovery.

Low chatter and the scraping of silverware sounded in the distance. The staff rushed back and forth between the kitchen and dining room where guests waited for their food. The quiet melody of the soothing music drifted through the air.

I missed the old Adrian. The one I grew up with. The one I knew before everything got complicated between us. The way he'd make me breakfast or take me to see a Russian Opera performance while fighting the urge to doze off. There weren't many Russian things I loved but opera was one of them.

Fuck, I miss him. Things were good between us. Until we got married. Then something went wrong and I had yet to figure out what and why. I couldn't forget all the good years we'd had. All the trust and happiness. Yet now, I was left without it. It was hard to see people around me get their happily-ever-after while I missed out.

I had been avoiding my family like the plague. Isabella and Aurora had been relentless - checking up on me, taking me to my appointments with the therapist and my doctor who was treating my injuries. Their eyes were always on me, watching me with worry and offering advice. I didn't need any. I just wanted these stages to be complete so I wouldn't hurt so much. Why did it take so fucking long to go through this grief?

Today, I thought I'd get a reprieve. Vasili and Sasha offered to take me for my final checkup, then decided to treat me to lunch.

So here I was.

My emotions shifted, turning from anger to pain.

My blank eyes stared back at me. Like the ocean, reflecting a soul trapped in its depths where monsters lurked. The harder I reached for the surface, the faster I drowned.

And nobody could see me. Nobody could hear me. My screams were silent.

My face was paler than usual. The bruises had faded to nothing. But on the inside, I still felt them. In my heart, in my soul, even in my bones. It all hurt.

A shudder went through me.

My heart twisted, being yanked out of my chest, inch by inch. Pain clawed at me as I stared at the blood staining my white pants with desperation. With a dull ache deep in my soul.

Something squeezed at my throat, stealing all the oxygen from my lungs.

Lost. It was all lost.

I'd be all alone. Forever. Sasha would eventually marry. Vasili had his own family. Even Alexei had his own family. In this world, men preferred younger women. Virgins. I was neither. The men in this world could have as many women as they wanted. But women, we were only allowed to find love once, like it was some fucking rule. I had my chance for a family with Adrian and it died, along with him, on some godforsaken road in the middle of nowhere. Violently.

Sudden panic expanded in my ribcage. *Oh, God.*

I couldn't breathe. I couldn't think. Oxygen was replaced by a wildfire, eating away at everything in its wake. The feeling of loss choked me with a vengeance. I couldn't handle it anymore. Four weeks of pretending I was okay. My control cracked.

I snapped, then reacted. Fire burned through my veins. My red Christian Louboutin clutch flew through the air and hit the mirror. Again. Then again. The metal trash can followed. It shattered the mirror, the sound of glass hitting tile echoing through the bathroom.

Hello stage two… anger.

My ears rang. Whether from the glass or blood rushing through my veins. Or maybe it was the screams that pierced the air.

The hot buzz shot through my veins. My vocal cords scratched my throat.

The air escaped me in a rush as hands came from behind me, one wrapping around my mouth and the other around my waist.

"Tatiana, snap out of it," Vasili growled.

It should have been my warning. His words were rougher. His Russian accent came through. But I was too far gone.

I clawed at his arms. Bit his hand. Then I screamed. I screamed until my throat ached and I tasted blood on my tongue. I screamed until my ears buzzed. I screamed until my soul bled.

Until there was nothing left but emptiness.

And then I blacked out.

I woke up with tears staining my face and sweat rolling down my back. Panic still tore through my chest, stealing oxygen from my lungs. My lip stung and I licked the cut on my bottom lip. I had no idea how I got it, but it hurt like a bitch.

"She has to get help."

Vasili's voice was a hushed whisper. My body shifted back and forth as Vasili drove like he was pissed off and ready to lose his temper. It must be bad if he was driving like a maniac. He rarely did that anymore since he had his kids.

A little green monster slithered through my veins. Envy and hate were a bitch. I had never experienced them before. Not like this. Not so strong. Until now.

I kept my eyes closed, listening to the hum of the engine.

"You're not shipping her off," Sasha hissed. "It's our job to help her. It's only been a month. She's slowly getting better."

He didn't believe it. Even I could hear the doubt in my brother's voice.

"She just destroyed a restaurant bathroom in her rage," Vasili hissed. "She bit me. Hit me. And sliced her lip in the process. How in the hell do you think she's getting better?"

Silence followed. I didn't bother moving. Let them think I was asleep. It was better than participating in this shitshow of a conversation.

"What set her off?" Sasha asked. "Did you say something?"

"No," Vasili clipped. "I went to check on her since she was taking so long and found her beating on the mirror, her hands bloodied from shards of glass cutting into her palm."

Silence, louder than a gunshot, followed. It was thick, heavy, and ominous. Deafening.

"She'll get better," Sasha grunted. "It's not like our family is great at grieving. Our own mother went to extremes. Father wasn't far from it."

"Tatiana is nothing like Mother and even less like Father," Vasili snapped.

But we all knew that was bullshit. Every one of us had our parents' qualities. Good and bad. Our control was non-existent, our jealousy deadly, and our fury destructive.

The car came to a stop, but I heard cars passing by us. Had to be a stop sign.

"Just take her to see the doctor," Sasha muttered. "Her hand will probably need stitching."

"Isabella can do it."

"No!" The single word, hoarse and raw, came out without realizing I'd spoken out loud.

My brothers turned in unison. "You and Bella are best friends," Vasili reasoned.

"Please, just take me home," I whispered, shifting up into a sitting position. Vasili's eyes flickered to my pants. Blood now stained most of my white pants and I grabbed someone's jacket to hide it.

"You need stitches," Sasha reasoned, keeping his voice soft.

"Then take me to a doctor," I reasoned, keeping my eyes lowered. "I don't want to go to your place, Vasili."

"Why the fuck not?" he demanded to know with a growl. "We're family. I won't let you isolate yourself."

The silence grew so deafening, it licked at my skin. Like a cold sweat against damp skin.

We didn't sit in silence for long before a horn blared, making me jump. Sasha shoved his hand out the window and flipped them off. Vasili turned around and resumed driving, but Sasha remained watching me.

"I'm taking you to my place," Vasili declared. Hatred filled me with a searing burn. Not at him. Not at my best friend, but at life, destiny, and the unfairness of it all. I took a deep breath, then another as my vision blurred. I needed to get myself together. "Isabella will fix you up, and then you'll stay with us."

"I don't want to go to your place," I screeched, losing my shit. Again. "It's all happy and joy there. I don't want to see that."

Admission and jealousy left my lips and bounced against the metal of the car. It was too late to take the words back.

"You need to move on," Vasili said quietly.

"Move on," I repeated quietly. "He was my everything. How do I move on?"

"Tatiana–" Vasili started but I cut him off.

"No, listen. Fucking *listen*, Vasili." I took a deep breath in but instead of calming me, it only fed the bitterness and rage festering inside me. "What if it had been Isabella? Would you just move on? I am not going to your place. How do you think it makes *me* feel? Seeing everything you have that I will never have. I have *nothing* left. Fucking nothing."

Vasili's eyes flickered to the rearview mirror, connecting with mine. I regretted the words instantly. The raw bitterness was meant to be hidden, not held against the world. Especially not my brother. He deserved happiness.

Tears streamed down my cheeks. I had barely said ten sentences, but I was panting by the time I uttered them. My lips trembled. My hands shook. Blood trickled down my palms and dripped onto the jacket.

"We'll take you to the hospital," Vasili finally said. "We have a doctor on the payroll there."

It was only the beginning of my painful journey.

SEVEN
TATIANA/ KONSTANTIN

Tatiana

D ay before Christmas.

Aurora and Bella fussed over the Christmas tree. I didn't bother putting one up, but my sisters-in-law were as stubborn as they were annoying. With their babies surrounding me with their toothless grins and cooing sounds, Aurora and Isabella decorated the whole tree while I sat and watched, feeling none of the joy. None of the hope.

Fucking nothing.

"Do you want the honor of putting the angel on the top of the tree?" Aurora asked, keeping her voice light despite the worry furrowing her brow. I shook my head. I didn't want the tree up, what made them think I'd want to put the star on.

"Come on, Tatiana," Bella urged.

"No."

I sat on the floor, my hair a matted mess. It had been a few days since I last showered. I think. I wasn't sure. I knew I reeked of alcohol but thankfully my little nephew and niece didn't seem to mind at all.

Probably because they reeked of baby puke and poopy diapers. Bella swore on her life they'd grow out of it soon; I didn't believe her.

Little Kostya, Alexei's son, crawled up my lap, gripping my shirt tightly. He cooed something, and it almost felt like a scold. Or an order. *Go take a shower*, he probably demanded, staring at me with those pale blue eyes.

"You go take a shower," I muttered. "You stink too."

"Mine," he babbled. The kid thought everything was his.

"Ummm, are you talking to Kostya?" Aurora asked, pulling my attention to her and my best friend. They looked like two idiots, swinging back and forth on the chair, trying to reach the top of the tree. They were both shorter than me, so unless they grew a few inches, that star would remain where it was.

"So what if I am," I snapped. It was my place; I could do whatever I wanted here. I didn't invite them here. Couldn't I just be left alone?

"Just don't expect an answer back," she joked.

I rolled my eyes. "How long are you staying?"

The two of them shared a look. Tension was palpable in the air. I didn't have the energy for it. I just wanted to be alone. Grief was *my* prison. Not theirs. The agony I suffered wasn't for anyone to witness. Seconds ticked by slowly, each heartbeat more agonizing than the last. Every second passed slower than the last.

I'd say sleep would be better but then the dreams plagued me. The scent of citrus, sandalwood, and spice would linger in the air, then something I couldn't identify would rear its ugly head and my heart bled. My screams pierced the air and sliced through my soul.

The pain was so raw that it cracked my insides piece by piece, they'd never fit together again. My heart and soul were forever altered, even the pitter patter of my heart refused to beat the same.

There was something I needed to remember, but I couldn't. It was tearing me apart.

Why can't I remember?

A soft slap on my face startled me and I glared at my nephew.

"What was that for?" Little Kostya just gave me a toothless smile, his small body comfortable using me as his own personal jungle gym.

"You keep this up and I'll be forced to choose a favorite nephew," I warned in a low voice. "Nikola has never slapped me."

Clearly Kostya, just like his father, didn't give a shit because his little chubby palm slapped against my cheek again.

I sighed. "I don't have time for this," I muttered under my breath. With him in my arms, I shifted off the floor and stood up, then strode towards the mini-bar. "I need a drink if you all will be nagging me today."

Taking the crystal lid off the top of the decanter, I poured myself a glass.

"I'd offer you some, but Alexei would kill me," I said, looking at Kostya seriously. His eyes watched my every move, and he listened intently like he could understand my every word. Of course, he couldn't. The only thing he understood was pooping and peeing in his diaper, and eating. Let's not forget slapping his aunt.

"I'll pay you back when you start dating," I mumbled under my breath, then tilted my head and downed my drink. The warm liquid trickled down my throat, and into my empty belly. The heat was almost instant.

Unfortunately, the oblivion wasn't.

My first Christmas without him. Even before we started dating, Adrian was around for Christmas. He always celebrated it with us. For almost twenty years.

"Hey, pipsqueak," Adrian greeted me with that dreadful nickname. Sasha said it was a term of endearment. More like embarrassment. "Merry Christmas!"

Adrian knew the term grated on my nerves. I just turned eighteen; I was a young woman. A damn grown up, not some little kid. When would Adrian start looking at me as such? I wanted to be his girl-friend, not the baby sister of his best friend.

"Why are you looking at me like that?" he questioned with a tilt to his head and a knowing smirk on his lips.

I tried to school my features like the grown up I was supposed to be. "I'm not looking at you in any particular way, Adrian," I retorted with a huff. He refused to look away. Stubborn man.

"Merry Christmas," I sighed, reluctantly giving up my disappointment.

"I got you something," he continued with a grin, holding out a small package wrapped in gold paper.

I stared at it, stunned. In all the years he'd been coming here for Christmas, he'd never given me anything wrapped in a golden paper. "What did you get me?"

He laughed and shook his head. "Why don't you just open it and find out."

I looked at the box he'd placed in my hands. It looked to be the right size for jewelry. Maybe it was a ring. Just the thought of it had my heart drumming faster. Maybe Adrian finally felt what I'd felt since I first met him! We were destined to be together. Did he talk to Vasili? Maybe I'd marry him and we'd have a fairy tale.

Tearing the paper off eagerly, I tore at the shiny paper and opened the box. My heart sank to find a pair of gold stud earrings staring back at me.

But I wasn't the giving up type. This was a start. It showed that he no longer saw me as a child. I could work with this.

With a smile plastered on my face, I met Adrian's green gaze and said, "Thank you. They're beautiful. I'll cherish them. Always."

Just like we'd cherish each other. Always.

The memory hurt. *You left me, Adrian.* His love had gone cold, leaving me alone, intertwining between reality and nightmare. Or maybe it was just one and the same.

Another crack in my heart. A lump in my throat. The unbearable suffocating feeling in my chest.

Walking back to where Isabella and Aurora still struggled with the tree, I lowered little Kostya down next to his little cousin. Then without a word, I headed for the master bathroom. Grabbing a bottle of vodka and a glass as I passed the mini bar, I rushed through the bedroom, signs of Adrian still everywhere. My designer outfits lay scattered all over the bed and floor, leading into my walk-in closet, which looked even worse.

The usual order and luxury was overtaken by grief.

Ignoring it all, I stepped into the bathroom. The moment the door shut behind me, my back rested against the door and a sob escaped me. My hand pressed against my mouth to muffle the sound, and I slid down until I found myself on the cold marble tile.

A shuddering breath mixed with my sobs. Loneliness swallowed me, pulling me into darkness and I had no way of getting out of it.

Don't you fucking give up. A deep voice whispered. It wasn't Adrian's voice. Whose was it? *Tatiana, give me your hand.*

My heart screamed. My soul bled. The weight pressed on my chest. The silence was too heavy and too thick, stealing my oxygen.

I craved the numbness. Needed oblivion. This was too much to bear.

A soft knock on the door.

"Tatiana." I startled as Isabella's soft voice came through.

"I'll be out in a moment," I said, my voice cracking. Each word felt like raw sandpaper scratching against my throat. I couldn't breathe, the walls were closing in on me and threatening to smother me.

Isabella pushed the handle down, cracking the door open and leaving me no choice but to shift around so she could enter. Isabella might be soft, but she was stubborn as fuck. You'd have to be to survive my eldest brother.

Once inside, she lowered herself down, taking a seat on the marble next to me. She wore simple jeans and a baggy white t-shirt. Her dark hair bounced with life, making me even more aware of the pitiful state I was in.

Her hands wrapped around me and turned me around to face her. My best friend. My brother's wife. She had everything. A husband who'd give her anything and everything. Children who love her. Happiness, love, family.

I had nothing.

My best friend and I have been through a lot. Four wild college years. Her miscarriage. Her pain. My rebellion. We were sisters more than friends. I loved her. She loved me. But right now, I couldn't handle being around her.

It fucking hurt to see everything I'd never have - a loving husband, children, a warm home. A family.

I loved her, I really did. But bitterness slithered through my veins, right alongside the alcohol, like poison. It suffocated, slowly like a pillow smothering your face. You hoped for death, but instead, the cruel destiny eased up and let you breathe. Just so you could suffer more.

That was how I felt. Day in and day out.

"God, Tatiana," she murmured softly. "I hate seeing you like this."

"I'm fine," I muttered, reaching for the bottle and taking a gulp. A glass wasn't enough to wash down this bitterness. The vodka burned my throat, dulling my senses.

"Vasili is worried," she rasped. I lowered my eyes, suddenly interested in the creases in my clothes. They were a mess.

"I'm fine," I repeated.

"You're not fine," she murmured, keeping her tone low. "We keep waiting for you to come to terms with Adrian's death. But you're getting worse. It's been two months since his death. We don't expect you to be your old self but by now you should at least be doing a bit better." I remained silent, my eyes darting back to the bottle of vodka. I needed one more drink. Just one more and nothing would matter. I'd survive another day. "I know what you're going through–"

"No, you don't," I cut her off, sharper than I intended. Hurt flashed in her eyes and I attempted to temper the sharpness of my voice. "You still have your husband. Even if he died, you have your children to help you carry on. I have nothing. Fucking nothing."

She opened her mouth to say something but then closed it. The pain in her eyes told me I had said something wrong. I had hurt her. Yet, I said nothing. I was sorry; I really was. But my lips refused to move.

"Tell me how to help you then," she whispered, taking my hand in hers.

"I'm fine," I answered automatically again. "I don't need any help."

"Tatiana–"

"I said I'm fine," I snapped and a pained expression flickered across her beautiful face.

Instantly, regret washed over me. I didn't like hurting her. Nor my brothers. And that was all I've been doing lately.

"You're not fine," she said firmly. "You were there for me when I needed you. Even when I didn't want you there witnessing my pain. So whether you like it or not, I am here and will be here to stay."

"No, you're not," I hissed in a low tone. "You have your kids. Your family."

I stared stubbornly at that spot on the floor straight ahead. The single faulty piece of marble that didn't fit in with the rest of the tiles. It made no sense, but when I redecorated our bedroom, I insisted that they install that piece of tile, despite throwing off the entire bathroom. It gave it an extra something. Adrian disagreed. He said it took away something. Whatever.

"Tatiana, I know you're thinking life is over." It was fucking over. "I thought so too when I-I–" She gulped, swallowing her own emotions. "When I had that miscarriage. When Vasili dumped me. But it's not the end of it. It's hard in the beginning, but you keep pushing. Find things to live for and then when you least expect it, life throws you the most wonderful curveball. You helped me when I needed help. I fully intend to help you. That's what family is for."

That dark day rushed to my mind. I was terrified when I found Bella curled up on the floor of our dorm bathroom, blood staining her clothes. It scared the living daylights out of me. My first instinct was to call my brothers, but she refused it. So the two of us powered through. When I rushed her to the hospital, seeing her bleeding out in my car, I was terrified.

I was petrified of losing her. I was mad at myself for missing all the signs. She'd needed my help, but I didn't see it until I found her bleeding out. Maybe she was returning the favor. Maybe my best friend was seeing something I couldn't.

After all, she kept me at arm's length. She wanted to grieve alone and I refused to give her space. She needed me and I was there for her -

whether she liked it or not. I was never too good of a listener. If I ignored her, would she eventually go away?

"It's okay to admit it, you know," Isabella whispered softly. I turned my head and gave her a blank look. "That you're hurting. That something inside of you cracked when Adrian died." It was so much more than a crack. It all shattered. "It only means it can be repaired. Adrian is dead but you are very much alive. Your life didn't end. You have to move on and live. Adrian would want you to live. And I know you can do it. You're strong, Tatiana. Stronger than most women I know."

She leaned over and pressed a kiss on my cheek. "Whenever you need me, I'm here."

A little, golden box with a rose bow landed on my lap. Like it was a foreign object. A box wrapped the same way as Adrian's first gift to me. I stared at it, unwilling to reach for it, afraid to open it. What if it was something Adrian ordered before–

"What's this?" I croaked.

"It was just delivered," she said, getting back to her feet. "I assumed you'd ordered it. I'll let you open it in peace."

She left the bathroom and my fingers slowly reached for the box. I turned it over in my hand, searching for a message. For an address. Something.

There was nothing.

I slowly pulled on the fancy bow, letting it unfold like a wilted rose. My fingers shook as I opened the box. The smooth velvet box sat inside the golden box. Pushing the little button, the box opened.

A diamond necklace sat in the box, but it wasn't that which caught my eye. It was the rubies in the shape of a red rose with green emeralds for thorns in the setting, like an embedded pendant.

A single card laid under it and I pulled it out. Two words. *Memento Mori.* What the hell did that mean?

It had to be delivered to the wrong place. Shoving the note into the box, I closed it and tossed the velvet box onto the counter.

I made it back into the room twenty minutes later, Aurora and Isabella still struggling with the stupid star.

"Give it to me," I grumbled, approaching them with an extended hand. My sisters-in-law acted like I'd just asked for last rites. Their eyes widened as they watched me like I grew a second head. "Just don't let me fall."

"Ummm, should we wait a bit?" Aurora suggested. "Maybe you can eat something and have some water." When I narrowed my eyes on her, she continued quickly, "Sasha would fucking murder me if something happened to you. And Alexei wouldn't be pleased either."

A scoff left me. "As if Alexei would let anyone touch you." I extended my hand further, tapping my foot impatiently. "Besides, I'm Russian. I can hold my liquor."

The two shared a glance, then finally handed me the star. My steps hesitant, I climbed the ladder, one step at a time, one sister-in-law on each side of me, their hands hovering and ready to catch me.

"There. The star is on."

"Amazing what a few inches can accomplish," Aurora grumbled.

"Maybe we're not done growing," Bella joked.

I descended the ladder, then turned around to face my sisters-in-law. They were trying so damn hard, and I wasn't making it easy on them.

Locking eyes with them, I finally uttered those keywords, "I need help."

Stage three... bargaining.

A fleeting shared glance between Aurora and Isabella. "Anything," they said at the same time.

It would have probably been better if I was sober for this, but I didn't want to delay it.

So I swallowed the lump in my throat and readied to say his name. I had yet to say it out loud since his death. At least not when I was awake. It was an echo in my brain, a shadow following behind me. But something about saying his name out loud felt final.

"I want to know what got A–" His name faltered on my lips, struggling to be uttered. But I was determined. I needed to find out what happened if I wanted peace. "I need help finding out what got Adrian killed without my brothers being all over it."

The silence that filled my penthouse was so loud, I could hear our heartbeats. I waited, holding my breath, waiting for an answer. Thunder rumbled across the sky and the three of us jumped at it.

"I have contacts in the FBI," Aurora answered with determination. "I can run some data and see what I can get my hands on." Aurora's eyes darted to Isabella. "Do you have any contacts at the hospital that Tatiana was taken to after the accident? I still don't get how they have no record of someone bringing her in."

Isabella shook her head. "I know a few nurses there. But none of them were on duty that night. It's just bizarre that they let that happen. A complete stranger dumping an unconscious woman, and they have no damn record of it."

"That's bullshit," Aurora grumbled, chasing the voices away. "There's protocol about that stuff."

"Do they know if it was a man or a woman?" I asked. A deep voice played softly in my head. *You're going to be okay. Because our story has barely begun.*

Bella shook her head. "Considering the chaos of an emergency room, it could have gotten lost in the mayhem but it still seems really strange that *no one* noticed. A woman was dumped that night and yet, there's no record of it."

The silence expanded with each breath until it became a living, breathing entity between the three of us. Right along with the shadows of the unknown.

Isabella chewed on her lip. "I'll check Vasili's office and see what information he has."

"Thank you," I choked out. Tears pricked at the back of my eyes. Maybe after I learned what happened to Adrian, I'd find peace.

Or at least answers.

Konstantin

Christmas morning. Russia.

Two months since that prick, Adrian Morozov, met his death. Two months, and the goddamn chip was still missing.

I watched my sister rip the packages open.

She might be approaching her twenty-third birthday, but she still reminded me of that little girl who'd eagerly try to stay awake all night to catch Santa bringing gifts. She used to write him a letter every year. It was easier to fulfill her wishes back then. Now she kept her wants and needs close to her heart.

Turning my head, I stared out at the snow covered horizon. I couldn't see past the castle yard thanks to the snow storm, yet I knew it stretched for miles. For the last few years, we celebrated in Paris where my sister attended college. While growing up, we alternated between Russia and California, where she attended boarding school.

"Thank you, Brother." Isla's voice pulled my attention away from the window and back to my sister. "You always get me way too much."

I shook my head. "I need to do more for you."

She sighed and picked up a gift, then padded over to me with her bare feet.

"This is your gift," she said. "I have one for Maxim too, but I guess he won't make it."

My twin brother was fucking up. He was crossing the line from a casual drug user to a regular one. He was a liability. It had been years since his woman died. Years to come to terms with it. And all he'd done was years of fucking it up worse - starting with going after Branka Russo and against Sasha Nikolaev. It didn't matter that our father had made a deal with Branka Russo's father.

The deal was for Maxim to marry one of his daughters. Maxim decided he wanted his whore instead, so Russo killed Maxim's woman to get her out of the way after he used her for his own depraved pleasures. My brother hadn't been the same since. He became reckless and set his sights on Branka. Russo's daughter's life for his whore's life. The only obstacle Maxim didn't plan on was Branka being the obsession of that insane motherfucker, Sasha.

"Yeah, Maxim won't make it," I replied dryly. He was probably high as a kite somewhere.

Leaving the topic for later, I opened the gift my sister had wrapped with such care. She loved everything red and gold so of course the gift was wrapped in those colors.

Ripping the paper, I opened the box and a beautiful frame with a picture from the past stared back at me. It dated back seven years ago when Maxim and I took her to D.C. for her first concert as a solo violinist. In the photo, she stood with her precious violin between Maxim and I, barely reaching our chest, but her grin compensated for her lack of height. She lit up the entire city with her music that night.

It was that night that I saw Tatiana Nikolaev for the first time. It wasn't until years later I learned who she was. Imagine my surprise when I saw her approaching the table where I sat with Sasha Nikolaev, discovering she was his sister.

"I love it, kroshka." Isla's big smile lit up her whole face and I pulled her into a hug. "I'll treasure it forever," I vowed. "Thank you."

A soft giggle escaped her, and it vibrated through my chest. It fucking made my heart swell. I'd burn down this world to keep her safe. To protect her. Everything I'd done over the last two decades was to keep her safe. Away from our world.

Unfortunately, I had to protect her from her own mother too. My father spiraled fast after my mother's death. He fucked anyone and anything with a pussy, as long as their hair didn't resemble our mother's light blonde mane. It was how Isla came to be - a young whore that father picked up in one of the brothels. Apparently, he was too drunk to roll on a condom, but not too drunk to knock her up.

"You're welcome." She gave me another hug. "Now, let me go check on our Christmas breakfast."

She shot to her feet and ran out of the room, just as my cell buzzed. I retrieved it and slid the message open. Unknown number. A recording, waiting for me to press play.

A bad feeling formed in the pit of my stomach. With Adrian's death, these should have ceased. Slowly, I pressed play and watched.

There was no need to watch it to know how it played out. It showed me pulling a pistol from my jacket. *Pop.* The gunshot reverberated through the screen. The L.A. senator slumped forward, his head smashing against his fancy mahogany desk.

Drip. Drip. Drip.

"Sniff around my family again–" I heard myself say on the screen, "–and I'll end your entire fucking family."

The moment the video finished playing, it was wiped clean. Same signature as the videos we'd received in the past.

Goddamn it! It didn't matter that the fucking senator felt it was his right to touch my sister. Or that he had done that to other young girls. The only thing that would matter, if this leaked, was that my empire would crumble.

My grip tightened around the phone. The crack followed, protesting the abuse.

Then it vibrated and I answered. "Yeah?"

"I just got a video." Marchetti barked. "Same digital signature as before."

"I got one too," I confirmed. There was no need to even run a digital scan. I could tell right away it was done the same exact way as before. "Did the others?"

"Yes."

"His wife better not have anything to do with it," Marchetti growled. "Or I'll–"

"You won't fucking touch her," I snarled. It didn't matter that I slipped. The night of the accident became clear that I'd fight the entire Omertà to keep Tatiana alive.

It was so much more than lust for her. There was something both tender and violent about my desire for her. This possessiveness went beyond anything rational. All I cared about was protecting her and destroying anyone who'd hurt her.

Even at the risk of exposing my whole family. The terror I felt when I saw her body twisted in that car was unlike anything else I had ever experienced.

I needed to protect her. At all costs. I wanted to unravel *her* and all the secrets she hid.

The question was, did I miscalculate her involvement?

F ury, pain, and betrayal sliced through me as I stared at him. Sometimes it felt like I didn't know him at all.

I waited for an explanation, anything, but the silence in our penthouse remained deafening and tense. His dark eyes stared back at me, that stubborn tilt of his chin, while his lips thinned in displeasure.

He **owed** me an explanation.

"Why not?" I demanded. "We're married. You could at least provide me with an explanation, Adrian. I'm going to be twenty-seven soon. You never claimed not to want children when we married."

His answer was swift. "You never asked."

"Because I assumed—"

"That's right," he interrupted. "You assumed."

I never asked him specifically, but I assumed he loved kids. He was good with Vasili's kids.

"Explain to me why," I demanded. My temper simmered under my skin; I could feel it and tried my best to keep it contained. I felt robbed. Of the future I dreamed of. Of the family I wanted.

"Illegitimate kids are not a desirable thing."

My brows furrowed at the stupid explanation. "We are married," I snapped. *"What do you mean by illegitimate kids? I don't care if the baby is blue, green, or illegitimate. It will be ours. We don't live in the medieval age."*

"No," he snapped. "No matter what you say, the answer will be no. No children. Our world is not meant for children."

"You are barely even in that world, Adrian," I screamed. "You run a successful security company. We have more than enough to provide for a family. Even if you quit, I have enough money of my own to—"

"You have your brothers' money, not your own."

"It is in my name." The anger inside me boiled over. "So it's my money. There is something you're not telling me, and I want to know what." My ears rang from the adrenaline rushing through my veins. The anger blinded me. It was as if I was a raging maniac. I reached for the nearby vase and threw it through the air. Adrian ducked down just in time to miss it hitting him. It crashed against the wall, shattering all over the floor.

He turned around to see all the broken pieces all over the hardwood. Then he returned his eyes to me and shook his head.

"Mistake," he muttered. He might as well have stabbed me right in my heart. "This was such a fucking mistake."

My stomach tied into a knot. Pain sliced through me and the words etched themselves into my soul. You couldn't take something like that back. Anger bubbled inside me, inflating until I felt like it would burst violently.

Instead, I reached for the first item next to me and threw it across the room. Our wedding, or rather elopement, photo stared back at me, shattered; pieces of glass scattered across the floor.

Without another word, he walked away from me, the door to our penthouse slamming so hard, it shook the entire apartment.

And another vase fell off the table, broken pieces scattering over the cedar planks. Moonlight reflected in the shattered glass, like raindrops against crystal. Kind of like my heart.

I watched them, frozen, as a tear splattered against the hardwood. A single dark drop, slowly expanding. Like this feeling in my chest.

Except, I didn't recognize it. I had never felt it before. It felt awfully close to hate.

I didn't like it. I wanted to erase it. Leaving all the mess where it was, my steps moved towards the back of the penthouse where our bedroom was. I stripped my clothes off, leaving me in a bra and panties, then crawled into the bed.

I'd sleep off the ugly feeling. It was best to sleep it off and start anew.

Closing my eyes, I focused on the buzzing of Adrian's gadget. Beep. Beep. Beep.

Until my heavy eyelids shut and dreams pulled me under.

Only to be startled in the darkness of the room. There was someone here. The squeak of the hardwood. My heart thundered, cracking my ribs.

My eyes shot open. A hand closed over my mouth, cutting off the air to my lungs.

I frantically searched his face. My husband's eyes.

Dark. Resentful. Furious.

"This isn't you." My muffled voice didn't register. This face wasn't my husband's. But it looked like his face.

It was the beginning of our end.

NINE
TATIANA

I shot up into a sitting position, heaving and choking, my fingernails digging into the sheets.

My scream traveled through the empty penthouse, vibrating against the walls and creating a horrid echo. The moon shone through the large windows, glowing over the city of New Orleans and witnessing my misery. It offered no advice, only watched me numbly.

The shadows danced across the walls of the home that had become just another tomb. The one housing a living, breathing human.

I glanced at the clock, the red digits showing it was 1:00 A.M.

"Happy New Year," I whispered, the words going nowhere. A nightmare plaguing my dreams wasn't the best way to start a New Year.

The day after I had asked Aurora and Bella to help, Aurora returned to inform me that she'd found something. While she wasn't able to uncover much, what she found out was surprising.

Adrian provided security for her father, a corrupt politician, and hacked into his competitors' network for him. It made no sense. It went against everything his company stood for. If he did that for him, who else did he do that for? The answers wouldn't come tonight.

Tossing away the sheets, I jumped out of bed and headed for the mini-bar.

The alcohol taunted, promising oblivion. And I fell deeper and deeper under the influence. I needed the numbness. I *needed* the relief it brought on. Agony fueled through my veins as I poured myself a drink with shaky hands. It wasn't until I was on my second glass that the bitter satisfaction swelled through my chest. Sinking to the floor, I held the glass and the bottle of vodka.

Deep down, I knew it was bad. Deep down, I knew it was a dangerous road for a Nikolaev to take.

Yet, I couldn't stop my self-destruction. It has been two months since Adrian's death. Two months of chances to move on. Instead, I chose to lose myself in the bottle. Every glass brought a temporary liberation as the anguish left me. Or maybe it just buried itself deeper.

One glass became two, then three, then as many as I needed to rid myself of the despair. It was the only way that I knew how.

It was the wrong way.

But I was too weak to stop. As the alcohol finally overtook my senses, I put the bottle down between my legs. Still on the floor, my back pressed against the wall, I stared out at the skyline of New Orleans, one of the most vibrant cities in the world. Known for its distinctive music, its celebrations and festivals; it was considered a colorful and happy city. A free to do as you please city.

Yet, I felt chained. I'd never be free, not for as long as questions about that night haunted me. Every waking and sleeping moment.

Who killed my husband? Why?

A knock sounded on the door, startling me. My eyes darted to the hallway, almost expecting to hear Adrian say 'I'll get it' but of course, those words never came.

Who in the fuck would be coming? Shifting onto my feet, I headed for the front door with unsteady steps. The world slightly tilted, making me unbalanced. The path to the front door seemed to take forever, when in fact it only took seconds. I opened the door to the empty hallway.

My brows furrowed. I heard the knock. I really did. Didn't I?

My eyes darted around the empty hallway, then something caught my eye on the doormat. Holding on to my door handle, I slowly lowered to my knees and reached for it. White, it felt like a… I turned it over and my next breath caught in my throat.

A photograph. The one of Adrian and I on the day we eloped.

What the fuck is the meaning of this?

"Hello?" I called out but the only voice that returned was my own. "I know you're there," I yelled, paranoia creeping through my veins. "Asshole, show yourself."

The elevator dinged and I screamed in fear, falling to my ass. The elevator door opened and Yuri stepped out of the elevator. Alarm shot through his eyes and his gaze darted around the hallway, but found it empty.

"You alright?" he asked, concern lacing his voice.

No, I'm not alright. "Yes, I'm fine." I swallowed, clutching the picture in my fingers.

"How much did you have to drink?" Yuri asked, disapproval clear on his face. I gritted my teeth and let him help me to my feet. If I said anything, he'd blame it on my alcohol levels. So I remained quiet and headed back inside.

Even if I was mad, I'd find the people that brought me to the point of madness and I'd make them pay. I'd get to the bottom of it. I'd find the assholes who killed Adrian and tore my life apart.

The thirst for revenge outweighed my thirst for alcohol. I needed to make those bastards pay. For what they did to Adrian. For what they did to me. Not doing anything wasn't an option. It could destroy me - slowly but surely. It had started already.

The nightmares were getting worse.

As long as my questions remained unanswered, I'd keep losing myself inside the web of assumptions and what ifs. My solution was in seeking answers.

And in revenge.

New Year. New me. New life.

Okay maybe there weren't so many new things, but I needed to get some answers. My eyes roamed the penthouse. Things were the same, but then they weren't. Traces of Adrian were slowly fading with each passing day.

The only room I hadn't entered yet was Adrian's mancave. Or his gadget room as I called it. I had been steering clear of it, keeping it locked, but now that I needed answers, it seemed the best place to start.

"There have to be some answers here," I murmured to myself. My eyes flickered to the end of the hallway. His gadget room was on the opposite side of our bedroom. I had to go check what was in there. The deeper into the penthouse I went, the heavier my steps felt.

I made it all the way to the door of his room. Once there, I stared at the door, uncomfortable entering into his domain. I had stepped foot into it once before when I first moved in and never cared to do it again. He had so much shit in it that you could barely move through the room. But Adrian always knew where to find what he was looking for.

My fingers gripped on the handle, but I couldn't make myself push it open. I stood frozen, Adrian's scent that I had come to know so well, was always stronger here.

Closing my eyes, I inhaled deeply. I could almost hear his laughter. His footsteps. Feel his touch. The way he teased me.

"I hear you and your friend took a bath in the fountain," Adrian *mused, his eyes sparkling like emeralds. I glared at him, rolling my eyes. "What happened? Was the bathroom in the dorm broken?"*

"Haha," I grumbled. "Very funny."

He let out a chuckle. "I thought it was. I'm trying to picture it and keep failing."

"Well, your imagination must suck."

He laughed. "Trust me, pipsqueak, I have a good imagination. I just think it's too dangerous to picture you without clothes in a fountain."

Embarrassment washed over me and I waved my hand in the air. "We kept our clothes on."

"Ahh, it makes sense." We both knew it made zero sense. Bella and I were drunk and took the party a bit too far. "Is this kind of like that time you and your friend broke into the nearest pool house drunk?"

I stuck my tongue at him, childish and bratty but what was I to say? Yes, we fucked up and got caught. Those cocktails were so tasty and gave me so many brilliant ideas.

"If it's any consolation, pipsqueak, I'm sure every boy in a hundred mile radius probably loved the sight. And now, I'm gonna have to kill them all. Or blind them, depending."

"Man, you're so damn sweet," I retorted dryly. "If you can't handle competition, maybe you should do something about it. Until then, leave those boys in a hundred mile radius alone."

His laughter followed me all the way out of the room. He didn't see a smile on my lips. It was a tug of attraction we kept playing. I'd been attending Georgetown for two years now and somehow every time I came back home, Adrian was here.

He started to see me. Like a woman. Like a friend. No longer a little girl.

Those years of college, I learned to flirt. I experimented. But I saved myself for Adrian. I knew he'd make a move eventually. I felt it in every look he ever gave me. Until one day, anger intertwined with his desire, pricking me like thorns.

With all those good memories, the bad ones came too.

His anger during those last few months. The obsessive, almost paranoid way he kept checking surveillances. The way he'd lose his patience unlike ever before. Whenever I'd question him about what he was looking for, he'd dismiss me.

"Go back to your shopping. The role of a princess brat is more up your alley, Tatiana."

I slapped him that day. It was the only time I had ever slapped a man. Our gazes burned into each other. His words and that look on his face was etched in my brain. *Hate. Anger. Disgust.*

Something heavy pressed down on my chest. My hand trembled uncontrollably. Was it alcohol or the things that lurked in the shadows?

Straightening my spine, I pushed the handle and entered. Surprise washed over me. The room was clean, only a handful of computers and laptops stretched over a large U-shaped desk.

"What the heck?" I murmured. "Where is everything?"

I could have sworn this room had more electronics. It was almost like things had been taken out of here but that was impossible. Yan and Yuri wouldn't touch anything inside this place without running it by me. Nobody else had access to the penthouse. My heart fluttered in my chest. I'd heard footsteps in the night. Was someone stealing shit at night? I shook my head. No, it couldn't be. Nobody but Adrian and I had the key to the penthouse.

Maybe I'd finally just lost my mind.

As I moved through the space, my eyes darted here and there, almost expecting all those missing electronics to appear out of thin air.

When did he empty out this room? I wondered.

He'd never said anything about clearing it out. I'd never *seen* him carry anything of it out. Padding across the room, I sat down at the laptop he always walked around with as if it was a part of him. Powering it up, I waited for the welcome page and instead was greeted by a logo.

A red rose wrapped in thorns.

"What the fuck is it with these roses and thorns?" I mumbled softly. There had to be a reason why it kept coming up. I still didn't know who sent me that gift on Christmas day. It had arrived with such a strange note, one I'd yet to decipher.

Moving the mouse around, I clicked on the logo and instantly a password prompt came up.

I stared at the logo and my mind whispered those strange two words that came with the jewelry. Could the password really be that simple?

I ran to my bathroom, the box still sitting in the same spot where I'd left it. I opened it, grabbed the note along with the box, and rushed back, murmuring the words.

"It sounds like goddamn Latin," I murmured to myself. I bet Bella would know. She had to take Latin class as part of her degree. I'd ask her later.

Once back in the gadget room, I sat in front of the screen. My heart thundered as I typed letters into the password field. *Memento mori.*

"Welcome." A digital voice had me jumping out of my skin.

Rolling my shoulders, I put my palm over the mouse and started navigating. One file was just a list of codes that made no sense to me. I moved onto the next file. That one contained a list of what looked to be IP addresses. I wasn't techy enough to be able to trace them so I moved onto the next folder. It included a long list of MP4 video files.

A name caught my eyes. *Tatiana's mother.*

I told myself not to click it, but in the end, curiosity got the best of me. I clicked on it and images played. Voices shouted. I watched my mother, who I never knew, and Papa, who I barely knew, argue and fight. She threw dishes at him. Then another. Her screams pierced the air, even through the screen.

I held my breath as she stormed out of there, slamming a few more things onto the marble floor. My father headed in the opposite direction, unfazed by her tantrum. Shattered pieces flew everywhere, and from the looks of it, Mother stepped on some of it. She rushed into a room, then came out with a baby in her arms.

My eyes flickered to the corner of the video, reflecting the date. It was right after I was born. I held my breath, seeing my mother hold me. I didn't have a single picture of myself with her and something about seeing it on this video made my heart warm.

She must have drawn comfort from holding me.

She climbed another set of stairs, then started pacing. She almost seemed hysterical. Crazy. She leaned against the rail, almost dropping me and a loud screech filled the room. Then as if the volume was turned up, the screaming became louder. The baby... I was screaming at the top of my lungs.

Mother kept muttering something and I leaned closer.

"He doesn't love me. I'll never be enough. He doesn't love me. I'll never be enough."

She was talking about Papa. She was right. He didn't love her. But what she did was wrong. My spine steeled seeing little Sasha appear.

"Mama," he called out and her pacing stopped. Honestly, she looked like a crazy woman. He should stay away from her.

"Sasha, get back to your room." Not surprisingly, he remained in his spot. "You look at me with your father's eyes. I can see him in you."

The hate in her voice was unmistakable and my heart clenched for my brother. I loved all my brothers, but I was closest with Sasha. Maybe because we were both stubborn. Or maybe because we cooked up things to drive our big brother crazy.

"Where's Papa?" Sasha asked her, his voice so different from the man I knew today.

"You're always going on about Papa. He doesn't love you," she snickered, shuffling the baby roughly between her arms. "He doesn't love me. I don't love you. Round and round we go."

Hate slithered through my veins for our mother. How could she say that to a little boy? To my Sasha. She was lucky to be dead or I'd kill her myself. I watched a little boy who'd grow up to be one of the best men I knew, rub his chest as if he wanted to ease his pain.

Mother roughly switched the baby again and a soft gasp left Sasha's lips. His eyes were on the baby, like a protective wolf ready to pounce.

"Where's Papa?" he asked again.

"He's chasing his little whore and her bastard," she hissed. "No matter what I do or give him, he chases his whore."

"Father is good," Sasha retorted, squaring his little shoulders and glaring at her.

"You're just like him. Worthless." Now I rubbed my chest, seeing how cruel our mother was to Sasha. I should stop playing it but something urged me on. "You brought a curse to our family, Sasha. You weren't enough. He found another woman because I was busy with your constant crying and whining." She lowered her gaze to the baby. "Just like this baby. Always crying. Always whining." Her eyes returned to Sasha, her lips curled in disgust. "You're so unlovable. No woman will love you. Just like your father. Unlovable."

"But you love him," Sasha pointed out in a small voice. He was so fucking smart and made me so proud.

"Never enough," Mother muttered as she started to pace again. "Never enough. He doesn't love me. I'll never be enough. You can't make someone be yours."

She kept going round and round, muttering to herself and ignoring the baby's screams. My screams. My chubby little face had turned red, then suddenly Mother stopped and lifted me as if I was a football to be thrown through the air.

M-maybe that wasn't me. No mother would behave like that and act as if she was about to throw the baby through the air. But deep down I knew.

"Mama!" Sasha called out to her. "Give me Tatiana. I'll feed her the bottle."

Mother lowered her eyes and stared at Sasha. Then somehow he managed to take me and cradled me like he knew what he was doing. I'd bet all my money he'd held me more than my own mother by that point.

"I'll never be good enough," she muttered. "Just like you've never been enough."

She started walking, passing Sasha when he called out, "Mama?" She didn't answer as she opened the doors and air pushed through. "Mama?" he tried again.

She glanced over her shoulder. "I'm going to jump, Sasha."

"No, Mama." My chest squeezed for my brother. He should have never witnessed something like that. "No, please." She cackled, crazed, her hair flowing through the wind. "Please, Mama. Stay."

He reached out with one hand, while still holding me. "Stay for me. I'll be good."

Just as I hoped she'd see reason and how lucky she was to have Sasha, she uttered the words that would make me hate her memory.

"You'll never be good enough. Not for me. Not for your father. Not for anyone. Nobody will stay for you. Better get used to it now, Sasha."

She took a step forward and her body flew through the air. And as her body hit the ground, the sound of her skull cracking filled the air, but I felt nothing.

She was lucky to be dead, or I would have hunted her down and killed her myself.

TEN
KONSTANTIN

What-the-actual-fuck?

Marchetti, Romero, and I watched the videos on our phones. Our own pasts taunting us, the valuable information meant to break us. Not that it would. We'd destroy whoever was behind it.

The Thorns of Omertà might have been an old organization that started in Sicily, but it has since evolved. After the five kings of Italy had fallen, they started rebuilding in the shadows. It was no longer just the kings of Italy. We were kings of the world. The empire was vast and powerful, stretching wide - north, south, east, and west.

My eyes trained on the screen, just as Romero's and Marchetti's were trained on theirs, I watched another sin play out in front of my eyes.

It was the meeting I'd held with Sofia Catalano Volkov. Her husband was the Pakhan of Eastern Russia. Since his death, she'd been playing in that field, taking her revenge. The woman was a bit deranged if you asked me. Loved her blood play. I had killed and would kill many more times before my time was over. It was a necessary evil of my position. For her, on the other hand, it was enthralling. Killing had a direct link to her lust.

Like I said, deranged.

She wanted into the organization. We said no. She tried again. We said no again. But the fucking video didn't have sound - first time ever. Goddamn it. To anyone outside our own organization, it'd look like I worked with the madwoman.

I didn't bother to watch how the video ended. After all, I'd been there that day, so I knew firsthand. Instead, I got straight to work. Logging into my computer, I started tracking it. It went to North Korea, then to Japan, London, even Russia, only to end up back in the U.S.

In New Orleans.

The IP address that belonged to Tatiana Nikolaev. The very same one that used to belong to Adrian. Motherfucking shit.

There was no way she could be part of it. Either she hid her IT talent brilliantly or someone was trying to frame her.

Just as the video came to an end, the IP addresses disappeared, leaving in its wake only a black screen.

"Anything?" Marchetti asked through clenched teeth.

"Same shit," I responded, keeping my cool. "The IP address bounced around then got wiped." My eyes traveled to the window that overlooked the city I ruled. The state I ruled. The whole fucking coastline. There was no better play to hide corrupted shit than in Hollywood. And in D.C. but that was a different story. One ran by Nico Morelli.

"But?" Marchetti prompted. We'd worked together long enough to know how the other thought..

"But this time the starting point was Japan," I told him. "The starting point was always the U.S. in the past. It's peculiar that it's suddenly Japan."

Tension rolled through me like an avalanche ready to explode.

The truth was it had nothing to do with these videos. This shit was part of our everyday work. We'd find the culprit. We'd eliminate the culprit. We'd move on and someone else would try to fuck with us, only for us to end that person.

It was the way of life.

My tension had everything to do with a grieving widow across the country. I had waited years for her. Bided my time. Waited for the opportune moment. The moment I learned it was her husband who was fucking with our organization, I knew I had found it.

I didn't hesitate to end him. I'd do it again without a second thought.

Because Tatiana Nikolaev was my queen. And the king always eliminates the threat to his queen.

ELEVEN
TATIANA

I looked out the window of the penthouse, my fingers twisting the thorned rose pendant necklace in my hand. Somehow that piece of jewelry seemed a lot more than a Christmas gift now. And all the while the videos I had watched played on replay in my mind.

Initially I thought it was a mistaken delivery, but now, I was certain it was sent to me by Adrian.

He must have anticipated what was to come. He *knew* he was about to die.

"What did you get yourself into, Adrian?" I whispered as I clipped the necklace around my neck. It had something to do with those videos. I was sure of it. They had been plaguing my mind for days.

There was damning evidence in there. Against many people, my brothers included. The question was why did my husband have those videos? I was under no illusions that my brothers or anyone else in the underworld didn't do some shady stuff. Or kill people.

Call me morally ambiguous or a hypocrite but that didn't bother me.

The unwritten rule of not killing innocents, women, and children let me sleep at night. So my moral compass was skewed a bit - fucking

But some of the things I'd seen on that video still hit a very uncomfortable mark. It was easier to be okay with it when you never had to witness it. Having a front seat to it was an entirely different thing.

I let out a heavy breath.

If those videos were anything to go by, the pool of suspects was vast and included my own brothers. Could I avenge Adrian against my own brothers? Were my brothers capable of killing my husband?

Yes, they were. But they'd never hurt me. I came out of the accident in bad shape so that eliminated my brothers as suspects. They'd be more likely to barge into our home and shoot Adrian point blank than risk a car chase with me in the vehicle.

The doorbell rang and pulled me out of my thoughts. Glancing at the clock, I noted it was barely eight o'clock in the morning. Unease slithered through me. Maybe someone learned that I watched those videos and had evidence against them.

Ding. Dong. Ding. Dong.

It would seem those videos made me paranoid too.

Bang. Bang. Bang.

Okay, maybe not so paranoid. I didn't know anyone that frantically rang the doorbell then banged on the door like a fucking maniac. Well, maybe Sasha but he would have called first.

Reaching for the coffee table, I put my hand under the table and patted around until I found the gun Adrian had tucked there. For security, he always said. I didn't argue against it. Sasha and Vasili used to keep guns in every fucking corner. It was easier to find a weapon in our house than chocolate.

I grabbed the gun and put it behind me as I headed to the front door. It was at times like this that I wished I had live-in staff like Isabella. But we couldn't have it all, could we?

I released the safety latch on the gun once five feet away from the door when someone started pounding on it again. I just about jumped out of my skin.

"Come on, Tatiana," Isabella shouted. "I know you're in there. You never were an early bird."

Releasing the breath I hadn't realized I was holding, my shoulders slumped and the tension left my body. I shook my head at how ridiculous I was being. It had been months since Adrian's death and nothing had happened. Why would someone come kill me now?

For fuck's sake, I had to get my head screwed on straight.

Putting the gun away in the nearest drawer, I opened the door and came face-to-face with my best friend.

"You scared the bejesus out of me," I grumbled as I pulled her into a hug.

The expression in her eyes was one of disbelief. "Are you drunk?" she questioned.

"Not yet," I grumbled, suddenly feeling very thirsty. But I had a rule of not drinking till after 10.00 A.M. at least. Before it, you were just labeled an alcoholic. My mind mocked that stupid rule, but I ignored it.

"Good."

She shut the door behind her, and I realized she was alone. "Where are the kids?"

"I left them with Vasili," she retorted. "To keep him busy. Aurora is doing the same with Alexei. She's on her way."

Warning shot up my spine. "What happened?"

"She found some stuff and so did I," she explained. Just as I opened my mouth to ask her more, another bang on the door sounded and I startled.

"It's probably Aurora," Isabella noted, completely unfazed.

"Jesus, I should just give you all a key," I muttered as I took a few short steps and opened the door to see my other sister-in-law standing there. Sweaty and panting like she had run a marathon. "You know, you're all wet and stinky. I could have had you picked up."

"Haha," she retorted dryly. "I ran five miles."

Isabella and I shared a glance. We hated exercise with a passion. Aurora was the runner though. Apparently, she liked self-torture. No wonder she and Alexei fell for each other. Two psychos!

"You are nuts," we said at the same time.

"We'll see who's nuts when you two have hips and I don't," she remarked smugly, making a shape with her hands.

"Vasili loves my hips, so whatever," Isabella announced grinning, but her smile quickly faltered and her eyes flickered my way cautiously.

I waved my hand nonchalantly, but something deep in my chest squeezed. Those two had a rough patch but they came through and their marriage looked like a fairy tale from where I stood. Of course, I was happy for them, but the green monster of envy wouldn't let me be.

Adrian and I had a rough patch. A long rough patch, but our story ended differently.

Unlovable. Like my mother.

I pushed the thought away. My mother was a lunatic, through and through. I wasn't quite there. Not yet anyhow.

"What's the reason for this interruption now?" I asked, hiding my jealousy and pettiness. I turned on my heel, heading for the living room, taking my seat on the couch. My yoga pants felt loose indicating I had lost more weight. Thankfully, my off-the-shoulder long sweater hid it well.

Letting out a heavy sigh, I studied the French manicure on my nails, deciding next time I'd go for something louder. Red maybe. Like blood. After all, Valentine's day was coming.

Fucking love day! Did Adrian love me? Comparing our relationship to my big brother's with Isabella, it looked drastically different. Adrian hadn't looked at me the way Vasili looked at Isabella.

"Tatiana!" My best friend's voice pulled me out of the fog, her hand gripping my trembling fingers and rubbing them together.

"I'm fine." I wasn't. We all knew I wasn't, but I'd claim it until I turned blue. It was the stubbornness in all us Nikolaevs. My best friend had a front row seat to all of it and had become used to it.

Bella tilted her head pensively, studying me with a worried expression and I let out an exasperated breath.

"Let's just get to the purpose of your visit," I grumbled.

Aurora sat her sweaty ass on the couch opposite of me, while Isabella remained sitting next to me. I'd prefer if she sat next to Aurora, but what were friends for if not to annoy you.

And to ensure you're alright, my mind whispered.

"Okay, I'll go first," Isabella said, clasping her hands in her lap. Unlike Aurora who kept her eyes open wide in regards to Alexei's business, Isabella liked to remain slightly oblivious. After seeing some of the videos, I couldn't blame her. Not that I'd close my eyes to it. Fuck that, and fuck oblivion. Look where it left me with Adrian.

"I found a document on Vasili's desk," she started. "He was going to buy out Adrian and you."

"What?" That made no sense. Adrian would never sell the company. Vasili's part of the ownership transferred to me when I married Adrian. If he needed it back, it was fine by me. But it made no sense for Vasili to buy out Adrian. "Why?"

She shrugged. "I don't know, but it talked about violating their original agreement."

My brows scrunched. I never heard about any of their agreements. I just thought Vasili helped Adrian with the capital to get him started.

"What was their original agreement?" I questioned.

Isabella let out a heavy sigh. "I couldn't find the original contract. I'd hoped you'd have it."

I shook my head. "I was never really interested in Adrian's–" I winced. I guess it was my company. "I'm not much into that stuff."

"Maybe what I found out will help explain," Aurora chimed in. Both Isabella and I looked at her expectedly. Aurora cleared her throat uncomfortably. "You might not like what I'm about to say, Tatiana. Are you sure you want to go down this road?"

A thick silence crept through the room, promising of what was to come. But could it be worse than those videos I have found? Could it be worse than the insinuation that Adrian was storing shit against my brothers?

"Yes." A single word that would change the course of my life.

This time it was Aurora who looked nervous, twisting her hands in her lap. She chewed on her lip nervously and each second that ticked by felt like a bomb exploding in my brain.

"You know what my brother Kingston went through." I nodded, although none of us knew exactly what he went through. Truthfully, I didn't know the details of what Alexei went through aside that whatever it was, it was horrific, so I could only imagine Kingston was in the same boat.

"It's okay," Isabella comforted her. "Whatever it is, we know that he's a good man."

"He's a survivor," I agreed. "Like Alexei."

Aurora offered a grateful smile. "Thank you."

"We're family," I whispered, scared of the truth that was to come. "No matter what." Vasili pounded that into me, in the best way possible. He always took care of us all, regardless of hard times we'd given him. "Now tell me what you know, please. I'm going out of my mind here."

"Adrian blackmailed Kingston." The bomb dropped. My heart stopped. My lungs filled with poison.

But denial came along too. I shook my head. It couldn't be. Adrian would never do that to our family. *My family.* He knew they were *everything* to me. When Aurora married Alexei, her family became my family. Our family.

Then why does he have those videos on that laptop, my mind whispered.

I shut the doubts down, and in my brain, I went through the videos I'd found. None of them were of Kingston. I'd stake my life on it. I'd met Aurora's brother, and it wasn't a face you'd easily forget. Kingston's face reminded me of the god of war. Jesus, which Greek god was that?

Shut up with ridiculous shit, I scolded myself silently.

"Why would he blackmail him?" I asked. "We don't need money."

Aurora locked eyes with me. "He wanted information on an organization that contracted Kingston for assassinations, but Kingston refused to give him the information." I stared at her dumbfounded. "Maybe that was the agreement he violated? Or maybe he did it to someone else that's close to Vasili?"

Aurora shrugged, not elaborating further. These bits and pieces of information weren't helping. They only piled up more questions than answers.

"Well, what else happened?" I barked. "Did Adrian just let it go?"

My sister-in-law looked uncomfortable. "I don't think we–"

I shook my head. "No, you can't give me crumbs and then not expect me to want to know the whole story. What happened then? Did Kingston give him what he wanted?"

"No."

"No?"

Aurora let out a heavy sigh. "No, Kingston refused. So Adrian blackmailed him with some surveillance that my brother didn't want anyone to see."

"What surveillance?"

"I don't know, Tatiana," Aurora snapped sharply. Then immediately regret passed her expression. "Kingston doesn't want to share details of his last twenty years with me. I won't ask him those questions. He's been through enough.

"How do you know then?" I questioned her.

"I overheard Alexei and Kingston talking. Your brother wanted to make sure nobody was after you." I scoffed softly and Aurora narrowed her eyes on me. "Alexei cares about you and wants to protect you. All your brothers do."

"I know, but they tend to hide shit from me," I muttered. "Being blind and oblivious to things makes you more vulnerable. You should know that better than anyone, Aurora."

She shook her head, disapproval clear on her face. "Well, after the accident and reading the investigation report, your brothers panicked. They wanted to make sure it was understood you had nothing to do with Adrian's dealings."

I stilled. "What dealings?" I asked cautiously. How much did my sister-in-law really know?

Aurora shrugged. "I don't know. Shady dealings. Alexei knows more, so you should really talk to him."

"Or Kingston," I remarked pensively.

"No, not Kingston," Aurora said firmly. "He's been through enough. He doesn't need more shit on his mind."

She was right. Kingston had gone through enough shit, just like Alexei. Yet, questions kept piling up. This explanation was just as clear as those videos I found on Adrian's laptop. *Not!* It pushed me further into confusion.

Couldn't any revelation come with an open book and explanation?

Nothing worth having or knowing comes easy.

It was the only lesson my papa had taught me.

Of course, I had no fucking idea what it meant. I guess that I had to find out what Adrian was up to. Nothing good, it would seem.

Yet, I struggled to reconcile the boy I knew all my life to the hint of the man he left behind. The one who had incriminating crap on his laptop. *Blackmail. Video evidence.*

What was going on with Adrian? Was I too blind to see? Too wrapped up in wanting a baby to help him?

Maybe Papa was right. I'd have to find out so I'd have peace and move on.

TWELVE
TATIANA

Valentine's Day. The first one without him.

And I was still clueless on what Adrian was up to - except that he started to work against our... no, *my* family. He couldn't possibly have thought of us as his family if he'd stored blackmail-worthy videos against my brothers, Aurora's brothers. I'd have to assume he had more material somewhere else. Who knew how many, probably countless, others - friends or not - he had videos on! Maybe they were stored on other laptops. He used to have many more than just what was left in that room.

The creak of the iron gate of the cemetery sounded like the screech of crows. Dark and threatening.

Walking down the rows of graves seemed surreal, too cheery with tourists and their guides who preached New Orleans' history. Carnival had begun and it wouldn't be long before Fat Tuesday arrived, which meant Mardi Gras was in full swing, inviting even more visitors into the already crowded city.

I made my way towards the above-ground tomb that became Adrian's final resting place. My black Chanel heels clicked against the stone. My tailored dress felt loose on my body.

For the first time ever, the color black no longer flattered me at all.

It made me look washed out. I'd lost weight over the last four months. Alcohol wasn't helping, but somehow I found myself constantly going back to it.

It turns out it was easier to form an addiction than shake it off. Who knew, huh?

The dull ache between my temples throbbed in that familiar way. Like I should remember something, but my mind recoiled each time I tried. The therapist said not to force it. He labeled it memory suppression. He told me that my memories would come back when I was ready to handle them or when something triggered them. I shuddered, not wanting to think about what *that* could be.

Still, I couldn't wait. I had to remember. It felt like a matter of life and death. Hopefully, not mine.

The cool breeze swept through the air, sending a shiver down my spine. Temperatures in February weren't freezing, but they felt colder than usual with the wind blowing.

I found his niche plate. For a long moment, I just stood there and stared at the words, unable to read them. Unable to process them. Never in a million years would I have thought our story would end like this.

With trembling fingers, I reached out to trace the engraved letters.

BORN IN THE SHADOWS. SWORN IN BLOOD.
A VOW BROKEN AND BETRAYED.
JUDGMENT DELIVERED.

I hadn't seen it before. The words were ludicrous. Why would anyone put that shit on my husband's final resting place? I read the words again, my lips moving as if reading them out loud would give it meaning.

It didn't.

I had no idea what it meant, nor who came up with the ludicrous engraving. Maybe some fucked up mafia funeral, although my own father had a simple, normal engraving on his plate.

Not this.

Besides, Adrian wasn't really part of the mafia. Although he seemed to have gotten on their bad side. Still he didn't deserve to die so young. Our life together had barely started. I could still smell him in our penthouse. I could still hear his laughter in my sleep.

Except, he didn't laugh a lot those last few months. I feared things had changed. I didn't know if it was my constant demands to have a baby or something else.

But none of what happened could diminish that Adrian died to protect me. He died because he loved me. That was what my brothers told me. That he got me out of the car somehow.

It didn't make me feel better. His sacrifice had left so many holes — in my mind and soul.

"I wish you hadn't left me behind," I croaked through a broken voice. It hurt to breathe. My eyes stung, but no tears came. I didn't think I had any tears left.

"I wished you told me." Whatever it was that was going on. Maybe I could have helped him. Maybe my brothers would have helped. After all, Vasili brought him to our family. The image of Adrian the first time we locked eyes flashed through my mind.

"I hate the cold," I grumbled, my breath fogging the window. Pressing my finger against it, I drew a sun. I needed hot weather and a pool. Russians didn't mind winter. Papa always said that. Well, I minded it. "I'm not Russian. I'm American."

The dark sky promised another winter storm, wind beating against the windows as I stared longingly out of it. I hated being in Russia. It was always cold and dark during the winter months. But Vasili insisted. So we'd been here for two weeks. It wasn't so bad when he was home all day with us.

He'd do my hair. Play chess with me. Read to me. Sometimes he'd teach me Russian. Even though I already knew it. He and Sasha argued too much in Russian for me not to pick it up.

I stood on the windowsill in the old library, my face planted against the cold window, my nose flattened against the glass.

My pigtails hurt my scalp. Sasha attempted it and nearly ripped my scalp off, but now I was scared to pull them out. He might attempt to fix them. My five-year-old head couldn't handle his hands styling my hair again.

I scratched my scalp, hoping to relieve some of the tightness.

"My hair will fall out," I grumbled. "And it will be all Sasha's fault."

The ice banged angrily against the windows, matching my own frustration. I pressed my hand against the cold glass door. It was then that I spotted Papa's car approaching. It sped down the road towards the house, like the devil was on its heel, until it came to a stop.

I began to pound the window. Papa exited the car, but I didn't pay him much mind. Papa didn't like me; he always frowned when he looked at me. When I saw a familiar tall figure with broad shoulders towering even over Papa, I banged the glass harder.

Vasili's head turned slowly my way and our eyes met.

I grinned, jumping up and down from excitement. He gave me that warm smile he reserved only for me. Well, Sasha too but mostly me because Sasha was naughty and a troublemaker. Those were Vasili's words, not mine.

Jumping off the windowsill, I rushed through the room and out into the hallway, just in time to see Papa and Vasili enter.

"Vasili," I squealed as I ran to him and threw myself into his arms. Papa headed for his office, never stopping to greet me. I didn't pay him any attention either. It was hard to think of him as my papa when Vasili and Sasha did everything for me. "Where have you been for so long, Vasili? I missed you."

My oldest brother effortlessly lifted me up onto his big shoulders. "You just saw me this morning," he teased.

"You left before you did my hair," I scolded him.

"Seems you managed," he remarked. "I like your pigtails."

"Sasha did them." Holding on to Vasili's hair with one hand, I reached for my scalp again. "They hurt my head."

"He needs to remember you're a girl." He turned around and it was then that I spotted him. The tall, dark stranger with green eyes as fresh spring grass. "Tatiana, this is my friend, Adrian."

I stared at the tall boy. Maybe a man, I didn't know. Adrian. I'd heard his name mentioned a lot, but I'd never met him. Papa trusted him, but Vasili didn't like to bring anyone around me. Just family and guards that had been around since he was a boy. And he refused to leave me alone with them too.

"Hey, pipsqueak," Adrian greeted me.

Instantly I straightened up. "I'm not a pipsqueak!" I retorted undignified. "I'm Tatiana Nikolaev."

He chuckled. "You don't say."

I shot him a glare, but before I could say anything else, Vasili interrupted. "Sister, you're gripping my hair so tight, you're going to pull my hair out. It hurts my scalp."

"Now you know how it feels when Sasha does my hair," I snapped.

A heartbeat of silence and the hallway erupted with their laughter.

Since that day, Adrian had always been around. But not even he was allowed to stay alone with me. Not for a very long time. Even when Adrian and I became an item, Vasili wasn't thrilled. However, he finally let me make my own choice.

Could it be that there was more to Vasili's objection? Was Adrian's job putting him on some kind of front line?

Pressing my hand to my forehead, I searched my memories for anything he might have said. For any clues that he was in trouble. Yet, nothing came. Absolutely nothing. Adrian did a good job of keeping his work separate from our personal lives.

Somehow our personal life became a dark room without windows. Nobody knew that my relationship with Adrian slowly deteriorated. At least I didn't think so.

My memory flickered back to the day of the accident. Right before we left the party, I caught Vasili and Adrian arguing. Maybe my brothers knew our marriage was in trouble.

"It's bullshit," Vasili hissed, his broad back turned to me. "How in the fuck do you accidentally record that?"

Alexei and Sasha kept their gazes on Adrian. "Where are the documents?" Alexei asked in a cold voice.

"Better come up with them, motherfucker," Sasha grunted. "Today."

Sasha had to stop going around calling everyone motherfuckers.

Click. Click. Click. My heels clicked against the floor as I approached them. I could tell the moment they all realized I was within earshot because talk ceased. Silence followed.

Maybe I was the only blind one. Everyone knew something or everything while I walked around oblivious.

I scoffed softly. *Our personal life.*

When did it all go sideways with us? Was it the reason for the tension in the last few months? Maybe I missed signs that were there all along. If I paid closer attention to what was happening around us rather than putting demands on him, could I have seen the signs? Maybe I could have saved him. We could have fixed things together.

And Adrian would still be here. I'd still have him. We'd have the possibility of a future.

Pain, raw and angry, grabbed me by the throat. It clawed at my heart. It stabbed at it. My ears rang and frostbite spread through my chest, suffocating. I blinked hard as a soft sob escaped me. I cupped my mouth to stifle it.

"I wish you would have said something," I choked on the words, but tears still didn't come. "Anything."

I pressed my palm against the cold stone. Maybe his spirit would rest here, but his body wouldn't. *Ashes.* My husband has been reduced to ashes. I'd give anything to remember what had happened.

An excruciating ache shot through me. A reminder that I'd never get a chance to say goodbye properly.

I pulled out my phone and dialed the number. I had come to listen to his voicemail a lot. Too much to be healthy.

The answering machine picked up and my heart skidded to a halt. "The number you have dialed has been disconnected."

"No, no, no," I muttered, looking at the screen. Maybe I dialed the wrong number. So I dialed it again. The same answer. "The number you have dialed has been disconnected."

My heart sank. It was bound to happen. "Fucking efficient people," I cursed, although truthfully it wasn't efficient. It had been weeks.

I ended the call and slid my phone in the pocket of the dress. Thank fuck they made dresses with hidden pockets.

The wind picked up and I shivered, wrapping my arms around me. My eyes drifted over the cluster of headstones surrounding the mausoleum. Another dedication caught my eyes.

> HERE LIES A ROSE. MY ROSE.
> WITH BROKEN THORNS.
> A DEBT PAID, BUT NOT SATISFIED.
> A BLACK ROSE AND POISONOUS THORN.

Adrian always referred to his mother as a rose. I found it bizarre but then my brothers referred to our mother as 'psycho bitch' so who was I to judge. At least 'rose' sounded affectionate. I read the dedication again.

It was a coincidence; it had to be. Nobody else knew about Adrian and the nickname for his mother. Not even my best friend. Definitely not my brothers. I searched for the date of birth and death but there was none. Just this cryptic poem, or maybe a message, carved on a plain tombstone.

Shaking my head, I averted my gaze back to Adrian's resting place and my brows furrowed. Then I realized. They had a theme. Yet, I knew Adrian had no family here.

We, the Nikolaev family, were his family. At least I thought so.

Who came up with these dedications? None of them made any sense.

With a last glance on the crypt, I turned around and left more at a loss than ever.

The cemetery offered no answers. Only more questions.

An hour later I stood in front of the building of New Orleans Municipal Cemeteries on Tchoupitoulas Street.

I didn't need to turn around to know that Yan was close by. He always lingered in the shadows, watching over me. Something I despised before, but now I found comfort and safety in it.

Pushing the heavy door open, I made my way inside. The website had given me the name of a superintendent for New Orleans Municipal Cemeteries so I searched the directory board for it. Second floor.

Jane Ford, Cemeteries Superintendent.

I shook my head at the title engraving against the door. At least it was easy to find.

Smoothing my hand down my black Valentino dress, I ensured nothing was out of place. There was no need for strangers to know what a mess I'd been since Adrian's death. Or that I'd turned to alcohol.

I blew a breath into my palm to ensure I didn't reek of alcohol. I only smelled mouthwash.

Knock. Knock.

"Enter."

I pushed the door open and entered, then stopped and glanced over my shoulder. "I'll be okay in here, Yan."

A terse nod and I shut the door. An elderly lady with soft features and white hair done in a bun met my gaze as I approached her desk. She recognized me; I could tell by the flicker of awareness that filled her green eyes.

Taking a seat across the desk from her, I crossed my legs.

"How can I help you, Mrs. Morozov?" she asked, confirming my suspicion that she knew who I was. "Or do you prefer Ms. Nikolaev?"

I ignored her question.

"I want to know who ordered my husband's niche plate engraving," I retorted, not wasting time. There was no need for unnecessary pleasantries. "And I want to fire whoever put that shit on it."

Her expression never faltered, the same smile curving her lips.

"Let's see," she said, reaching for a folder on her desk. She shuffled through some papers, but somehow I got the impression it was just busy work and she already had an answer. *As if she was expecting this visit.* What the fuck?

"Aha," she exclaimed. She pulled out a piece of paper, her eyes roaming the page, then lifting to me. I watched her mask, the expression on her face untelling but something in her eyes kept tickling the back of my mind. A feeling in the pit of my stomach warned, but I couldn't pinpoint what was bothering me about her. "The engraving was ordered by you, Ms. Nikolaev."

She dropped the bomb and my mind blanked. I stared at her, repeating her words in my mind slowly. Maybe I misunderstood her? Maybe my English and Russian were mixed up. After all, I did sustain a concussion from the accident.

"Excuse me." My voice sounded distant. A rush of noise swept through my brain. Whispers. Warnings.

"The engraving on the plate was ordered by you," she repeated slowly, like she was talking to an imbecile.

"That's impossible." I'd never write something so morbid. So fucking mafia. "Do you have a copy of the order?"

Her lips curved into a cold half-smile.

"I thought you'd never ask."

Holding the paper, she extended her hand across the desk. Warning alarms shot through me, but I ignored them as I grabbed the paper. I read through it, each word more confusing than the last one.

Until the last line.

My signature on the dotted line stared back at me, questioning my sanity.

THIRTEEN

TATIANA

Time didn't bring more answers. Only more questions.

Frustration gripped me. Anger boiled my blood. Melancholy swallowed me.

Maybe I reverted to stage two. Or maybe I was on stage four. Depression. Was there a stage for losing your mind?

Last night I swore I heard a radio playing. The song that Adrian and I danced to. While the moon lingered high in the sky, I heard those words repeating 'walking in the shadows' by Jillian Edwards. Except, the whole song didn't play. The same words played over and over again. *I go on. I go on. Standing in the shadows.*

Too terrified to get out of bed, I covered my ears with the palms of my hands and hunched into a ball while hot tears burned my skin. I was scared of ghosts. Of turning into my mother. Of going crazy.

Yes, the stage for losing your mind was probably dedicated only to the Nikolaev members. Jesus Christ!

I had no fucking clue where I was, that was the honest truth.

Weeks flew by. My snooping through Adrian's stuff only provided more questions, no answers. Weird notes came up here and there. Call N. Who was N? Itinerary N and J. Who in the fuck were those people?

Months of digging through information only to end up more

confused. Information I found in Adrian's room shed no light on anything. He didn't seem to have focused on a single person with his secret and damning videos. It was all over the place - politicians, underworld members, doctors. There was no rhyme or reason to what he was doing or who he was targeting. But the videos I uncovered included some very scary shit. If any of them knew about these, they'd want him dead.

God, maybe they *all* wanted him dead.

Then, Alexei's words from the morning of the funeral shattered through the fog.

He wasn't good for you. Not anymore.

That required elaboration. I'd have to corner Alexei and ask him what he meant by it. Just not today. Today, I needed this. A seed of doubt whispered in my mind, mocking my words.

How many times had I said, '*not today*'?

My sweaty fingers gripped the flask, the only medicine that kept me going. All my cuts and bruises had long healed, but my mind hadn't. If anything, I started to question it all.

What had I done?

What had Adrian done?

What in the fuck was going on?

A weird type of anger gripped my chest and refused to let go. I blamed it on my husband's death. I blamed this fucking life. The underworld. I blamed everyone. Everyone including myself.

I was hearing voices at night. Things in the penthouse were here one day and gone the next. The man I married wasn't who I thought he was. It was all becoming too much. I felt like I had lost my mind, and I was scared to let anyone see it. What if my brothers decided I was crazy like our mother and locked me away?

It was better to hide it all - with alcohol, anger, anything.

Panic about my state of mind made it hard to breathe. I needed to somehow relieve this anger. Get rid of the bitterness. Get rid of the addiction I was clearly nurturing.

I just didn't know how. It had become a part of me.

My hand shook as I brought the flask to my lips and tipped the bottle. A pitiful drop touched my lips, tasting bitter. I shook it, again and again. As if that would produce more alcohol. I needed more of it, so I could feel less. So I could drown out these thoughts in my head. There were too many.

My feet moved across the paved streets. People passed me by. Men. Women. Children. Families. Nobody paid attention to another drunk on the street. There were plenty of those in this city. Or maybe they all paid me attention but thought I deserved it.

Spoiled Nikolaev princess at her lowest. Or maybe there was still room for me to fall even further.

My thoughts were scrambled, coming and going. Some made sense; most didn't. It was the alcohol in my veins. It made it hard to think. Was I going crazy?

God, I hoped I wouldn't turn into my mother. I couldn't turn into my mother. That would be bad. Very bad.

I crossed the street, my small heels clicking against the pavement. I caught my reflection in a shop window. The old-fashioned seventies style dress, white at the top and black skirt swished with my every move. It flared from my waist down to my knees, flattering my figure that had gotten way too thin in recent months.

It was peculiar how our exterior never reflected our inner selves. Everyone expected a polished and up-to-date fashion clad Tatiana.

So here I was. Looking polished and put together on the outside while on the inside, I was a jumbled mess. Maybe I was an alcoholic. Maybe I was just insane. After all, it ran in the family. Those fucking genes - there was no escaping them.

I let out a heavy sigh. I should have just stayed in bed. At least I had a fully stocked bar at home. Or maybe I should be smart and dig through more of Adrian's stuff. Look for answers.

Instead, here I was, roaming these lively streets while lack of sleep pulled on my muscles.

Whispers echoed in my mind. Words that made no sense at all.

He left her to die. The words were spoken. I was certain I'd heard them except I couldn't remember anything else about it. Who left me to die? Who uttered those words?

Pissed off at the words I didn't understand, I sped up my steps. Yan and Yuri trailed behind me, but I'd gotten good at ignoring them. It was a constant since the accident. The only time I didn't have them following me was when I was in the penthouse or with my brothers.

The coolness of New Orleans filled my lungs and touched my skin. The warmth of the alcohol baked me on the inside, and I couldn't decide whether it was helpful or not.

The city buzzed with life. The ambiance of the old New Orleans was in the air, smelled along the breeze, heard in the music, and felt in the colors all around me.

But the atmosphere didn't match my mood. The Crescent City floated as I drowned. The vibrancy of the city highlighted my dark mood. I used to be a talker, happy chatter, but now, I preferred my own company. I couldn't even recognize myself.

Alcohol swam through my blood, making me feel relaxed, dulling all my senses. Although it failed at dulling the self-disappointment in the pit of my stomach. I promised myself I'd stop drinking. I really tried, but the sweats started, then tremors followed. My hands were unsteady. Withdrawals were bad.

I turned down the alley, opting for a less busy street. I couldn't stand all the laughter and music anymore. The constant click of my heels and my bodyguards in the distance was the only thing I focused on, ignoring all other noises.

But then the second set of footsteps stopped. It happened so fast. By the time I registered it and went to turn around, it was already too late.

Unyielding hands slammed my back against the wall and a hand covered my mouth. My flask clanked against the pavement. My breath was cut off from the impact and that hand that blocked my airway. My vision blurred from the impact. I blinked, then blinked again, staring at the stranger's face.

High cheekbones. Hair as dark as a raven's feathers. Dark, cold eyes. Beautiful skin. He'd be beautiful, if not for that sneer curving his lips. And cruelty in his eyes.

"Where is the chip?" His voice was rough. Heavily accented. Unfamiliar.

My eyes shifted to the left, then right, frantically searching for my bodyguards. They were nowhere to be found. My heart thundered hard against my chest, cracking my ribs.

I guess I'm on my own.

Yet, I knew. I was no match for this guy. Not in my buzzed state.

I lowered my eyes to his wrist and my heartbeat faltered. A Yakuza tattoo sleeve decorated his skin. *Yakuza in New Orleans?* Shock slammed through the alcohol induced fog in my brain.

I wasn't drunk enough to not realize this was bad. Really bad. The Yakuza were ruthless. Merciless. Dangerous. And their fighting skills were unmatched.

Sasha always tried to teach me self-defense moves. I'd never been particularly interested but things somehow stuck. So I went for it. I relaxed my body, fooling him into thinking he'd overpowered me. Then I kneed him into his balls. *Hard.*

"Fucking bitch," he hissed, pain crossing his expression but his grip on me refused to ease. Goddamn him! The alcohol swimming through my veins wasn't helping.

The next second, he jammed his elbow into my ribs. "Ouch," I yelped. That fucking hurt.

"Last warning before I snap your neck," he growled. "Your husband's chip. Where is it?"

My voice was muffled as I answered. "I-I don't know. What ch-chip?"

One second I saw his fist flying through the air, the next the man's body slumped onto the ground. It happened even before my brain could process it all.

I blinked, staring in shock at the man lying at my feet. He couldn't have been a high ranking Yakuza member. His pants were decent but not expensive. His white t-shirt was Tommy Hilfiger. Not cheap, but not overly expensive either.

"Are you all right?"

The first thing that registered was the scent. Citrus, sandalwood, and spice. Adrian! Alas, the wrong voice.

"Adrian?" My voice was a hoarse whisper.

The corner of my mind understood it couldn't be him, but still my eyes shot up with hope, expecting to see the familiar face.

My husband's.

The sinking feeling was instant, overwhelming me with such power that my knees started shaking. My heart shuddered and my lungs expanded, taking a deep breath. The scent seeped into my marrow, so potent it intoxicated me more than all the alcohol.

I closed my eyes, letting it wash over me. Just one more moment of oblivion. Hope. But reality came too soon.

"Are you okay?" The same, unfamiliar voice.

I opened my eyes. The man who stood in front of me wasn't my husband. But he smelled like him. Just the way I remembered from our first time together.

"Why do you smell like that?" I croaked. My voice trembled. My muscles shook.

"Like what?"

Like the man I love. Like the man who was everything to me. Like the man who kept secrets from me.

Instead I shook my head and remained numb, drowning in his dark eyes. They were harsh and dark, pulling me into their depths. Yet I wasn't scared. The scent fooled me, thinking he was someone he wasn't. And I let it, living in that oblivion that it offered.

It was short lived.

He shifted and I instinctively took a small step back, pressing myself flat against the wall. He paused, then slid his hands into his pockets and rocked on his heel. The same hands that just mere seconds ago knocked this man out with brutal force.

He tried to appear non-threatening. *Tried* was the key word here.

Nothing was non-threatening about him. There was darkness in this man. Underneath that stunning male beauty lurked something savage. Something terrifying.

My heart thundered heavily in my chest. The particles in the air charged and sizzled. My skin heated and my breaths turned shallow.

Run, Tatiana. My instinct warned. A smart person would run. Yet I forced myself to remain still, studying him. I had just seen him at the graveyard. He wasn't exactly someone you'd forget. Running into him twice was suspicious.

He was tall. Very tall. Probably about six-foot-four, maybe even six-foot-five. He was wearing a black shirt and white pants. Extremely good quality clothes. Tailored. Expensive. This guy was *someone*. Everything about him screamed money and elegance. Self-confidence.

It was that which fascinated me more than anything else. His charisma. And the intimidation of his demeanor. This man was dangerous. I'd recognize his type amongst millions. I grew up with that type.

The question was what did he want, and why was he here? It couldn't be a coincidence.

Heart hammering, we stood there, watching each other. Studying each other. Reluctantly I wondered what he saw - a drunk, a grieving widow, a Nikolaev.

I swallowed hard. This was bad. If it was just a street thug, I'd be able to handle it. It was better when nobody was after you than somebody. But this guy, it'd be hard to overtake him. He was too big, his eyes too sharp, and the intelligence in them daunting.

My eyes frantically searched around him but he was alone. Maybe I was wrong and he was just a passerby, a good Samaritan, who tried to assist a woman in distress. Usually men like Vasili had muscle behind them. There had to be at least one wingman but this guy had none.

My eyes flickered to his face and I knew instantly, I was fooling myself. A cloud of harshness surrounded him. The kind that spoke of things he witnessed and bad things he'd done. His face was unmoving, unblinking. Hard.

But his eyes pulled me into their dark depths, swallowing me into their savagery.

This man was exactly where he wanted to be.

"Are you okay?" he asked again. His voice brushed the side of my cheek, deep and indifferent. A strange feeling fluttered in my stomach.

An even stranger sense of familiarity. Yet, my brain was too deep in the buzzed fog to identify him.

And all the while his dark eyes decrypted every inch of my soul.

"Yes." My voice came out small. I hated to look weak so I pushed my shoulders back. "I had it handled, thank you very much."

His brow cocked and the corners of his lips tipped up. Barely. There was no empathy in his expression. No feigned worry. He stood there, unmoving. Unblinking. As if he was waiting.

The itch beneath my skin deepened. His closeness seared, like standing too close to the fire but you refused to step away because the cold would then swallow you whole.

"You better get back to the busy street," he instructed, the citrus and sandalwood scent filling my lungs. "I'm going to wait for the cops."

I almost snickered. *Almost.*

I didn't know who he was fooling, but it wasn't me. His kind didn't use cops to do the right thing. Or the wrong thing. His kind got their hands dirty just like those men, including my brothers, in the videos I watched.

Was he in one of those videos on Adrian's laptop? It could be where I saw him before and the reason he seemed familiar.

I couldn't shake off the feeling. I knew this man.

FOURTEEN
KONSTANTIN

A red mist covered my vision.

My brain cells were burning faster than the breaths I inhaled in an attempt to calm my rage.

I had been watching her. Stalking her. Waiting for the right moment.

A day was coming when she'd find that which belonged to me. What belonged to Marchetti. What belonged to every goddamn criminal on this planet. And that alone put her life in danger. Unfortunately, some fuckers didn't know the meaning of patience.

Like the goddamn Yakuza.

I had just returned from California. My driver dropped me off in the French Quarter. Then I spotted her. I had two of my most trusted men tailing Tatiana since Adrian's death. The moment I got out of the car, the men fell back while I walked on foot, following the woman who still seemed to be mourning her late husband.

It had been over six fucking months. It was time she moved on. He wasn't worthy of her. He was a peasant; she was a queen. He was treacherous; she was loyal.

Fuck, how that irked me. The fucker wasn't worth the ground she walked on. Definitely not her tears. She deserved better. She deserved the whole goddamn world.

The stars in her eyes were gone. But I vowed the day I left her in that hospital bed that I'd take the stars from the night sky and put them back where they belong. In her eyes. I'd see them in her eyes again if it was the last thing I did in this life.

Completely oblivious to her surroundings and lost in her thoughts, Tatiana sipped from her flask. It wasn't hard to guess what was in there. I hated that she developed that habit, but that wouldn't last. Not once I got her where I wanted her - in my home and in my bed.

After all, I'd waited a long time for her. Adrian was a fool and his fuck up was my gain. The moment I learned his true identity, he was a dead man anyhow.

And then the goddamn Yakuza got to her. Dared to touch her. The one I said was off limits. Only I was allowed to torture her, and my kind of torture would produce screams of pleasure, not fear.

They'd knocked out Yan and Yuri, the two bodyguards that always trailed behind her, which left her vulnerable. My own men fell behind, per my instruction, since I intended to watch her myself.

A mistake I wouldn't repeat.

After I handled the fucker and he laid passed out on the ground, I met Tatiana's gaze. Her pale blue eyes widened and her breath hitched. She watched me, searching my face and something in her expression had me pausing.

Waiting.

"Are you okay?" I asked her again, worried that asshole hurt her and I came too late.

"Yes," she croaked, gripping the bunch of her dress. She looked beautiful. Like the Grace Kelly of the twenty-first century. Then as if she realized she sounded too weak, she added. "I had it handled, thank you very much."

There she is, I thought satisfied. My fearless queen.

Tatiana Nikolaev wasn't a woman to cower. She was just as stubborn as her brothers and just as impulsive. Her life was one of impetuous decisions and reckless actions. She lived her life to the fullest. As if it was her last day on Earth.

It had to be the reason I couldn't handle seeing the light leave her eyes. Seeing my mother executed left a mark - on both Maxim and myself. Seeing Tatiana end up the same way would break me. Although I feared if the news of her connection to Adrian's chip spread, she'd end up like my mother.

Unless I married her before anyone found out.

The most important question was did she work with Adrian, and, if so, how much did she know?

"You better get back to the busy street," I told her softly. "I'm going to wait for the cops."

As if. I'd have my men shove this fucker into a van and then I'd teach him a lesson.

She watched me warily and I held my breath. Did she recognize me? For the past seven years, she had been a constant whisper in my mind. When I finally learned her identity, it turned into a downright obsession.

I knew her favorite foods. Her favorite book. Songs. Designers. You name it, I knew it.

She frowned. "Have we met before?"

I let out a sardonic breath, annoyance flaring in my chest. Jesus Christ, this woman! I'd been obsessed with her for years and she didn't even remember meeting me. That night in the gazebo fueled my obsession, and she had no fucking clue that it was me who was buried deep in her tight pussy as she moaned, begging for me.

Lovely! That certainly boosted my ego.

"You tell me," I retorted wryly. "Did we meet?"

"Whatever." She waved her hand, as if my answer didn't matter. "Anyhow. Thank you, I guess." I cocked my eyebrow.

"You guess?"

"Like I said, I could have handled him," she repeated, narrowing her eyes on me. "I'm not a damsel in distress."

She shifted between her feet. The woman was smart enough to know she couldn't have overpowered him.

"Go home." I needed her and that scent of roses to be gone before my control snapped and I touched her.

A terse nod and she hurried away from me. My attention remained on her until she rounded the corner. The moment she disappeared from my view, I called Nikita. He answered on the first ring.

"Follow her and make sure she gets home safely."

"Got it, Boss."

My driver, Lenosh, showed up next and stopped at the end of the alley, blocking the view. Boris, my second-in-command and my driver jumped out, both eyeing the man sprawled on the ground.

"Are you sure this is a good idea?" Boris asked. "The Nikolaev brothers won't be happy if they find us in their territory."

I shrugged. "They start shit, I'll take it all from them. They need to be reminded it was my family's territory before it was theirs."

They were here by the grace of my old man. He didn't want this territory after snatching my mother and marrying her. So he tipped Nikola Nikolaev. My old man even sponsored him. I'd honor the agreement, but I had to get my hands on that chip. If that shit ended up in the wrong hands, like Interpol or the FBI, it would be bad.

For everyone, including the Nikolaevs.

Never mind if our enemies got their paws on it. We'd all go down. Just the thought of Sofia Volkov getting her hands on a piece of information like that would send a ripple through the underworld. That crazy, vindictive bitch would destroy us all.

After all, it was my father who overtook her husband. The old Volkov was the Pakhan but he was weak, losing territories to the Italians, French, Greek. So my old man swept in like fucking Alexander the Great, with the backing of Thorns of Omertà, and became Konstantin the Great.

Yeah, I was well aware of the fucking irony.

"Definitely trouble on the horizon," Boris, my second in command, muttered. He jogged over to me, picked up the body, and returned to the vehicle, throwing the unconscious body into the trunk before tying him up.

Once we were back in the car, the driver sped up. Boris retrieved his phone, scrolling through it quickly. Probably checking on any potential hackers, and then there was the fact that we hacked into Nikolaev's network.

My attention was zeroed in on the surroundings and my whole body tensed as we passed Tatiana, her steps slightly unsure as she headed back towards her penthouse. Disappointment washed over me when she didn't look over. I was so damn obsessed with the woman, and she couldn't even remember me.

But by the time this was over, she'd remember me. Every fucking touch. Every word. Everything.

She had gotten thinner, but her features were the same - delicate, beautiful and so fucking tempting. How could have she mistaken me for Adrian? I fucking lived for those sounds she made. Those moans were impossible to erase from my memory, no matter how hard I tried.

I shook the image out of my head or risked getting a hard on. It was hardly the right time.

Instead, I called up a connection I knew wouldn't rat to Marchetti. The famous, rather infamous, Bitter Prince.

Amon Takahashi Leone.

The second-in-command of the Yakuza organization, not just a branch in a certain country but in the world. Truthfully, he should be the head of it. He only had to seize it. He was the only man who had connections to Yakuza and indirect connection to Marchetti. Maybe Enrico had had enough waiting. Although I'd hope he'd give me the courtesy of a goddamn notice.

He answered on the third ring. "Yes."

"Did you send the Yakuza after Tatiana Nikolaev?" I growled.

If he had, I'd wipe him off this planet. Regardless of how much I admired the fucker and how much he accomplished.

"No."

"Did Marchetti?"

"No."

"But you know who put the hit on her," I declared. Nothing happened in Yakuza without the knowledge of Itsuki Takahashi, his cousin.

"Yes." Fuck, him and his short answers.

"Your cousin is a problem."

Amon didn't comment. Not that I expected him to. Instead, his reply came in a cool voice, in his perfect British English, "It's not the last attempt. Hide her."

"Keep your cousin the fuck away, or he'll end up dead."

A heartbeat passed before Amon's next words shot fury through my veins. "Maxim provided the tip."

Anger spread like fire through me and a red mist covered my vision again. The idea of Tatiana's lifeless body and never again seeing that gleam in her blue eyes made my stomach tighten. My hands clenched with fury as I ended the call. Maxim. My fucking twin brother. I would have never expected such betrayal from him.

Inhaling deeply, I released my breath, then repeated it again. It took several minutes to calm the rage that swallowed me whole. Anyone else, would be dead within an hour.

Maxim would be dealt with too.

In the meantime, I'd teach Amon's cousin a lesson. Maybe I'd even go the extra mile and end the cousin. Then Amon could take over that kingdom.

Today though, I'd shred the guy that dared to touch Tatiana. Tear him fucking apart. Maybe I'd have his heart delivered to Itsuki Taka-hashi with a message.

Yes. I liked that very much.

The car came to a stop in front of one of the warehouses we bought outside the city. Its location was perfect, right on The Mississippi River. It made disposal of assholes like this one easy. Alligators loved to eat humans.

Lenosh had the guy out of the trunk and already dragged him inside the warehouse before I even stepped out of the car. I stalked inside, letting the anger simmer my blood and spread through me.

Who the fuck was he to believe he could touch her? Some little Yakuza errand boy. Even if he was the head of the Yakuza, he wouldn't be allowed to put his filthy hands on Tatiana.

I entered to find him rolling on the concrete floor and groaning as he gripped his nuts. My lips curved into a half-smile. I was so proud when I saw her kick him in his balls. Tatiana was a fighter, and it was time to remind her.

That's moye solntse. My sun. *Moya luna.* My moon. My everything.

Finally noticing me, he wrestled himself into a sitting position. I let him. No sense in binding him to the chair. There was nowhere he could run that I wouldn't get him. His wrists were already tied behind his back. I almost hoped he'd run. It would make killing him all the more enjoyable.

His dark, slanted eyes met mine.

"W-Who are y-you?" he stumbled over his words in his heavily accented English.

"Nobody."

I pulled out my gun as I approached him, then the silencer, taking my time attaching it. "Have you taken the oath of Omertà?"

His eyes widened and sweat broke across his forehead. "Yes."

His gaze was locked on my movements as I stalked toward him.

"You touched what's mine," I said, as I placed the muzzle to his forehead. "Bad move."

He spat a string of words in Japanese. I knew enough to understand he was cursing me.

"Ah, you're asking to be sliced up," I drawled. "I can accommodate that."

I smiled and grabbed my knife. His tongue was the first thing he lost, but certainly not the last.

By the time I was done, he had no blood left in his body. It poured out all over the warehouse floor.

The last move was cutting out his heart.

"I'm going to ship this to your boss," I said to the dead corpse.

He didn't object.

FIFTEEN
TATIANA

lcohol still in my veins, my steps faltered as I passed the
threshold of the penthouse I used to share with my husband.
Shutting the door behind me, I leaned against it while my
heart still pounded against my chest.

I slumped against the door. It was only then that I let out a relieved
breath. My eyes traveled over the desolate penthouse. There was furniture throughout the penthouse, but the little things that made it a home
weren't. Photographs in frames were stored away; somewhere where
they wouldn't stare back at me, reminding me of what I had lost. But
memories weren't as easily erased. Every memory lurked in the
corners of my mind, telling me it was time to move on. Maybe let go of
some things.

Like this place, I thought silently.

This place no longer felt like home, but it was safer than out there.
Jesus, that was intense.

Yakuza.

Was that who killed Adrian?

What the fuck was going on? Adrian got wrapped up into something that he shouldn't have and I had yet to learn what.

Somehow it felt like I didn't even know him. Maybe we weren't as good of a fit as I thought.

This place for example. Adrian preferred his place outside the city. I didn't. I preferred staying here. This penthouse was in the middle of the city. The French Quarter could be seen from the windows. There was some comfort in knowing there was the buzz of the city right outside the window. It made me feel not so desperately alone.

Or maybe it was even lonelier to be amongst millions of people, laughter, and music and this was my way of torturing myself.

Crap!

Yan and Yuri were still out there somewhere. I should go look for them. I couldn't look their families in the eyes if something happened to them because of me. Just as I debated whether to go back out in danger, a soft knock on the door sounded.

My whole body stiffened and I stopped breathing. Did the Yakuza have more men and they followed me home?

Scared to even breathe, I kept my hand on my racing heart to calm it down.

"Tatiana." A swish of air left my lungs. That was Yuri's voice. Then just to be sure I wasn't imagining things, I peeked through the peephole. Yes, it was Yuri.

I unbolted the door and opened it, then threw myself on him.

"I thought they killed you," I whimpered, my voice shaking. My nerves were shot, although the alcohol might have something to do with it.

"No, they just gave me a lump on my head," he grumbled. "It's more important that you're okay."

"Don't say that," I scolded him softly. "My life isn't worth more than yours. Just ask your family."

He smiled and my eyes darted behind him. "Where is Yan?"

"He's downstairs. Coordinating a check around the building, ensuring there aren't others around."

"Please tell me you haven't said a word to Vasili." My brother would put everything into overactive protective mode. He was as lovable as he was overbearing.

"Not yet, but we must."

I shook my head. "No, we must not."

"Tatiana–"

"No!" I glared at him. "First, he'd blame you for letting yourself be taken out. Then, he'd assign a whole army on me and possibly remove you. Let's keep this between us."

"Yan's not going to like it."

"Tell Yan, I pay you, not Vasili." Yuri raised his brow as if to claim all my money was Vasili's anyhow. Well, that wasn't true. I had my own trust fund and I did well managing it. "That's final. Now come in," I demanded.

Yuri shook his head. "No, I'll watch out here. I can't see the threat from inside." With that, he turned around and pulled the door shut. "Lock yourself in."

I did as he asked, then leaned against the door again with a relieved breath. Yuri and Yan were okay. I was okay. Relatively speaking.

"Chip," I muttered as I hung my coat on the rack beside the door and went to the kitchen, my steps heavy and slow. "What did he mean by it? Is that what—" The realization hit. It should have sunk in earlier but the alcohol in my veins probably wasn't helping. "That must be what these men are after!" Now, I had a direction. A purpose. I'd find it and get my answers. "Where is that damn chip?"

It felt important. That man clearly thought I had it.

I made my way to the window and stared at the people below me, rushing to their final destination, while my thoughts wandered.

Was this the reason Adrian didn't want to have kids? It is possible he knew he was in so deep that it would endanger our family. The memory of that last week together flickered through my mind.

I was stubborn, demanding to get my way and oblivious to what was going on apparently.

Adrian and I sat on the couch, each one of us on the opposite side of it. An old Grace Kelly movie played. Flash. Luxury. Cameras. Dresses. But I didn't see any of it. The wheels in my brain spun furiously ever since he dropped the 'I' bomb yesterday. INFERTILE.

Initially, it was a shock. I didn't know what to think of it. Or feel.

But since then, I have had time to think it through. It wasn't an obstacle. Days of research showed me there were many children that needed a family. I wasn't willing to give up on our family just because he was infertile.

"We could adopt," I whispered.

If only I could show Adrian that a child would be a blessing. They needed love and affection, a caring family. My brothers would love their niece or nephew, regardless if we adopted or gave birth.

The temperature in our penthouse dipped into the Siberian freeze-your-fucking-ass off winter.

"Drop it, Pipsqueak." Adrian's warning was vehement and harsh.

But I wasn't the giving up type of girl. The stubbornness was part of my genetics. So I pressed.

"I've researched a few agencies," I continued, while tension pulled tight in his shoulders. "There are some here in the U.S.; although, it might be faster if we adopt from an international one." He didn't look at me but the tension grew palpable. It was so thick, I could almost taste it. "Maybe we could adopt from a Russian agency?"

After all, he came from the streets of Moscow. He knew some kids that grew up in Russian orphanages. We could give them a better life.

"I don't want a kid," he spat out, not even deigning me with a glance.

Then he shot up and started to walk away from me. Blind rage was like an injection and I jumped up too.

"Give me a reason," I shouted. "A good reason why. You refuse to even consider what I want or need."

"Tatiana, you've been spoiled your whole life," he said, not even turning his head. "You'd never understand."

Dumbfounded, I stared after him. It took a minute for my lips to form a question. "Understand what, Adrian?" I asked in a hurt voice. Yes, my brothers gave me all they could, but I didn't think I was spoiled. I never demanded unreasonable things, and I was always willing to work for what I wanted.

"Adrian, don't walk away from me," I called out. "Talk to me."

The door slammed and my voice echoed throughout the empty penthouse.

He had left me. Again.

Ultimately, he left me for good, hadn't he?

But we were happy initially. There'd been life here before. Happiness.

We had a life together. I moved in. We laughed. We watched movies. We made plans. And then, it almost changed overnight.

My eyes traveled over the empty room.

Adrian's gadgets used to lay everywhere. My fashion magazines. His combat boots he'd just kick off and leave laying in the middle of the hallway. It used to drive me nuts. He'd say he'd put them away, but he never did and I'd get irritated.

It seemed such an insignificant thing to be fussing over now. In the light of death and forever gone.

So many memories. Most of them were packed away. Some were forgotten. The day it all ended lingered in the darkness, waiting to come out of the shadows.

Another shudder rolled down my spine. This place was too dark and empty.

Kind of like me, I thought to myself.

After the accident, I ceased eating, bathing, and living for a while. I couldn't take care of myself, but I refused to let anyone else care for me too. And now… well, I wanted the truth and answers.

Abruptly, I whirled around and went to the kitchen.

I opened the refrigerator and found it empty except for two slices of cheese. I had no idea how old they were so I opted not to eat. I sat at the empty kitchen table, the only thing on it was a vodka bottle. My constant companion. I gazed over the empty table, the empty counters.

The place has been empty. No visitors for weeks. Only me.

Both Isabella and Aurora kept gently reminding me to move on. Neither one of them were able to get more information on the agreement between Vasili and Adrian. Aurora was clear she wasn't willing to dig through Kingston's past to figure out what exactly he was involved with.

Aurora's words were, "Certain things are best left in the past. Let's all move on."

Except I couldn't.

Every night a reminder would come. Every night ghosts would visit.

I let out a sigh, almost fearing the next time I'd close my eyes. The more I drank, the less I remembered from the dreams. But I knew my brothers were right. I couldn't keep it up. I'd destroy myself, or my liver at minimum.

Another sigh echoed through the house. It was so damn quiet. Too empty.

"Can you let me sleep tonight?" I asked, half-expecting a response.

From whom though? Ghosts? Memories? Adrian?

I closed my eyes, my heart aching in that familiar way. It didn't go away with time, but it dulled. The pain was inside my chest, a constant companion and reminder of what I had lost.

Moving on shouldn't be this hard, this painful.

A shuddering breath filled the space. It echoed against the walls. It traveled through the darkness along with a pitter-patter against the windows. I looked out the large floor-to-ceiling window. It had started raining again. The last few months brought a lot of rain. It made for depressing weather.

A tear fell, sliding down my cheek, leaving me alone with memories of my dead husband.

I poured a glass of vodka and downed it in one gulp. Then I poured another one. It tasted bitter. I didn't like the taste of it, but I still refused to give it up. I needed the shot of numbness that came along with it. It took no time for my body to relax and the buzzing in my ears to grow. The world was spinning, but I didn't care.

I picked up my glass with one hand and the bottle with my other, then headed into the bedroom. I put them both on the nightstand, then my fingers moved to the zipper, the sound slashing through the air. I let the dress fall down my body, pooling at my feet.

The air must have been turned off because it was hot in here. I could hear the blaring of the sirens in the distance. Someone below me must have slammed the door because the entire building shook.

I drowned it all out.

Reaching for the glass and bottle, I sat on the bed and poured another drink. I downed it in one gulp, then closed my eyes.

I still couldn't shake off that feeling. The same feeling that came every night. Someone was watching me.

The glass and bottle from my night stand shattered all over the floor. My heart cracked. My breaths came out panting. I brought my legs up to my chest and curled up into a ball. I squeezed my eyelids shut hard, hoping to erase all the images in my mind.

"Sleep, sleep, sleep," I murmured as I rocked back and forth on my bed. Pipsqueak. Moya luna. Pipsqueak. Moya luna.

Why was my mind whispering the stupid words on repeat over and over again?

Glass was everywhere. I hung upside down. Voices argued. Blood covered my face. Adrian was gone. I looked around for him, he was nowhere.

Did he just leave me?

A hand stretched towards me. A man's hand. A strong hand. Not Adrian's hand. But he smelled like my husband. Citrus and sandalwood.

My heart was in my throat.

"I won't let anything happen to you." It wasn't my husband's voice. But I knew that voice. I knew it, damn it. But from where? "Grab my hand."

I cried. The pounding in my heart grew louder, competing with the screams and buzzing in my head.

"Please don't let me die." I wasn't ready to die. Tears flowed down my face. The saltiness of them stung. Burned. Something burned. It felt too hot. It hurt.

"Just an inch," the stranger's voice demanded. "Give me just an inch and I'll keep you forever, Tatiana."

Who are you? I wanted to ask. But all that came out were whimpers and cries. I had to get to him. The man ducked down and now I could see him. Our eyes met and blood simmered in my veins. It circled around me like a tornado engulfed in fire.

Or maybe that was the burning of the car I was trapped in.

I reached out my hand. Glass cut into my skin. The shattered windshield cut into his forearm, but he ignored the gash and blood seeping out of his wound.

"I'm here," he said, his voice deep. The Russian accent. "Just a bit more."

Our fingers touched and it was all he needed. He gripped the tip of my fingers, pulling me. My bones cracked, but I didn't care. He'd save me.

Flames licked at my back.

"Please," I sobbed. My fingers slipped out of his grip and my hand fell down onto glass. Exhaustion, heavy and overwhelming, drowned me. Black dots swam in my vision. I forced myself to lift my head, searching his darkness.

His eyes flashed, darkening in fury and determination.

"Don't you fucking give up," he roared.

Pieces of glass stuck to him and me. Warm, sticky blood ran down my skin.

His. Mine. Ours.

Pain sliced through me, exploding in my head. My hands were coated in blood. My insides were on fire. Every muscle in my body ached.

"Tatiana, give me your hand," he demanded. "Don't you fucking dare close your eyes!"

Blackness kept coming, tunneling my vision. I could barely see him. I tried to move my hand; I really did.

His eyes remained on me. Dark. Consuming. Demanding.

I woke up with a piercing scream traveling through the air and jerked upright in bed, my entire body soaked in sweat. My heart pounded, and my eyes darted around the dark room as my chest heaved up and down, taking in gasping breaths of air.

Inhaling deeply, again and again, I kept telling myself it was just a nightmare. A dream.

My fingers curled around the blanket, forming fists and I curled back into a ball. My eyes squeezed shut as I heard the faint voice. I sat up, listening. I heard it again. And again. It kept repeating the same word. Like a broken record playing over the speaker.

Over and over again. "Your betrayal. Your death."

It was Adrian's voice that traveled through the darkness and sent shivers down my spine.

For the rest of the night, I sat frozen, staring at the empty doorway as images of ghosts played in my mind. I even convinced myself I heard voices whispering in the darkness, promising retribution.

With the first flicker of dawn, I knew what I had to do. It was time to search for the truth and quit the booze.

But first, I'd move the fuck out.

SIXTEEN

KONSTANTIN

Marchetti and Agosti stood outside the restaurant outside Rome where Marchetti usually held meetings. The place Rose Spinosa, translation Thorned Rose, was owned by him.

Even under the moonlight, I could see they were both dressed impeccably in dark suits, looking more like respectable businessmen than the heads of one of the five Italian families. At least here in Italy. DiMauro, Agosti, Leone, Romero, and, of course, Marchetti were once known as the kings. And then their empires fell.

But while the world wasn't watching, each one of those families had come back stronger and more powerful. Remaining in the shadows, thanks to Konstantin technology, which gave them the extra leg to stand on. We made an unusual alliance. Came back as kings.

A row of black SUVs parked around the restaurant with several soldiers patrolling the street.

My own driver came to a stop, and I climbed out the second my door opened. Adjusting my cuffs, I sensed Enrico Marchetti's and Giovanni Agosti's eyes turning my way. One set of dark brown eyes and one set of green. The former was in his mid-forties, while the latter was in his thirties.

Enrico owned a large estate in Rome and businesses all around the world. Giovanni Agosti would be the sole heir to his uncle Matteo Agosti's business in Italy. Matteo Agosti ran the Boston Italian mafia and the word was that his wife wanted more time with her husband. Giovanni was a sound choice. He stayed under the radar and followed the rules, unlike Matteo Agosti's brother. That one was a prick.

"Konstantin," Agosti and Marchetti greeted me at the same time.

"I'm not late, I hope." It was just me. I opted not to drag Nikita nor Lenosh with me. I left them to watch after the woman with pale blue eyes. She needed more protection than me.

"Right on time."

Truthfully, I didn't give a shit whether I was late or not. I knew exactly why Marchetti demanded this meeting. He wanted the progress on Tatiana. The video recordings of our sins had resurfaced and started taunting us, causing havoc among the underworld. The fact that it came from Tatiana's IP address didn't fucking help.

Then there was the whole fucking deal with the chip. If that chip that Adrian created got in the wrong hands, it'd put the whole shadow world of the Omertà at risk. But that wasn't the worst part.

At least not for me.

That chip contained a list of all the powerful men and their illegitimate children. Those illegitimate children roaming this world would be targeted. Some of them were clueless about who their parents were. Like my sister, Isla.

She was the main reason I continued my agreement with Marchetti that our fathers and grandfathers started. Not that getting out of the vow was an option. Not unless you had so much dirt on all the members that you could use it against them. But even then, you'd have to watch your back forever.

The Omertà was a vow and commitment for life - for my grandfather, my father, me and many generations to come. For centuries, the kings of Italy managed their empires and criminal underworld with pride, believing themselves untouchable. The Yakuza destroyed that illusion, three generations ago, in a matter of months. They crept in and slowly started crumbling the empire of the five families.

It wasn't until Marchetti's grandfather reached out to mine, that a pact was made. Information, sharing ports and common goals. And then there was the vow. One way in and one way out of that vow.

Omertà above all else - except I wasn't willing to let my woman pay the price for it like my father let my mother bear it. Nor her gardener who threatened exposure of the organization.

"Everyone's here," Agosti said.

"How is the widow doing?" Marchetti wasted no time.

"Fine," I gritted. Just thinking about it had my temper flaring. "Aside from the Yakuza sending an assassin after her."

And my brother, but I'd deal with that my own way.

Marchetti clicked his tongue. "Yakuza are getting harder to control."

"Impossible you mean," I snorted.

Marchetti smirked.

"Oh, it's possible." I agreed, and one way to make it happen was by letting Amon take down his cousin and his brother, but that would mean that one of the men at this table would have to be condemned to death. "Let's get inside and come up with a plan," Marchetti announced.

"There's no firepower inside," Agosti declared and I nodded.

I'd keep my knife. It was all I needed to end every single one of these men. But they weren't my enemy. Not today. Although if they even attempted to even hint about eliminating Tatiana, they would be.

Agosti entered the restaurant, leaving Marchetti alone with me.

"You okay?"

"Yes."

Was I okay? No, I fucking wasn't. My own brother conspired with the Yakuza. If the men at this table learned of it, they'd easily believe that I was in on it too. Trying to switch sides. It was a known fact that the Yakuza had tried for years to take over the Thorns of Omertà. It'd give them power over Europe.

It was the last fucking thing I needed right now. And the fucking videos were back. Jesus H. Christ.

"Your woman okay?" *My woman.* It was the first time anyone had called Tatiana my woman. It felt right. It fucking sounded right. I nodded. "It was the right choice to keep her alive. But we need to get to the bottom of the videos."

I eyed him suspiciously. Marchetti wasn't the kind to easily change his mind. And he didn't believe in second chances. What was his motive here? The bastard never did anything just out of the kindness of his heart.

Sensing my suspicion, he clarified, "We need to know exactly who was part of this conspiracy against us."

I nodded. It was a sensible thing to learn, yet something about his idea of using Tatiana for it didn't sit well with me. I'd filter whatever he needed to learn, but I wouldn't let him question my woman.

Still, it was good to know Marchetti had my back. The agreement between us dated back decades. But it didn't mean we were friends. Friends and the underworld didn't go hand-in-hand. It was the vow of Omertà, and then family. Past that, nothing mattered.

"We should get this meeting over with."

We walked into the building. The restaurant had a Mediterranean feel; the walls painted with motifs of vineyards, Roman ruins and statues, and the beaches of Sardinia. The tinted bulletproof windows blocked the view from the outside, and kept the elegance inside.

I took in all the men around the table. As expected, Enrico Marchetti, Giovanni Agosti, Aiden Callahan along with his brothers, Dante Leone, his half-brother Amon Takahashi Leone, also known as Bitter Prince, and Tomaso Romero.

Bitter Prince. An alias that stuck with him thanks to his bitter beginning.

"Gentlemen," I greeted them all, taking inventory of the tension in the room.

Each representative from the five families in Italy was seated at the table. With the exception of Luca DiMauro who was represented by the Callahans. It might be a while before he decides to come around.

The Callahan twins moved to stand at the opposite end of the room. After the whole fiasco with Margaret Callahan and the DiMauro family, it was a surprise to see them here. They took a vow and represented their family as well as DiMauro's. I'd wager there would be some years before Luca DiMauro agreed to have a civilized conversation with a few individuals here.

Turning my head, Amon's dark exotic eyes met mine for a second. He tilted his head in acknowledgment, his silent vow that he hadn't shared my secret with anyone.

If he had, Maxim would have been dead already.

"Konstantin," Dante Leone said, standing to shake my hand. "Good to see you."

The corner of my lips barely tipped up into a semblance of a smile. I'd prefer Amon in Dante's seat, but the Italians were nothing if not traditional. Besides, Dante was the older brother, although only by a few days. The two couldn't be more different yet somehow they got along. Go fucking figure.

Amon had connections in the east, and was not only second-in-command for Yakuza, but also an ally for the Leone empire and even the Thorns of Omertà.

Courtesy of his father's extramarital affair.

He was an asset through and through. The Yakuza have been a threat since the inception of our organization. Their ultimate goal was to control the vast territories under us. So far they'd been unsuccessful and having Amon Leone with his one foot in their organization helped us keep tabs on them. If Amon ever turned his back on the Thorns of Omertà, we'd be at a serious disadvantage.

Dante resumed his seat and each of the others greeted me in turn.

Aiden Callahan was the last one. "I'm surprised to see you join the crowd," I admitted. As far as I knew, the Callahans had no reason to linger in the shadows. Besides, most of the underworld already knew them and what they represented. Especially those twin brothers of his. Younger than Adrian, they tended to be on the wild side. God help the family who'd arranged the marriage of their daughter to one of those twins. She'd be getting more than she'd bargain for.

"This is good for us," Aiden answered cryptically. Luca probably wouldn't agree but whatever. I'd bet my entire fortune they were protecting the interests of their niece, Penelope DiMauro. None of them were too thrilled about the wedding contract that Marchetti made for one of his sons to wed their daughter.

Luca was the head of the DiMauro family but he wasn't willing to forgive. Not quite yet. The Callahans came to a reluctant peace with Luca, for their sister's and niece's sake. I could only imagine those Christmas dinners once their kids marry.

I took my seat at the round table, Marchetti on my left.

"So what's the reason for this meeting?" I opened it up. It wasn't as if getting together would give us any answers on the videos we'd been receiving for the past year before Adrian's death. "I had to make a detour before my long weekend in Paris."

I could see by the look on everyone's face, they wondered too. Although they didn't dare to voice their opinion.

Tomaso Roman ended up being the one to start. "I need to know where we stand with retrieving information from the Nikolaev woman."

Jesus, here we go again. I locked eyes on him. He didn't look well. Worn out. Dark shadows under his eyes. And he only had daughters, which would potentially leave his seat at this table empty. An opportunity for someone else.

"I can't have my identity slip," he continued in a hiss. "It'll leave my daughters vulnerable."

"So will a lot of other children," Aiden chimed in. "Your daughters at least have protection with the Omertà. Other illegitimate kids are truly left vulnerable. Most of them don't even know of their connection to this world."

I frowned, studying Aiden. Was there more to his vow of Omertà than just protecting Penelope DiMauro's interests? I didn't need to dig into him nor hack him to know he was trying to protect someone. By the looks of it, it was someone he cared about a lot.

"I can't have my daughters connected to this world," Romero snapped. From the corner of my eye, I noticed Amon stiffening. Barely. It was enough though. "We need that chip, Konstantin. They don't know about any of this. Reina will stir up a riot if she finds out about the whore houses."

"Maybe you should end flesh trading all together?" I remarked, leaning back in my seat. Usually, illegitimate daughters were dragged into whore houses by any member of the underworld who participated in human trafficking. They were prized above any other woman and sometimes sold at a premium price. The Belles & Mobsters agreements had nothing on this shit.

No amount of protection could guarantee the safety of illegitimate children. It was the reason I had been concealing my own sister's identity. I could count on one hand how many people knew about her, including Maxim and myself. Romero's daughters weren't illegitimate, but without a male heir, they'd be left vulnerable.

"And that would stop the Yakuza how?" Romero snapped. "If they get that chip, they'll probably expand the number of whore houses in all our territories. We need that chip."

"And you shall have it," I said.

"Are you sure she wasn't working with her husband?" Leone questioned.

Fuck, how I hated hearing those two words. *Her husband.*

"Yes, I'm sure," I gritted.

"Maybe ending her would have been a better course of action," Romero chimed in again. Panic made Romero more paranoid than usual. "There is nobody else that could be dropping these videos. It's either her or one of the Nikolaevs. But our sources indicate they actually had a fallout with him when he tried to blackmail Kingston Ashford into exposing us. So it has to be her."

Kingston Ashford. Our contracted killer when we needed him. Alexei Nikolaev's brother-in-law.

"That woman–"

I stood up and leaned over, resting my palms against the cold mahogany table and narrowed my eyes on Romero. "You should worry more about *me* than Tatiana Nikolaev right now." I let the words sink in before I continued. "I keep all your information out of every single database in the world. Fucking dare bring up Tatiana's name again, and I'll ensure your name is blasted on every goddamn site."

Okay, this wasn't smart, but fuck it. It was too late the moment I laid eyes on Tatiana again. Maybe she and I were inevitable from the moment we were born.

"I don't know her well but my brother-in-law knows her and her brothers. Tatiana Nikolaev is part of the underworld," Aiden Callahan chimed in. "Her family is everything to her. Unlike her late husband, she'd never let that chip fall into anyone's hands. That is, if she even has it." He paused, his eyes locked on Romero. "She'd rather die than harm or bring danger to her family."

I shifted my gaze around the table. Leone's thoughts seemed to have drifted somewhere else. Agosti didn't seem to care one way or the other. It was Marchetti who settled the score at the end.

"All the evidence points to the fact that Tatiana Nikolaev would never betray her family," Marchetti declared vaguely. Fuck if I knew whether it meant he was on my side or not. His eyes turned to me. "Konstantin will bring the chip once he retrieves it. But we have to figure out who's sending us these videos. Is Maxim able to help?"

"No."

Maxim was the expert when it came to tracing IP addresses. It was his niche, once upon a time. These days, my brother couldn't help himself, never mind anyone else.

Fuck, maybe Nico Morrelli could unravel that mystery. He was a genius in his own right. Everyone in this room has tried to decipher the digital signature of the video messages. Unsuccessfully. There had to be someone smarter than that fucker Adrian.

I nodded, then stood up. Marchetti did the same, signaling the meeting was over.

"I'm glad to see we're all on the same page." I buttoned my jacket. "Gentlemen."

They remained seated as I turned to the door. Marchetti was on his way out too. Maybe he'd also had enough of this shit.

"Romero will fall in line," Marchetti said once we were outside. "He worries about his eldest due to her disability."

I didn't envy him. Having daughters was a worry that never went away. Romero had no male family that would protect his girls once he was gone. It made them more vulnerable, and it didn't help that they were oblivious to this world.

"He needs to consider wedding one of them to someone powerful," I said. "Before he keels over."

"The disability of the oldest daughter makes it hard to arrange a marriage," he admitted. "And his youngest is a cheerful rebel. A breed of her own. Stubborn."

"Aren't they all," I retorted dryly.

Coincidentally, Romero's daughters attended the same boarding school as Isla back in California. The three bonded and went on to attend the same college in Paris. His youngest one was twenty-one or so while his eldest was Isla's age. Twenty-three and deaf.

"Romero is entertaining arranging a marriage between his youngest and Dante Leone."

"Bad move," I answered dryly.

Enrico watched my face, his eyes narrowed on me. "Why?"

I raised a brow. He should really observe the younger generation more. "Dante has a temper. He doesn't need to marry a hellion, but someone that will calm him down."

His eyes narrowed. "Well, do you have a candidate for Reina?" I kept my mouth shut. They'd find out soon enough. It was Amon's battle to wage. "I know it's not you," he remarked dryly. "Not after you vouched for the Morozov woman."

I gritted my teeth. I hated hearing that last name attached to Tatiana. I stopped by my waiting car and turned to face Marchetti.

"Just a fair warning," I started, locking eyes with him. Usually I towered over people but Marchetti was as tall as me. We stood eye-to-eye. Right now, I'd love to tower over him though. "I will take any attempt at Tatiana's life as a direct hit at me and my family. And my revenge will be swift and brutal. Just ask the Yakuza asshole who dared to get close to her."

He studied me for a moment. I didn't give a shit if I revealed too much. I wanted it known whose wrath they'd have to endure if they touched a single blonde hair on that woman. I was the only man allowed to touch her.

"Why do I feel like you have a plan for the Yakuza?" Marchetti remarked wryly.

A cold smile touched my lips. "Actually, I'm only assessing and assisting where needed. Someone already had a plan going. I'm speeding it along."

Marchetti's lips curved into a smirk and he extended his palm for a handshake.

"Good. I'm looking forward to it."

This was the reason the two of us worked well together.

The next morning, I woke up in my Paris home to loud music and a killer headache.

"What the fuck?" I grumbled, jumping out of bed, and pulling up a pair of pajama pants. I never knew who'd my sister have over and having girls barely in their twenties gawking at me in my boxers wasn't on my agenda. Like fucking ever.

I left the bedroom and followed the sound of voices all the way to the dining room.

Surprise, surprise. I hadn't seen my twin brother since my last trip to California. He'd been hiding and conniving, probably making some fucked up mess that I'd have to clean up.

I entered the dining room to find Maxim and my baby sister Isla sitting at the long dining room table, along with four of Isla's girl-friends - Phoenix and Reina Romero, Athena Kosta, and Raven Jameson. And damn if they weren't drinking alcohol. At fucking breakfast.

They hadn't even noticed me walk in. In a dark mood already, I strode over to the stereo and shut it off.

The silence followed. Awkward. Tense.

"Illias!" Isla cried out, jumping to her feet. She ran towards me and threw herself into my arms. "I thought you decided not to come when you didn't show up yesterday, so the girls and I are just hanging out."

"Drinking in the morning," I scolded her.

She shrugged. "It's just mimosas. They are meant for the morning."

When in the fuck did my baby sister grow up?

My chest tightened as I hugged her, kissing her forehead. My half-sister was half my age. Too good to be around men like me. Maxim and I had done our best raising her away from prying eyes and the dangers of the underworld. Nobody could connect her to us. Her friends were clueless about who we were, right along with Isla. It was the safest life for her. And them!

"How are you?" I asked her, her petite frame barely reaching my chest. The abundance of her ginger curls made her seem even smaller than her five-foot-three. Almost as if a strong gust of wind could break her frail form. Sometimes I wondered how she managed to hold her violin for hours as she played.

And she could play. I'd seen grown men weep when she played that violin. She had a way of getting those tunes right into your soul and making your heart bleed.

"Much better now that you're here," she beamed.

When she looked at me like that, she reminded me of that little girl who always watched me with unfiltered adoration and admiration. No matter how sullied my hands were, that little girl depended on me. To protect her. To shield her from our world. Especially from the men in our world who'd find a way to get to her and exploit her.

My eyes flickered to her friends and traveled over them. It was always the same crowd. Somehow Isla connected with the illegitimate daughters of other mafia families. It always surprised me to see them together. They were all so different - a violinist, a painter, a writer, a fashion designer, and pianist.

It was the last two girls that I was always surprised to see. The Romero girls. The old Romero didn't have a good handle on his daughters. I'd venture that their wealthy grandmother had something to do with it.

"So what's going on here?" I asked, flicking a gaze to my brother who looked fucking high. He sat slumped in the chair, looking at the girls with glee in his eyes that made me sick to my stomach.

I clenched my jaw, the need to teach him a lesson and then to punish him drummed through my veins, deadly and cold. He'd be dealt with one-on-one.

Our sister didn't need to hear any of our *business* shit. And her friends even less. The Romero girls were just as oblivious to the dealings in the underworld. The others certainly knew nothing about it.

Oblivious to the tension traveling between her brothers, Isla shrugged as she turned to her friends. "Maxim showed up yesterday and said you wouldn't be coming so I called the girls. We were going to hit up a few clubs but–"

"We can go back to our apartment," the youngest Romero daughter said as she pushed her chair back and started signing to her deaf sister. *Let's go to our place.*

All the girls started to nod, obviously understanding the sign language perfectly well.

"No, that's okay," I said. "You ladies stay. Maxim and I have some business to deal with anyhow. We'll leave you to it."

"Are you sure?" Isla whirled around, watching me curiously.

I smiled, although right now I wanted to stride over to my brother and wring his neck. "Yes. But tomorrow, we're spending time together. Okay?"

A smile spread across her expression and her entire face lit up. "You got it, brother. We'll go to my room then."

I nodded and the girls scattered away. Maxim got up, preparing to leave too.

"Not you," I said in a cold voice. The tension in my jaw and shoulders was ready to snap, but I had never lost my temper with him. Through all the years, right or wrong, I had always protected him. But now, he went too far.

We had never looked less alike than we did right now. His abuse of drugs had aged him. His eyes were dull and unfocused, his hands slightly shaking.

"Have you run the paperwork on the new manufacturing plant for me?" I had given him the task two weeks ago. It was a two day job. I had taken care of it already, but he had been too high to notice it.

"I will. Next week."

I shook my head. "Have you acquired more servers?"

He shrugged.

Once upon a time, Maxim could run circles around the top programmers and could set up a dark web within seconds. Now, I ran it all and oversaw everything, covering for his shortfalls. I started to wonder if I didn't do him a disservice by going easy on him our entire life.

But now I felt a stronger urge to protect Tatiana from my brother's demons and whatever her dead husband had brought to her doorstep.

"How did your meeting with the Yakuza go?" I asked casually.

"Fine." Then realizing he slipped, he sat up straighter. "Why would I meet with the Yakuza?"

His eyes darted around as if he contemplated running. I loved my brother, but it was hard to miss how far he had fallen.

"I'm wondering the same, Brother," I challenged. "I distinctly remember stating to stay-the-fuck-away from the Nikolaev family."

Especially after he put a hit on Sasha's woman years ago, after the unhinged Nikolaev warned him Branka Russo was under his protection. It was thanks to my twin brother that I owed Sasha any favor he'd need. Anytime. Anywhere. I gave him my word as the Pakhan and a Konstantin. It was either that or Maxim's certain death.

I still remembered the exact words I told him once Sasha roughed him up and left.

"No harm is to come to any Nikolaev family member. One day, our families will merge, and I'll fucking strangle you if you cause issues with your fucking vendetta they never started. Understood?"

Maxim's one eye already turned blue, swelling shut. His face was bloodied. But I knew that stubborn tilt of his chin and that stupid gleam in his eyes.

"I mean it, Maxim," I vowed, my voice colder than the winters in our motherland. "There are only so many chances you'll get before I'll kill you myself."

"Like Papa killed our mother," he spat out, blood trickling down his lip. "Like you killed Papa, and now you'd kill your brother?"

I let out a sardonic breath. I'd had enough of cleaning up after him to last me two lifetimes. Family didn't do the shit he did. With him out of the way, life would be a walk in the park.

"What do you think?" I answered his question with my own.

I was responsible for thousands of men and women, not just Maxim. Including Tatiana. If it came down to him or Tatiana - the choice would always be her.

He opened his mouth and I raised my eyebrow, daring him to say something else. He might get another beating if he wasn't careful.

He closed it.

"I won't go around the pale devils," he promised reluctantly.

I passed him on my way out but stopped. I lifted a shoulder and turned to him. He really needed a lesson. So to ensure he remembered the lesson, I clenched my fist and the next second it collided with his jaw.

"Don't fucking break that promise," I warned, then walked out the door.

"I haven't been near the pale devils," Maxim's voice pulled me back to the present, shrugging his shoulders nonchalantly. Fucking drug addict and a liar.

My jaw tightened and I sent him a look that promised retribution.

Silence. Thick and dark crept through the room.

I knew he'd try and run before he even moved. The chair slammed against the wall, but I was faster than his doped ass. My hand wrapped around his throat and I slammed his body against the wall, rattling it with the impact.

"Don't push me, Maxim," I growled. "You won't like what comes from it."

Our gazes burned into the other's, clashing with years of animosity. He hated me for being strong; I hated him for being weak. My twin brother was so fucking bitter about losing his whore that he reeked of it. I promised him I wouldn't get involved in his relationship. He could fuck whoever he wanted, but when he started impacting our business and attacking people that should be our allies, my promise went down the toilet.

"You're just like *him*," he hissed. There was no need to question who *him* was. Our father. The unforgiving, cruel man who made us into the men we were today.

I released the grip on his throat and shoved him away. Then taking a step back, I reached for the nearby drawer that worked on my fingerprints only. I pulled out my .45, twisted the silencer on as Maxim's eyes widened, registering my movements. I pulled the trigger. The silent *pop* reverberated around us. I shot him in the arm and he hissed in pain as he slid down the wall.

"Stay the fuck away from Tatiana Nikolaev. Last warning." Then to ensure he remembered, I added, "Same with Sasha and his woman. There'll be no more chances."

I put the gun away, shutting the drawer with a click before walking toward the door. I opened it, my hand on the handle.

"The great Pakhan pussy whipped," he snickered. "I wonder if you'll pull the trigger on her like Father did Mother."

The insinuation and the thought of Tatiana's beautiful blues void of life sent raw feelings to my heart.

My voice was unnaturally calm as I stated the next words.

"You better hope she lives longer than you," I said without looking back at him. "If something happens to her, I'll gut you alive regardless if you are guilty or not."

Then I walked out the door and locked him in there.

SEVENTEEN
TATIANA

Questions came. Answers didn't. Time didn't fly. It dragged in slow motion.

At least it seemed that way.

I was lost. Nothing made sense. Not the information I found on Adrian's laptop in our home. Not the signature on the funeral documents. Not the necklace that showed up on Christmas along with the password to Adrian's kingdom.

Maybe Adrian knew he'd die and wanted to protect me by passing along information.

Except, none of it made any sense.

So here I was at Alexei's penthouse.

Flicking a glance over my shoulder to Yan and Yuri, I nodded, signaling them to stay there. It was okay for them to enter my place, but Alexei preferred nobody outside family to enter his.

My hand shook as I knocked on the door. After the first five knocks came up empty, I raised my hand again, prepared to pound on it, but the door opened before I could make contact.

Alexei stood there with his son on his shoulders, and for a moment, I stared at my brother. Two years ago, I couldn't have imagined this scenario. I'd bet that neither could he. Yet now there he was - with his own family. Content. Happy even, despite all the horrors life had put him through.

He tilted his head. "Come on in."

I reached out and brushed my fingers over Kostya's soft cheek.

"Hey, buddy." He grinned, then took my finger into his mouth and bit. "Kostya! That's my finger," I protested.

"He wants his pacifier back," Alexei explained. As if that made it ok to bite my finger.

I shook my head, then marched past him and into his penthouse, while nursing my poor finger.

"You're lucky you're family, buddy," I grumbled softly. "Or I'd bite you back."

The corners of my brother's lips tugged up.

"Where is Aurora?" I asked, glancing around, expecting her to appear any second.

"She's meeting her brother for lunch."

I raised my eyebrow. "You weren't invited?"

He shrugged. "I was. Byron has some shit going on. Kostya didn't need to listen to it."

"Oh." I wondered what shit Byron Ashford got himself into. Not that it mattered. I had enough problems in my own life. "I could have babysat Kostya."

The moment I said those words, I realized how dumb they sounded. I had hardly been a reliable sister since Adrian's death. To Alexei's credit, he didn't voice that opinion. Just watched me in that unnerving way that I had gotten used to.

He waited for me to continue. My eyes flickered to Kostya, then back to my brother. Tattoos marked most of his skin, even his face. We shared our eye and hair color, just like Sasha and Vasili. But unlike any of them, I didn't have any ink on my skin. Their stories were harsher than mine. Compared to them, my life was fairly easy. Minus being a widow.

Sunrays flickered through the floor-to-ceiling windows, throwing shadows on Kostya's hair, so similar to his father's. To mine. To Nikola's. There was no mistaking our family trait. I wondered if my child would have had the same coloring.

A sharp pain pierced a hole through my chest. Bitterness filled it.

"Tatiana." Alexei's voice softened, his eyes seeing through me.

I swallowed the lump in my throat, burying all the feelings deep down.

"Yeah?"

"What are you wearing?" It was an odd thing to question. My eyes lowered. I wore Adrian's sweatpants and white t-shirt. It wasn't the hottest nor most flattering look.

I returned my attention to my brother.

"On the day of the funeral…" My voice cracked, remembering that day. The pain was still fresh, although healing. *I think.* Maybe I graduated to the next stage of grief. I sighed shakily, realizing I was probably fooling myself. "You said something," I rasped as I continued.

He wasn't good for you. Not anymore. His monotone voice repeated the words over and over again, like an echo in an empty room.

Alexei nodded, but in his typical way, he didn't elaborate.

"Why did you say that?" I questioned, watching him. Not that I expected my brother's mask to crack. It never did - for anyone - but his wife and son.

He studied me wordlessly while I held his gaze. But I didn't squirm. I didn't break eye contact. I was ready for whatever was coming my way.

"You're not going to like it."

My lungs closed up, but I refused to stop now. I came for some answers, and I refused to leave without any.

"There are many things I don't like, but I deal with it," I choked out.

His eyes remained on me. A heartbeat passed.

"Adrian transferred your part of the company to his own name." My brows furrowed. I shook my head, confusion clear on my face.

"How?" I didn't sign any papers transferring ownership to Adrian. Granted, I wasn't interested in the company, but I'd never sign it over without speaking with Vasili first.

"You must have signed the agreement."

I shook my head vigorously. "I didn't," I claimed with conviction. "I always read every document I sign. Vasili pounded it into me. I swear, I never signed it."

But you signed funeral papers with that weird niche plate inscription and you don't remember, my mind whispered. I wasn't willing to admit it. Not yet.

"Vasili wasn't happy about it when he found out," Alexei continued in his cold voice. "He confronted him the night of your accident."

I remembered seeing Vasili and Adrian argue the night of the Halloween celebration, Alexei standing there in his usual form. The moment I approached them, they ceased talking and I thought nothing of it.

"Why didn't Vasili say anything?" I breathed and Alexei's gaze flashed with something fierce. Dangerous.

"You didn't need to deal with that stuff."

"But didn't he wonder why I would sign over the company without talking to him?"

Alexei shrugged. "Once Adrian died, it didn't matter."

I winced at his words. But in typical Alexei fashion, he didn't apologize. He wouldn't have meant it, and somehow I appreciated it. I'd rather he gave it to me straight than bullshit.

"Who does the company belong to now?" I questioned.

"You."

He watched me with eyes of the palest frozen oceans, the dark secrets thriving in his depths, while only confusion danced in mine.

"But–" There was something he wasn't telling me.

"There is a clause preventing us from erasing Adrian's name from the legal papers."

"What about the breach of the original agreement?"

Alexei's eyes turned colder and his gaze met mine. "Who told you about it?"

I pressed my lips together. It was one of my tells when I was adamant about not telling on someone. Alexei could read me as well as

Vasili and Sasha. Maybe it was the Nikolaev blood that ran through our veins. Or maybe it was just Alexei.

"Did Adrian discuss it with you?" Alexei asked evenly. But the undertone of displeasure was there.

My brows furrowed. "Adrian? No, why would he–"

He shrugged. "An assumption. Adrian told Vasili he told you about the agreement, and you were adamant about transferring it all to him," he replied coldly. "It was your idea to be fair to him."

What in the heck was going on here? "I absolutely didn't say that."

"It doesn't matter anymore. The company is yours," he remarked coldly. "Now that he's dead."

A frustrated breath escaped me. "For the love of God. Just once Alexei, please elaborate!"

My brother's lips tugged up. "Upon your husband's passing, every-thing passed on to you. There are a few things that Vasili is working out. Vasili froze the assets until everything is in your name. The company among other things."

Silence followed. Thick and deafening. It felt like there were too many things that still remained unanswered.

"Alexei?"

"Yes."

I studied my brother for a moment. Most people shit themselves just seeing him and usually steered away from him. The tattoos on his face weren't even the reason for it. It was that unnerving expression that always lingered in his eyes. For some odd reason, he never scared me. Maybe because I grew up with two unnerving brothers or because I'd heard enough about what went on in the underworld to understand that no man ever came out of it unscathed.

Alexei was no exception. And he was family - so he'd always gotten extra points. We always looked after our family. Those were the words that Vasili hammered into all of us. He might not think so but he did.

"The day of the funeral," I started. He nodded and I had a sense he knew exactly where I was going with it. "What was the real reason you said that Adrian wasn't good enough for me anymore?"

One heartbeat passed. "He had started to do some shady stuff and was putting the family at risk. You included."

"Like blackmailing Kingston?" I felt like each syllable of those two simple words was too heavy to say. Or maybe I wasn't ready to hear the explanation.

Alexei shrugged. "Like blackmailing Kingston. Like starting shit and putting you in harm's way."

Nothing was as it seemed.

I left Alexei's place more confused than when I arrived.

But I was certain of one thing. Adrian wasn't the man I thought he was. Yes, I loved him. He had been part of my life for far too long to erase all the love and affection I had for him. However, it had become obvious that I didn't know the real Adrian at all.

The videos I'd found and the blackmail scheme against Kingston were bad enough but now I was told that Adrian was actually stealing from me. What else was I supposed to think? He'd forged my name on some fucking papers to transfer my half of his security company to him. I may be going crazy, but I know I didn't sign any goddamned papers.

Nothing was as it seemed with my late husband. And that was the part that bothered me the most. Adrian didn't trust me to share his problems with me. It was clear he had some problems, although it remained to be seen what they were.

Instead of going home, I headed to Adrian's office space in the building he owned.

There had to be a reason behind all he had done. I had to find out at least some answers to all these questions I had.

I combed every inch of the office space, hoping to find what exactly Adrian had gotten into. I had discovered two things. Adrian didn't believe in paper trails or paper at all. And he liked to leave gadgets everywhere. Just like at home. My husband had little pieces of electronic shit everywhere.

The whole building was intact. Vasili invested in Adrian's company to help him get started, but when I married Adrian, Vasili transferred the ownership to me. Except, tech and business wasn't something I was interested in. There wasn't much I was interested in aside from fashion when it came to business.

My brothers were shocked when I picked Political Science for my undergrad degree. Adrian even more so. He always found me to be flighty, and I feared he stereotyped me as a dumb blonde. I objected to that. Maybe I wasn't as brilliant as he was, but I wasn't dumb. I had my strengths and weaknesses. So I opted for the stupid, useless degree in order to prove to my brothers and Adrian, I could be just as sharp as they were.

Was it smart? No, it wasn't. I passed with flying colors, but those four years of studies were enough to drive a saint to become a devil. The only good thing that came out of that degree was Isabella. My best friend.

I loved her and she had made our family richer. She made Vasili happy. The happiest I'd ever seen him.

Taking a seat at my husband's executive desk, which I knew he rarely used, I pulled his laptop closer. It sat in the same position as the last time he came to work, frozen in time for over six months.

I snickered silently. I could totally relate. I have been in limbo just as long.

My fingers hovering over the keyboard, I stared at the screen.

'**Blood and Thorns**' stared back at me as a user ID, reminding me of his morbid niche plate. There have been so many strange discoveries, I didn't know what to think of it. I reached for my necklace, twisting it left and right.

It was the strangest user ID I had ever encountered, but Adrian had a weird logic sometimes. I mean, just look at the way we finally ended up together.

I sighed. It was the wrong time for memories so I pushed those thoughts away.

"I just need a password," I grumbled. If the user ID was any indication, it would be a difficult password to guess. "Just a tiny obstacle."

Could the password be the same as the one on his home computer? It seemed too simple, yet maybe…

My brain registered the scent of citrus and sandalwood before I heard his first word.

"Indeed a tiny obstacle." A voice came from behind me, and I shot out of the chair. In the blink of an eye, I reached for the gun in the drawer and pointed it at the intruder.

Broad shoulders. Black suit. Expensive watch. He didn't seem concerned with the fact I held a gun pointed at him.

And then it clicked. *Pakhan.*

The stranger who saved me wasn't a stranger at all. I'd heard of him. I might have met him too. Somewhere. Oh shit. I couldn't remember where I'd seen him nor his name. I stared at the same dark eyes. I knew he was *somebody*. Name. What was his name again? I cursed myself for forgetting his name. It was dumb to forget the names of your friends, but even dumber to forget names of your potential enemies.

He must have seen recognition cross my eyes. The corners of his lips barely curved, but his expression sent chills down my spine. Like he was pissed off.

And while I wracked my brain, he leaned against the door frame, looking quite like a villain himself. Maybe a devil in D&G. I snickered silently at my clever title.

My eyes traveled over him and his strong frame. His tailored suit must have cost him a small fortune.

"Dolce & Gabbana?" I asked, lowering my gun, then putting it away before I sat back down. If he wanted me dead, I'd be dead already.

His eyebrow shot up. "No. Illias Konstantin."

That's right!

How could I forget! I kept my expression blank. Konstantin. There were two of them. Twin brothers. There was a rumor about a sister, but it was just a rumor. What was he doing here?

"The suit," I said, rather than asking him a question. "Dolce & Gabbana suit. I don't care who *you* are."

The corners of his mouth barely tipped up but I saw it. "Now, that's not the way to talk to your savior."

"How presumptuous," I grumbled. "I told you. I could have handled it."

He didn't believe me, but he let it go.

"I have no idea who made the suit," he answered honestly. Then his eyes traveled over me and suddenly my cheeks flamed. Still wearing Adrian's sweatpants and a plain white t-shirt that was five sizes too big. The clothes hung on me, making me look like a rag doll. Then to finish the look, I wore a pair of plastic crocs in baby diarrhea green.

Lovely!

I looked my worst, and he looked like one of the best dressed men I'd ever known. I narrowed my eyes on him, daring him to say anything. It was always the day you dressed down that you ran into someone you didn't want to.

"Well, it's D&G," I grumbled, wishing I had at least put on jeans. "Your suit," I added.

"And you're wearing…" My nipples tightened under the scrutiny of his eyes and his gaze lingered a heartbeat too long over my breasts. Shit, I forgot to put a bra on. Goddamn it!

"None of your fucking business," I snapped, folding my arms over my chest to hide the state of my nipples. The fleeting smirk on his face when he met my gaze told me he noticed exactly what had happened. In fact, I'd stake my life that there wasn't much that could escape this man.

He saw everything.

"Tatiana Nikolaev, I presume?" he questioned. He called me by my maiden name. Again. Didn't he know my last name was Morozov? "Nice to see you again."

I wondered if he referred to saving my ass from the Yakuza or whether he remembered our fleeting meeting in the Los Angeles restaurant.

I didn't bother answering him. Instead, my eyes flickered behind him. Where in the fuck were my guards?

"They're taking a nap," he declared, reading my mind. My heart fluttered, a tiny bead of fear slowly growling. I swallowed the lump in my throat. *He saved me from the Yakuza*, my mind whispered. He wouldn't have saved me if he wanted me dead. "You're safe from me," he added. "For now."

I blinked in confusion. "For now?" He nodded. "Well, if my brothers find out you harassed me, you won't be safe. Now or ever," I hissed, pissed off that he dared to threaten me.

Was it smart threatening the Pakhan? Totally not. It would seem that I was just as smart as my brother Sasha. Go fucking figure.

He smoothed a nonexistent wrinkle from his jacket, his movements sure and confident.

"That's good to know." He wasn't worried at all.

I shouldn't be surprised. Illias Konstantin was Pakhan of California and Russia, and one of the most feared men in Russia. The rumor was that he had a direct link to one of the most merciless families that ruled the world from the shadows.

Nobody knew who those families were nor what they did.

"What do you want?" My voice trembled, and I despised myself for it. I was stronger than that. My brothers taught me how to be a queen. Not a damsel in distress.

"I imagine we both want the same thing."

"I doubt that," I muttered.

He ignored me as he continued. "Your husband had something that didn't belong to him. Now, you have it."

There it was again. Somehow it seemed Adrian had even managed to piss off the Pakhan. Where did these secrets end?

I tilted my head, studying Konstantin. I wasn't a short woman, but he was at least a head taller than me. However, it was more than that. He gave out those larger than life vibes. *Kind of like my eldest brother,* I realized. Except, this man was dangerous on a whole new level.

"And what is that?" I questioned. Maybe he'd give me a clue. He didn't bite. Not surprising. You didn't get to be a Pakhan by being stupid. "Is that the reason the Yakuza attacked me yesterday?" He nodded. "Did you send him? A set up so you could meet me," I murmured in a quiet scoff. "You know, there *are* better ways to meet a lady."

Konstantin's lips tipped up, amusement passing his expression.

"If I'd sent him, you'd be dead already," he replied coldly.

Jesus. It was that simple for him. Just a word, and he could have me obliterated from this planet.

However, it didn't escape me that he didn't comment on the matter of introduction. Well, he had another thing coming if he thought I'd just take whatever he dished my way. I'd end him before he could end me.

It was at that very moment that the revelation settled somewhere deep down. Although I didn't recognize it right away, and it'd take me another few months to realize it.

I was never the giving up type. I wasn't ready to call it quits.

I'd have a future, children, even if I had to adopt, and I'd be damned if I'd let anyone take it from me.

EIGHTEEN
KONSTANTIN

She was a queen and the worst part was she knew it.

This woman could wear rags and she'd still look stunning. Like fucking royalty.

Her hair was tangled, reminding me of spun gold. Her face was pale, dark shadows under her pale blue eyes and those rosebud lips tempted to be kissed. Fuck kiss, those lips were meant to be devoured. Ravaged. Bruised.

It fucking hurt to watch her; she was so beautiful.

"Okay, so you didn't send him," she stated as she brought her hands to the laptop. They hovered over the keyboard, her brows furrowed. "You say I have something that belongs to you, and I'm telling you, I don't have it." Then those pale Arctic blues darted back to me. "And let's not forget you're trespassing on my property."

A muscle in my jaw tightened. Nobody ever fucking talked back to me.

"You have it," I told her with a dark warning in my voice. "You just need to find it. Or remember where it is."

Unbeknownst to her, I'd had my most trusted men watch her. I didn't trust families of the underworld not to do something stupid. She was a liability, the only human that currently had the identity of every member of our organizations at her fingertips. A list of all illegitimate children hidden in plain sight.

That chip contained evidence to lock up almost every member of our organization.

Her eyes flashed and those pale blues narrowed to slits. "So I put it in a safe place?"

"Probably."

She shrugged. "Well, that's helpful. I know exactly where it is then," she remarked sarcastically. "Besides, since it is *mine*, what makes you think I'd give it to you or share it with you?"

She stared at me, the expression on her face annoyed. The fire that I knew the Nikolaevs had, especially Tatiana, was a backbone and despite it all, I was happy to see it. All the reports I'd been getting so far indicated she was falling deeper into depression.

My eyes narrowed. "Because you know what's good for you, Tatiana. What's good for your family."

She tensed and lightning flashed in her gaze. "Don't you dare threaten my family," she hissed. "You might be the Pakhan but that won't matter if you hurt any of them. I'll murder you."

So she did remember me. The fire burned like blue flames in her eyes. A sardonic feeling pulled in my chest, mocking my obsession. From the moment I spotted her, the block of ice in my chest turned into something else. A fire that burned hotter than a volcano.

"Then let's help each other," I drawled. "And there won't be any need for murders. So how about a truce?" I offered.

She eyed me suspiciously. Maybe she'd prefer to murder me. Personally, I'd prefer to bend her over that desk and make her scream my name. Feel her pussy clenching around my cock. Hear her moans. The memory hit me like the high of a drug, tempting me to take her. Make her mine already.

I clenched my teeth, keeping the carnal hunger from my expression. It wasn't time yet.

Our gazes held. Time lagged.

She kept secrets behind those Nikolaev eyes. I had a few of my own.

"I don't know if I want a truce with someone who's breaking into my company," she said, leaning back into the chair like she was reigning over her kingdom. Little did she know, the ship had sailed on this little kingdom. I steered the boat and controlled the winds.

"It's just a shell, Tatiana," I remarked, keeping my voice nonchalant. "A real company needs customers." Her brows furrowed, surprise crossing her expression. "Don't tell me you didn't know you have no customers?"

"How do you know there are no customers?" she questioned, keeping her tone cautious.

Smart woman. Not that I doubted it. Her brothers had probably taught her to answer questions with her own questions when she had no answers.

"Because they all brought their business to me."

"I thought you owned malls and shit," she noted. "Your malls do have some really nice stores. It's almost like shopping in Italy." Then as if she realized she complimented me, she added, "Almost but not quite."

A sardonic breath left me. This woman was *something*. My malls carried all luxury brands and trended the latest fashions that were the best of Italian couture. My connection with Marchetti ensured that.

"Well, pray tell what's needed to make it just like shopping in Italy," I challenged her.

Her lips curved into a small smile. "Well, the ambiance," she noted. "When you step into one of your malls, the ambiance is typical American. When you shop in Italy, gelato, Italian music and vibrancy is what captures you."

She had a point. Now why didn't my mall manager think of that? I paid him big bucks to make it happen, so fucking typical. I'd have to fix that.

"You're right," I acknowledged and her eyes widened. "What? I'm smart enough to see when someone has a good idea."

"Hmmm." She leveled a questioning gaze my way. "Pray tell, Konstantin. Why would the owner of malls have something Adrian's customers would want? Security isn't something you can buy in a boutique after all."

"A discussion for another day, perhaps." She knew who I was. She knew full well what those "customers" would get from me, the minx.

"There's no time like the present," she remarked dryly.

My eyes flickered to the laptop in front of her. "So what are you trying to do?" I asked instead.

She sighed. "Log in," she admitted. "But I don't know the password."

She lowered her eyes to the laptop, her fingertips resting against the keyboard. All my intel indicated that Adrian didn't keep any of the information on his business laptop. It would have made it too easy to uncover it. Too easy to hack into.

Besides, I'd already been into that laptop.

"Why?"

She shrugged. "I want to find the company ownership papers." Then as if she realized she answered my question, she retorted dryly. "And it's none of your business."

"You know we could help each other," I noted.

"I seriously doubt that," she muttered.

What the fuck did I have to do for this woman to actually see me? They usually fell all over themselves for me, yet this one hardly remembered that we'd met before. Not once but twice. I might as well be fucking invisible to her.

By the time this is over, she'll only remember me. Her every breath will belong to me, I vowed.

She might have been my obsession for years, but I'd become hers too. We'd be two souls intertwined so thickly, nothing would be able to separate us. She hid fire beneath those pale blue eyes, I wanted to know how hot it burned. And then, I wanted to let it consume me. Consume us.

Because we'd be one body and one soul.

"Try 'Thorns and Roses' with a capital T and capital R," I told her, offering her the olive branch. "Underscore between the words."

She raised a brow, then pushed an unruly piece of hair back off her face with trembling fingers. It was the most peculiar combination when it came to this woman. She could be strong and vulnerable at the same time. Meek one moment and a spitfire the next.

Maybe it was that which made me vouch for her to Marchetti. Or maybe I'd been whipped by her virgin pussy all those years ago. Talk about a mockery.

I scoffed at my idiocy.

"Try it," I ordered her.

"So bossy," she muttered and typed the password. The screen unlocked immediately. "I'm guessing you've been on this computer already."

I didn't confirm it. Nor deny it. "How did you enter?" she asked.

"Through the door," I said dryly.

"You don't say," she mumbled wryly, then turned her attention to the computer. I watched as she moved her mouse left and right, clicking. It didn't take her long to realize there was nothing noteworthy there. Not even the company agreement she needed.

She leaned back in the chair. "He saved pictures on this one," she muttered, her eyes lingering on the screen.

"Do any of them mean anything?"

I fucking hated every single one of those photos. Adrian saved their happiest moments on that laptop. The images of the two of them sharing ice cream, on a merry-go-round, skiing. Tatiana's smile dazzled in every single one of them.

Adrian meant for me to find it. I'd stake my life on it. My father might have started the war when he killed his father, but Adrian took it to a whole new level. He was the boy I shouldn't have saved.

My father's words rang in my ears. *Boys grow up to become men. They come back to find you, and suddenly, the hunter becomes the hunted.*

The tyrannic bastard would fucking laugh if he knew how those words haunted me over the last few years. Maybe that was my punishment for killing the bastard.

Abruptly, Tatiana stood up. The chair fell behind her with a loud thud and she marched by me without another word.

But I didn't miss her bottom lip trembling before she disappeared.

NINETEEN
TATIANA

The pictures clawed at my soul.

But among the pain, one photo caught my attention. Every single photo had the two of us in it except for one. The gazebo.

I had to get to Washington D.C. The answer lay there. I was sure of it. At our beginning.

Despite all the secrets and some questionable things that Adrian seemed to have done, I couldn't just erase my love for him. It had been part of me for so long, but now I wondered what else I didn't know.

Probably many things, I thought to myself.

It was time to go see Sasha again. My favorite brother. It would seem today was the day for visits. If I add Vasili to the itinerary, the day would be complete.

On my way out, my guards were indeed napping. They were knocked out. In their stead, four other guards stood around, and I knew who they belonged to.

"They better be fine," I gritted, pointing at the two men who worked for my brother. "And when they wake up, you convince them not to say a peep to my brothers about this shit."

149

They just gave me blank stares, and I blew raspberries. "Now, wake them up. I need a ride and I'm not digging through their pants for the keys."

Nothing. They refused to move and frustration flared within me.

I sensed the presence behind me at the same time as that scent enveloped me. I really hated that he used that cologne. Of all the colognes in the world, why in the fuck did he have to use the one that belonged to Adrian and me?

Whirling around, I glared at him, blaming him for everything wrong in my life.

"Fix this." I pointed at my passed out guards, tapping my foot impatiently. If I'd worn my heels, the result would be graceful. Clogs made it look kind of awkward.

Gasps traveled from his guards and the sensible part of my brain knew that was not how you talked to the Pakhan. Too fucking late. Too fucking bad. I bowed to nobody.

I might be a grieving widow, but I was still a motherfucking queen. Not Konstantin's peasant.

"Say please, or I'll spank you." Shock rolled through me and something else. Like a spark lighting a match that would eventually catch into a full blown wildfire. There was something about Konstantin's voice that was pure seduction. It had my thighs clenching, like he was the only thing I needed between them.

No, no. *I don't want him*, I scolded myself. I inhaled a shuddering breath while my skin burned hot.

"Unless you're into spanking," he drawled.

My cheeks heated. The visions of me bent over while his big palm smacked my ass played in my mind and the image had my thighs quivering.

"In your fucking dreams," I breathed. This guy was the last man I'd want to get involved with. This was just a physical reaction after not being touched for so long. Then, because I couldn't keep my tongue in check, I snarled but my voice was too hoarse. "And if you ever try to spank me, I'll cut off your hands."

A soft chuckle traveled through the air. The threat was ludicrous. I knew it. He knew it. But I feared he also recognized my body's reaction for what it was.

Lust. Desire.

He flickered a silent command to his men and they rushed to help Yan and Yuri wake up from their forced nap. I tapped my foot impatiently, chewing on my bottom lip. The sooner I got out of here, the better.

The moment my bodyguards realized who knocked them out, they eagerly agreed not to say a peep to Vasili. It didn't do much for the confidence of my safety if they could be so easily persuaded, but for now, it worked in my favor.

Yan rushed to the car and opened the door before I got to it. Usually my exit would be a lot more graceful but in my current wardrobe, it was slightly less than mediocre, not that I cared. I just wanted to get out of here.

"Running?" Konstantin's voice came from behind me. My heart thumped to an odd beat, sending a shiver through me. I didn't like this reaction to him. I'd like to convince myself it was fear, but I knew it'd be a lie.

My steps halted, Yan holding the door and looking straight ahead. If I was smart, I'd get into the car and ask Yan to slam the door so I wouldn't have to hear another word from the Konstantin devil. But I never claimed to be, so I turned around. Slowly. Maybe even sensually.

"I never run. Do you?"

I could feel his heat. I could smell that scent that became my aphrodisiac from my first sexual experience. During all my years in college I experimented with my sexuality. A lot. But contrary to everyone's belief, I held onto my virginity. Until that night with Adrian in the gazebo. That night, the inexperienced virgin became the experienced woman.

"I never run," Konstantin responded in that deep voice.

He closed the space between us. My breasts brushed his chest and heat, unlike any before, shot straight to my core. A soft gasp parted my lips and his hand curled around my nape, grabbing a fistful of hair. He closed the distance, his lips hot on mine. My stomach dove, stealing my breath. His tongue swept over my bottom lip as butterflies erupted in my lower belly, then spread fire through my veins.

Addicting. It felt so goddamn addictive.

His tongue brushed against mine and a rough sound vibrated deep in his chest. My ears buzzed. My blood seared.

Then he bit my lip hard enough I yelped. I fell back a step, staring at him in confusion while my bottom lip tingled like he branded me.

"This is not a goodbye, Tatiana Nikolaev." His voice was soft, like black velvet, set to catch me with his hooks.

His twin brother I could probably handle. But this guy, definitely not.

He stepped away from me and suddenly, my lungs filled with air. I could finally get some oxygen into my brain. Just in time to realize what an idiot I was to play with someone as powerful as a Konstantin. This Konstantin. But I'd be damned if I'd stop.

Like a glutton for punishment, as I slid into the back seat of the Mercedes, my eyes darted to the tall dark figure.

"I really hope it's a final goodbye," I told him dryly, then offered a fake sweet smile. "For your sake. You seem a bit too obsessed with me. It's not healthy."

His gaze flickered with something akin to dry amusement, and I quickly pulled the door shut so I didn't have to hear his reply.

The tension in Yan and Yuri was visible in their shoulders as they drove me to Sasha's home. Damn Konstantin. This man was making me feel things I haven't felt in so long, and I feared latching onto it. He overwhelmed every fiber of my being. He made me feel wanted unlike any other man, even Adrian before things went askew.

Jesus Christ!

I was a grieving widow. I couldn't go around kissing well-dressed men. And this one was nothing like Adrian who preferred to wear jeans and combat boots. This guy was all suave and charismatic. Powerful. Dangerous.

In short, bad news.

Adrian was the man who I loved and missed. He was my life.

But he kept you in the dark, the corners of my mind whispered. *About so many things.*

"Not a word to anyone," I warned my guards, ignoring the whispers in my head. They both nodded and I reached for the little flask sitting in the console. I gulped it down, this time it wasn't vodka. It was a fruit flavored brandy. Instantly the alcohol slid into my blood and warmed me from the inside out.

I had somewhat reduced my alcohol consumption, but I still resorted to it. It was just to take the edge off.

Like now.

So technically, it was the damn Pakhan's fault.

By the time the car pulled up in front of Sasha's home, I had one too many sips from my flask. Self-control wasn't my strong suit and alcohol filled the hollow in my chest.

At least temporarily.

I entered Sasha's home, the one he kept in the French Quarter, to find him in his office. Unlike Vasili who spent the majority of his time in the office, Sasha was rarely there. It meant he was strategizing how to fuck someone up. And I had a feeling I knew who.

"I hear Branka Russo is engaged." The dark look he gave me was my confirmation, and I knew that Branka would never tie the knot with that man. He remained silent. "Do you want to know who the lucky guy is?"

He didn't bite. Not surprising. My brothers were stubborn and scary fuckers. Truthfully, I was surprised he hadn't learned the identity of her future husband. The underworld could be like a little village sometimes. It was how I learned of it a few weeks ago.

"Killian Brennan."

I dropped the name and the way Sasha' expression iced over I knew the Irishman might not live much longer. I threw myself into the chair and took another sip out of my flask. That shit was pretty tasty.

"So you gonna kill him?" I asked curiously. I propped my long legs on the table, stretching them. At least sweatpants were good for stretching.

Sasha threw me a worried gaze, ignoring the bait and taunting I threw his way.

"Sestra, you can't keep this up." Sasha's voice was serious, a concern lacing it. He only called me sister in Russian when he was uber-worried. "You're killing your liver."

I waved my hand and drops of alcohol splashed out of the flask. Damn it. Maybe the alcohol was working overtime.

"Livers can be repaired."

"So can your heart," my brother reasoned.

I met his gaze, that loss from so many months ago still gnawing at me. Although, the kiss I just shared with Konstantin flashed in my mind, dulling some of the ache. *Pathetic!*

"Then why are you chasing the Russo girl?" I asked, rather than evaluate my reaction to the Pakhan. My brothers would go bananas if they knew I had been alone with that man. Taunting him. Playing with him.

"Tatiana, you have to let him go. You have to find a way to move on. And searching for clues, drinking vodka–" his eyes flickered to my wardrobe, " –and wearing sweatpants is not the way to move on."

I tsked, dismissing his advice. It didn't surprise me he knew I was searching for answers. He knew me too well. And I was certain Aurora mentioned something to Alexei who in turn said something to Sasha.

"Like you're looking for ways to move on from your obsession that is engaged?" I remarked sarcastically as I put the flask down. Then I stretched my legs some more. Exercise and alcohol all in the same minute. Now that was multitasking.

Thankfully, he changed subjects.

"What do you know about Branka and Killian's arrangement?"

I shrugged. "Only that they're getting married and Branka refused to walk down the aisle until her friend was back safe and sound." Then

I snapped my fingers, the idea dancing in my head. "Of course, that's assuming her friend gets out of Afghanistan."

I didn't think my brother could handle getting his happiness at the cost of someone else, but it didn't hurt to test him. Judging by the expression on his face, I was right.

"You know, Killian Brennan is practically family," I said casually. To say our familiar relations were complicated was an understatement. Alexei's wife, Aurora, was related to Davina Brennan, wife of Killian's father Liam Brennan. Step-father. Whatever he was.

I let Sasha steam on it a bit, but there was no doubt he'd come up with a plan. And get what he wanted. Which apparently was Branka Russo. He'd better hope our big brother didn't get wind of Sasha's plans, whatever they might be.

Exhaling, I lowered my feet and stood up. "By the way, I need your help."

Sasha's eyes, that signature Nikolaev pale blue, met mine. He waited and waited. I could ask him to go with me, but I thought it would be better if I went alone.

"Any chance you have someone, aside from you, who could take me to D.C. for the weekend and keep it a secret from Vasili?"

He pushed his hand through his hair, that ink marking his skin flashing his own life story. His skin told his story and while it had been somewhat of a hard story, I really hoped he got his woman and happily-ever-after. For a while, I thought the woman he loved died, but apparently, I was wrong.

"Why don't I go with you?" he offered.

I shook my head. "No, this I have to do alone. But I'd prefer if you assigned someone to go with me and lend me your plane."

His brows furrowed. "Is something wrong with Yan and Yuri?"

I shook my head. "No, but they have families and Yan has small children." It was a half-truth. "They work too much as it is. I don't want to pull them away from their families."

He didn't exactly buy it, but considering I asked for protection, he was willing to let me get away with it.

"Yeah, when do you need to go?" he asked.

"Tonight?"

"You could go with Byron Ashford," he offered. Aurora's brother. It had to be a sign and the best part was that the Billionaire King wouldn't bother asking any questions.

As Alexei noted, he had bigger problems to deal with and wouldn't pay me much attention.

S he was on the move.

Lenosh sat next to me, watching Tatiana make her way through the luxury backyard of the residence. I remembered it well. How could I fucking forget! It was where I first spotted Tatiana all those years ago. Second time was in my restaurant - Constantinople. Yeah, the name was not very discreet. My little sister named it.

Unbeknownst to the Nikolaev family, I had a tracker inserted in Tatiana right after her accident. A simple dental procedure while she was at the hospital. Maybe it was a little overboard. Tatiana's safety was more important than her right to privacy.

I had questionable morals. Fucking sue me.

For the first few months, there was absolutely no activity. Then the fighter that I knew her to be, she started digging, seeking answers. Marchetti was getting impatient. So were the others.

But nobody dared to attack. Except for the Yakuza. They weren't members of the Thorns of Omertà, but they had an indirect connection to it through Amon. But as far as I knew, they weren't blackmailed. Not like the members of our organization. So that meant they wanted to get their paws on the chip so they could expand into our territory.

Putting those thoughts on hold, I focused on the woman I'd been watching for years. Since Adrian's death, I'd had men on her twenty-four seven. Yes, her brothers had bodyguards on her too, but that wasn't good enough. They gave her too much freedom, which meant too many opportunities for someone to get to her.

She had landed in D.C. late last night. Byron Ashford didn't even realize how close he was to dying. She flew with him and the fucking '*gentleman*' escorted her inside the Waldorf Astoria hotel to check-in. Two minutes. He was alone with her for two minutes. A hundred and twenty seconds. One more second and he would have been a dead man. If he came back that night, he'd have been a tortured dead man.

Fucker!

I watched her roam the property on the Patapsco River. It was where we first met and she didn't even remember it. I let out a sardonic breath. She was all I had thought about for the past seven years and she didn't even remember me.

Fucking irony.

Her heels sunk into soft ground and she muttered something I couldn't hear, then continued tiptoeing, bypassing the house. She headed straight for the vast landscape in the back of it that backed up to the Patapsco River.

Sunset threw shadows, slowly lowering down the horizon. The property belonged to me so even if I hadn't been tracking her, the alarm would have been set off the moment she stepped foot on the property.

Images of my first encounter with the woman who became my obsession flashed through my mind. The way she strolled into the party like she owned it. The way her eyes glimmered like sun rays reflecting over the Caribbean Sea.

Then that note. That fucking note asking me to fuck her. Jesus Christ, I was many things but a saint wasn't one of them. So I followed her into the gazebo and fucked her brains out. Unfortunately, or maybe fortunately, she left an impression.

Just as we found our release, my cock buried deep inside her tight pussy, her fucking bodyguard came back. I didn't know her name back then, albeit I was determined to find out.

But Adrian started playing his games. He was always in the fucking way, even back then when I didn't know who he really was. Motherfucker! I should have shot him as he approached, then got back to fucking her and listening to those moans and whimpers.

Regardless, shortly after my sexual encounter with Tatiana in this very gazebo, I convinced the owners they wanted to sell.

I was never sentimental, but I fucking needed this place. It was a sacred temple that I'd been determined to bring her back to and worship her all over again. The home wasn't bad either - the white manor on the Patapsco River with plenty of acreage to afford privacy and protection.

I could fuck her any time, day or night. Inside and outside. Perfect fucking dream.

Fuck!

The way Tatiana strolled through it like she owned the place. In that pink dress, her thighs played peekaboo each time she took a step.

Sasha Nikolaev's voice faded into the background. So did my twin's.

Jesus, I couldn't quite decide whether she looked like an angel with that light blonde hair or a seductress. Everything about her was enticing. Like a femme fatale determined to act innocent. And then she blindsides you with an insinuating message. Or those fucking moans I'd dreamt about since that night in the gazebo.

Blood rushed to my ears and heat to my groin.

I had to know who she was. The universe threw her into my path. It had to mean something. It had to be a fucking sign.

Reaching for my phone, I kept my gaze on her as I typed my message to Nikita. ***Need a name. Woman in the pink dress. Now.***

The soft pink satin gown hugged her curves, her long legs giving way to the slit that stretched almost to her hip. Every man in the restaurant was eyeing her. Some men on dates were being discreet but others couldn't peel their gazes off Tatiana's catwalk.

Jesus, the woman even walked like a queen. And she was headed straight to our table.

Did she recognize me? Had she been looking for me like I'd been looking for her?

God, someone had to punch me. I acted like a pussy whipped teenager. Or even worse, a giddy fucking girl.

A man leaned forward and the woman's steps faltered. Her eyes left my general direction and she turned to glance at the guy. She mumbled something, then left him without a backwards glance.

"Then your mouth can find my cock."

The table, full of men, roared with laughter. Red mist covered my vision, making her pink dress appear different shades of red. The whole restaurant noise was distorted by the rage rushing through me, pounding at my chest and eager to make the fucker pay. Right. The. Fuck. Now.

*It took all my self-control not to pull out my gun and kill the fucker who dared talk to a woman - **my woman** - that way.*

I shot to my feet, but my brother's hand wrapped around my wrist. My head whipped around, ready to punch him when he gave me a curt shake.

***Not now,** his gaze relayed. It was one of the rare moments he bothered with the well-being of anyone but himself. It used to be different between us. We used to be close. Then one bullet tore us apart.*

I gritted my teeth and sat back down, keeping my eyes on the woman and that table. I'd kill that fucker and teach the others a lesson for even glancing at my wife.

I ran a hand through my hair, well aware I was getting ahead of myself. But fuck it, I knew what I wanted when I saw it. And she was IT for me. I'd marry her, have babies with her, and keep her with me forever. This life and the next.

Her eyes flickered to our table again. As if she knew exactly who I was and what thoughts ran through my mind. Except... she was looking at Sasha Nikolaev. I followed her gaze, but the fucker's freaky pale blue eyes were focused on something else.

***Someone** else.*

Returning my attention to the queen, I noted her muttering some-

thing under her breath and the guy reared backwards as if shocked by whatever she said.

My phone still in my hand, I sent out another text message to Nikita. ***Table 5. I want the prick with the cheap suit and ugly face. Keep him in the back room.***

The scent of roses filled my nostrils and invaded my lungs. In the best fucking way.

"Brother, you know this restaurant is more for dates than a quick lunch. Right?" The question was in Russian. Fuck, that voice. My heart sped up, heat running through my veins and to my groin. I was already painfully hard, I feared my control might snap and I'd fuck her right here. Bend her over the table and thrust into her tight pussy, while getting drunk off the scent of roses.

It was only then that her words registered. Brother?

Sasha was on his feet, already taking her hand. "You're early," Sasha grumbled. "You're never early."

His sister cocked an eyebrow. "And here I thought you'd appreciate me trying to appease you. It'll be the last time, ever."

"I doubt it," Sasha retorted wryly, then his eyes flickered to my brother and me. "Gentlemen, nice seeing you and doing business with you."

Not so fast, you unhinged motherfucker. "Introduce us," I demanded.

I was still the Pakhan, and while I allowed the Nikolaevs autonomy, he still owed me respect and allegiance. Not that I fooled myself that they'd ever fall to their knees for me.

"My sister, Tatiana," Sasha gritted.

Tatiana. Fuck, the name suited her. Fairy queen.

My mother's favorite story was A Midsummer Night's Dream and the Queen of the Fairies, Titania.

Our gazes met, her cute button nose scrunched and... she glared at me. Fucking glared at me!

I could have laughed, yet there was absolutely nothing funny about it. I was inside her tight pussy, jacking off at the images of her for years now, and she fucking glared at me like I was a speck on her pretty pink pumps.

"And you are?" she asked, her eyes darting between me and my brother. "Aside from twins, which is obvious."

It was obvious she'd be more worried about me putting a stain on that pump than me.

I stood up to my full height, towering a good head over her. Nobody, and I meant fucking nobody, ever showed less interest in meeting me.

"Illias Konstantin," I drawled. "You'll do well to remember your Pakhan's name."

A flicker of recognition flashed in her eyes. At least she knew of me, if she didn't fucking remember me.

Her lips curved, barely. "Well, Mr. Konstantin, I'll try to remember the name. At least to appease your fragile ego."

Jesus Christ, this woman!

My lips tugged up, amused. It would seem my little seductress didn't remember our encounter. I'd be sure to remind her of it. She'd remember my name and my fucking cock in her pussy for the rest of her life.

"Tatiana, Illias and Maxim occasionally make deals with Vasili." Sasha's voice was cautious but distracted. His attention was elsewhere. It kept flicking to the entrance where two women whispered urgently back and forth. Maxim spotted them too, and for some dumb reason, he seemed to be fascinated by them.

Kind of like I was fascinated with Tatiana.

"That's fascinating," she remarked dryly. Was the magical woman reading my thoughts? Then I noted the undertone of her sarcasm. God, I wanted to spank her. I needed to spank her and teach her a lesson.

But I'd be satisfied with beating the shit out of the fucker who dared talk to my woman like she was a common whore.

I buttoned my jacket and straightened my sleeves, signaling to my brother it was time to go.

"We'll leave you two. Enjoy your lunch. It's on the house."

Maxim left us before I even got to finish my sentence. My twin brother was acting downright stupid lately. Like come-the-fuck-on... was I the most feared and ruthless Pakhan or what? My brother clearly was close to going off the deep end. My future brother-in-law had more interest in my restaurant's reception area than anyone else at this table.

And my soon-to-be-bride - her attention was elsewhere right along with Sasha's. Not that I cared about the psycho fucker's attention. Hers... it was something entirely different.

"You know what," Sasha muttered. "You're right, this is a couple's restaurant. Let's go grab something off the food truck."

Tatiana snorted. Legit snorted. "Fuck you, Sasha. I'm not eating off the food truck."

He paid no attention to her, pulled out his wallet and threw a stack of bills on the table.

"Sasha—" she hissed, blue lightning filling her gaze.

"Let's go, my lady."

Whatever the fuck that meant, I had no fucking clue but it got his sister glaring at him. Thank fuck! I didn't think my heart could handle another glare from her.

He tugged her arm and she gave me some flimsy hand wave. "Laters, Pakhan."

I shook my head. I might have been at my limit today so I shrugged it off. She'd remember me when I made an arrangement with her brother to marry her.

Right now, I'd go and torture the fucker with the filthy mouth. Excellent stress relief.

I found Nikita in the "back room" as instructed. It was more a cellar but who got hung up on formalities here. Fucking nobody. The men that dared to laugh at the crude joke their friend uttered would be taught a lesson. Stand up for the woman in the future. The fucker who dared to say them. Well, things wouldn't end very well for him.

"Gentlemen, thank you for meeting me," I drawled in a bored tone. I walked toward them, slowly, like a predator ready to pounce. With each step, their tension and fear grew, fogging the air.

"What is this?" one of them asked, his tone undignified. Of course, it'd be the fucker who dared suggest my angel suck his cock.

I let my rage loose and grinned sadistically.

"This is me teaching you manners," I answered before my fist flew into his jaw.

The three sets of eyes popped open wide. Terror radiated from every single one of them.

"W-whatever you think—" One of them stuttered.

*My voice was deadly calm when I spoke again. "Your friend here talked to my future wife with disrespect." They were petrified. All three of them. "Unless you'd like to bear his punishment, I suggest you shut the fuck up and observe. Don't worry, you won't be slighted though." He opened his mouth and I clicked my tongue, narrowing my eyes on him. "But if you say another word, make a fucking sound, I'll teach **you** a lesson first."*

His lips instantly tightened, scared to make a single peep. I grinned savagely, tasting his fear on my tongue.

"We didn't know it was your wife." The fucker who dared talk to Tatiana pleaded. Then to my amusement, he pissed himself. "I was joking when I said I'd tear her ass up. I-I'm not into ass fucking. N-nor rape. I-I w-wasn't gonna rape her."

I flashed him a ferocious smile while red slowly seeped into my vision. It took all my control to keep my cool. Not to go on a murder spree with these three assholes who hung off my cellar ceiling.

Turning to my left, a table lay with all our tools neatly organized. There might have been a blood stain. Or two. We purposely left those. It worked magic when it came to instilling fear.

I reached for the scalpel and twisted it in my hand as I neared the ringleader. The guy who dared even utter rape when talking about my woman.

"What's your name?" I asked, letting the savage wash over me.

"T-Tom."

"Well, Tom. You and I, we're gonna get acquainted so fucking well."

He shook his head. "I-I don't want to get acquainted."

My eyes darted to Nikita. "Let's teach the fucker what happens to rapists in my town."

And I did. For hours and hours. By the time the light in his eyes was extinguished, his buddies hated the idea of non-consensual anything.

"We have to get that chip soon." Lenosh's hard voice pulled me out of the past. "The others are tired of waiting."

I tapped my fingers against the wheel, watching the slim figure wearing all black make her way here and there, as if she was trying to remember something. Her long blonde hair wasn't matted and messy today. It fell down her back, the stark blonde even lighter against her black Chanel outfit. It seemed to be her signature outfit.

I couldn't help a soft scoff. At least she wasn't wearing those hideous sweatpants. It took all my restraint not to rip them off her yesterday. Although it was more attributable to the knowledge that it belonged to her late husband.

"They'll have to wait for as long as it takes," I said firmly.

Lenosh thinned his lips but said nothing else. It was why we got along so well. He knew when to object and talk, and when to be quiet. So did Nikita, but he had some urgent business to tend to.

My gaze slid back to the woman who was now on her knees, her hands skimming over the lawn.

"Jesus, what is she doing?" Lenosh muttered.

"Searching would be my guess." The question was whether she was searching for the chip or something else.

"Maybe she's drunk and finally lost– " Upon seeing my thunderous expression, he paused, thinking better of finishing that sentence.

"You can go," I told him. "I'll hitch a ride with our little explorer."

He nodded and I exited the car, slamming the door shut more forcefully than needed. I wanted to make sure Tatiana heard me. And sure enough, her head whipped around, her eyes connecting with mine.

I could practically hear her groan from here as she rolled her eyes and jumped to her feet. Taking my time, I strolled towards her and drank the sight of her in. The dress she was wearing flattened against the curve of her breasts and waist, then flared down to her knees. Her cheeks were flushed red and her full lips so goddamn tempting.

Of course, it didn't help that memories of the last time both of us were here swarmed my mind.

It was here. In this gazebo.

I stole her innocence that night, but she stole my fucking soul. I was a fool to let Adrian take her, but now she'd be mine. Completely. Figuratively. Literally.

In every sense of the world.

"Hello again."

"God, I hoped I'd never see you again," she snapped, her anger covering up the fact that I'd startled the shit out of her. "What are you doing here?"

"Careful," I warned her softly, stopping five feet from here. "Or you'll earn yourself a punishment."

"And you'll earn yourself a bullet."

Fuck, her fire was such a goddamn turn on. Nobody, and I meant *nobody* ever spoke to me like that. It made me want to tame her even more. To see how her eyes turned a shade darker when she craved my touch. My mouth.

Just like she did that night.

I beckoned her with a finger. "Come here."

A hunger roared in my chest, deep and consuming, demanding another taste of her. I had been dreaming of her for years, and now that she was so close to me, it was hard not to go all in. Demand her submission. Her body. Her soul.

Her eyes flashed like two blue lightning bolts. "I'm not a dog, Tyrant."

God, I'd love to fill her mouth with my cock. Heat rushed to my groin and instantly my dick twitched, on board with that image. Though judging by the look on Tatiana's beautiful face, she would more likely try to bite it off.

Contempt spread through my veins like a Siberian winter. Her soft curves under that hideous black tempted and invited. She was mine. She had always been mine.

In one swift move, I grabbed her by the chin using two fingers.

"No more hiding shit," I drawled. "What have you found?"

TWENTY-ONE
TATIANA

His fingers were rough and possessive.

It didn't hurt but it did something to my insides. Confusion swelled inside me. What was happening to me? Every time this man came around me, my body responded. My blood ran hotter and my heart thundered harder.

The note burned in the palm of my hand. It was written in Adrian's handwriting.

I go on. Standing in the shadows.

It was cryptic. Confusing. Bottom line, the note made no fucking sense.

Sliding it into my pocket, I decided to deal with one problem at a time. First, I had to handle this devil who seemed to be stalking me. Fucking villains. Always stalkers. I bet he'd get along swell with my brothers.

Ugh.

"You should come with a warning sign," I grumbled. "Stalker alert. Beware!"

Konstantin leaned closer, his cologne, citrusy and so damn familiar, swelling all my senses. Forgetting the scrunched up note in my pocket and my attitude, I closed my eyes, fighting this unfamiliar urge deep inside me. To submit. To let him dominate me.

For the first time ever, I wanted to get on my knees. The urge confused me. Terrified me.

Yet, now as our gazes clashed, confusion swam thick through me. The past and present blurred in my mind. Adrian and Konstantin. There was a key piece of information I was missing. Or maybe I forgot it.

I couldn't blame the alcohol. I hadn't touched it since I arrived in D.C.

"Tell me what you found, *moya luna*," he drawled in a lazy tone that did things to me. Something tickled the back of my mind, but refused to come forward. "Tell me and I'll reward you." This villain wasn't easily distracted for sure. Although his seductive tone certainly distracted me. "Trust me, you'll like it." His breath brushed against my earlobe. His scent was addictive and mind numbing. "In fact, you'll like it so much you'll be screaming my name for the entire state to hear."

A shudder rolled down my spine. Every inch of my skin was on fire. I felt the drumming of blood in my ears, but my stubbornness took over. I pushed my lightheaded, intoxicating feelings out of my mind, leaving me with determination. To focus. To make sure he didn't find the clue Adrian left me. If Konstantin decided to search me, he'd find it. So I'd use my wiles.

I met his gaze and my heart stilled for a flicker of a moment, before speeding up in an unnatural way. There was something dark behind his eyes, pulling me to him by an invisible force. As if we were bonded together.

I stepped closer, our breaths only inches away. I felt him on every inch of my skin, even though his fingers only touched my chin. I was parched - for a taste of him, for something that would trap me beneath his darkness. Alcohol had nothing on this feeling.

My lips hovered close to his. The kiss was a single breath away. I wanted to bite and lick his lips. My breasts brushed his chest with each breath, sending heat straight to my core. Clenching my one hand, I ran my other up his abs, curling my fingers into his chest.

I wanted to claw his clothes off his body and feel his chest - hard and warm - under my fingertips. Against me. He smelled so fucking good, I was lost to him.

Our lips connected and my stomach swooped with butterflies working overtime. I didn't know who closed that final inch. Maybe we met in the middle, splitting that inch in half. My lips parted and his tongue pushed into my mouth, stealing my breath.

It was hot. Wet. Addictive.

Pure lust erupted inside me, drowning me in its waters. My head swam and my world turned so fast, I grew dizzy behind my eyelids. I held on to him as my tongue slid across his. A rough sound vibrated deep in his chest, echoing my own volcano erupting through my veins.

My heart pounded. His thundered under the palm of my hand.

The note forgotten; the plan of seduction forgotten. I rubbed myself against him, needing more of this friction.

And then he bit my lip hard enough I yelped. Again.

This Russian motherfucker.

I glared at him. "What the fuck?"

His gaze burned like the fires of Hades. If we were gods, he'd be part of the hellish dominion and I'd be... well, I wasn't sure where I'd be. Maybe somewhere between purgatory and heaven.

"You're playing with fire, Tatiana," he warned, his voice all velvet and seduction. But the tick of his jaw and lust in his eyes betrayed him. His hand came to my throat, lightly grasping it. I held my breath, waiting and goosebumps broke over my flesh as he caressed my fluttering pulse with his thumb. All it would take was him squeezing against it and he'd snuff the life right out of me.

"So?" I breathed.

I was burning up. I needed more of him. There was no going back. Just here and now.

"You ready for it?" For what, I wanted to ask but my throat was dry. My ears buzzed.

My lips burned from the heat of our kiss. I could still taste him on my lips. The hint of citrus and something else, I couldn't quite place. It was so fucking addictive that I knew if I crossed the line, there'd be no recovery from the addiction called Illias Konstantin.

As if he read my mind, he added with a rough lilt to his voice, "If we cross this line, there's no turning back."

The tone sent a tremor through me, warning me of the risk I was about to take. The electric pull of his gaze tempted me. I hadn't enjoyed myself in so long, but now... with him... I wanted to play. I wanted to seduce. I wanted to win.

I was never the type to like dropping to my knees. I'd preferred it the other way around. All you motherfuckers drop to your knees and worship me like a queen. But with him... God, help me. I wanted to drop to my knees and make him feel good. I wanted his hands on me.

Yes, it was about winning, but also about feeling good for the first time in a long time. A very long time that stretched before Adrian's death.

Slowly, keeping eye contact, I lowered myself down to my knees. Surprise flashed across Konstantin's expression and his eyes darkened to black pools. I didn't care that we were outside. Or that someone could be watching from a distance.

This felt like a need that I couldn't deny.

So I reached for his belt and unbuckled it, my thighs clenching. The scent of citrus and sandalwood swarmed my mind, like the strongest alcohol I had ever consumed. He didn't stop me and as I freed his cock, my hands didn't tremble. It was as if my fingers had known him. Had touched him.

"Are you sure?" His voice was restrained, like he was teetering on the edge. My hand wrapped around his rock-hard length, pre-cum glistening and I proceeded to jack him off. Up and down. Up and down. He was big, much bigger than what I was used to.

"Tatiana. Are. You. Sure?"

Staring up at him, I leaned over and licked the precum from the tip and sucked him into my mouth. It was the only answer I had for him.

A deep groan spilled from his lips, but his half-lidded eyes zeroed in on me. I quickened my pace as I clenched my thighs with the arousal that had hit me like a tsunami. This was empowering. Maybe I was on my knees, but he was unraveling for me. It was me who was giving him pleasure. I controlled his pleasure.

I let him hit the back of my throat, his fingers clenching in my hair and gripping almost painfully. His grunts and appreciative noises were all for me. My hands gripped his thighs and my nails dug into his pants.

He thrust his cock to the back of my throat. Again and again. My gag reflexes kicked in, but I refused to stop. I let him fuck my throat, his fingers holding my head immobile as he hit the back of it over and over again.

I moaned around his length and his dark eyes flashed with something victorious. Consuming.

He pounded in and out of my mouth. His hips controlled the rhythm, and as if he had always known me, he thrust in deep and hard. All the way in. He was so big and so thick that he still wasn't completely inside my mouth.

His other hand came to grip my jaw. And all the while, our eyes locked. Darkness and light. Past and present. Maybe future. Tears pricked my eyes, then spilled down my cheeks.

Konstantin powered in and out of my mouth with a mad rhythm, his control nonexistent. My thighs tightened with each ram inside my mouth. My eyes fluttered shut and arousal drenched my panties as I lost myself in this lust.

"Open your eyes, moya luna," he ordered, his tone savage.

I peeled my eyelids open, seeing the brutal edge on his features. His grip tightened on my hair and he kept going on and on. Fucking my willing mouth. All my thoughts evaporated, leaving me alone with him. Drool dripped down my chin. My jaw ached, but I refused to stop. I wanted to see this man fall apart. For me.

"Open your mouth wider," he grunted and I obeyed before I even processed his words. Heat bloomed in my stomach and lower between my thighs, sending a wave so strong, I thought I might have orgasmed by him fucking my mouth. I never particularly cared to be bossed around, but with this man, it did things to me.

"Fuck, that's it," he praised, his head falling back.

He tugged my hair back while his hips thrust into me with a ruthlessness that stole my breath and every thought. Sparks of pleasure was the only feeling I could focus on.

There was only one time I felt like this before. Ironically, it was in this same spot. At this gazebo. I stuck my tongue out the slightest and moaned, my mouth full of his cock.

His groan rumbled from deep in his throat.

"*Fuck.*" His voice was rough, raspy and sent an unfamiliar raw wave of warmth through my body.

And with that, he came all over my tongue and down my throat. I swallowed his cum, but there was so much, some of it dripped down my chin. He looked magnificent when he orgasmed. It was hands down the most beautiful sight I had ever seen. His veins strained in his neck. The bliss on his face. But his eyes! They shimmered like black diamonds.

My skin grew hot under his gaze. He pulled out, then brought his thumb to my lower lip while his other hand still gripped me by the hair. His breaths came out heavy as he wiped my chin and brought it to my lips.

My tongue darted and licked his finger, then sucked it clean.

He tucked himself in with one hand and zipped his pants, then fastened his belt. And the whole time, he kept his gaze on me.

Then he pulled me up to my feet. We stood toe-to-toe. Chest-to-chest. My breathing was ragged, but his wasn't much better. The cold of D.C. slowly registered and felt like frost against the scorching sun. It was slowly melting me.

"Whose mouth is this?" he demanded to know, his grip on my chin firm.

"Mine."

His lips curved up, as if he expected that answer.

"We shall see about that." He leaned over and licked my lips. It was so filthy. So erotic. A shudder rolled down my spine. This was different, but kind of familiar. "Now you will tell me what you found, Tatiana."

"Nothing," I answered quickly.

Too quickly.

TWENTY-TWO
KONSTANTIN

I 'd learned from a young age to spot lies.

It was about that subtle eye movement or change in posture, a fake smile. Even a change in the pitch of the voice. But the most telling was the quickening of the pulse. I could see Tatiana's vein pulse in the neck speed up.

I'd tortured men for answers, and I knew I could drag it out of Tatiana. Except that just the thought of Tatiana in pain made my heart twinge. It made bile rise in my throat. So we'd have to learn to talk it out.

It was a new thing for me, but for her, I'd learn it.

"Wrong answer." My voice was deadly calm, hiding the volcano deep inside me. The one that demanded I get the answers and the one that demanded I don't hurt her. "One more try."

She blinked twice, but she held my gaze. Fuck, her cheeks were still flushed from the arousal and her lips sticky from my cum.

Her eyes darted to my left, then to my right. I recognized the signs even before she kicked her shoes off. My hands wrapped around her wrist before she could bolt.

"Not so fucking fast," I growled, pulling her back. She jerked her arm and my hand wrapped around her throat, tilting it back and

175

squeezing it gently. "Want to run? Do it. I will love every second of hunting you down. But fair warning, I will fuck you hard once I catch you."

Her body tensed and she remained silent, watching me with those beautiful eyes. She didn't even fight back. But I wasn't fooled into thinking she had given up. This woman wasn't the giving up type. Not long term anyhow.

"So much for a thank you," she grumbled. "At least you could give me a head start for a blow job well done."

There she was. The fighter I knew her to be. And a snarky one at that.

"Maybe next time." She rolled her eyes. Fucking rolled her eyes at me with my hand wrapped around her neck. God, I had to put some fear into her. Men pissed themselves around me and this woman was rolling her eyes. "Now, show me what you found."

She put her hand into her pocket and pulled out a note, fisting it in her palm. I stretched out my hand and waited for her to hand it to me.

She blew a raspberry, her blonde hair flying off her face. She just slapped it into my hand and growled.

"That's the last time I give you a blow job."

I smiled. "Don't taunt me," I purred. It most certainly wouldn't be the last time. We'd only gotten started. "And don't worry. I'll return the favor."

The stain on her cheeks deepened to crimson and I smiled, loving the look on her. I'd dreamed of her for years, and I knew the moment I met her, nothing would be the same. When she married Adrian, I convinced myself it was for the best. She seemed happy.

Letting her go was my first and last selfless act. If only I'd known it was all part of Adrian's plan for revenge. If I knew back then who he was, I'd have claimed her and killed him back then.

I glanced at the paper she put in my hand, while rubbing my thumb gently over her strong pulse.

I go on. Standing in the shadows.

"What does it mean?" I questioned her.

She shrugged, her brows furrowed and a pensive look in her eyes.

"I don't know," she said with a hint of annoyance in her voice. Then as if she realized it made her sound something less, she added, "Yet."

Putting my hand on the small of her back and nudging her forward, we headed towards her rental car.

"I have no doubt you'll unravel it," I told her, then extended my hand. "The keys. I'm driving us back to the hotel."

"What if I'm staying with a friend?" she said wryly.

Dry amusement filled me. No friend, no family, no enemy would keep me from her.

"Then you better warn your friend, I'm coming too."

Twenty minutes later we were in her hotel room.

Of course, she got the best room the Waldorf had to offer. The Presidential suite. Nothing less would be right for the queen she was.

The moment we entered her room, she dropped her purse on the little side table, kicked off her heels and stretched out her toes. It was such a simple act, yet something about it was so soothing. So fucking right.

I could practically envision her doing that every day when we got home. Together. Fuck, I was getting ahead of myself.

She glanced over her shoulder. "I don't need company," she sneered, like the idea of coming home with me was nauseating to her. Too fucking bad. She'd have to get used to it.

I checked the time on my watch. "Well, you're going to get it."

When I raised my head, it was to find her eyes flashed with annoyance, glaring at me.

"Well, don't expect any entertainment."

I let out a sardonic breath. She certainly didn't bother stroking my ego. Without another glance, she sauntered to the little mini bar and poured herself a glass of wine. I noted the pills that sat next to the fully stocked bar and my brows furrowed. I didn't like her taking that shit.

She was so focused on the alcohol she missed me stalking closer to her. Before she could bring the glass to her lips, I moved it out of her reach.

"What the hell are you doing?" she hissed, taking a step backwards as I took one towards her. I could see her pulse thundering under her pale skin. Her eyes slightly widened but she refused to cower.

"No alcohol today," I ordered.

Her eyes narrowed with contempt and her pulse quickened. She didn't like being told what to do. From all the intel I had on her, and from what I had seen, her brothers doted on her. Probably compensating for the lack of a mother and an absent father.

"You're not my father."

I placed the glass back on the counter, not sparing it another glance.

"Vok tak." *That's right.* She took another step backwards and I followed.

"You're not my brother either."

"Vok tak." *That's right.* Another step backwards and her back hit the hotel wall. "But I am a man of my word." A whisper of darkness laced through my voice as I closed the distance between us. I pressed my hands against the wall on either side of her and lowered my head. She sucked in a breath as my lips skimmed up her neck. "There will be no blaming alcohol after we fuck, Tatiana Nikolaev."

A visible shudder rolled down her body and her slender, delicate throat moved as she swallowed. Fuck, she was beautiful. Like an angel thrown to this Earth to tempt me. To humble me.

"W-Why don't you ever call me by my married name?" she stuttered softly. I nipped her sensitive flesh - hard - punishing her for even suggesting it. "Ouch."

"Don't push me, moya luna," I murmured against her flesh. "You're mine and I don't want reminders of anyone else." I bit her again. "Understood?"

She didn't even realize she tilted her head to accommodate me. *My defiant queen can be tamed*, I thought amused.

I eased the sting by sucking on her pulse and then licking it. She tasted like ice on a hot, humid day. It was the only time I loved the smell of roses. Around her. The scent that I hated since my mother's betrayal came full circle.

Lifting my head, I could already see my mark on her porcelain skin and something savage swelled in my chest. *Mine.* It screamed loud and clear. Not Adrian's. Not her family's. She was fucking mine.

Meeting her eyes, I let myself get lost in her pale aquamarine gaze. She didn't push me away, but she didn't exactly pull me to her. I needed her words. It had been months since Adrian's death. She was ready to move on, despite her stubbornness to hold on.

"I need to hear you say it." A dark obsession grabbed hold of me. I wanted to study every inch of her body, touch it and kiss it. I needed her moans like they were my next breath, but first I needed her willingness. Compliance. "I need your words, Tatiana. Tell me you want to be fucked."

Taking a strand of her hair between my fingers, I inhaled deeply, letting the scent of roses invade my lungs and carve a place there. Just for her. Just for us.

"Say it," I growled against her neck.

"Okay," she murmured, tilting her head to accommodate me. "Yes."

"Yes what?" There'd be no easy way out of this. She'd go in eyes wide open and with her words clear.

"Fuck me already," she said exasperated, clenching her thighs.

In one swift move, I was on her. My mouth smashed against hers, my hands ripping her mourning dress off. She belonged in colors, not fucking black. Her hands wrapped around my neck, her fingernails scraping against my scalp. Fuck, I was hard for her again. Like a goddamn teenager who just got hit with hormones. At the age of forty-one, it was hardly desirable. This obsession with her was growing too fast, consuming me.

She stood in front of me, wearing only a black laced bra and matching panties. Against her pale skin, it was such a contrast. Seductress and angel. Innocent and sinful. It didn't matter. As long as she was mine.

I unclasped her bra, letting it fall to the floor, joining her dress. I leaned in and took her naked nipple into my mouth, lapping my tongue around it.

Her soft moan vibrated through the air. Her fingers gripped my hair, pulling me closer. I bit down on her nipple, then eased the sting by sucking on it. Her back arched and she moaned again. The scent of roses was everywhere - on my fingers, on my skin, in my pores - and I hadn't even fucked her yet.

My fingers hooked around her panties and I lowered to my knees, as she shimmied out of them. Her skin was soft under my knuckles, her arousal scenting the air. My eyes traveled over her naked body flushed with need. It spread over her fair skin like an overflowing dam.

"Do you want me to taste this cunt?" I asked, brushing my mouth over her mound and watching her body shudder in pleasure. Her juices glistened, making my mouth water for her. "I can give this pussy what it really craves. Just ask."

I watched her neck bob as she swallowed. If I didn't know better I'd thought she was drunk the way she watched me through her half-lidded eyes.

"Please," she moaned, her hands in my hair as her hips arched into me, hungry for my mouth. "Just once. Casual sex."

A dark chuckle sounded between us. "There's nothing casual about us."

"I-I... "

She struggled to put words together. Unlike me, the Russian accent never came through when she spoke. But her words quivered when she was excited. Her skin flushed, but she never hid any of it.

Tatiana was a queen. Always had been and always would be. I should put all my cards on the table, but I was so fucking far gone that I couldn't think straight. Nothing about this woman was casual. It never was and never would be. But she wasn't ready to hear that.

So I'd show her.

My fingers trailed between her legs, parting them. Fuck, she was soaked, her glistening arousal in full view. I stroked her sex lightly, then brushed my fingers over her clit, loving the feel of her slick heat.

Her breath hitched and her eyes glazed with lust. I'd take that. For now. I hooked her leg over my shoulder, giving me better access to her pussy. My mouth latched onto her clit and her hips rocked against my mouth. Demanding more. I nipped her clit and she gasped, then moaned as I sucked on it.

I slid two fingers inside her, my mouth still on her. Her walls clenched around my fingers greedily. Her eyes went soft, unfocused, and I could feel her getting close to her orgasm. Her juices dripped down my fingers, welcoming my touch and my mouth. I worked my fingers in and out of her pussy, her body so fucking responsive that it was addictive.

Lapping her creamy arousal, I growled against her pussy. She tasted so fucking perfect. Her fingers clutched my hair as if she was scared I'd stop. There was nothing in this fucking universe that could make me stop. My cock was so hard, it ached in my pants. But this was for her. I needed her orgasm before I'd take another one.

Her hips ground against my face. I could feel her body beginning to tighten, her breathing harsher and faster. I removed my fingers and pushed my tongue inside her entrance. In and out. In and out. I tongue fucked her, sucking every single drop of her juices.

Her grip tightened, making my scalp burn. Her gaze turned distant, and her pussy rippled around my tongue. I didn't stop lapping her until her contractions stopped.

She still watched me, her eyes hazy on me, waiting. Her lips were parted and her cheeks flushed. She looked like a thoroughly pleasured woman, and I loved that look on her. I needed her badly, her tight pussy gripping my cock and milking my cum from me.

Standing up to my full height, I locked my eyes on her as I discarded my clothes. She didn't help, just watched me. My every move. Once I was naked, her tongue swept across her bottom lip as her gaze traveled over me.

Appreciatively. Hungrily. Boldly.

It was only then that she reached out, her fingers trailing softly over my shoulder, down my biceps, then my abs.

"You're beautiful. And that scent, it's like Viagra," she whispered so low, I'd almost missed it. It was the second time she commented on my cologne. It was a custom cologne built by one of my companies. It had never gone on the market. It surprised me she seemed to recognize it.

Those aqua eyes met mine, and it hit me then how different we were. Her pale blonde hair and eyes, her porcelain skin against my dark hair and eyes and my tanned skin. Light and dark. Angel and devil. Rose and thorn.

My fingers wrapped around my hard shaft and I stroked myself. Once. Twice. The look in her eyes told me she liked the view. Her words confirmed it.

"Do it again," she breathed. Fuck, she was perfection in the flesh.

"Next time," I grunted. I needed to feel her pussy. I needed to consume all of her now.

"Are you going to fuck me now?" she rasped. Her eyes told me she wanted me to. The question was whether her heart wanted it too.

"Do you want me to?" I asked, my voice hoarse. Fuck, I'd explode any moment. I needed to feel her tight pussy strangling my cock. She nodded. "Words, *moya luna*. I need your words."

"Yes."

I shifted us towards the bed. Pushing her down, her back hit the mattress and her boobs bounced with the soft impact. Fuck, she had magnificent breasts. Perfect for kissing, biting, fucking.

I straddled her in a swift move, my knees on either side of her parted legs.

"Your arousal is the best aphrodisiac," I admitted as I aligned my cock with her entrance. She arched her hips, greedy for my cock. Her swollen pink flesh glistened, and I wondered how it'd look when she was finally pregnant with my child. Just the thought of her pregnant had me flying high.

"I love your taste too." *Holy fuck.* A quiet, breathy admission.

Those words alone could make me come. Although I wasn't sure whether she meant to say them aloud. Her eyes were lowered, staring at the spot where we almost connected. Her heat at the tip of my cock. "P-please, don't make me wait."

In one forceful thrust, I powered into her tight pussy, filling her to the hilt. Tatiana cried out, staring down at where we were joined. I didn't blame her; I watched us too. It was impossible to peel my eyes away from where our bodies were connected.

"You're too big," she choked out.

"You'll get used to me," I gritted, keeping myself still. God, she felt like heaven and hell. Beads of sweat formed on my forehead, fighting the urge to start fucking her hard and fast. I thrust into her with slow, shallow movements unable to hold myself still any longer. Her eyes sparkled like fucking stars, pulling me under her spell.

"Look at us, Tatiana," I grunted as I moved in and out of her. Her walls clenched around my cock, strangling me. Her fingers gripped the sheets, wrinkling them as she ground against me. But her eyes were locked on where we connected.

"More," she whimpered. "Konstantin, p-please."

I slammed inside her, more than happy to give her more. Once I filled her to the hilt, all bets were off. I fucked her harder and faster, her walls welcoming my every thrust. Her whimpers turned into soft moans, then high-pitched screams as I powered into her tight heat. Over and over again. Flesh against flesh. Groins slapped against one another. Her hand came to my biceps, but it wasn't to push me away. Her fingernails dug into my flesh, urging me on.

"Fuck, fuck, fuck," she panted between moans, her head tilting back and her eyes squeezing shut. Strands of her blonde hair fanned around her head, giving her a halo and her rose-scented perfume filled the air between us. I breathed it in, letting it overtake all my other senses. With her, the rose scent was an aphrodisiac.

"Look at us." She thrashed against the sheets, her pussy taking me higher and higher. She was close, I could feel it in the way her body coiled.

Her eyes sparked as she opened them, then lowered them between our bodies. I thrust inside her, hard and fast. It was like I had lost all control and fucked her to oblivion with the intent to own her. Possess her.

"You and me. It was always you and me," I groaned.

Her small whimpers urged me on, begging for release. I pulled almost all the way out and her growl vibrated in her throat, but before she could say anything I drove back in.

She fucking glowed as she came apart under me. Her throaty moans and her fingers digging into my biceps as she shook underneath me. It was all I needed to find my own release. My balls tightened, that familiar feeling in the back of my spine and my own release came crashing harder than ever before. I emptied myself into her.

Her body slack underneath me and both of us breathing hard, I pulled her to me as I rolled over on the bed. Her head nestled into my chest and a deep sigh left her mouth.

God, I fucking missed her sounds. It only took one to hear and I needed them for life.

"I'm never letting you go this time," I whispered, pressing my kiss against her temple, as her eyes closed with a dreamy smile on her lips. Fuck, that alone could bring me to my knees.

I'd loved her for far too long from the shadows to let her go now. I'd hammer through her walls and keep her prisoner in this cocoon we'd created. In our world.

"Adrian," she murmured softly as she dozed off and my fucking heart froze.

It only took one name, a single word, to rattle me to my bones.

Suddenly, I wished I could kill the fucking bastard all over again.

Tatiana Nikolaev needed a lesson in what it meant to be owned by a Konstantin. It was time to teach it to her.

TWENTY-THREE
TATIANA

We danced under the stars in the snow covered, gravel parking lot, not a single building around us. The moon and headlights from our rental afforded us our only light. It was a cold Russian night, right outside Moscow and our breath fogged the air.

"It's cold," I grumbled, closing an inch of space between us.

"I'll keep you warm," Adrian vowed. We slow-danced, snow crunching at our feet. I wore my white sweater dress with red Ugg boots and a matching colored jacket. The fleece leggings blocked some of the cold, but it wasn't enough. I could honestly say that my Russian heritage extended only as far as my last name. I was an American girl through and through.

"Always remember, Tatiana." Adrian's mouth moved against my scalp. "No matter what happens, I go on."

I lifted my head to look at him. Adrian's voice was dark and so was his expression. His words made no sense, unless he was just quoting the song.

"Why are we here, Adrian?" I asked him softly, letting him lead me as we danced to the music that played through the speakers of the rented car. Jillian Edwards' song "I Go On" wouldn't have been my *choice of a song for us to dance to. Especially not the first dance after we just eloped.*

We had been married for almost twenty-four hours. It wasn't exactly the dream wedding I'd always envisioned, but I had his ring on my finger. It was enough.

"This is where my father died," he rasped and my eyes flickered around us, almost expecting the ghosts to appear. "His body was never found. He's buried here somewhere." His eyes grew distant as he glanced around us, but somehow it seemed the two of us weren't seeing the same thing. "This is where my future was set."

I furrowed my brows. "I thought your father was a drunk and mother–" My voice trailed off, not wanting to call her a junkie, but I couldn't come up with another word.

"Junkie," he finished for me. I swallowed and nodded. "My adoptive parents. He was a deadbeat drunk and she was a junkie," he elaborated. "My real father was a good man. He just got involved with the wrong person."

"Your biological mom?" I rasped.

His green eyes darkened, rage so strong swimming in them that my feet tripped. "They loved each other very much, but someone else claimed her."

Seemed like a complicated family history. But then we had enough of those ourselves.

"I'm sorry." It hadn't been easy for him.

Vasili and Adrian became friends when they were kids, both growing up in Russia, way before I was born. Then when Father expanded into the States, they brought Adrian along. He had been around for as long as I could remember - in one way or another.

"This will be our wedding song," Adrian changed the subject.

I chuckled softly. "It's kind of a depressing song."

Adrian's face was a blank mask, devoid of emotions. His eyes were a darker green than I'd ever seen them. They almost appeared black. But his strong frame still held me firmly, in his warm arms. Something was off, but I didn't know what.

"There is blood here," he said casually as flurries fell all around us. "Do you see red splattered all over the snow, Tatiana?"

My eyes traveled over the white snow, light under the moon. I didn't see any blood. Just fresh fallen snow like a warm white blanket over the earth.

"A clue, Tatiana," he gasped. "It's a clue right where we're dancing."

But then I heard it. **Bang.**

A single gunshot. Red splattered on the white snow, then slowly spread, drenched the snow covered ground with red. Like paint over the white canvas. Adrian lay there, crimson liquid dripping from his mouth.

His eyes clouded over before life extinguished in them, leaving darkness. A terrifying darkness pulled me deeper and deeper into it, suffocating me.

I fought against it. I didn't want to die. But if I let it take me, I would. I'd be left in its terrifying darkness forever.

I shrieked so loud, my ears popped.

My body shook. My head lolled. Then I startled awake in warm arms. Another man's arms, strong and protective, embracing me.

"It's just a dream." A soft whisper. A strong scent. Konstantin.

He held me in a sitting position, in the middle of the large bed, his palm stroking my sweat-damp hair away from my face.

My shaky fingers covered my mouth and I sobbed. Sobbed for what was and never would be. The dream. That night. Adrian. They were all gone.

Konstantin took my chin between his fingers and brought my face up, his eyes drilling into me.

"What did you dream about?" he asked in a soft voice. *Answers.* But I didn't tell him that. I couldn't trust him. Not yet.

"I can't remember," I murmured.

I was still staring up at him, the dream fresh in my mind. I knew what I had to do next.

It was time to visit Russia. The freeze-your-ass country.

Something smelled delicious.

Like citrus, sandalwood, spice, and heat. Like home. Like love.

I snuggled closer to the source, squeezing every inch of my body to it, using it like a soft blanket. It felt like a solid warmth beneath my cheek.

I yawned, my muscles pulled by a familiar exhaustion. Muscles I never thought I had twinged in protest.

Forcing my eyes open, I latched onto the bare expanse of skin. And for a fraction of a second, my heart lifted. I looked up, but the wrong pair of eyes stared back at me. These were dark, almost black. Unlike Adrian's green ones.

I had cheated on my husband.

Your husband is dead, my mind mocked. *He'll never come back.*

It didn't make me feel better. It was too soon. I wasn't ready. Too late. I should have thought about it yesterday. I should feel the nauseating betrayal swell through every fiber of me. Surprisingly, I didn't.

Have I arrived at the fifth stage of grief? Acceptance, here I come.

"Good morning." Something was off about him. His voice was hard, matching the expression in his eyes. Here I was congratulating myself, and he'd been staring me down like I had just murdered his puppy.

Wrapping the bedsheet around me, I pulled my knees up to my chest and I eyed him. Maybe he was regretting this.

"Morning," I muttered.

When he said nothing else, I got out of bed. I pulled the sheet along with me, gripping it to my chest, while pushing my free hand through my tangled hair subconsciously. Adrian always said I slept like I was dead. Sometimes I drooled too. Discreetly, I brushed my fingers over my mouth but thankfully there was no drool on my face.

"You didn't have to stay the night," I grumbled, painfully aware of my nipples hardening under his look. My skin flushed with arousal. Apparently my body had a mind of its own. I didn't want to be attracted to this man, but clearly my body did. "It's just a hookup."

It had to be the wrong thing to say because Konstantin's expression turned even darker.

"Refrain from hookups going forward," he warned, his voice cracking through the air like a whip. The menace in his voice didn't escape me and something about the way he glared at me made me want to spite him.

"I can do whatever I want," I hissed.

It didn't matter that I hadn't hooked up since college. It was none of his business. The cold contempt that stared at me from those dark, devilish eyes made me regret my bravery. His next words even more so.

"Touch another man and I'll kill him," he snapped. "Then I'll fuck you in his blood, Tatiana." I stared at him, frowning. I wasn't sure if he was joking or not. I feared he wasn't. That comment was wrong on so many levels. Maybe the Pakhan was a psychopath.

"Understood?" he growled.

The simmering anger traveled through the air. My mouth parted and my mind blanked. I couldn't think of a single thing to say in my comeback. Except, something had to be wrong with him. Or me because my thighs clenched with the thought of him fucking me again. Alas, I could go without blood nearby. That was certainly not my kink.

I stared at his face. It was hard with granite features but beautiful. I actually ached inside to look at him for too long. Something in his eyes shook something deep inside me. Like he could peer into my soul and retrieve every single secret out of me.

But he wouldn't uncover Adrian's message. I'd uncover all those secrets on my own terms. If I had to, I'd use this man to help me, but I wouldn't be his pawn. He'd be mine.

His eyes narrowed and he stalked towards me until there was no distance left between us.

"Do. You. Understand?" His tone, though quiet and soft, sent a dark shiver down to the deepest corner of my soul. My body immediately went on alert, craving him. *Again.*

I swallowed, then nodded. "Words, Tatiana. I want your words."

"I don't have time for other men, so I guess I understand you." My voice sounds strangely hoarse, breathy even. What was this guy doing to me?

"You'll never have time for another man again." The words were soft with a hint of warning and vehemence showing through. "You've signed over your pussy and your life to me. Nobody else will ever touch you again." *Jesus Christ!* The intensity in his eyes held promises of burning down the world if someone dared to touch me. I couldn't quite decide if I liked it or not.

"I will ruin you, break you. Then put you back together." His voice lowered to a dark rasped, but the message was loud and clear. "Only I'm allowed to do that. Nobody else - not if they want to live."

I sold my soul to the devil and he'd be collecting. For the rest of my life. All for one night of sexual release. How did my life get so fucked up?

I wasn't a meek woman. There was no room for those in our family. Even Isabella with her nurturing heart was a fighter. You had to be to survive this family and this world. But something about the way Konstantin's gaze darkened had me choking on my next breath.

The two of us stood, toe-to-toe, a battle of wills dancing around us. The game was thrilling and dangerous.

"Well, I have to–" I rasped, taking a step back. Then another. He didn't move, but his eyes followed my every move. "Pee."

I rushed into the bathroom and locked the door with a loud click, like the lock on my heart. As if that could stop him.

Maybe playing with the devil wasn't such a grand plan, but there was no going back now. I'd just have to make sure he didn't steal my heart and soul.

As I stumbled into the shower, turning it on, I felt taken unlike ever before. Owned. Possessed. Consumed.

Actually, scratch that. I had only felt like this once before. The first night Adrian and I were together. It had never felt that good again. It was okay, but never that good.

That night, in the gazebo, when he took my virginity. It was the most amazing night of my life. It was the night when I took charge and sent Adrian a note to meet me in the gazebo. The pleasure that he gave me made me an instant addict. After that, I waited and waited for him to make a move. He didn't - not for years.

The ache between my legs throbbed with that sweet, familiar pain. I tried to use Konstantin to ease that ache. It backfired because I was the one that felt utterly used and consumed. Not in a bad way either. In fact, it felt so fucking good that it was tempting to go down this road again.

The waterfall cascaded down my body, freezing at first, then gradually warming up. I still felt him on every inch of my skin. I still smelled him deep in my lungs.

A mirror surrounded me and I caught a glimpse of myself in it. My lips were swollen and red. The expression on my face was one of a thoroughly pleasured, or better yet fucked, woman.

A red mark, a hickey, marred my skin where my neck and shoulder met. Another one on my left breast. And another one on my right hip. I twisted around and caught more marks. Light bruises in the shape of his fingerprints on my ass.

Konstantin had marked me.

But it felt so much more than just a mark on my body. There was a mark on my soul too.

My gaze locked on my thighs where the warm liquid trickled down my legs. Cum.

We didn't use a condom!

Maybe... Letting out a sigh, I pushed all the hopes and dreams that have been crushed before out of my head. Besides, getting pregnant with the devil would result in the spawn of Satan. Hardly a perfect scenario.

I turned off the shower twenty minutes later, then wrapped myself in one of the luxuriously fluffy hotel towels. Tucking the towel around me, I stilled as I listened for any movements. Tiptoeing to the door, I pressed my ear against the smooth wooden surface.

Still nothing.

I softly cracked the door and found the room empty.

"Konstantin?"

No answer.

It was then that I saw the piece of paper sitting in the midst of the tousled sheets.

Padding across the cold hardwood, I made my way to the bed.

There. Are. No. Other. Men. For. You.
Your hands, mouth, tits, cunt, and ass are for me only.
Remember that before you do something stupid.

How fucking romantic.

TWENTY-FOUR

KONSTANTIN

Weeks ago, although it felt like years, I left Tatiana in D.C. and returned to California for some urgent business. Reluctantly. But it was clear the woman still hadn't moved on from Adrian. A grinding, crunchy noise registered, and I realized it was me. I clenched my teeth so hard, my molars protested.

Motherfucking Adrian. He was always in the way. Even when he was dead.

But even after she'd spoken his name as she fell asleep and she dreamt of nightmares, her brows furrowed and her forehead glistening, I wanted to comfort her. I couldn't stay mad at that woman. I needed her. Watching her thrash through her nightmare was like a knife pierced through my heart. I wished to scoop the nightmares out of her skull so she'd find peace. She didn't deserve the torture that came along with those dreams.

I, on the other hand, deserved them plenty. So did most men in the underworld. But not her. Never her.

My fists clenched around my glass and I fought the urge to throw it across the room. It'd be witnessed by all and I prided myself in keeping my cool. I succeeded in it until Tatiana came into play. Then it

I stared out the window. Downtown Los Angeles spread in front of me and the ocean view behind all the buildings stretched for miles. This was my empire. California. The West Coast. Russia.

The glass wall behind me separated my office on the top floor of my building from the staff. This was my legitimate front. Nothing to hide. At least not in this building. White Spanish tile brightened the entire top floor, making my dark mood even more apparent.

I'd been in a foul mood for weeks. The smell of roses followed me everywhere. The thoughts of Tatiana were with me like a constant shadow. Apparently, the same wasn't true for the blonde angel. It took her far too long to answer my fucking messages. She had been avoiding me.

Of course, the same was true with me. I didn't trust myself not to take her to bed again, and if she called Adrian's name, I'd set this world on fire.

Fucking Adrian. It was the first time my father had ever spared anyone's life. He did it for me, but his warning rang in my ears for years now.

"No!" I shouted, reaching for my father's hand as he pointed the gun at the boy who sat next to his father's dead body. "Papa, no! Please."

Maxim cried, his small body clutching our mother's dead corpse. Much later, I'd come to learn it was that day that broke my twin brother.

Papa's big hand came to my shoulder and clutched it so hard, I feared he'd rip my left arm out of the socket.

"Mercy is for the weak," Papa hissed. "Boys grow up to become men. They come back to find you, and suddenly, the hunter becomes the hunted."

I didn't understand his words. Father hated hunting.

"He's just a boy," I argued. Lenosh stood next to Papa, his eyes grim and focused on the boy. As if he waited for the final execution. "He didn't do anything."

"Keep your gun trained on the boy in case he runs," Papa said to

Lenosh, then turned to me. It was the only time I had ever seen his eyes glisten with moisture. Tears. He held it all in.

"Illias, one day you'll take over my position," he said, his voice hard and cold, despite the shimmering tears that refused to fall from his eyes. "You have to use a hard hand or others will view you as weak. Weakness attracts greediness and vengeance. It's best to not go down that road."

I nodded, although I didn't understand his words. "Tomorrow," I said, holding myself taller than my young age. "If he comes back tomorrow, no mercy. Today, he lost a lot. He might not even survive tonight. Let him go, Papa."

Our eyes locked. He knew we were made out of the same cloth. Just like Maxim was made out of the same cloth as Mama. He might have looked like Papa and I, but he was too soft. Just like Mama said.

It wasn't his fault. Just as it wasn't this boy's fault that his papa and my mama decided to betray the Pakhan. My papa.

The moment I heard Papa's resigned sigh, I knew he'd let the little boy live. He rarely gave in, but tonight, he gave me that little mercy.

"Fine, my little Illias," he caved in. "But remember my warning. Boys grow up to be men. And they come back for revenge. Be ready for him."

My phone rang and I answered without checking who it was.

"Yes," I barked.

I wasn't ready for Adrian. He became a forgotten boy with no name and no face.

And then it was too late. I never saw him coming.

His revenge was in full swing by the time I narrowed it down to him. He was prepared to take down not only me but the Thorns of Omertà and every family associated with it. So it was ultimately my responsibility to handle him.

"Are you there?" A voice bellowed over my cell. Fuck, I forgot I answered the call.

"Yes, and stop shouting." I glanced at the caller id and was surprised to see who it was. "Sasha Nikolaev."

"I heard you went to Afghanistan to rescue a lady," I remarked dryly. "I kind of hoped you'd stay there. "

"I bet you did, fucking Pakhan," he grumbled. "Nothing would make you happier than to see my tombstone, right?" He was wrong. I knew how much Tatiana loved her brothers and that was the only reason I wouldn't want to see him dead. "Well, likewise, motherfucker."

He'd try to kill me if he knew my obsession with his sister. Not that he'd succeed. I'd stake my life that Tatiana didn't share our encounter with her brothers, which left only one other reason why Sasha would call. He wanted to collect on his debt.

Seven years ago, Maxim fucked up and went after Sasha's woman. My twin brother wasn't too smart when it came to his dick. But then there weren't too many men who were. The problem was that Maxim didn't know how to kill people nor hire killers without tracing it back to himself. So when Sasha found out that my twin brother went after Branka Russo, he was set on killing him.

In order to spare my brother's life, I offered to owe him. I'd stake my life, Sasha was finally ready to collect.

"So, you're ready to collect the debt," I drawled.

"Yes, yours and your dumbfuck brother's," he snapped.

"Careful, Nikolaev," I snarled. "There are only so many liberties you'll get."

"What-the-fuck-ever." My lips curved. Sasha hadn't had it easy. He'd been pining after Branka Russo for years. Blue balls probably took a whole new meaning with him. "I'm collecting and I need a plane. Your brother will have to produce a motorcycle."

I didn't even fucking want to know what he needed a motorcycle for.

"When?"

"Two weeks from now," he grumbled. "First Saturday of summer. What a fucking joke!"

"Spare me your theatrics, Nikolaev," I said in a cold voice. Knowing Sasha, he'd probably crash the wedding, kill everyone, and then kidnap the screaming bride. "You can have my plane. Just text me the information on the departure city."

"It's certainly a pleasure doing business with you, Konstantin."

God, it fucking irked me to be called Konstantin. Didn't he fucking know that my first name is Illias? Actually fuck it, I didn't fucking care what he called me. I'd make his sister call me Illias. She was all that mattered.

"I wish I could say likewise."

Maxim walked into my office twenty minutes later.

Fuck, he looked like shit. Reeked of shit too. White powder and alcohol. Possibly piss.

"Where in the fuck did you get it?" I hissed, glowering at him. I owned every drug dealer on the West Coast, and they all knew what'd happen to them if they sold to my brother.

"Get what?" he grumbled, his pupils dilated. He was high as a kite right now. Goddamn him. Having a drug addict for a brother was a liability. I couldn't trust him with any work anymore.

"What did you use this time?" I hissed. "Crack, heroin, some other opioid?"

Maxim's lips thinned, refusing to answer. It didn't fucking matter. Whatever it was, it was bad.

"Who gave you the shit?" I repeated. I was two inches taller than Maxim. It was enough for me to tower over him.

My brother blinked, his eyes unfocused. Fuck, he was so far gone, I didn't think I could reach him anymore. Each day he fell deeper and deeper into depression, wallowing in his own hell and refusing to move on. Some days I wondered if maybe Maxim's hell hadn't started the day we witnessed our mother's death.

"Who, Maxim?" I roared, gripping his collar.

"Takahashi."

The name sent an echo through my office, a threat so calm and deadly it stilled the air and washed over me.

I knew it. I just fucking knew it at that very moment, I'd have to choose between my brother and Tatiana.

And soon.

TWENTY-FIVE
TATIANA

Another beep. Another text message.

I sighed and picked up my phone sitting next to me. It was Konstantin. Of course it was the Pakhan. It has been two weeks since D.C. and the freaking guy was so goddamn demanding. Did I figure out the cryptic message? Did I find the chip?

As if I would tell him if I had.

"What made you decide to move?" Isabella asked as we unpacked boxes in my old home. It had been years since I'd been here. After Isabella had been attacked there, Adrian took me to his place and Vasili took Bella to his compound. I hadn't been back since, but this was my home. It made sense to come back here.

So here I was. Back at the beginning.

I shrugged. "Figured it was time," I muttered as I reached for another box. This one contained remnants of Adrian's gadgets. Three laptops, five external hard drives, and a server. I'd gone through every single item in that box. My husband clearly recorded things that shouldn't have ever been recorded. Those things clearly didn't belong to me nor my late husband and shouldn't be in my possession. The problem was, it looked like they were backed up somehow, and I didn't know how to destroy it.

Of course, there was always the old fashion way. Bonfire here we come, but I feared that it would push those items to the cloud. I was a dummy when it came to IT, but I knew backing up any data to the cloud would be a mistake.

So here I was.

Jesus, Vasili better have the whole goddamn army surrounding my house. The shit in that box would have a shit ton of people after me. Was that the chip? My gut told me no, but I wasn't sure. Maybe I should ask Konstantin to look it over. Except I didn't know how much I could actually trust him.

He could view it as something against my family and that I couldn't risk. Storing the box in the safe room that Vasili had installed here, I headed back to the dining room for more unpacking. That was where I was while Isabella was unpacking a box in the kitchen, little Nikola dragging a pot and pan, one in each hand, over my fancy and expensive Italian tile.

I shook my head. She let my nephew play with all the dishware. She was a great doctor, but a horrible homemaker and an even worse cook. God knew what we ate when we visited Isabella.

I sighed. It made no sense to scold my little nephew. If a single tear glistened in his eyes, I'd feel guilty about it. I'd just wash all the dishes after they left.

The movers just brought in the last box, and we had another three hours' worth of unpacking to do. With little Nikola, it might be six hours. I swore everything we put away, that little kid pulled back out and scattered all around.

"How about we go get something to eat?" I suggested. I'd rather unpack the rest later when I'm alone.

Isabella's eyes widened. "Are you sure?" It had been a while since I recommended we go out together. My stomach grumbled in answer. Her whole face lit up. "Yes, yes. Of course. Let's go to Nola's."

I raised my eyebrow in surprise. "Did Vasili buy Nola?"

She shook her head. "No, but I've heard their food is great. Maybe they'll share a recipe?"

My brows met my hairline. I'd never understand why she insisted on figuring out the whole cooking thing. It was clearly not her strong suit. Frankly, it wasn't even her weak suit. I wasn't an expert, but at least I could scramble eggs. Even make decent pasta. But Isabella managed only to burn food - best case scenario. Worst case was burning down the house. She came close once. Maybe twice.

Lowering to my knees, I met Nikola's eyes. "Hungry?" He nodded. "Then let's go," I said in a light voice for the first time in almost a year.

Isabella's eyes watched me with hesitation while Nikola eyed me curiously. It had been a while since I'd been his aunt. Since I played with him. Since I smiled.

Maybe I graduated from the five stages of grief, I thought proudly.

"Are you all better now?" he asked, his blue eyes never wavering from me. The concern I had seen in everyone's eyes since Adrian died mirrored my nephew's gaze too. It always hit me the worst seeing it in little Nikola's eyes.

"I am," I murmured softly. *I think,* I added silently.

"I'm going to be six soon," he declared, drawing a smile out of me. "My baby sister will be two."

"I know," I said, brushing my fingers over his cheeks. "And I am so proud of you for taking care of her. We always protect our own, don't we?"

He nodded with a big smile on his face. I bet Vasili had told him those same words a few times.

God, I loved my family. I loved my niece and nephews. I'd kill for them. I'd fucking burn down this world for them. I shouldn't have kept away for so long. It was what made us stronger - Nikolaevs stick together. And I'd protect them with everything I had. If getting on the Pakhan's good side was what it took, I'd do it.

Besides, it wasn't a terrible inconvenience. My body still remembered him. Every inch of my skin craved him since that day. Replacing one addiction with another wasn't smart. So I'd take it easy.

Good plan.

I grabbed my purse and the three of us walked side by side. Hand in hand. Something in my throat squeezed. The lump grew and grew, choking me until each breath became painful. A wheeze.

"Auntie, are you all better?" Nikola questioned softly, his small hand squeezing mine.

I cleared my throat. I inhaled a deep breath, then slowly exhaled. It was easy to get emotional.

"Yes," I assured him softly. "Yes, I'm good. Thank you."

We left the house, Isabella's guards right behind us. We got into the large Mercedes Benz, the three of us in the back, while her two guards got in the front. There was another car driving behind us.

I stared out the window, feeling Isabella's eyes on me. She wanted to make sure I was okay. Completely healed. I wasn't. Not yet, but I would be.

The driver pulled up in front of the restaurant, a large sign hanging over the door. We strode inside, past the dark red fabric and windows facing the streets. The atmosphere was cozy and warm. The air smelled of delicious food and pastries.

"Geez, it looks busy," Isabella muttered. "I should have made a reservation."

"You won't get a seat if you don't have a reservation," the hostess said, her eyes on Isabella. She had an earpiece and by the look on her face, she was ready to dismiss us. Then her eyes came my way, her hand touched her earpiece and she tensed. Her eyes flickered to the left and I followed her gaze. She stared at the glass wall as if she sought answers there.

Snow White theme going on here, I mused. *Mirror, mirror on the wall. Can these two pass?*

I snickered at my own joke. Isabella gave me a questioning look. My lips curved into a smile and I mouthed, "Mirror, mirror on the wall, who's the fairest one of all?"

She followed my gaze to the mirror and chuckled, then quickly stifled it. It had to be a one way mirror.

"I know that movie," Nikola exclaimed. The little bugger was too smart. "The evil witch said it."

Okay, I wasn't calling the hostess an evil witch. This could be taken wrong.

"This place is always packed," a guy behind us chimed in for no good reason but to gawk at Isabella and me. "I made my reservation a month ago."

Isabella and I shared a glance, then shrugged our shoulders.

"Oh, in that case–" Isabella never got to finish her sentence.

"I have an opening," the hostess said quickly. Surprised gasps came from behind us. My eyes flickered to the mirror. There had to be someone back there. Unease lurked under my skin. I sensed eyes on me, watching me. A familiar awareness.

Like a warm breeze. Or a caress. It made no sense.

"Ready?" The hostess pulled my gaze away from the mirror, and I realized everyone was staring at me. They must have called me several times.

I nodded and as the hostess led us deeper into the restaurant, I glanced over my shoulder one more time. There was nobody there.

The hostess seated us in a booth with a window to the street. Isabella slid in, Nikola followed, and I took the seat across from them.

The hostess handed us our menus, then asked, "Would you like something to drink?"

She handed me the drink menu and I read through it. Slowly. The tempting names - Chardonnay, vodka, brandy, Sazerac, beer. Sweat trickled down my spine. My hand trembled as I lowered the menu down.

It had been a few days since I'd had a drop of alcohol and my body craved it. It *needed* it like oxygen. At least it thought it did. It was time to wear big girl panties and stop this addiction. My brothers were right.

Gosh, they'd love it if I said those words out loud.

"Nikola will have orange juice," Isabella quickly chimed in. "I'll have a glass of sparkling water. We've been unpacking all day."

"Ah, that explains the wardrobe," she remarked.

Isabella's eyebrows shot up at her unspoken rudeness. She wore her signature jeans and a black Chanel top. I wore a dress. We didn't look bad, but none of it mattered to me because my mouth watered and the only thing I could focus on was the drink menu.

The need for at least a beer clawed at me. "Water," I croaked.

With a nod, she left and was back in no time with our drinks. We placed our food order and she disappeared just as fast.

"Wow, I'm impressed," Isabella noted, propping her elbows on the table. "They have superb service. Although slightly snobby if you ask me."

I shrugged.

The entire room had been lit up and the atmosphere was busy. The buzz of the restaurant wasn't unpleasant. The ambiance was warm and the music light.

Reluctantly, my eyes went back to that mirror and my eyes widened, noting our hostess disappeared through the hidden door. An awareness touched my skin. A familiar feeling expanded in my stomach. Restlessness grew and this time it had nothing to do with alcohol.

"I need to go to the bathroom," I told Isabella as I stood up.

"Want me to order something for you if the waiter comes?"

"Yes, whatever you're having."

I headed for the bathroom when the same hostess came up to me, appearing out of nowhere. Awareness trickled down my spine and grew stronger with each step I had taken. I glanced around. Nobody was paying attention.

"Can I help you?"

"No," I told her. "I'm just headed for the restroom."

"Lovely," she answered, smiling like her life depended on it. I gave her a double take. "Please let me show you to our VIP bathroom." I narrowed my eyes. *VIP bathroom?* That sounded almost like an invitation to the room where forbidden things happen. "This way."

She pointed towards the glass door and I reluctantly followed through the secret door and down the dark hallway, my heels clicking against the floors. I pushed the door open and entered the most luxurious restaurant bathroom I had ever seen.

Black marble tile gave the room a dark vibe. The waterflow sink ran a constant flow of water into a red porcelain bowl, making it appear like the constant flow of blood. My eyes flicked to my reflection. My messy bun framed my face, my blonde hair in contrast to the black marble. My black Chanel dress fit right in with the black marble.

I put my hands under the flowing water and washed my hands, then dried them off. Truthfully, I didn't need to use the bathroom. I just needed to shake off the feeling of being watched.

The door opened behind me and I lifted my eyes, meeting the dark eyes I have been avoiding since Washington. A shiver rolled down my spine and he hadn't even spoken yet.

"Hello, Tatiana. You've been avoiding me."

His voice was velvety, smooth as silk, but with depth to it that sent electricity through every fiber of my being. Even from this position, he exuded an intense masculine vibe and such controls that I itched to ruffle his feathers. That signature smell, citrus and sandalwood, traveled through the air, slowly starting to represent Illias Konstantin and erase Adrian.

Strained silence swept into the bathroom as he watched me with a dark, half-lidded stare. His eyes were too obscure to read, an unsettling conviction in his gaze sending warnings through every cell of my being. Did I run? Heck no.

Turning around slowly, my gaze met his dark one head on. We stared at each other, and a thick tension filled the air. It almost suffocated, draining oxygen in the space that seemed too small for the two of us.

"I haven't been avoiding you," I lied with a soft scoff.

"Yes, you have," he claimed. "And you haven't been answering my messages."

I rolled my eyes. "I didn't have answers," I snickered. "I mean how many times do you want me to type that up."

Konstantin's dark hair was cut shorter than the last time I saw him. His dark suit molded his toned body, accenting his broad shoulders and the crisp lines of his muscular body. It was the kind of body that women swooned over. But most of all, it was the intelligence behind those dark eyes that fascinated me.

He beckoned me with a finger and I shook my head.

"Again, Konstantin, I'm not a dog," I snarled softly, fighting my legs that wanted to move towards him. This stupid body. I should demand a new one.

"Don't make me repeat myself, Tatiana," he purred.

"Or what?" I challenged against my better judgment.

He tilted his head to the side as if he read my thoughts and was entertained. "Or I'll spank you."

I blinked. He couldn't be serious.

"You're crazy," I spat out. My brothers were crazy, but somehow their crazy didn't touch this man's. "Lay a finger on me, and I'll murder you."

His expression flickered with something, then darkened. Despite the murderous expression, I remained rooted in place. I refused to let him scare me. If he thought he could control me, he had another fucking thing coming.

"Careful, moya luna," he drawled. "Threatening me isn't wise. Now stop playing and come here. I hate repeating myself."

"God forbid you don't get your way," I muttered as I slowly approached him, swaying my hips. Was I doing it on purpose? Yes, I was. Good Lord, I was in seduction mode. This man!

He watched me, calculating, his calm façade a front. But his eyes betrayed him. They *burned*. And I knew it was for me. I didn't know how I knew it, but I did.

One moment, I stood facing him, the next my back slammed against the door. It rattled under the contact and a gasp of air escaped me. He took my wrists in a vise-like grip and held them above my head.

I panted, fire spreading through my veins. A languid sensation pulled on my muscles. His lips pressed against my ear and a shiver rolled through me.

"You always have to get the last word in, don't you?" He looked at me - his eyes traveled over my body. My breasts rose and fell with each breath. Every inch of my skin became hyper aware of his eyes on me. Almost as if he had already touched me. "You're smart, Tatiana. But sometimes you're blind."

His voice was taunting, and it made me want to kick him in the balls. What the hell did he mean by that? His gaze met mine. Coal black. Obsession. Desire. Possession.

I could see it all lurking in his eyes. It mirrored my own.

He pressed his face into my neck and inhaled. A deep groan sounded in the back of his throat, sending a tremble through me. I tilted my head to bare more of my neck, needing his mouth on me.

His lips skimmed over the sensitive area where my neck and shoulder connected, then bit. *Hard.* The spot throbbed, matching the pulse thrumming between my legs.

He pushed his big body against mine. God, he was so big. Even with my heels adding three inches to my five-foot-seven, I had to crane my neck to look at his face.

My breasts burned under the heat of his chest. The material brushed my nipples, sending sizzling sparks beneath my skin. My heart beat so hard, I feared it'd crack my ribs.

The side of his mouth quirked up. He knew exactly what he was doing to me. The impact he had on me. But I refused to act like some swooning school girl. I let my eyes roam down his body, enjoying his wide shoulders, defined arms, to his narrow abs.

Next, I ran a finger over his shoulder, then down his chest and his abs, and a small smile touched my lips noting a bulge in his pants.

"I'm not blind enough not to see this," I purred, cupping his bulge. My next words were soft and sensual. "What's the matter, Konstantin? You had to come back for more?"

I had lost my mind, taunting him like that. He tasted like a bad decision. Sometimes a villain turns into a hero. That'd never be the case with **him**.

It still didn't stop me from playing with him.

He watched me with a half-lidded stare and my heart thundered to an awkward beat. A glance from him could light me on fire. My soul grew claws, clutching him for survival.

My lips were a breath away from his. Close enough to kiss him and feel the shadow of stubble gracing his jaw. Heat shot straight to my core and my thighs clenched with the need to feel the roughness of his stubble between my thighs.

The warmth emanating from him was stronger than any alcohol I'd ever consumed. I ran my hands up his abs and curled my fingers into his chest. He was hard and warm, tempting and exhilarating. Even the obvious danger of him tempted me.

His hand curled around my neck and he grabbed a fistful of hair, then pressed his mouth on mine.

"You want more too, Tatiana," he rasped, my stomach clenching as his tongue brushed against mine. He was right. I did want more. So much more. He stole my breath, kissing me like it was the last thing he'd ever do. "I know exactly how to get you off. I know exactly what it takes to make you writhe, to make you moan, to make you scream."

"Yes," I moaned. My voice was hoarse, the single syllable giving him all the confirmation he needed. His tongue slid across my bottom lip, then tangled with mine. Butterflies fluttered through my veins.

He put his leg between my parted legs, his hard thigh pressing against my pussy. My body moved of its own will, needing friction. His hard cock pressed against my hip and as I ground against his thigh, my head tipped back against the door.

"Harder." The word slipped between my lips on a throaty moan.

His mouth skimmed my jaw until his lips brushed my ear. My heart pounded in my ears, and his thumb caressed my wild pulse, then pressed down on it slightly. I couldn't catch my breath. My body was burning up, and I knew I needed more of him.

Needing something to steady myself, I reached up and gripped his biceps. His muscles were hard under that expensive dark suit, my fingers curling into his muscles. I tightened my grip and then his hand made a slow path up, moving under my skirt. His hand on me, rough and expert, moved higher and higher, until it brushed against my panties.

"You're soaking wet." His voice was a dark rasp, sending a shiver down my spine. "Is that for me, moya luna?"

"Yes," I croaked, watching him through heavy lidded eyes. He rewarded me by slipping his fingers under the material of my panties and running his fingers along my slit.

A low satisfying groan left his throat. "Good girl."

He traced circles around my clit and my hips bucked against his hand. My skin buzzed like a live wire and my breaths came out short. I tilted my hips up, a moan ripping from my throat when he pushed two fingers inside me.

My eyes fluttered shut as he pumped his fingers in and out of me at a slow, agonizing pace.

"Please, Konstantin," I panted. "Faster."

A dark chuckle filled the space, sounding like a distant noise. I ground myself on his hand, greedy for more friction on my clit. His expert fingers felt so good, and I needed to come undone.

He dipped his head, his teeth scraping against the sensitive skin where my shoulder and neck met. Another shudder rolled down my spine. And all the while, his fingers worked me, in and out. My hips rocked under his touch

"Konstantin." I clenched around his fingers, his name a moan on my lips.

"You'll call me Illias," he ordered in a rough tone.

Then in one swift move, his arms wrapped around the backs of my thighs and he scooped me up and shifted us around, to sit me at the edge of the counter.

Then he lowered to his knees, his head between my thighs. With a dark gaze that reflected heaven and hell, he met my eyes, his mouth barely inches from my clenching core. He might be on his knees but there was nothing meek about him. He licked my pussy through my silky panties and I spread my legs wider. His tongue was hot, too close yet not close enough, sending a deep rush of pleasure through me.

"My name," he demanded as he fisted my thong.

"Konstantin," I moaned.

The shredding sound rang through the air. He dropped the thong to the floor, not sparing it another glance. I shuddered under the hot, wet touch of his tongue against my core. He took lazy, leisurely laps from the entrance to my clit and then his tongue pushed into my entrance. I made a throaty noise and my fingers gripped his hair, my nails scraping against his scalp.

His mouth left me, only for his smoldering gaze to find mine.

"What's my name?" he asked in a sharp tone.

"P-Please," I breathed. His eyes flashed and before I could think the next thought, a feeling of fullness came over me. He slipped two fingers inside me, roughly, igniting pleasure through my bloodstream.

"My name, Tatiana," he demanded harshly, pulling out his fingers and then plunging them inside harder. A tremor went through me as pain and pleasure mixed. "Say it and the pleasure is all yours."

"Why... Why do you care?" I choked out, rocking my hips against his fingers. It was hard to think with his fingers inside me. "Don't you know your name?"

He pulled out his fingers and a dark, deep chuckle left his lips. His gaze locked on my exposed pussy and his hot breath brushed against it. I shuddered with the intense need to beg him to close the distance.

"I want to make sure you know whose name you'll be screaming, Tatiana," he rasped. "My name. Always my name."

The battle of wills pulled back and forth between us. I had to be a weak, weak woman because I caved in.

"Illias," I breathed and the reward was instant. His mouth found my clit, licking and sucking, while his fingers moved in and out of me. A deep groan of satisfaction vibrated from his throat and straight to my core, like this was as pleasurable for him as it was for me.

My hands tugged at his hair, my hips grinding against his mouth. I needed more but he was taking his time, slowing down when the pressure ignited and I was right at the edge of the cliff, ready to spiral into an abyss.

Then he'd slow again. My fingers gripped his strands tighter. "*Please, Illias,*" escaped my lips.

As if that was what he waited for, he finally gave me what I wanted. He fingered me faster and harder, and his laps turned firmer. Nothing but deep, hot pleasure built inside me. His dark gaze found mine while still between my thighs and he curled his fingers inside me, hitting that spot.

The pressure exploded through my veins like wildfire. One hard press of his thumb on my clit and I flew through the space between heaven and Earth.

And I screamed his name.

TWENTY-SIX

KONSTANTIN

An hour later, I watched Tatiana head out of my newly acquired restaurant, her little nephew's hand in his aunt's. Even the kid had bleach blond hair and pale blue eyes. He looked more like Tatiana's son than her sister-in-law's.

I wondered if Tatiana's children would have the same coloring as their mother. Like little angels running around.

The image danced in my mind, tempting me. I wanted a family with her. It was all I wanted from the moment I found her.

I loved pleasuring her. I loved seeing her smile. I loved putting that smile on her face. I intended to show her - eventually. Until then, I'd bind her to me through pleasure. It was the only thing that currently worked.

I shook my head.

I was losing my fucking mind, and the woman barely spared me the time of day. Unless my head was buried between her thighs, or my cock buried deep inside her.

She said she found something. It might be something or it could be nothing. One thing she made clear was that her brothers knew nothing about it. Just like Aiden Callahan declared, Tatiana would protect her family with her dying breath. And I would protect *her* with mine.

Either way, I'd meet her later at her place, and we'd find out together if her discovery was relevant.

As if she could sense my eyes on her, she glanced over her shoulder and found me staring after her. Then she looked around before flipping me her middle finger.

I didn't know whether to laugh or be furious at her. The latter seemed impossible when it came to her so I settled for a laugh. I had been pining after her for over seven years. Now that she was within arm's reach, it was hard to take it slow. But I had to play my cards right.

One slip up, one revelation too soon, and she'd be gone. Forever.

Kidnapping her was a possibility but her brothers would move heaven and earth to find her. They'd burn everything in their wake. So that probably wasn't the best course of action.

But it was a possibility.

Nikita walked in, sizing up my back room in my new venture. Once the Nikolaevs received word of my new acquisition, they'd blow a gasket.

I let out a sardonic breath. Maybe I should corner them and force them to give me their sister. The day I learned Tatiana got involved with Adrian was like a nauseating pill I had swallowed and its effects refused to ease.

Of course, it was too late. I'd held it against him. I even held it against her for mistaking him for me.

Until she was mine - in body and name, my jealousy and obsession wouldn't ease. I knew it.

"Yakuza is back in town," Nikita declared. "I tried to get him, but he disappeared before I had a chance."

Tension rolled through me like lightning. Somehow I believed it was Maxim's doing.

"Do you have a location on my brother?" I asked.

"He's in New York as you demanded," Nikita answered. At least my fucking twin did one thing right.

I had always been logical. Maxim, on the other hand, while excellent with hacking skills let emotions swing him one way or the other, depending on his mood or how high he was.

When I ordered him to pay up his debt to Sasha, he went into a psychotic rage. He managed to throw a fit even under the influence of narcotics.

The two of us looked almost identical, but that was where our similarities ended. Sometimes when he was around our sister, he seemed to get better only to spiral out of control once he left her. Maybe I should demand he spend all his time watching over our little sister, but I worried about his influence on her.

"Put extra men on Tatiana," I told him. "I don't want anyone but her brothers and immediate family getting close to her."

With a nod, he left to execute my order.

I came alone.

It was Tatiana's condition. No man or woman dared to put ultimatums and conditions on me, but this one had me wrapped around her little finger. I wouldn't have brought any of my men into her house, but the knowledge that I was so deep under her influence was concerning.

My car stopped in front of a black metal gate, but no guards stood there. She said she'd get rid of them, and it turned out she really meant it. Tatiana must have been a handful for her brothers when growing up. Isla, my own sister, never caused issues. When I asked her something, she did it. I had yet to see her rebel.

The black metal gate, as tall and as high as the one at my own home, slowly opened with a loud creak. As I drove through the gate, I surveyed the security. My own men lingered around the house, unbeknownst to the homeowner.

The house sat at the end of the long driveway. The moon projected on the white stone of her home. It wasn't large, but it suited her. Elegant. Cozy. Large enough for a family but not too big where you'd get lost in it.

Parking my black Aston Martin, I got out of the car just as Tatiana opened her front door.

I raised my eyebrow. I expected her to have staff to do that. "I could have been here to kill you."

She waved her hand. "I saw you through the security monitors at the gate."

I shook my head. It was still careless, but today wasn't the day to lecture her. Instead, I let my eyes travel over her. She wore a hot pink tank top and a pair of matching shorts, her long bare legs on full display. She was barefoot, her toes the matching sparkling pink. It was nice to see her outside her signature black Chanel.

Her thick blonde hair fell down her shoulders and between her fingers, she rolled a scrunchie.

"Come in." She stepped aside, my suit brushing against her as I walked in, closing the door behind us.

I turned around, watching the sparkle in her eyes. It was gone those first few months. I swore that I'd see it back in her blues even if I had to bring down the stars from the sky. The stars were safe for now.

"Lead the way. This is your home."

The strap fell off the slim curve of her shoulder. She didn't bother pulling it up, holding my gaze. This lust for her was embedded like thorns in a rose. It was engraved in the very marrow of my bones.

It was part of me, and I didn't even want to purge it.

The question was whether she could handle my love. My mother wasn't able to handle my father's, and it didn't end well for her.

"Just take a seat anywhere," she said in a frustrated breath. Her hands pulled her hair out of her face and she attempted to braid it. The scent of roses filled my lungs and spread like a drug through my veins. "I just need to get this mess under control."

I reached out and took the scrunchie from her hand. "Here, let me."

Her mouth parted and her gaze met mine.

"You know how to braid hair?" she murmured, surprised.

"I know how to braid hair," I answered quietly. I had enough practice over the years.

My eyes darted around the foyer, lit up by an antique chandelier.

There were antique pieces sitting around in different corners, blending with her other furniture. Tatiana loved her antiques, I realized. She'd love my castle in Russia.

I spotted an old sixteenth century Spanish bench chair and I nudged her toward it. She sat down without a protest, her posture rigid as if she expected a prank.

I started braiding her hair, remembering the last time I braided my sister's hair. It had been years.

"Where did you learn to braid hair, Pakhan?" she asked, her shoulders slowly relaxing.

"A little girl demanded them every night," I told her. "So I learned how to do them."

"Your kid?"

"She's under my protection," I answered vaguely. If she was anyone else, I wouldn't have even told her this much.

I alternated right and left sides, bringing the side section up and over the middle until I'd reached the end. Once satisfied her braid was nice and tight, I secured it with the hair tie. Her fingers came to the back of her head and she traced it down.

"Not bad," she murmured, glancing at me over her shoulder. "For a Pakhan. What would the world say if they knew the bad, big Pakhan knew how to braid." The corners of my lips tugged up. Tatiana could be charming when she wanted to. She glanced over her shoulder at me and her eyes shimmered as she tapped her chin pensively. "I might even use it to blackmail you."

I let out an amused breath. "You can try."

She grinned. "Oh, I will. You just wait and see. I own you now."

The woman already owned me. She'd find out soon that I'd own her too.

"Now, let's get down to business," I said. "Lead the way to those hard drives."

She jumped to her feet and turned around. Our bodies stood close, chest-to-chest. Toe-to-toe. My black suit to her pink tank top and shorts. She was the light to my darkness.

She was my reason for everything. She was mine for the taking. Mine to own. Mine to possess.

And nothing less would do.

"Illias," she started, biting her lower lip nervously. It was unlike her to show her emotions but she was worried.

"What is it?" I asked, cupping her cheeks.

"Whatever you see on those hard drives, stays here." The plea in her eyes was impossible for me to deny her, but I couldn't make that promise. Not until I saw what was on them. "There's stuff about my brothers and…" Her teeth tugged at her bottom lip and she averted her gaze. She was concerned I'd use it against her brothers. "They don't know what's on there, and I'd prefer it that way. We can delete it, permanently, so it can never come back to my family."

Those blue eyes, lighter than the clearest sky, met mine, searing themselves even deeper into my chest. Fuck, she might have become part of my DNA for all I knew.

"I promise," I vowed. "Anything concerning your family will remain between us."

She nodded satisfied, then headed through her house. "You live alone?"

"Yes and no," she remarked, going deeper down the hallway. Then stopped and faced the wall. Her hand roamed the wall until she found it. A trigger that opened the wall. "Usually there are guards around here."

"Why did you leave the penthouse?" I questioned her. Truthfully, it was easier to watch over her on this property, despite several blind spots. The penthouse was a security nightmare with other tenants that were unpredictable and brought in all types of guests. But she resisted moving for so many months, it seemed abrupt.

She shrugged as she punched in the code. The door slid open and a safe room came into view. Empty but for a single box.

"That was Adrian's place," she retorted. "This is mine. It was time to move."

I agreed. It was long overdue.

She entered the safe room and I followed.

"This is the box with laptops and hard drives," she explained, pointing to it. She sat down on the floor, then crisscrossed her legs. Her eyes crinkled amused as she tilted her head up where I still stood. "Sit down wherever you wish. The floor is yours."

I shook my head, then sat down on the ground and crisscrossed my legs too. "If I knew we'd be sitting on the floor, I would have dressed accordingly," I remarked dryly.

"Don't be a party pooper," she teased. "It's like being back in college. Don't you miss those days?"

I scoffed. "Not really. I had to run my business and attend classes."

She cocked her eyebrow. "Well, you could have always ended your *business*."

"Aiming for my job, Tatiana?"

"You couldn't pay me enough money to do your job," she remarked dryly, using air quotes when saying job.

Opening the box, she pulled out a laptop and hard drive out of the box then handed it to me.

"Are you good with technology?"

Dry amusement filled me. She really didn't know much about me at all. But then that was the way we operated in the Thorns of Omertà. Sticking to the shadows was our motto.

"I'm okay," I told her. "Not as good as my brother, but he's unavailable for hacking anymore."

"Your twin brother, Maxim." I nodded the confirmation. "I hear he's quite grouchy. Are you usually grouchy, too?"

"Mmmm." As if I'd ever admit it.

"Are you close with your brother?" she questioned, studying me closely. "I mean you're twins but somehow the two of you seem different."

"We're not as close as you and your brothers," I responded dryly.

"Why not?" I shook my head. I hadn't realized my woman was so nosy.

"He has an addiction problem," I told her honestly. "The woman he loved died years ago and he has become unreliable."

"Oh." She stared at me, waiting for me to elaborate. When I didn't, she continued, "Maybe your brother is the emotional type while you're a block of ice." If she only knew how little like a block of ice I was when it came to her. "It's not easy getting over people you love." I locked eyes with her. If she dared to go on about Adrian and her love for him, I'd dig for his ashes and kill him all over again. That selfish prick didn't deserve her. He put her life in danger with his actions. "People don't just forget about their loved ones," she added quietly. I gritted my teeth. It was better than saying the words that were on the tip of my tongue. After a moment, she shrugged as if trying to shake off her thoughts. "Well, whatever. He's your brother," she muttered.

There wasn't much else to say about it. Besides, Maxim was the last topic I wanted to discuss. So I opened the laptop, the password blinking at me.

"The password is *Memento mori*," she announced. I raised my eyebrow and she put her both hands up in the air. "I didn't come up with that password."

"The literal translation is '*Remember you must die*'. That's quite morbid for a password," I noted. "Did you know what it means?"

She sighed, then nodded. "Latin is not my strong suit. I had to look it up."

I typed in the password and the welcome screen appeared. I clicked on the first folder. One, two, three… I could see why she was worried. Adrian recorded some shit on Tatiana's brothers. I started deleting the videos from the drive as well as the history so there'd be no traces of it.

The video of her mother almost killing Tatiana hit me right in the chest. To think her life almost ended so soon after it began. Sasha didn't know it, but I'd forever owe him for saving his baby sister.

"Is this it? The chip?" she asked, pulling me out of my task. Her fingers played with her necklace, twisting it nervously. I'd deleted dozens of videos, but there were many more. Nothing on the members of the Thorns of Omertà.

"No."

She let out an exasperated breath. "Ugh, I hoped it was so it can be put behind me." Silence followed for a heartbeat. "What does the Yakuza want with this chip?"

"Probably to protect themselves," I answered vaguely. "A lot of powerful families want that chip. Adrian recorded shit onto that chip that could put a lot of people in jeopardy."

Including my sister, but I kept those words to myself.

"But none of them attacked me," Tatiana argued. "Except for the Yakuza. So it means they're desperate for the information on it."

I had my suspicions why the Yakuza wanted to get their hands on it first. Then they'd own every other member of the Omertà. But it wasn't easy to throw this on them without concrete evidence. It could be easily said that they grew restless and worried about their exposure on that chip.

While I was there, Tatiana disappeared a few times and came back with cookies and drinks. *No alcohol*, I noted pleasantly.

I didn't comment but she must have noticed my look, because she added, "Umm, I'm not keeping any alcohol here."

I didn't want her drinking because I fully intended to have her knocked up. Then I'd marry her before she could say 'baby' and we'd have our whole life ahead of us. I'd burn this whole fucking world if it'd make her happy.

Her eyes were clearer. Her smiles, no matter how small, were more frequent. She wasn't back to her normal self, but she was well on her way there, and it made me the happiest man alive to see her like this. Fuck everything else, she was the only thing that mattered. I considered her my family.

"Good," I answered curtly.

It was a step in the right direction. I was proud of her. Adrian didn't deserve her tears, her nightmares, never mind her liver. So I drank Coke while she sipped on water. It took three hours to go through it all. Adrian had gathered data on a lot of people, but what I needed wasn't there.

With the last drive completely erased, I shut down the laptop.

"All done."

Her eyes met mine. "No traces of videos on my brothers, right?"

"I've gone through all the videos and they are all erased. Do you know why he had them?"

"No." She shook her head, chewing on her bottom. "It makes no sense. He's been around our family forever and having that stuff almost feels like–"

She didn't finish her sentence but the meaning lingered. It bothered her. I could tell by the expression on her face. By the way her lower lip trembled. By the way her hands fidgeted.

Loyalty was part of Tatiana's DNA. It wasn't part of Adrian's.

"Well, it's gone now," I commented. "But we're still in need of that chip."

"I don't know where else that damn thing could be," she uttered with a heavy sigh. "I looked everywhere."

She was either an excellent liar or she truly didn't know where it was.

I believed the latter to be true.

TWENTY-SEVEN
TATIANA

The world outside seemed not to exist while we sat in this room.

It was just the two of us. The handsome lines of his face fascinated me. The darkness in his eyes spoke to me. The longer we stared at each other, the further the tension stretched.

But it wasn't uncomfortable. In fact, there was something just the opposite about it. He helped me. We did this as a team. Adrian had never included me in anything. He hid things from me, leaving me in the dark.

The realization hit from somewhere, and it made me appreciate Illias even more.

Truthfully the two were nothing alike. Adrian rarely ever dressed up, always opting for jeans, t-shirts, and combat boots. Illias Konstantin, on the other hand, wore a suit better than God himself.

He screamed sophistication, status, and power. It wasn't just the way he carried himself but also his wardrobe. Adrian had tattoos marking his body. Illias had only one. On his back – the skull wrapped in roses and thorns.

Why did the theme of roses and thorns keep reappearing?

"What does the tattoo on your back mean?" I asked, breaking the silence.

Our gazes locked. His gaze burned, studying me for too many seconds. The memory of our night in D.C. heated the air and crawled beneath my skin. Suddenly the safe room felt hotter than the furnace. My heart beat, fast and hard. A heaviness settled between my legs.

Oxygen seemed to be lacking. My head buzzed while adrenaline rushed through my veins.

"Why do you want to know?" he questioned.

I shrugged, hiding my fluster. "Maybe I want to trace it with my tongue."

I blurted out the answer, but now that I said it, I *wanted* to do it. The desire simmered through me like my life depended on it. But I kept my head and, more importantly, my lust in check. I needed to know what the deal with that tattoo with the roses and thorns was. The answer somehow seemed important.

"The skull represents death, the thorns represent sacrifice, and the red roses represent the love a vow can cost you."

"Morbid," I muttered. Truthfully, I was surprised he answered. But since he had, I was eager to know more. "Why are the roses stuffed in the skull's mouth, ears, and eyes?"

As far as tattoos went, it was pretty cool. Albeit, dark. Personally, I'd make it pink or something girly, but his was really ominous with red roses. It was as if it symbolized blood coming out of the mouth, ears, and eyes.

"See no evil. Hear no evil. Speak no evil."

My brows furrowed. "But men like you, that's all you do. See, hear, and speak evil." Before he could comment, I continued, "My brothers might have protected me, but I've never painted them as saints. I don't see them through rose-colored glasses, no pun intended. So don't bother denying it."

He seemed amused. "I wasn't going to. But the evil we see, hear, and speak is contained. It never leaves our most confident circle."

Unless someone recorded it. *Like Adrian.*

"Do you ever regret it?" I asked seriously.

"Regrets are for fools." I scoffed at his response. That sounded like such a Vasili response. "What? You don't agree?" he challenged.

I shrugged. "It sounded like an answer Vasili would give me."

"Smart man."

When I was growing up, I viewed Vasili like he was a god. He always seemed larger than life in my eyes. Now that I was a grown woman, I still viewed him as a force to be reckoned with. But he was a man, and I knew his faults as well as I knew mine. He was no longer a god but he was my brother, and I knew he'd always have my back, no matter what. And I'd have his.

A comfortable, yet deceitful silence consumed us both. We might not be saying anything, but there were so many words that filled this room.

I waited, holding my breath. He hadn't touched me. But my skin lit up like he had. His citrusy scent I loved so much filled the closed space of the safe room.

"You smell like roses. That scent has become my addiction after I hated it for years," he uttered softly. I gasped, his words shocking me. Then the meaning registered.

"Why did you hate it?" My voice was soft, vulnerability lacing it. It was stupid but I didn't want him to hate *me*.

"My mother's perfume was similar," he admitted, keeping his voice even. Cold even. But underneath it all, he hid his own vulnerability. I could feel it as if it was my own. "She betrayed my father as a husband and as the *Pakhan*."

The meaning lingered in the air. There was no need for clarifications. You didn't survive betraying *Pakhan*. It opened the door for weakness and more attempts.

"I'm sorry." The word paled in comparison to what he had to feel learning of his mother's betrayal. "How old were you?"

"Six."

"So young," I murmured.

"You were even younger," he remarked, keeping my gaze. So he'd seen the video. I hoped he'd just delete them without watching them, but then that would make him a lousy criminal. Wouldn't it?

"I didn't see it. I didn't feel it. I imagine it hurt Sasha more."

He nodded.

How in the hell did we get here? Enemies to what... reluctant friends. Friends with benefits? Or maybe lovers? Either way, my brothers would tell me to be cautious trusting this man. Scratch that, they'd lock me in this room and keep me here until I forgot about him. Not that I ever could.

That sharp jawline. Those eyes that pulled you into the pits of hell and for some reason you liked it. God, the things he could do with that beautiful, smug mouth and those strong hands. How in the hell wasn't this man taken?

Maybe singlehood was a hazard of his occupation. After all, he was the Pakhan.

My eyes traveled over him. He should look ridiculous wearing his expensive black Brioni suit, sitting on the floor, but he looked graceful. Like a panther resting, ready to pounce if needed.

My pulse sped up. My skin buzzed with anticipation. My breaths felt choppy.

I reached for my glass of water, my fingers trembling lightly. The tension between us sparked like fireworks on the 4th of July. My body craved his touch, and I started to wonder whether I replaced one addiction for another.

But at this very moment, I didn't care. He shared a piece of himself with me and I wanted another. In all the years I'd known Adrian, he had never shared anything from his childhood. Not a single memory. The most he had ever shared was that night we danced in that parking lot in Russia.

Illias' eyes were on me, studying me. His gaze filled with something soft and dark, like he'd waited for me his entire life. It was ludicrous, but I couldn't shake off the feeling.

Crawling on my knees, I closed the distance between us. On all fours, I brought my face an inch from his. The smell of him made me feel dizzy. I pressed my lips to his, then trailed my mouth down his jaw, to his ear, down to his collar. He inhaled a heavy breath and the woman in me felt victorious.

I made an impact on him. It was me who made his heart beat hard in his chest.

My eyes fluttered shut as I gave in to the kiss. His tongue expertly thrust into my mouth and a big warm hand grabbed my nape, holding me in place. Sparks burned, setting my entire body on fire. It was just a kiss but it was so much more.

The entire world faded away. All the past. All the worries. The only thing left was the intimacy of the two of us and the magnetic force that pulled us towards one another.

His tongue slid across mine, and with a rough sound from deep in his chest, he sucked on it. I moaned and he swallowed the sound. His warm breath intoxicated me, sending waves of shudders down my body. He explored every corner of my mouth, claiming it for his own, and I freely gave it.

My nipples hardened under my tank top and my inner muscles clenched on a growing empty ache. Want filled my veins and swam through my bloodstream. My head swam as a low, rough sound rumbled in his throat. He kissed me back with such savage hunger, his arms caging me in his iron grip.

This brutal lash of desire threatened to burn me to ash. I had never felt such raw and carnal need - not with Adrian, not with anyone.

I had no idea when he'd laid us on the hard floor, my back pressed against it and his big, strong body hovering over mine. My hands frantically pushed his suit jacket off his wide shoulders. It slid silently onto the floor. His tie followed. Then I worked on his buttons. The pressure of his abdomen against my lower belly sent sizzle through my blood. He nipped my bottom lip, then licked it and a moan traveled up my throat as he licked my lip, soothing the sting.

My fingers pushed inside his shirt, feeling his hot skin under my palms. The wet glide of his tongue inside my mouth mirrored the push of his hips against my core. It sent a tremble through me. The heat of his body and the way he kissed me stole my breath. I couldn't breathe.

My nails dug into his shoulders and my legs wrapped around his hips, grinding my throbbing clit against his hard erection. A ragged groan escaped his throat, and his hand swept down my body, touching every inch of me.

Roughly, he pulled my tank top up over my head and his rough palm closed over my right breast, kneading it.

"Illias," I breathed, arching my back into his touch. His lips still crushed mine, his kiss consuming me just as his touch did. My hands slid up into his hair and gripped a fistful of his silky strands. "Get rid of your clothes," I rasped.

The need in my voice was alarming. I didn't heed the warning. Heat tugged in my lower stomach, and I rolled my hips, grinding against him to relieve the ache inside.

My hands fumbled with his belt. Desperation was eating at me, clawing my insides with the raging need for him. The jingle of his belt registered in the far corner of my mind. His fingers hooked on my shorts, grabbing panties along with them and pulling them down my legs.

He inhaled deeply. "Your arousal... I can smell it."

He discarded the rest of his clothes, leaving us both naked. In one swift move, he pulled us into a sitting position. My legs still wrapped around his waist, straddling him and my breasts pressed against his hard chest. He placed a kiss on my neck, then nipped it hard, marking my flesh as his. A shudder erupted beneath my skin.

"You and me, moya luna," he murmured, tracing the edge of my ear with this tongue. "Don't you ever forget it. Every inch of your body and soul - I want it all."

I wanted to tell him *no*. I wanted to tell him this was just physical. But his lips against the hollow of my neck had me forgetting English and Russian.

Instead, I tilted my head, offering him better access. I was his. Every inch of my body and he knew it. My body hummed for him. My soul sang for him.

I'd be terrified later. Right now, desperation ate at me. We'd barely gotten started, and I already needed him inside me with an ache that was increasingly becoming hard to bear. I wanted him so badly my body trembled.

I ran my hands up his bare chest, over his biceps, and into his thick hair. He let out a rough breath, watching me lazily with a dark expression. His erection lined up with my entrance, the heat of his body had my insides clenching. I couldn't help it; I rocked against him.

A fire lit inside me. I wanted more. I shifted on his erection, feeling his hard cock at my entrance. I slid down, feeling the tip of it inside me and my head fell back with a moan.

"Look how prettily your pussy takes me," he rasped, grabbing a fistful of my hair and forcing me to watch as his cock disappeared inside me. He stared at our joined bodies with a reverence in his eyes, dark and possessive. There was such intensity in his gaze, calling to my soul and sending ripples of waves through it.

"You see that, Tatiana?" he rasped, his voice laced with a thick accent. "It'll always be like this. You and me." A shuddering breath left me, as I watched him, my eyes half-lidded and hazy. "Ride me. Fuck me," he groaned. "Let me see you get yourself off."

The thick lust in his voice drifted between us, filling my stomach with heat. He bent his head and captured a nipple in his mouth. White light shot behind my eyelids. While he sucked and licked one breast, his rough palm kneaded the other.

His palm landed on my bare ass with a slap. "Fuck me, Tatiana."

My ass stung from the palm of his hand. My arousal dripped, making a mess of both of us.

A dark chuckle vibrated from Illias. His jaw ticked. His heartbeat raced against mine. Something dark lingered in his eyes; he looked on the brink of losing control.

I moved slowly, rocking my hips in a circular motion, feeling him deep inside me and my walls clenching around him. I ground my clit against him, shuddering with the pleasure that already swam through my veins.

"That's it, moya luna." His mouth was pressed against my ear, his words heavy with a Russian accent that for the first time in my life I loved. It showed he was losing his control. For me. "You're taking me so well."

His hands were everywhere - on my neck, up and down my spine, gripping my hips. Every breath I took was intoxicating. My mouth trailed over his neck, nipped on his jaw until our mouths clashed again.

He gripped my hips to grind me harder against him.

"Ohhhh," I whimpered. Pleasure built and built, igniting sparks that reached higher and higher. I rode him, up and down. My tits bounced. He slapped my ass again, nipped my throat, sucked my nipples, then bit down on them hard. "Jesus–"

"Illias," he groaned, grinding me on him hard and fast. My insides shuddered. He was everywhere. "The name is Illias. Don't you forget it, Tatiana."

He slapped my ass again and the orgasm was instant. I screamed his name. I came so hard spots flew behind my eyes. The fire inside me spread like wildfire, sending a tingling sensation through my body.

When I came down from my high, it was to his eyes on me.

"I love seeing you orgasm," he rasped, nipping at my lip.

A blush spread over me. His words filled me with feelings stronger than I had ever felt before. It was terrifying and thrilling at the same time.

"My turn to see you orgasm," I murmured and his eyes lit with fires that burned hotter than inferno as I reached back, leaning my hands on his thighs. It gave him a better view of our joined bodies, his cock buried deep inside me.

His eyes traveled over my body, from my flushed cheeks, over my parted mouth, down my bouncing breasts to where he slid in and out of me as I rode him. My arousal dripped down my thighs, the erotic noises of slick flesh against slick flesh filling the safe room.

I could feel him deep in my womb. I watched with half-lidded eyes as he gripped my hips, then pulled me chest-to-chest and then slammed me down on his erection. Hard.

A joint groan. Locked gazes. Then he pulled me up, only to bounce me down on his cock again. Up and down. Again and again. My moans filled the space. My fingers came to his shoulders, clawing at his skin.

"Illias," I whimpered. "Oh, God…. Ahhh."

He thrust in and out of me with such force, filling me like never before.

His fingers gripped my braid as he devoured my lips and my tongue. He pounded in and out of me with such brutality that I'd fear he'd branded me on the inside. With his other hand, he pinched my nipple and I moaned against him.

The rhythm with which he fucked me was savage. Consuming. He twisted my nipples over and over again, pain and pleasure intermingling. He powered into my pussy, while his palm slapped against my ass and I saw stars.

The sound of my pleasure was unmistakable. Fuck, I never even knew I'd enjoy the pain as much as the pleasure. The sting enhanced the pleasure, and I knew my body would never be the same.

Shamelessly I reached for his hand and put it on my clit. "P-please," I gasped.

He didn't even hesitate. He rubbed the heel of his palm against my clit, then in one swift move slapped it. My heart thundered so hard, it threatened to break my ribs. He reached for my swollen clit then and twisted it.

"Ohhh…"

His pace increased to a maddening level, his thrusts piercing me. His groin hit hard against my clit.

"That's it," he murmured against my mouth, his eyes hooded. "Come apart for me."

The second orgasm hit me with monumental force, and I screamed his name so loud, my throat was raw. Throaty moans mixed with his name. He continued powering into me relentlessly, my walls clenching around him.

With a last punishing thrust, he shuddered, his face buried into the crook of my neck and finished inside me.

High on the pleasure and post-orgasmic bliss, I pressed my body against him and rested my face against his neck. Our breathing was heavy. Our hearts beat wildly.

Thick wet arousal, a mixture of both our liquids, slid down my thigh, leaking out of my pussy. His hand caressed my back, never ceasing its soothing movement and my eyes drooped in fatigue.

"I need to clean up," I murmured sleepily, attempting to move but my muscles refused to support me.

"I've got you," he assured softly.

Deep sleep pulled me under.

That night I dreamt of little boys and girls with pale blue eyes and dark hair.

TWENTY-EIGHT
TATIANA

I had to find a way to get to Russia.

Since there was no other information among Adrian's possessions, I was back to my original plan. Adrian's hint. It had something to do with that parking lot in Russia. So, to Russia I must go.

There were just a few minor obstacles. The men that Konstantin had on me. The men that my brothers had on me. And then there were the damn Yakuza. What the fuck did Adrian involve himself in?

Illias got an urgent call and left sometime in the night. I woke up to a bouquet of roses on my nightstand and a note.

I had to take care of a debt. I'll be back. Wait for me.

My lips curved into a soft smile and I buried my face into the pillow. His scent still lingered on the sheets and I inhaled deeply, letting it seep into my lungs.

Wait for me.

I reached for my phone and quickly typed up a message. **Touché, Pakhan. Goes both ways.**

That was weeks ago.

Having Yan drop me off in the heart of the city due to crowds, I exited the car and walked down the hot pavement, the weather humid. None of it bothered me though, as I watched people from all over the world flock to the French Quarter.

The smell of jambalaya, gumbo, beignets, and unfortunately urine in certain corners invaded my senses. The cuisine of New Orleans was known for its spices, but it was the sweets that were my favorites.

Elaborate decorations all year long were the signature of the city. Tourists gathered around the street painters and cheered on local street bands. Music, laughter, and cheer were always present in this city.

And for the first time in so many months, the desperation and sadness didn't swallow me whole; although it was still there. In a dark corner of my soul, hiding from the light and laughter.

A young woman with a baby caught my eye. I watched the baby laugh excitedly as they danced together to the local music, the rare summer breeze sweeping through. Instant sorrow wrapped around my heart and constricted so hard that tears stung my eyes.

I wanted so badly to have a baby of my own. Adrian was so set against it. I couldn't understand why. Acid ate at my heart, the green hole growing bigger and bigger with each breath.

For months before his death, he seemed more like a stranger than the boy that kept calling me a pipsqueak.

I stood in front of Adrian in my Valentino dress that barely reached my knees and matching pumps.

He took a sip of his drink, probably vodka as his eyes traveled over me, impassive and cold. Those green eyes that used to send my heart racing in anticipation, now only managed to disappoint and flare my anger.

I didn't know what had shifted between us. Something had happened and he refused to acknowledge it. Stubbornness was part of my DNA. My brothers ensured that.

"What?" I snapped.

He took another sip of his drink and looked at me in annoyance.

"Are you trying to start shit, Tatiana?"

I clenched my fists. I could feel my anger rising inside of me, as well as his burning through me. Our eyes clashed, resentment in his blue depths sending my heart spiraling until it fell to my feet.

All the years I had known him, he had never shown me this side of himself. I didn't know it even existed.

"Adrian-" My voice cracked, the pain in it evident. "What happened?" I choked on the words. I had loved him for so long. First as my brother's friend, then friends and ultimately as my crush until he became my lover.

This tension swimming through the air was suffocating. The invisible chain wrapped around my throat tighter and tighter.

My lip trembled and I cursed myself for not being stronger.

Vasili and Sasha had always protected me, but they also taught me how to protect myself and be strong. Physically strong. But emotionally I was too sensitive because both my brothers always babied me too much. Even I knew that.

"If you don't want this marriage, just say so," I croaked.

Something passed his expression, but it was gone so fast, I couldn't be certain. Each thud of my heart ached as I waited for his answer drowning in his green eyes.

The green eyes of deep forests.

I swallowed the lump in my throat and ignored the ache in my chest. I waited for his answer, but it never came. He stared somewhere past me, almost as if he couldn't bear to look at me.

"Why else wouldn't you want to have a baby with me?" My voice broke, just as my heart was breaking. Slowly but surely.

"Don't do this," he said, his voice almost sorrowful. Almost desperate. The heartbreaking silence stretched on, tearing us further and further apart.

"Do what?" I murmured, my eyes welling with tears. I wasn't enough for him. Deep down in my heart I knew it as well as I knew my name. "Beg you for a family of our own?"

"I told you," he said, his voice cracking. "I don't want to bring a

child into this world. Mine was plenty fucked up. I don't want that for my children."

"You and I are nothing like our parents," I pleaded. *"We are better. We'd offer our children a better life."*

All the years of damage that Adrian's childhood cemented into his DNA couldn't be remedied. I could see that now, but back then, I was too blind to see it. I failed him; he failed me.

Round and round we went.

Someone elbowed me in the side and startled me out of my memories. I gasped, then turned around sharply to bark at the jerk who dared to get too close to me when I came face-to-face with a man smiling at me.

Flawless chiseled face and deep, dark, beautiful eyes that sparkled. A soft, full smile filled his expression, and I swore my heart might have skipped a beat. Maybe two. He was gorgeous. The kind that painters would want to draw down to memorize his features for all eternity.

A strong jaw. High cheekbones. The kind that would make any woman jealous. His mouth. And that goddamn smile. Until the awed gawking faded and his gorgeous features finally registered as danger.

He could be a Yakuza.

Before I could panic, he put his hands into his expensive suit. *Expensive Italian custom made suit,* I noted.

"Might want to find your way inside before some men get too brave," he suggested softly. I listened for an accent, but I couldn't quite place it. It almost sounded... mixture of Italian and posh British. Barely a hint of it though, so I couldn't be quite sure. "I'll keep them away."

I blinked, surprised at his offer. I wasn't stupid enough to trust him. Drop dead gorgeous or not. "Who are you?"

He tilted his head slightly, his eyes sharp on me and the surroundings. "Amon Takahashi Leone."

Geez, even his name sounded kind of sexy. Then the name registered. Was that Japanese and Italian? Unusual combination for sure.

My eyes darted around and I spotted a man across the street. I froze at his grim expression. There wasn't an ounce of warmth on his face.

"So you *are* Yakuza?" I choked, my voice barely audible. My hand smoothed over the black and white button-up dress, my eyes flicking to the other man. Once my fingers clutched onto the white button, I kept twisting it nervously. I could possibly outrun the other guy but this one, no fucking way.

Amon T. Leone looked to be in top shape. Strong and athletic.

"Yes and no," Amon retorted, smiling. "I'm just offering favors in turn for future collections." He tilted his head and his eyes darted to my guards as well as another set who I'd wage belonged to Konstantin. "They'll keep you safe until you get inside wherever you're going. I'm going to keep the others busy."

Jesus, how many men were actually watching me?

It would be stupid to question it now though so with a terse nod, I rushed towards Yan and Yuri.

We were a block away from the building when bullets started to fly. I jumped and before I knew what was happening, Yan jumped on me and tackled me to the ground. "Stay down," he grunted. I shifted my head to find Yuri shooting at a Mercedes driving by

Adrenaline pumped through my veins. My palms burned against the pavement. My heart lodged itself between my ribs and each heartbeat hurt worse than the last. Maybe I cracked my ribs. Jesus, I was scared. I wasn't ready to die.

"Fuck, it's the Yakuza." There was shouting. Alarms. Police sirens. It all happened in a blur, and the only thing that I registered was the hot pavement. And the stench of a New Orleans street. Piss and beer.

God, I couldn't die. Not like this. A breeze swept through, cooling and gentle. It soothed my burning skin. The sound of the city penetrated through the fear and my survival instinct kicked in.

"Yan, we have to get inside," I rasped, my heart drumming in my ears. "We're sitting ducks here."

He must have agreed because he barked orders. I was only able to process some of his words.

"Okay, Yuri and your friend will have our backs," Yan hissed.

"W-what friend?" Jesus, I stuttered. So much for being badass. Next time, I comforted myself. I wasn't prepared today.

"The one you were gawking at," Yan retorted dryly, slight annoyance in his tone.

I rolled my eyes. "That's Amon Leone. You'd gawk at him too if you saw him up close."

"Jesus," he muttered. He looked behind him, a terse nod and he jerked me upward. "Let's go. They have our backs."

With my bodyguards at my back and my breathing erratic, I entered the building and rushed up to our old penthouse. Once inside, I paced back and forth, waiting on Yuri and Yan to come up.

My heart thundered in fear and worry. I hoped the two of them were safe. I hoped I didn't make a mistake coming up here, cornering myself. I shook my head. No, no, no. They were safe. I knew they were.

A knock on the door. I stilled, holding my breath.

"Tatiana!" A relieved breath left my lungs as I rushed to the door and opened it.

"Yuri, is everyone alright?" I asked, my eyes darting behind him. "Where is Yan?"

"He's good. Everyone's good."

I pushed my hand into my hair. "Vasili is going to hear about this, won't he?"

"I can't make any promises, but we'll try to keep you out of it," he promised. "Now, go and do what you must. Lock the doors."

I wondered if he suspected I was looking for clues. Rather than question him, I just nodded and returned inside.

Like a zombie, I headed into the walk-in closet I used to share with my husband. There were still clothes here. His. Mine. I had only moved items that I knew I'd need. Things that reminded me of Adrian, I left behind.

I aimlessly pushed them on hangers, back and forth. Back and forth.

I loved fashion. Chanel. Valentino. Armani.

No matter my attempts at curbing my taste for luxurious fashion, it was impossible to stop it. I blamed my brothers for feeding the monster inside me whenever I was sad or upset. But the fact was that I thrived on it.

I studied political science only to prove to Adrian I was smart. The truth was, I didn't care about being smart nor sophisticated. I just wanted to lose myself in different designs, decorate maybe some little shop with beautiful dresses that anyone could afford.

My fingers trembled as I traced them over the fine material of his clothes. He rarely wore them. Many still had tags hanging off them as he rarely dressed up, always opting for casual wear. Somehow being back here, the reminder of Adrian was daunting.

I let out a heavy sigh and headed for the bathroom.

My reflection stared back at me. I felt better than I had in a long time. The mirror attested to it. My hair was shinier, My eyes brighter, my complexion clearer. There was color to my cheeks and the dark shadows under my eyes had faded into nothing.

The doorbell rang, then a loud knock and I stilled. My family knew I moved back to my own place. It wouldn't be them. Maybe the bad guys? I shook my head at the absurdity of it. What bad guy rings a doorbell?

The door opened. I held my breath as I realized all the guns in secret places were no longer here. I moved them all to my own home. "Tatiana?"

A swish of air left my lungs as relief washed over me. "In here," I called out to Yan. "Master bathroom."

I turned away from the mirror, my eyes lingering on that single tile that Adrian and I argued about when I redecorated his penthouse. It stood out.

Yan appeared at the door and I peeled my gaze away from the tile. "This just got delivered."

I frowned. I had forwarded all my mail. "How come it didn't go to my house?"

Yan shrugged. "A personal delivery."

He handed me the box. "Thanks, Yan."

He nodded. "I'll be right outside the penthouse."

I sighed. "You know, you can stay inside the penthouse."

He gave me a half- smile. "But then I'd miss anyone trying to approach outside. Yuri is outside the building and I'm inside the building. It's how we work."

He turned on his heel and left me to it as I ripped open the box. Once open, I found an iPhone in it with a screen saver 'Play me' flashing on and off. Suddenly, the brightness of the day dimmed.

I held my breath as I slid the phone open. It was all it needed for a video to start playing.

The video showed Sasha strangling a man. Nobody I recognized, but he was brutal about it. That look in my brother's eyes was crazed. That unhinged smile on his lips promised pain. God, how many of these damn videos were circulating. It wasn't one of those that were on Adrian's laptop. So it couldn't be it.

What was going on? Who was after my family?

I watched the video play out with a knot in my stomach. Until the body slumped onto the floor, the head almost disjointed from the man's body. *Jesus Christ!*

It wasn't until the end that I saw it. A reflection against the glass. A reflection of Adrian as he reached for the camera and slid the tape out.

"I'm erasing all the traces of our visit," he told Sasha. Yet, it was playing right here in front of me. He never erased anything. If he had, I would have never seen this.

Disappointment and anger washed over me. Adrian had put my family at risk by keeping these videos. He might be dead but he left a clusterfuck for me to clean up in its wake.

I turned around and met my gaze in the mirror.

"My brothers," I rasped to my reflection in the mirror. I stared at it blankly, wondering if there was anything I really knew about Adrian. Did I know my husband at all?

My heart hardened. No, not hardened, just numbed. But that was good. I didn't want to feel Adrian's betrayal. It was like I had just lost him all over again.

He knew how much I loved my brothers. My family. They were all I had. Why would he do that?

My shuddering breath fogged the mirror. The wounds that started to heal cracked back up. Silence echoed all around me, the sound of my heart bleeding almost an actual sound.

Drip. Drip. Drip.

The vise around my heart squeezed. The lump in my throat grew, until it hurt to do such a simple act as breathe. And betrayal burned the backs of my eyes.

"I need a drink," I said to my own reflection, but before I turned around, my eyes landed on that piece of tile that Adrian and I argued about. He hated it, I liked it. He threatened to remove it. I threatened to tear into his computers.

But then abruptly, one day I got home to find him fixing that same tile in our bathroom.

"What are you doing?" I questioned him suspiciously. "You better not touch my accent tile or I'll touch your accent laptop. Roughly."

Adrian shook his head, one of those rare smiles playing around his lips. My chest warmed and I fought the urge to just hug him.

"Pipsqueak, you've got to relax."

I rolled my eyes and groaned. I hated that nickname.

"I just came back from the spa. I'm relaxed," I snapped sharply. I wanted a sweet, lovable nickname. Like he called me that first night in the gazebo. **Moya luna***. Now, that was a nickname for your wife. Not fucking pipsqueak. "Stop calling me pipsqueak," I demanded, glaring at him with my hands on my hips. "Why don't you ever call me moya luna?"*

He gave me a blank look. Oh no, he didn't! Did the fucker really forget?

Now that really got my temper flaring. It was our first time together. The hottest night of my life. He fucked me in the gazebo while the party went on inside the manor and he acted like it was just another night.

"You touch that tile and I'll go ballistic." I whirled around on my heel, when his voice stopped me.

"Come on, Tatiana," he drawled. "You were right and I was wrong. The tile grew on me. I'm making sure it's cemented properly."

I didn't think much of it, but why would he cement it? It was tiled. Unless—

My breath caught in my lungs. Unless he dug it out then put something inside it. Without delay, I rushed through the penthouse in search of a hammer. I found a small box of construction tools and grabbed a hammer. Returning to the bathroom, I swung the hammer into the air. A heartbeat later and I brought it down onto the single tile.

It instantly cracked. So I did it again. And again. I lowered to my knees, my hands digging through the mess. I cracked the surrounding tile too. The debris was everywhere. I scooped up the pieces and shoved them aside.

A glittering shine of metal caught my eye. My fingers sifted through the dirt until I found it.

A tiny key.

Another clue but no answers.

⁂

Hours later, I entered Vasili's building. With each step nearing my big brother's office, his deep accented voice vibrated through the walls. It was the first indication he was pissed off. His accent became thicker when he was mad.

I found another clue but personally, I had a setback. Disappointment tasted bitter. Like Bacardi vodka without the fruity flavor. My senses dulled and so did the self-disappointment, but I knew in the corner of my mind that it would come back tenfold.

"I said find a bride, not kidnap one," Vasili roared so loud that I feared the glass on the building would shatter.

"Semantics," Sasha retorted in a bored tone.

I should have known it was Sasha who wound him up. He mostly lost his temper around our slightly psychotic brother. Personally, I thought there was sense to Sasha's madness but then maybe that showed how fucked up I was too.

My hand on the handle, I blew a breath into my other and smelled it. Fuck, it smelled like alcohol. I kicked the habit but after seeing that video and clear evidence that Adrian clearly lied to my brothers, I fell off the wagon along with my resolve to get my act together. I resorted to a glass of vodka to calm my nerves. Then to another glass to drown out my sorrow. And another to numb the fact that the man I loved betrayed me. My family. It turned out, I hadn't known my husband at all.

Well, it spiraled from there. At this point, I wasn't certain how much I drank.

I waved my hand around as if that would eliminate my alcohol breath, then opened the door and strode in.

"So I hear you're starting a war," I said jokingly. Sasha needed Vasili to back off. He deserved to get the woman he loved. And so fucking what if he had to kidnap her? It wasn't as if Vasili was a goddamn saint. "Can I join in?"

The stormy look my eldest brother shot me could have killed a lesser person. Lucky for him, I could handle him. I took a seat and leaned back, watching my brothers. Vasili was too riled up to sit, instead he kept pacing back and forth.

"You two are worse than my toddlers," Vasili bellowed. "That's it. Enough is enough." He pointed a finger at me. "You will stop drinking. I don't want to smell alcohol on you and-"

I've been good, I wanted to protest. Fucker caught me on a bad day. Instead, I had to come up with a smartass comment.

"I'll spray more perfume," I retorted, my speech slightly slurred. Damn it, that shit hit me harder than I thought.

"The fuck you will," Vasili roared. "You will stop drinking and taking sleeping pills. Every goddamned thing."

I flipped him the bird. He was crazy if he thought he could boss me around. I was a grown ass woman. He pushed his hand through his hair and turned his eyes to Sasha.

My poor brother.

"And you, Sasha, will return the bride," my big brother demanded.

"Nah, I'll pass," Sasha answered nonchalantly. "I'm keeping her."

"I agree," I chimed in, against my better judgment. "Why should you be the only one to get what he wants and needs?"

I winced at the bitterness in my voice. It was hard not to feel the acid of envy after the video I had just watched. It seemed I didn't even know Adrian.

"The two of you will be the death of me! Tatiana, you get your shit together or I'll do it for you. And you, Sasha. You will go to Alessio and deliver his sister, then apologize."

"The fuck I will," Sasha answered, then blew a bubble with the gum still in his mouth. "His sister is mine."

Vasili pushed his hands through his hair.

"Jesus Christ. I thought you had the hots for Autumn, not her friend."

I snickered. Vasili should pay more attention to his siblings. On the other hand, maybe it was best that he didn't.

"Your mistake," Sasha retorted, shrugging his shoulders.

"We cannot go to war with him," Vasili attempted to reason. He must not know our brother well if he thought that would dissuade Sasha. "Cassio and his gang will back him up. He's even close with Raphael."

"I never liked the devil anyhow. He thinks he's more of a brother to Bella than Alexei. I bet you Alexei would be on my side."

On cue, Alexei walked in wearing his signature black cargo pants and t-shirt. A knife sliced through my chest. Adrian loved wearing the same kind of stuff. Ignoring it all, I focused on my brothers.

Alexei sat himself down. "So you got yourself a bride?" His voice was casual, unemotional.

"Yeah," Sasha replied almost proudly. "I need to lay low for a bit. But first I need some ink. Want to hold my hand?"

Alexei cocked an eyebrow. "I'll keep you company. But there'll be no hand holding."

"I'll hold your hand," I offered, my speech a tiny bit slurred. "As long as you buy me a drink. I'm feeling depressed."

And that was putting it mildly. It wasn't every day you found evidence of your husband's betrayal. He had enough shit on my brothers to put them away for twenty goddamn lifetimes. Maybe destiny intertwined and spared us all the pain.

Well, except for me.

The problem now was to figure out who sent me that video. Adrian was dead and obviously someone had it. Maybe a blackmail note would follow. Or demand for something. *A chip*, my mind whispered. It could be that a follow-up demand would come for that chip that everyone seemed determined to get their hands on. Maybe it was in Russia and Adrian left me a clue to the chip.

"It's possible," I muttered to myself while my brothers started their usual bickering. Well, it was more like Vasili preaching and Sasha egging him on.

I tuned them all out, my drunken brain working up some kind of plan. Any kind of plan. I'd been going through options for weeks, trying to figure out how to get to Russia and go to the spot where I believed another clue waited for me. Vasili raged and bellowed, while I schemed a way to get to Russia.

A pair of dark brown eyes flashed in my mind. Would Konstantin help? Except, he was the last person I wanted with me when I found that message. Assuming there was even a message.

Jesus, what a damn mess.

"Take Branka Russo back," Vasili threatened. "If you don't, I will."

Sasha got to his feet and fixed the sleeves to his suit. "Touch her and you won't have to worry about a war with others, Brother," he declared calmly. The two stared at each other like two stubborn Russians. "Because you'll have one with me."

Without another word, Sasha left his office, Alexei right behind him, leaving me alone with my eldest brother.

We stared at each other as an invasive silence crept along at my skin. The first droplets of rain started to beat down on the glass. Somehow it reflected what I felt inside. As if my soul was weeping, right along with the dark skies.

The distance to healing seemed to have suddenly gotten longer rather than shorter. That familiar dull pain in my chest was back. A tremor shot through my veins. The cloudy sky cast gloomy shadows over us, the slow thunder rolling through the sky.

"I'm sorry, kroshka." Vasili's voice startled me, and I ripped my gaze from the window.

Our eyes connected. He watched me with furrowed brows. I feared he'd see too much. Or maybe not enough. I wanted to tell him what I found but I feared what it would mean. Maybe it was best to let ghosts rest. Adrian was dead; he couldn't use any of that data against my brothers. Against anyone.

Inwardly, I shook my head. I couldn't go there. Not now. I wouldn't think about Adrian now, I couldn't. It would tear me apart.

"It's not your fault."

Lowering my head, I stared at my clenched hands, my knuckles turning white in my lap. My black dress mocked me.

"I shouldn't have let you get involved with him," Vasili muttered.

My head shot up. "Why?"

Did he know already?

"I didn't want you in this world," he continued. "I wanted a good life for you. Fashion. A design house. Not underworld and crime."

I swallowed.

"Adrian wasn't part of the underworld," I croaked but the lie was bitter on my tongue. My chest squeezed painfully at the sense of betrayal that plagued every fiber of me since I saw what my husband had stored in his gadget room. The pain was deep, and it wrapped layers around my heart.

I still cared for him, but even that seemed like a betrayal. I remembered the boy who always called me pipsqueak. Pulled on my braids. But then it all turned into anger somewhere along the way, inflicting such destructive suffering. The harsh truths slowly crept through my mind, but I refused to listen to it.

Maybe I was just a glutton for punishment and chose to believe in Adrian. After all, he wasn't here to defend himself.

"He wasn't good enough for you," he claimed. "I vowed to protect you and I failed."

I sighed. "So I keep hearing," I said, slightly annoyed. "Yet, nobody said a word while he was still alive." Our gazes locked and despite the alcohol in my veins, I found the will to rebel. To fight.

"I never signed the shares over to him," I uttered softly. The surprise in Vasili's eyes told me Isabella kept him in the dark about what she shared with me and my chest warmed. She'd always have my back. Just as I would have hers. "You taught me better than that, Vasili. I would never do something like that. Not without speaking to you."

"Fuck, kroshka," he grunted. "I just want you to be happy. I didn't want to burden you with business stuff."

"If it involves me, I should know," I claimed. I regretted drinking so much prior because my speech was slurred but my head was clear. For the first time in a very long time. "Vasili, how did Adrian and you become friends?" I asked, changing subjects. There was no sense of beating the dead horse.

Vasili's expression darkened. "He had it rough. Living on the Russian streets. His no good parents. Then father learned of a connection he could possibly provide and pulled him in."

Those words Adrian whispered when we danced in that shitty parking lot echoed in my brain.

"Did you know those weren't his real parents?" I asked.

Vasili's brows furrowed. "Yes, they were."

I shook my head. "No, they weren't."

"How do you know?"

"He told me when he took me to some shitty parking lot in Russia," I murmured. "He said his father and future died there. Murdered."

"What the fuck?" he hissed. "He took you to where his father was shot?"

I nodded. "There wasn't much there," I remarked, although Adrian and I didn't see the same parking lot when we stood there. Then Vasili's earlier answer registered. "What connections did he have that father wanted?"

Vasili shrugged. "There's some secret, powerful organization. Papa thought they held Marietta and Alexei. Then when he realized it was a false lead, he thought they could help find him. Obviously, he was wrong."

Yeah, he was wrong. Our mother stole Alexei and Marietta found refuge in the arms of the Spanish cartel. Like I said, we had all different shades of fucked up family history.

"Papa trusted him that much?"

Vasili shrugged. "After months and years, Adrian had proven his loyalty."

And then betrayed it. But those words remained sealed behind my lips and buried deep in my soul. My brother said nothing about Adrian's betrayal, and I saw no point in telling Vasili how far Adrian's self-protection went.

Rising to my feet, I strode to my brother and wrapped my arms around his waist. "You protected me, Vasili. I am possibly one of the most normal women in the underworld." He tilted his head and gave me a pointed look. "Okay, I had a very normal childhood. Actually, normal and Nikolaev don't go in the same sentence. The point is you didn't fail."

"I hate seeing you like this, kroshka."

The pain in his voice cracked my heart some more. At this rate, it would be impossible to repair it.

"I'm getting better," I rasped.

One step forward. Two steps back. Goddamn Adrian and the bullshit he left behind.

A hard-carved face with a strong jaw and piercing eyes flashed before my eyes. The pain in my chest dulled, giving way to a fire so strong it stole my goddamn breath.

Vasili's eyes searched out mine. Whatever he saw in them must have satisfied him, because he nodded.

"Never forget, my little kroshka. We're family. Your brothers and I will burn down this world for you. All you have to do is ask."

And I would burn down the world for them. They didn't even *have* to ask.

Then Vasili kissed the tip of my nose. Just like he did when I was a little girl.

TWENTY-NINE
KONSTANTIN

The air was humid. The windows were open. The music was loud.

Some brass band playing a corner in the French Quarter, probably competing for tourists' attention. My desk was positioned close enough to the window to see the street, but far enough so passersby couldn't see me. Not that they could see through the tinted windows.

My phone beeped. The same unknown number. Motherfucker!

Slowly, like each movement was at the slowest speed available, I pressed play.

My sister's face was the mirror version of the woman on her knees. The same curly red hair. The only difference was the green eyes. Isla's were vibrant green. The eyes of the woman in the video were dead, even before I pulled the trigger.

She stared somewhere in the distance, not seeing me. She was lost to the living even before I killed her. Papa saw to that.

Bang.

One clean shot. Her body fell over. Blood seeped from her temple. It was too fucking similar to what had happened to my mother.

It wasn't a good picture. Isla wouldn't forgive me.

I stared at the video, no longer seeing it. Instead, memories from twenty-two years ago rushed to the forefront of my mind.

A sense of foreboding slithered down my spine as I watched my father with the girl who had to be younger than me.

I looked much older than most of my peers at eighteen. Even Maxim, and his build was similar to mine. I guess being a killer and my father's right hand aged me.

The girl, who couldn't be older than eighteen, climbed the cake-like marble steps, my father clutching her hand. Her curly red hair shone like fire under the Russian sun, throwing off the colors of a burning sunset.

Then my papa and his new woman stopped in front of me and the lead settled in my gut when I noticed her bump. She was younger than I thought. Yes, she had tits, but her curves were all due to her baby bump. She still had baby fat in her face. She never had the chance to become a woman and lose that baby fat.

I gritted my teeth and shot a glare at my papa. How far he had fallen!

Ever since that night he executed Mama, he'd been going through women and whores. He'd done some shit that had me going ballistic.

"There is my boy," Papa greeted me. He didn't smile. I hadn't seen him smile since Mama's death. Maxim and I didn't have much to smile about either. Maxim had been on and off pills, going through periods of depression. And I had turned into the spawn of Satan. I learned how to kill a man, turn off any and all emotions, and I learned attachments were trouble.

Papa was more than happy to teach us that lesson. Hence the surprise he managed to knock up a woman. He was adamant about never marrying another woman. They were just something he fucked, then discarded when he was done with them.

"This is Pixie. She'll stay around for a while," he grumbled when all of us remained silent, Pixie's green eyes locked on me and Maxim. I saw fear in them, and I fucking hated it. I could kill a man without a second thought, but seeing fear in women's eyes never sat well with me.

My eyes lowered to her belly, then back up to her face.

Papa must have followed my gaze because he added, "She'll have a baby so you two might have a sibling. It remains to be seen whether it's mine or not. We'll keep her alive until she has the baby."

Papa didn't even try to be subtle about it.

Terror replaced the fear in her eyes, but she quickly tried to school her features, which blew because it meant she'd been through some shit.

"She'll be in the guest room closest to mine," Papa ordered me. He had yet to spare Maxim with a single glance. Just a glance from Papa would have Maxim crying. Sometimes, he'd lose his shit and snap by beating the shit out of him. Then I'd step in and take the bulk of the punishment because Maxim couldn't handle it. It was a joyous affair here. "She can still be useful to me." Then his eyes locked on mine. "I don't mind sharing her. After all, the whore can't be knocked up again."

I clenched my jaw so hard my bones ached. A terse nod and I extended my hand to her for a handshake.

"This way," Papa gritted, jerking her forward.

Poor girl. She knew she'd found herself in a pile of shit. I wondered how she ever even connected with someone like my father. She was too fucking young. She should be in school, not fucking an old man like my papa.

Papa and she headed into the house and up the stairs that Mama used to decorate for every occasion, including summer. She'd have flowers on every step, perfuming the air. Now, this place was just a large mausoleum where the Konstantin men ruled their empire.

I watched after the two of them until they turned the corner at the top of the steps.

"Is she a whore?" Maxim whispered. My twin brother was slowly dying on the inside. Each fucked up thing he witnessed caused him to die a bit more. Papa insisted he needed to become stronger. Good thing he wasn't around too much, busy with chasing the next skirt, leaving me to run the empire and shelter my brother from it all.

That night, I heard her screams. That night I lost my shit and snapped, not my brother.

I got to Pixie's room just in time to see Papa shred her shirt down the front, her full tits spilling free. He held the belt in his other hand and whipped it across her pregnant belly.

"Shut the fuck up," he hissed, reaching with his other hand and squeezing her tits. "You thought because you're pregnant, you're off the hook. You'll pay your dues until that bastard child is out. Then I'll decide whether it's mine or not; whether I'll keep it alive or not."

Rage boiled in the pit of my stomach. The baby was innocent. This fucked up arrangement of their parents shouldn't be for the baby to pay.

My eyes roamed the room until they landed on my old man's gun. The same gun that executed my mother. I reached for it, gripping its handle. I'd learned to shoot by seven, my training starting shortly after my mama's death.

"Get off her, Papa."

He whipped around to look at me, his eyes unfocused. He was drunk as a motherfucker. Alcohol and whores were his coping mechanism since mama died.

"You want to fuck her too?"

His pants were unbuttoned, his dick swinging around like a limp hot dog.

I didn't think; I just reacted, pulling the trigger without an ounce of hesitancy.

Bang.

The bullet hit him in the heart, the small red dot swelling by the second. He slammed back onto the bed, on top of Pixie. His hands came to his chest, over the wound, as he struggled to breathe.

I stepped toward him, my disgust growing with each step. This was what he had been doing since killing Mama. Raping women, young and old, willing and unwilling, whores and virgins. It didn't matter which one Pixie was. She fought against him, but he refused to back off.

Papa's eyes bulged out of his head with each second that death neared. He was my flesh and blood, but it didn't absolve him of his sins. His fear fed into my racing blood, but I felt no remorse as I watched the life drain from his eyes.

Ironic really.

Both of my parents were executed with the same gun.

By a family member.

It didn't bode well for our future. Fucked up family dynamics. It didn't matter though as long as my sister and Tatiana survived it all.

Everyone around the Konstantin family ended up dead. Isla had the best odds of surviving, keeping her mother's last name.

Isla was innocent. Gentle. Kind.

Unlike the rest of us. We breathed and cycled the violence. Over and over again.

I smelled the roses before I even heard her heels clicking against the marble floors. Reason warned me to put some distance between the blonde angel and myself. I didn't heed it. It'd be like lassoing the current and wind, a losing battle.

We were like gasoline and fire, bound to create a raging inferno. Together we could burn this world to ash.

Did it stop me?

Fuck, no. Let the world burn, as long as I had her with me. I had given her up once. Never again although I knew it wouldn't end well.

The world will burn when she learns the truth, my conscience whispered. Tatiana wasn't the forgive and forget type. She was the queen that would get even and smile while she watched the villain bleed.

And still I was unable to keep away. With the chip somewhere out there and the danger coming after her, I had to wed her and quickly. With my last name attached to her, she'd be under the protection of the Thorns of Omertà too.

The door swung open and Tatiana walked in, swaying her hips like she was intent on seducing me. Moot point. All she had to do was look at me and mission accomplished.

"What was that bullshit about 'wait for me' and then I don't even hear from you again," she greeted me, her tone bored but daggers flashed in her eyes.

"Miss Nikolaev, how nice to see you," I greeted her. My eyes traveled over her Valentino, or was it Chanel, black dress. She really had to give up on all that black. She looked great in it but the significance of mourning was getting goddamn old. The only man she should be thinking of was me.

"Jackass," she muttered.

"Do you own any other color besides black?" I questioned her, ignoring her insults. I'd seen her in pink and preferred her in happy colors.

She rolled her eyes as she was about to sit across from my desk, but I tsked, clicking my tongue, stopping her. I patted a spot in front of me.

"How many times do I have to tell you? I'm not a dog," she grumbled, but she still made her way to me. Much to my surprise. Just as she came to stand in front of me, my phone buzzed and her eyes flickered to it.

Her ass leaned against the desk, her front to me.

"Why is my brother texting you?" she questioned, those sparkling blue eyes searching me out.

"Maybe he likes me."

She snickered. "I doubt it." She hopped on the table, then crossed her legs as her eyes traveled over the room. "You have yourself a nice place here."

"Thank you."

"You won't have it for long once Vasili gets a wind of you poaching his territory."

I leaned back into my seat, watching her. She was fiercely loyal to her brothers. To her family and friends. Would she be loyal to me?

"I have you to protect me," I mused.

She chuckled, slowly swinging her long, slim legs up and down. "Somehow I don't think you need my protection. When did you get back?"

The corners of my lips tugged up. She almost sounded like a committed wife eager for her husband's return. "Last night."

"Could have told me," she remarked, her eyes still studying every corner of the space.

"Would you have invited me over and waited for me naked in your bed?"

She snickered. "Let's not get ahead of ourselves."

Whether she knew it or not, she was mine. I was just letting her come to terms but sooner or later, my ring would be on her finger. Adrian was already leaving her mind, and I'd evict him out of her heart and soul. There was room only for one tenant in there.

No sharing here, fucker.

"So why is Sasha messaging you?" I knew she wouldn't drop it. Curiosity killed the cat and all that.

"He needed a getaway plane."

"To?"

I debated lying to her for a fraction of a second but then decided against it. Sasha cashed in on his debt, he was owed nothing more.

"Somewhere." I'd tell her eventually, but I'd let her work for it.

Something flickered in her gaze and she folded her arms. Bracing my knuckles on each side of her, I leaned forward invading her space. She didn't move an inch.

"Why do you want to know where he is?"

She shrugged. "Maybe I want to crash his honeymoon," she retorted flatly.

Her golden hair cascaded down her back, tempting me to touch it. I caved, taking a strand of it between my fingertips.

"Do you not like his intended bride to be?" I asked her.

Her gaze traveled to the balcony, a distant look in her eyes. She let out a heavy sigh, but kept her eyes averted.

"I'm not thrilled to be the last one," she whispered.

I took her chin between my fingers and forced her to face me. "Explain."

"No."

"Yes."

"You're annoying." Then as if she thought that wasn't enough insult, she added, "When are you going to go back to wherever you came from?"

Sardonic amusement filled me. "I thought you just scolded me for not coming sooner."

She shrugged. "No, I scolded you for not letting me know you came back. Big difference."

I brought my lips closer to hers, letting her scent fill my lungs. "Stop avoiding my question."

She blinked, pretending confusion. "Not sure what you mean."

"Your comment about being the last one. What. Did. You. Mean?"

Those pale blues had so much light in them. I could stare into her eyes for days and feel peace unlike ever before.

She exhaled a heavy sigh. "He'll have kids, his own family. And I'll be–" She swallowed. "Maybe I need a few cats," she muttered under her breath.

She's scared to be alone, I realized. My whole life, ever since I witnessed my mother executed in front of me, I'd been alone, hiding behind the wall that my father built around us. But it was lonely. Even with a brother, it was always lonely.

He needed my strength and I... Well, I needed her. My entire life, I searched for her.

Somewhere along the way, I opted not to form attachments. My sister was the first one to start cracking my walls. It was impossible not to create a connection when you cared for a baby - changing diapers, feeding her, reading her stories... only to be puked on and do it all over again.

But all along, I'd been preparing myself that she'd leave one day. She'd get married, have children, find her own life and voice. This time, I'd be ready. I wasn't ready for my mother's loss. She was my first attachment and she was brutally erased from existence. So deep down, I was certain that it would happen again.

Maybe it was exactly that which resonated between Tatiana and I, but I failed to see it all along.

"Don't get a cat," I quipped.

She raised her eyebrows. "Why not?"

"I'm allergic to cats."

Tatiana grinned while her eyes twinkled mischievously. "All the more reason to adopt a few. Don't you think so?"

This was the woman I knew. This was the woman that captured me from that first fleeting glance and she didn't even know it. I remembered the day I spotted her like it was yesterday. It lived in my memory like a flickering light in the darkness.

Her rose scent invaded my nostrils and my hand slid to her cheek, palming it.

"You're not going to be alone," I told her firmly.

As if she hated that word and hated being seen as vulnerable, she snickered softly, but she remained silent and our bodies flush against each other. Her body trembled at my touch, and I couldn't help but wonder how receptive she was to Adrian's touch.

Fuck, I had never felt anything like this with another woman, and I'd had my share of women. The attraction between us was undeniable. It sizzled in the air. It was explosive enough to shake the French Quarter like a category five hurricane.

I parted her legs. Sliding my palms under her ass, I tugged her into position so she'd straddle my right leg. Her core was hot, burning me through the material of my suit pants. I angled her so her clit pressed against my muscled quad and a soft moan spilled from her lips.

I dipped my head down, her half-lidded eyes watching me. She wanted me, almost as much as I wanted her. Her lips parted for me and I took her mouth for a hard kiss while pressing my knee between her thighs. I could feel her muscles clenching.

Her breasts pushed against me. Like a cat rubbing against its owner. My tongue danced with hers as she kept rubbing against me. Anywhere. Everywhere. I cupped her face between my hands, deepening the kiss and trailing my mouth down her jaw, then her neck where her pulse beat wildly.

I drew a lazy circle around her racing pulse with the tip of my tongue, then sucked on it. Another moan vibrated through the room, mixing with the sounds of New Orleans.

"I'm going to fuck you and you're going to scream my name," I rasped against her throat. "For the whole fucking world to hear. But today, we'll start with New Orleans."

The two of us were like an inferno together. Match and fuse.

Her fingernails dug into my shoulders. "Whatever you want, just don't stop."

I chuckled darkly. There was no stopping. Even if the world burned right now, we'd burn with it. Together.

My fingers already worked on the zipper of her dress. One slash sounded through the air and the dress fell down to her waist. My mouth continued its journey south, over her dainty collarbone, then to her tits. I gently nipped her nipple through the lacy black material. She grabbed my head and let out a frustrated sound.

"Rip the bra off," she demanded. I bit harder at her breast and she yelped, her eyes narrowing on me. "What the fuck?"

"We fuck my way," I growled.

She rolled her eyes. Actually rolled her eyes. "Fine, old man. I don't have all day and night, so speed it up."

A sardonic breath left me.

"For that, moya luna, I'm going to fuck you for the rest of the day and night," I said, smiling slightly sadistically. "Until you beg me to stop."

"Fat chance."

In one swift move, I unclipped her bra and discarded it, then took her erect nipple into my mouth, sucking it. I moved to her other nipple, lapping, pulling and biting. Hard. She ground against my thigh, humping my leg shamelessly. Her thighs trembled. Her moans heightened. Her fingers reached for my zipper eagerly, but I wrapped my fingers around her wrist and halted her movements.

"Stand up." She blinked confused and a look of uncertainty crossed her face. "Dress off."

She obeyed, wiggling out of her dress, letting it pool on the floor around her feet like a black lake. Her chest rose and fell to the rhythm of her frantic heartbeats, her eyes darkening a shade as she watched me.

My eyes traveled over her body. Her skin was flawless, but for the small scars on her forearms and her stomach. My chest tightened remembering how she got them. In all my fucking life, I had never been so scared. Not when I saw my mother shot in front of my eyes. Not when my own life hung by a thread.

But that night, I tasted terror. Almost losing her was strong enough to tear me apart.

I reached out my hand and traced the faint scars. Her eyes followed the movements. I watched the invisible walls build around Tatiana, hiding her feelings. I didn't want her hiding from me. I wanted her fears, her happiness, her love. Her fucking everything.

As if she couldn't bear me touching her, she snatched my hand and wrapped it around the front of her neck. My skin was several shades darker against her snowy skin. But our hearts beat to the same frantic, wild rhythm.

I squeezed her neck, just slightly, testing the waters. "Does that turn you on, moya luna?"

A tremor rolled through her.

"Maybe." Her voice shook almost as much as her body.

"There is no maybe," I told her. She watched me with that cautious look in her eyes. As if she had been burned too many times expressing herself. "It's either you like it or you don't. No right or wrong answer here."

She remained quiet, her breathing frantic and her body tempting me. My dick was rock hard, urging me to fuck her my way.

"I prefer to fuck hard," I said, moving my fingers under her panties and into the folds between her legs. She spread her thighs for me, and I dipped my index finger inside her. A faint, soft moan and her eyes hazed over.

I took my finger out of her hot entrance and brought it to her lips. Her lips parted and she sucked it clean. Grabbing her hair from behind, I brought her lips to mine and stopped an inch from her mouth.

"Show me your true colors, Tatiana," I demanded. "And I'll show you mine."

"I like it rough," she croaked. "Borderline pain."

That was all it took for my control to snap. I rose to my full height and took her lips in a punishing kiss.

"You'll need a safe word," I growled against her mouth. She sucked in a breath, her eyes glimmering like the palest blue sapphires. "Actually, your mouth will be too full for talking. Tap any surface and I'll stop."

In one swift move, I ripped the underwear off her body, throwing them on the desk, then thrust her against the window overlooking the city. Butt naked. It was a good thing the window was tinted from the outside.

Her tits and pussy pressed against the glass. She was so wet, her thighs glistening with her juices. Shoving my dress pants down my hips, I freed my cock.

Instantly she whimpered, wiggling her ass, arching against me. I kicked her legs open and roughly palmed her round ass. I smacked it hard, leaving a pink mark on her beautiful skin. She gulped but no protest came. Leaning over, I reached for her drenched panties, rolled them into a ball, and stuffed them into her mouth.

She stilled, her eyes wider pools of the clearest lagoons. She gagged, her eyes watered but she didn't tap. I remained waiting, testing the water, but she didn't move. She splayed her fingers across the window, glancing over her shoulder and staring at me with lust.

A nod and I thrust into her in one go, filling her to the hilt. She cried out, but her panties muffled her moan. I began to move inside her, plowing into her rough and fast. I smacked her ass, then drove into her again.

She whimpered, but it wasn't in pain. It was in pleasure. Her back arched and she tilted her head, as if she was offering herself to me. My teeth sank into her neck. The scent of roses drowned all my senses.

I spanked her again. And again. Hard. Merciless. Rough. I was punishing her for the years I lived without her. Punishing her for loving Adrian. Fuck, I was too far gone.

I grabbed her jaw and turned her head to stare at me. Her eyes half-lidded, she watched me fuck her and by the look on her face, she loved what she was seeing.

"Touch your tits," I ordered roughly. "Show the world whose slut you are."

Goddamn it. I just about blew my load when she did as I said. She pinched her nipples, her body shuddered just as I drove into her. She tugged on her nipples, caressed the shape of her heavy breasts. I pumped harder and faster, watching goosebumps prickle on every inch of her skin.

Her muffled moans increased in pitch. My angel was just as depraved as I was, and I fucking loved it. I pulled her back slightly from the window and bent her over, so I'd penetrate her deeper. I needed more of her. Her pussy clenched around me while I pumped into her deeper. Her hand left the window and I was certain she'd tap, but instead, she pushed it between her thighs, opening her thighs wider and she rubbed her clit.

Her inner muscles strangled my cock, the friction on her clit wreaking havoc through her body. I grabbed both her ass cheeks and pounded her mercilessly. I craved this. *Her*. It was never this good with anyone, but her. She was the only one I wanted.

A bead of sweat trickled down her spine and I glanced down at her bruised ass. I loved the goddamn view, as I pounded into her, this position allowing me deep penetration. I wanted to put a baby in her belly. Put cuffs on her wrist and tie her to me forever.

She spat her underwear out, then screamed.

"Illias… Oh. My. Fucking. God." Her legs quivered. She fell on her hands and knees, our sweat dripping on the hardwood floor.

Her golden hair brushed against my sleeve with every movement and I wrapped it around my wrist, pulling her back so I could take her mouth again. Her insides tensed and she moaned into my mouth. I swallowed a muffled 'I'm coming' and relished in her inner muscles strangling my dick as she shook with the intensity of her release.

Her face was flushed and she looked thoroughly fucked. But I wasn't done with her yet. I wrapped an arm around her lower stomach, massaging her clit to milk another climax out of her. And all the while, I continued driving into her doggy-style. Like a madman. Like a possessed man.

This was a carnal fuck. A desperate fuck. A need so deep that I feared what left my soul as my balls tightened. I shot cum into her clenching, greedy pussy, emptying inside her just as she found her second climax.

Slowly, I pulled out, enjoying the view of my cum dripping from her cunt. There was something so fucking erotic and carnal about the view.

Tatiana collapsed, burying her face in her hands and her pink ass with my handprints staring back at me.

"Are you tired?"

Still panting, she met my gaze and her lips curved up. "Is that all you got?"

A deep chuckle vibrated in my chest. "We've only just gotten started," I drawled.

Her eyes widening was the only thing that betrayed her. But stubbornness was also Tatiana's downfall.

"Unless you want to rest," I quipped.

She shook her head and I had to stifle a grin. Heading for the bathroom, I grabbed a clean rag and soaked it under the lukewarm water. Then I returned to her and started washing her pink, swollen pussy.

Her shoulders tensed each time I wiped the wet cloth against her thighs, then discarded the rag into the trash can.

"Too rough?" I asked her.

Her chest rose and fell with each breath.

"No."

"Then what's the matter?"

Her eyes darted away from me for a second, then returned to me. "You left your clothes on."

I glanced down at myself. My pants were unbuttoned, my shirt halfway undone. I didn't remember doing it, though not surprising. When it came to her, all my control bolted out of the room, leaving me a hungry beast.

"Want me to strip?" I offered.

She sat up, turning around to face me, still buck naked. Fuck, her tits were gorgeous. Full and pear shaped, with pink nipples that would make any man mad.

"Might be better if we were both naked. You know equality and all that."

The only betrayal of her nervousness was the flush coloring her neck.

"I've never been much for equality," I told her, lifting her off the floor and sitting her on my desk.

Parting her legs, I admired her glistening pussy.

Mine.

She was all mine.

THIRTY
TATIANA

Illias' fingers felt so hot against my skin, it sent a shudder down my spine.

Truth was that my ass stung and burned against the cool mahogany desk. But I had to go and taunt him.

He leaned over, reaching into his drawer. His grin turned lazy as he pulled out a black box. I eyed it curiously as he lifted the lid. A gold-and-diamond piece of jewelry sat in the box, just for my taking. Yet something about it had me hesitating. What the—

No, it couldn't be.

"What's that?" I asked.

His grin turned so naughty that my heart actually fluttered. When Illias smiled, he was downright dangerous for a woman's heart.

"A butt plug."

My mouth gaped open. He had to be joking. The look on his face told me he wasn't. The dark lustful expression in his gaze told me he was dead serious about it.

I shook my head. Then just to ensure he understood what that meant, I said clearly, "No."

Konstantin's grip tightened on the box. "I don't like when you deny me."

"Well, tough shit." I shook my head incredulously at the nerve of this man. We weren't even an item and he was shoving a butt plug my way. "Get used to it. You're not touching my back door."

Illias' dark gaze burned into me, and I sensed he took my denial as a personal challenge.

"Yes, I am," he drawled.

"No, you're not," I sneered. "And what, you just happened to have an extra butt plug sitting around?"

My voice was laced with jealousy thinking about Illias doing anything with other women. I mentally slapped myself. This was just a hookup. Nothing more. Nothing less.

"I bought it for you and waited for the opportune moment to broach the subject." I shook my head. This man was mental. Or maybe I was. I sighed. We probably both were batshit crazy.

"It will never be the opportune moment to shove that thing in my butt."

The corner of his lips tugged up and I had to fight the temptation to lean over and trace my tongue over his lips.

"Now is the right time," he drawled, his voice pure seduction. "And you'll thank me for it."

I snickered. He didn't know me if he thought he could convince me to put that thing in my ass.

"The hell I am. This is over." I was just about to slip off the table when I paused. His smile never faltered, but something dark and smug flashed in his eyes. Maybe I could play this into my favor. "Unless–"

I waited… and waited. "Unless?" he asked with an arrogant expression. It took all my self-restraint not to smile victoriously.

"Unless you tell me where Sasha went with your plane," I said, the words pouring out in a single breath.

"Get on my lap and bend over."

"No." His dark gaze narrowed on my face. This man really didn't like to hear the word no. "First you tell me."

"You think I'd cheat you."

I shrugged. "First information, then I'll bend over."

My cheeks heated, which was ridiculous. I sat naked on his desk and such a simple word was making me blush.

"Russia," he said, his eyes flaring with heat and I had a feeling it had nothing to do with my brother's trip and everything to do with me bending over.

"Where in Russia?" I demanded to know, although my guess would be he went to our family estate there. "Russia is a big damn country."

"I didn't ask for details," he retorted and his smug smile of satisfaction spread across his beautiful face. "Now, bend over my lap and show me your ass."

My nipples hardened at his demanding voice and juices coated my inner thighs, quite possibly Illias' desk too. Sliding off the desk, the sticky wetness smeared a trail of evidence. I had never in my life been so turned on.

I bent over his lap, my ass jutted up in the air. I didn't know whether this position was humiliating me or turning me on. I shifted slightly and froze. His rock-hard bulge pressed against my lower belly and my thighs clamped together.

Definitely turning me on.

He trailed his finger gently, then his palm cupped my ass cheek. "Does it hurt?"

I glanced over my shoulder, but he wasn't looking at me. His eyes were focused on my red ass.

"No." A terse nod and he reached into the drawer again. "Please tell me you don't have two butt plugs. I can only handle one," I said exasperated.

"Lube," he answered as another deep chuckle vibrated through him. I felt it all the way down to my toes. My chest warmed for the first time in years. "Unless you are wet for me already?"

He lifted his hips, pressing his hard bulge into my belly. "Because I'm hard for you."

His fingers dipped into my opening, then smeared my wetness around my clit. I sucked in a breath, a tremor rolling down my spine.

"Oh, moya luna, you're soaked."

He flicked my clit and pleasure shot through me. He dragged the wetness back toward my ass and circled it, coating it with my own slickness. He applied the slightest pressure against my forbidden hole with his finger, then pulled it out.

I inhaled deeply, tensing.

"Relax." A soft, tightly reined in command.

I released a breath and he pressed his finger deeper into my back hole, and my hips pressed harder against his thighs. With one hand he reached between my legs and pushed his long, thick finger into my pussy, then started fucking it. In and out. In and out. He lazily finger-fucked me until I was panting and writhing against him.

"Look at you." His voice was deep and hoarse. Almost reverent. "Moya luna is so wet, her juices are dripping all over my pants."

"It's a nice Tom Ford three piece suit," I said, my voice breathless. How I recognized it was a Tom Ford suit was beyond me. "You sure you don't want to take your clothes off?"

He chuckled again, his finger never ceasing his finger-fucking as he teased my clit.

"I like you creaming all over my pants." He lowered his head, his mouth brushing against my ear. "It makes this suit worth so much more than anything else I own."

He pushed a second finger inside my channel and a whimper left my lips. Slutty and needy.

"I can feel your greedy pussy clenching around my fingers. But you want my cock, don't you?" Another moan. Another shudder. Pleasure built and built. "You want to be fucked senseless. Don't you, Tatiana," he drawled.

God, his deep voice saying dirty things was enough to make me shatter right now.

He nipped my earlobe, his teeth scraping against the sensitive skin. "Actually, you fucking love being fucked. Owned."

My pussy was grinding against his hand. My moans becoming louder. And my body tethered on the edge of an orgasm.

"Please."

It was a soft plea, whispered by a voice that didn't sound like mine.

"You begging me for your pleasure is the sexiest thing I have ever heard," he murmured against my ear. "Almost as good as your pussy clamping down on my cock."

His palm rubbed my clit hard as he kept pushing two fingers in and out of me. He refused to ease down, causing friction with each movement. Then something cool drizzled down my crack and I tensed.

"It's just lube." He pressed down on my clit and an orgasm shot through me like fireworks, white dots behind my eyelids. "I'm going to finger your asshole now. I'm going to own all of you."

I was still flying high when Illias circled my asshole, while he kept circling my clit. Pleasure stretched and my brain wasn't fast enough to send a warning through my body.

Another orgasm built and he breached the tight ring of muscle with his fingertip.

"You'll love my cock inside your ass," he growled. "I'll own every inch of you, Tatiana. You won't know where you end and I begin. It's how it was always meant to be. You're mine."

He pushed his finger deeper and I stiffened, attempting to push him out.

"Illias—"

"Don't you fucking keep me out of your ass. I own it, I will fuck it, and goddammit, you will let me in."

My second orgasm shot through me like a volcano and his finger pushed all the way inside the virgin hole, claiming it as his. As I rode a wave of pleasure, he pushed his finger in and out, and I writhed against him.

Then he pulled his finger out and he reached for the plug.

"Open your lips," he ordered. My mouth immediately parted and he brought the plug to my lips. "Suck."

And I did. Good God, I must have lost my mind, but there was something so filthy about it all and I fucking loved it.

Before my brain could process it, he already had it at my back entrance. His right hand resumed teasing my pussy and my clit, while he pressed the end of the plug against my forbidden hole with his other hand. A shudder rolled down my back.

"You're going to love having your ass filled with my cock." The dark seduction in his voice wrapped around me like a blanket. "For now, we'll just keep the plug. I don't want to hurt you when I fuck your ass."

He slid a finger into my pussy at the same time as the plug. Both my holes filled, I had never felt so full. Before I could even process it, Illias' palm connected with my clit with a sharp slap.

Sharp pleasure, the mind-blowing kind, burst through me and I swore stars played in my vision. He resumed fingering my sensitive clit, murmuring words into my ear.

"Your body is mine," he said, nipping my earlobe. "Your heart and soul will be too."

I should tell him off. Except, I forgot English, Russian. Any language. The only sounds falling from my lips were moans and whimpers.

Then he lifted me off his lap and bent me over the table. The utter possession in his darkness had me panting and my pussy clenching with the need to feel him inside me again. The sound of the zipper filled the room. Illias' fingers dug into my hips, his chest covered my back and his cock forced his way inside me. In one powerful thrust, he filled me and his groin brushed against my tortured skin. The friction sizzled; pain and pleasure mixed.

His pace built up, faster and harder. The slap of flesh against flesh and my moans echoed through the room. My breathing turned harsh. The orgasm hit me like a tsunami, crashing through me with such intensity it had my thighs quivering.

His hold tightened, digging harder into my hips and he spilled inside me with his own grunt.

His front covered my back. His breath brushed against my ear. Warm liquid filled my walls.

"We'll be doing this all day and all night, Tatiana. Until you give me your all."

THIRTY-ONE
KONSTANTIN

A sardonic breath pulled in my chest as I read her message.

Returning the butt plug.
Shove it up your ass.
P.S. I disinfected it so it's all ready for you.

Not only did she send me a sassy message but she also played me. She was enroute to Russia, landing in Moscow in about three hours. She even managed to shake all of her guards. I didn't know whether to be proud of the angel or angry with her. She played me to get information on her brother.

Lovely.

Pussy whipped might be the right term here.

Picking up the phone, I dialed Vasili.

"Konstantin," he grumbled. "Not a good time."

"Nikolaev," I greeted back. "I imagine there's panic in your household because you can't find your sister and your brother kidnapped his bride."

His silence was all the answer I needed. I didn't break it, letting him weigh his options. There were none of course. I had a tracker on Tatiana; he didn't.

"What do you know?" he asked and even over the line I could hear he was pissed off.

"Tatiana is in Moscow," I told him. If I was to claim her as my wife, I'd need her brothers on my side and working with me, not against me.

"What the fuck is she doing in Moscow?" he hissed.

"Maybe she's on the way to your family home there."

"She doesn't consider Russia home," he said pensively. "She avoids visiting there whenever she can." It shouldn't surprise me, yet somehow it did. "So why would she go to Russia willingly?"

That was a good question. Unless she had come up with a clue that Adrian left her and it led her to Russia.

"That's for you to figure out," I told him. "Your brother Sasha is in Russia too. He needed my plane, and it took him close to your ancestral home. I'd imagine he took his kidnapped bride there."

I ended the call and sent my pilot coordinates. And all the while the first time I touched Tatiana played in my mind. That gazebo at the edge of the property that overlooked Patapsco River. It was the week I flew into D.C. for Isla's concert. She went to a party with her friends while I handled some business.

I'd spotted her the moment she strode into the party with twin college boys on each of her arms. Those two boys were wrapped around her little finger. Nico Morrelli and I had just finished our meeting, and I watched her crash the party with two kids. Because that was what they were - boys.

I watched as a man, assumingly her bodyguard, pulled them away from her and led them out of the house. The pale-haired blonde angel just watched after them, annoyance on her face and her heels tapping impatiently against the marble foyer.

"Jerk," I saw her mouth, glaring after them.

She looked like a tempting woman that needed to be fucked thoroughly in that strapless, sparkling black mini dress, displaying her long legs. And that fucking blonde mane. Jesus, what I'd give to wrap it around my wrist and grip it as I fucked her.

Then something flashed in her eyes and she reached for the nearby eighteenth century desk. Shamelessly, she opened one drawer after another, searching for something.

"Aha." She victoriously pulled out a piece of paper and a pen, then wrote a note.

She reached out to a nearby server and handed him the paper, then disappeared into the back gardens that led out to the river.

To my surprise, the server came over to me and handed me the paper. When I raised my eyebrow in surprise, he just murmured, "She said to give it to you by the door."

I opened the note. There weren't many things that surprised me anymore. But Tatiana Nikolaev certainly managed to surprise me.

I re-read the note again.

You ruined my opportunity to get laid.

Now it's up to you to satisfy those urges.

Meet me at the gazebo.

Glancing up, I almost expected her to be back and admit her joke in poor taste. But she wasn't there. So I folded up the note, tucked it into my suit pocket and headed for the gazebo.

I headed through the backyard, the sounds of crickets and rustle of water filling the air. The path was cobblestone and the scent of fresh grass seeped into my lungs. I couldn't believe I was even entertaining this young girl's whim.

That was until I saw her. The night was dark but the full moon threw light over her, making her hair appear almost the same color as the moon. So fucking poetic but here I was, unable to tear my gaze from her pacing form.

So unlike anything else I had ever done, I let my impulse guide me. I closed the distance between us, the scent of roses mingling with the fresh air. She stilled and her spine straightened, but she didn't turn around.

She stood there waiting, staring away from me and waiting for my first move. My hand came to rest on her bare shoulder and she attempted to turn around.

I wrapped my other hand around her waist and urged her towards the wall made of vines and plants.

"Not sure how I messed up your opportunity," I hissed into her ear. "I'll satisfy your urges but you have to follow my rules."

A visible shudder rolled down her body. I pressed my body against her back and instinctively she leaned back into me. Something deep inside me wanted to pound its chest and roar 'Mine' to the world. I shouldn't have gone further. I should have ended it. But it was too late.

*I pressed my lips against her earlobe, the scent of roses even stronger there. Then I realized. It was her. She smelled like roses but the memories that scent usually brought never came. I stared at her light hair, mesmerized by the girl that wasn't even legal to drink, and I knew she was **the one.***

"Do you consent?" Desire for her made my Russian accent thicker. We had barely gotten started and she was tearing down all my walls.

"Yes." One word. It was all it took. In a swift move, I pulled my tie off and used to bind her hands with it.

My hands roamed the curves of her body, lower and lower, testing whether she'd stop me. She didn't. Goosebumps rose on her skin. A small moan sounded between us. And her ass ground against me. But there was something else.

Her arousal.

I could smell it. I could practically taste it. My fingers grabbed the hem of her dress and I yanked it up in one move. She wore only a thong, her round ass just tempting me to get down on my knees and bite it.

Burying my head into the back of her neck, a groan left my lips as I cupped her ass and squeezed. Hard. There'd be time for other stuff later. My mouth latched on to the curve of her neck, sucking and biting. Marking her.

Her moans and little noises vibrated through the air, driving me insane. Making me feel like a teenager fucking a girl for the first time. She shifted her head to the side, but I wrapped my hand around her throat and pressed her against my chest.

My dick pushed against her back and by the shudder she must have liked it.

Her breaths became small pants. Moans and whimpers.

"Eyes forward," I rasped, gravel in my voice thick. *"Understood?"*

"Y-yes."

Releasing her throat, my fingers latched on to her beautiful, thick hair that reminded me of ancient stories of a beautiful seductress with a mane the colors of gold. I forced her to bend forward, my feet nudging hers apart.

"Open for me, moya luna."

She instantly obeyed and spread those long legs eagerly.

"Please," she breathed.

Releasing her hair, I brought my hand and slid it between her thighs. She was drenched, her pussy grinding, eager for my fingers.

"So soaked," I grunted as she shuddered in response.

In one move, I shredded her thong off, then traced my finger over her pussy drenched with her slickness. I purposely took my time before brushing my fingers over her clit. Then finally caving into my own desire, I brushed over her clit and a violet shudder tore through me.

"Ahhhh." Her moan, her shudders. It told me she was close. I traced lazy circles over her clit then plunged a thick finger inside her.

"Please. More," she begged in a needy voice.

A dark chuckle vibrated through my chest. "You don't get to demand, moya luna. I choose how much and how hard to give it to you. Understood?"

"Yes, yes. Whatever you want. Just give it to me."

A sardonic breath left me. No woman, never mind as young as her, ever dared to be so vocal about her wants. It was refreshing to see this one wasn't ashamed of her desire. As she shouldn't be. It was beautiful to witness. She owned her pleasure.

"You want me inside you?" I growled, barely keeping myself in check. Not the most expert touch of a woman had ever impacted me as this. I knew there was something about this woman that drove it.

"Yes." It was all the confirmation I needed. *"I need you inside me. Please."*

A satisfied growl left me as I continued finger-fucking her, teasing her clit. Her moans became louder. Her pussy ground against my hand hungrily. Demanding her pleasure. I couldn't wait anymore to own her.

I pulled my fingers out and reached for the condom in my pocket. I tore open the condom, almost regretting having something separating us. But I never fucked without a condom. Rolling it onto my length, I poised my cock at her hot entrance and lost all my control.

In a single thrust, I plunged forward and buried myself deep inside her. Her scream tore through the air. Her body tensed. Her moan turned into a painful whimper.

"Fuck." I certainly hoped she wasn't a virgin. Her pussy walls strangled my cock, sending pleasurable shudders through me and urging me to move. To fuck her hard and senseless. But I needed to ensure she was okay. That she still wanted this.

"Don't you fucking dare stop," she hissed, surprising me. "Make it good."

I should have known at that very moment, she was mine. Or rather, I was hers.

"Your wish is my command," I rasped.

I pulled out slowly, her walls clenching me greedily, then plunged inside her again. Contrary to my instinct, I moved slowly, letting her adjust to my size. Her pussy was tight, clenching around my shaft like a vise.

Each thrust inside her was like heaven. Her moans were music to my ears. They became louder and louder. My fingers dug into her soft hips, not wanting to hinder her noises, but we'd get caught otherwise. I brought my hand over her mouth, as my hips plunged into her, harder and faster. Deeper.

I wanted to own her. Possess her.

I rolled my hips, pounding deeper into her, my fingertips sinking into her flesh. This animalistic need for her was foreign to me. But I knew it would bind our lives together. In one way or another. I fucked her harder, powering into her with a maddening speed. I kept one hand protective on her hips so she wouldn't fall down on her knees. My raw thrusts fed the hunger, stealing corners of her soul and merging it with mine.

This need between us was new, raw, and hungry. My pace

increased and my rhythm spiraled out of fucking control, which never fucking happened.

Her teeth bit into my palm, muffling her final hoarse scream. Her orgasm was the most beautiful sight I had ever seen. I fucked her like a madman through her orgasm, relishing in her pleasure and pain. I kept thrusting through her orgasm, her walls squeezing around my cock while her muffled screams vibrated between us.

Another thrust and I joined her, finding my own release. For the first time in my life, I wished I spilled my seed into a woman and got her pregnant.

Because this one was meant for me.

The feeling was too intense. Too strong. It consumed and burned through me like a raging inferno. Careful not to hurt her, I pulled out of her tight cunt and looked down at the condom.

A shock stilled me as I stared down at the bloody condom, sheathing my cock. Instantly satisfaction washed over me at the realization that I was her first.

"Mine," I rasped, raw possession washing over me. "You'll always be mine."

A set of footsteps registered, and I quickly pulled her dress down, then buckled my pants.

"I'll come for you, moya luna," I vowed, tucking her ripped thong into my pocket. "And you'll wait for me."

She was still dazed from her orgasm. But her soft, "Yes," gave me her promise.

I knew a day would come when our paths would cross again. I hoped it wouldn't, knowing she'd be my weakness open for exploitation. Something I'd fought all these years. It was the reason I had let her go once.

But I'm Illias fucking Konstantin. It was time to claim my bride.

THIRTY-TWO
TATIANA

I stood outside Moscow, in the same parking lot Adrian brought me to when we eloped. It seemed like a different lifetime. A different girl. Yet, it was a mere few years ago.

Somewhere in the distance I could hear the squeaking noise of an iron gate.

Squeak. Clank. Squeak. Clank.

My eyes traveled over the vast landscape. I couldn't see the home or establishment that it belonged to. Only the same deserted gravel parking lot that looked just as depressing in the summer as it did in winter.

The soft breeze traveled through the air. Summer in Russia could be pleasant. But it was Russia. The first thought that came with Russia was oppression. Medieval methods. Beautiful people, but I was an American girl through and through. When I thought of home, New Orleans came to mind.

Exiting the car, I slipped my duffle bag over my shoulder, cringing at the idea of someone seeing me with a duffle bag. But I had no choice but to pack in a rush using Sasha's duffle bag.

Jet lag and lack of sleep pulled on my muscles. Memories plagued my brain. Adrian's words from that night echoing, over and over again.

There is blood here. It's a clue.

"A clue," I muttered, the cool summer breeze sweeping through. "What clue, Adrian?"

I was too tired, my brain not sharp enough to see what Adrian wanted me to see. I dug my cell phone out of my duffle bag and turned it on for the first time since I landed. I had twenty missed calls from Vasili, five messages from him, and two missed calls from Konstantin.

"Only two," I scoffed, rolling my eyes. "No matter. Just a hookup," I mumbled under my breath, then checked my brother's messages. I couldn't help but let out a sardonic breath. It would seem the entire Nikolaev clan was enroute, if not already, in our Russian home, crashing Sasha's pre-honeymoon. I shook my head. I wondered if Konstantin slipped them a tip or if Vasili figured it out on his own.

No matter. They were on the same continent as me. Maybe that was for the best anyhow. If I learned of something critical, I might need Vasili's help. My brows furrowed. Maybe I should continue to keep him out of this.

I'd hate for the Yakuza to go after him and his family too. Yeah, maybe it was best I keep this to myself.

I slid my phone into my pocket.

Then, looking around, I tried to eye the spot where Adrian and I danced. The sun was setting, and I didn't have much time left. As I turned in a slow circle, I eyed the area, my Coach flats crunching against the gravel.

The shadows grew darker and so did my memories. That dance. The words to our song. A crawling sensation pricked at my mind and anxiety slid down my spine.

Step. Step. Step.

I paused on my third one. The gravel sounded different under my feet. I took a step to the left and the sound didn't repeat. Back to the right... *thud.*

Uncaring of my jeans, I lowered onto my knees and started shifting the gravel as tiny stones dug under my nails. I didn't care. I kept digging, until I felt it.

A box.

"Oh my gosh, he left a box," I muttered. It could mean only one thing. Adrian knew he was about to die. He was certain of it. He had been gone a lot before his death, traveling all over the world in secrecy. When I suggested coming along, he denied me. He claimed it was a project he was working on and couldn't risk anyone knowing about it.

By the time I finally had the box in my hands, my fingers were filthy and bleeding, but I was too focused on the box. I needed to know what was in it. I kept pushing the button but the box wouldn't open.

"Goddamn it," I grunted in frustration. I kept shaking the box, a lone thud back and forth. There was only one item in there. "How in the hell do I open this?" I groaned in a whisper.

Then I spotted it. A tiny keyhole. I groaned. Of course, I needed a key. It couldn't be as simple as finding a box and opening it to find out what the fuck was going on.

"Oh my gosh," I murmured. "The key!"

I reached for my necklace where the key hung right next to the rose thorned pendant. Taking it off my necklace, I attempted to put it into the keyhole. It didn't work. I tried again, pushing left and right, up and down. Nothing.

"Goddamn it," I hissed. With a sigh, I put the key back on my necklace and hooked it around my neck. It was all connected, I knew it. Why in the fuck couldn't have Adrian left steps one through ten, instead of this game of hide-and-seek?

A gust of wind swept through and Adrian's words came along with it. Or maybe my mind was playing tricks on me. *There is blood here, Tatiana.*

"Whose blood?" I muttered. My eyes roamed the area. He said his father died here. Maybe he wanted me to find his body. Or maybe he wanted me to avenge his death. Jesus, how many years ago was that?

Adrian never revealed who killed his father. He never even told me his father's name. He never really explained what had happened that night in this parking lot.

Raising to my feet, box in my hands, I shoved it into my duffle bag and headed back to my rental.

Time to visit Sasha and his kidnapped bride.

I walked down the hotel hall with the duffle bag over my shoulder and key in my hand.

The Carlton in Moscow was the epitome of style, class, and luxury in typical Ritz manner. But I preferred the American version of the Ritz. In my attempt to blend in, I stuck to speaking Russian. I didn't want to attract more attention to myself than needed.

Tomorrow I'd take a flight to our Siberian home and there'd be some family reunion going on. Unless Sasha kills us all and that was definitely not out of the realm of possibilities.

Finally finding my room, I stopped in front of it and swiped the key against the magnetic strip. The door clicked and I pushed it open. I slammed the door shut behind me and leaned against it with a sigh.

I was exhausted.

I took in the room. A large bed that looked inviting. Two night-stands, one on each side. A large sofa and a corner desk for busi-nessmen that were crazy enough to invest in this country. But the view behind the large window was magnificent.

St. Basil's Cathedral with all its magnificent domes and colors stretched in the distance, and for a moment, all I could do was stare and imagine hundreds of years of history. This cathedral had seen the rise and fall of an empire and the Romanov family. How many Tsars had gone to pray there? Any?

One of the earliest memories of Vasili's bedtime stories to me were of the Romanov princess that might have escaped. Princess Anastasia. Though she was murdered along with the rest of the family, there were fake claims for years that she'd survived. It was enough to get my imagination going. I kept asking my big brother to tell me stories about the princes roaming this world, hiding in plain sight from the evil Rasputin. *Anastasia* was my favorite movie, but I needed more fairy tales associated with it. My brother appeased me, although he always concluded with 'this is not real' statement.

I shook my head at the ridiculous stories.

Striding into the room, I dropped the duffle bag on the coffee table and headed to the bathroom. I took a long shower and scrubbed my skin raw, letting the hot water trickle down my body.

Once I stepped out, I felt refreshed. I padded back into the room and dug through the bag for something to wear to sleep. Once dressed in shorts and loose tank top, I crawled under the covers and fell asleep the moment my head hit the pillow.

A soft click woke me out of my deep sleep. I blinked. Did I hear it or dream it?

I held my breath. *Click.*

There it was again. My heart stopped beating for an agonizingly long second and I blinked my eyes, getting used to the dark. Keeping my movements to a minimum, I slid out of the bed on the side closest to my duffle bag and reached for the Beretta I had tucked into the side pocket. Then I remembered. I needed the silencer.

I couldn't have Moscow police on me tonight.

I screwed on the silencer. One. Two. Three twists. My hands were slightly unsteady but I got it on. I raised my arms and aimed, keeping my hands steady despite my wild beating heart.

My brothers would be so proud, I thought for no reason.

Without thinking, I put my finger on the trigger, keeping it aimed at the shadow.

"Stop there or I'll shoot," I called out. The shadows stopped. A man. I couldn't see his face. It was too dark. But he was tall and lean.

One step. "Last warning."

He started advancing, taking another step and I shot. *Bang.*

The body fell down with a loud thud and I waited, holding my breath. But nobody else entered. No other shadows moved. Slowly, gun still in hand, I padded silently towards the body. I kept my guard up and my eyes sharp. Nothing.

Then I flicked the light on. A body lay slumped; the face turned away from me. Cautiously, I pushed it with my feet, and the dead weight rolled over. Annoyance flared inside me.

"Are you for real?" I hissed.

The Yakuza in Russia. The world was going to hell in a handbasket.

THIRTY-THREE
KONSTANTIN

Tatiana fled to Russia and I followed.

I could have sent one of my local men in Moscow to retrieve her, but I didn't trust anyone there with her. Not fully. Not in Russia. Men let their savage free in Russia, knowing the corruption of officials would get them off the hook for anything and everything.

Besides, the fucking Yakuza roamed the streets in Moscow, and I didn't trust them not to try anything. I followed the digital trail thanks to the tracker on her. She was no longer in Moscow but while here there was only one stop she made, outside of the hotel and airport. So I headed to the exact location, following the coordinates.

"This is it," Boris announced, his voice tense. The moment I recognized the area, I knew why. "Why would she come here?" he questioned, reflecting my own thoughts exactly.

It couldn't be a coincidence. I didn't believe in them, especially so many. Not when it came to this fucking place. The very same place where my mother was murdered. The same place where my father spared a boy on my request and that boy came back with a fucking vengeance.

I never saw him coming. He took my woman. Then he used her and made her a target.

Anger crept beneath my skin, burning through me. The rage tasted like acid. The memories tasted bitter. Fuck!

"I have to talk to her." I have to find out what the fuck she knew. The enemies were closing in and I feared she'd pay the price. The only price I wouldn't survive. Her death. The Yakuza in Russia. In my city. Trying to kill my woman.

The fucker in that hotel room was lucky she shot him dead. Otherwise, his torture would have been long and painful.

The best way to protect her was to put my ring on her finger. I'd make her Mrs. Illias Konstantin. It had a nice ring to it.

So I followed her trail all the way to her Siberian Nikolaev home. A sardonic breath left me. We were practically neighbors all along. Of course, the first I ran into was her eldest brother.

"Konstantin, I'm surprised to see you." Vasili watched me warily. "Are you visiting as a Pakhan or as a neighbor?"

I raised my eyebrow. My Russian home was in Moscow, hardly a neighboring town.

He shook his head. "I swear, if Sasha has started some shit, I'm going to strangle him."

Vasili and I were the same height. He was a few years older, but our upbringing was similar. Both our parents raised us to be the heads of our family. Unlike me, his brothers were more helpful than mine.

"It's not about Sasha," I told him. "It's about Adrian."

Surprise flickered across his expression, but he quickly masked it. It was the last thing he expected.

"What about him?" he asked, keeping his voice even. "He's dead."

"He is, but the clusterfuck he started isn't," I said, my voice cold. "He started to fuck with the members of some powerful families."

"Goddamn it," he hissed, then let out a sigh. He didn't know about Adrian's dealings, but by the look in his eyes he didn't seem surprised.

"You don't seem surprised."

"He did a few things I questioned before he died," he admitted. "But he's dead and that's behind us."

I watched him with sardonic amusement. He knew better than to think I'd let that go. I walked past him and turned around when he remained glued to his spot.

"Why don't we go inside so I can announce this once?" I suggested.

He raised his eyebrow, rubbing his jaw and probably going through pros and cons in his mind.

His eyes narrowed. "Why do I get the sense I won't like whatever you've come to say?"

"Knowing you, you probably won't," I said amused. "But we might as well get this over with."

He shook his head, but caved in.

"This way then."

A few minutes later, we found ourselves in the library. I took a seat in front of the desk and brought up my ankle to rest on my knee.

"I'll be brief," I started, my eyes darting over Tatiana's brothers. "For Adrian's fuck up and yours, for letting him get as far as he did, I want Tatiana's hand in marriage."

There was no sense in beating around the bush. The bomb was dropped. Now let the games begin.

"Are you for-fucking-real?" No surprise, Tatiana's protective brother who saved her from her bitch mother spoke first. He could be a pain in my fucking ass. "Fuck you. Fuck no. Get the fuck out. Is that fucking clear?"

A deadly stillness fell over me. My grip tightened. Their sister would be mine, whether they liked it or not. She was worth starting a war for.

"Not fucking clear." I gave my head a shake or risked losing my tightly reined control. And if I lost it, I'd beat the shit out of Tatiana's favorite brother. "I can make you pay or you'll stay out of my fucking way."

"Fuck you, Illias," Sasha hissed. "You can't have her. You owe me."

Sasha's words were laced with venom and ready to fight glares. It wasn't surprising that Tatiana's brothers hadn't taken my demand lightly.

An amused breath escaped me. "You collected your debt. Remember? The kidnapped bride you're hiding here."

Sasha leaned forward but Vasili's wordless glare stopped him short.

Tense silence drifted through the air. Alexei stood unnaturally still, leaning against the wall with his arms folded and his eyes on the door and me. Vasili sat on the chair next to me and opposite of Sasha who kept flipping his knife. Open. Close. Open. Close.

It grated on my fucking nerves. My fingers itched for my gun. I could shoot him in the palm, just a tiny bullet.

"If you think this is a joke, I'm not laughing," Vasili commented. His furrowed brows and those pale blue eyes studied me as if he thought he'd decipher whatever was going on in my brain. Yeah, no chance of that. I had never expressed interest in Tatiana, and nobody knew about the encounter the two of us had in the gazebo.

Apparently not even the woman I had it with. I had to swallow the frustration in my chest. The irrational part that demanded I take her back to the gazebo and fuck her brains out so she'd remember.

Jesus Christ.

"Why her?" Sasha hissed, pulling my attention to the craziest Nikolaev. "You've seen her once."

I shrugged my shoulders instead of answering.

"She won't take well to being forced into marriage," Vasili remarked dryly. At least he was smart enough to consider it. He knew the repercussions of Adrian's fuck up, and how badly it reflected on their family. And that was putting it mildly.

"She'll come around." *Eventually.*

"Clearly you don't know Tatiana then," Alexei commented in a cold voice.

Alexei Nikolaev.

The tattoos on his face and every inch of his skin sent people running. It took a bit more to make me even consider it, but it seemed to work on most people. I knew it unnerved my twin brother, even before he decided to get lost in the drugs.

"Adrian's shady dealings and attempt to blackmail put Tatiana and your family in a peculiar position. His fuck up is viewed as hers and by default yours. You know as well as I do, revenge is the name of the game in our world. Tatiana's marriage to me would protect her."

Vasili shook his head. "Tatiana needs time."

"She's had almost a year." My voice was cold and my intent clear.

"She'll never agree," Sasha chimed in. "She'd sooner cut your balls off than marry you. I'm not much into balls but fuck it, for her I'd cut yours off."

"And I'd cut out your tongue just to stop hearing your goddamn voice," I said in an unnaturally calm voice. "I'll keep this short and clear so your little psychotic brain can process it. Tatiana *will* marry me. By the end of this year, she'll carry my last name."

My words were a razor-sharp demand.

"We can protect her," Alexei stated calmly. His and Sasha's temperament were like night and day. It was beyond me how the two got along.

"No, you can't." Our gazes burned into the other's while animosity danced through the air. "Your father pulled Adrian into your family in order to make contact with an organization. And as such, the Nikolaevs took the responsibility for Adrian's actions from that day forward."

Surprise flashed on Sasha's and Alexei's faces, telling me their big brother didn't share *everything* with them. Not surprising. When you play caretaker for so long, it is hard to switch off that mode.

Fury blazed in his blue eyes, but I had the upper hand. I'd take it easy for Tatiana's sake, but not her brothers.

Vasili's jaw ticked, and it didn't take a genius to know he was pissed. "My sister is not for sale. Nor will she ever be." I didn't comment, waiting for him to come to his own conclusion that he really didn't have a choice in this matter.

"Adrian's actions are his own," Alexei said dryly. "He was a grown man and made his own choices."

"Which now falls back on Tatiana," I answered sharply.

"Why her?" Vasili demanded to know, watching me as if he'd find the answer on my face. Yeah, good luck, fucker. "She's nothing to you. And she's everything to us." Fucking wrong. She was everything to me. Sun, moon, stars. The whole fucking world. "She's been going through a hard time since Adrian's death."

"Stop fucking explaining yourself to him," Sasha snapped at his brother. "I know my sister and she'd never choose you."

Wrong.

"This is non-negotiable." My voice came out as a dull roar, his words fueling the fire already burning inside me. Tatiana was mine and nobody would keep her from me. Not even her fucking brothers. Her protective brothers were her only downfall.

I stared at the three of them with cold fury; the men who stood in my way of getting what I wanted.

"She's not into you, Konstantin," Sasha grumbled. "You're not even her type."

The anger twisted in my chest with aversion before icing over. I recognized the feeling. It was the very same one that my papa often described when he learned of Mama's betrayal. She was his vice, and it ruined him just like that white powder was ruining Maxim.

I was well enroute of letting Tatiana become my vice. Or maybe I was already there. The need for her spread through my veins like lava. Hot and consuming. For as long as there was life in my body, there would be no giving her up.

I got up, buttoned my jacked and turned to leave.

"I'll let you process the merging of our families," I said as I opened the door and came face-to-face with my obsession. My eyes traveled over her slim frame, her signature black and white Chanel outfit hugging her body like a second skin.

Her eyes flashed in surprise and her cheeks colored crimson. She flicked a look behind me, then back to me, her gaze questioning what I was doing here.

"Tatiana," I greeted her, smiling smugly. Let her sweat a bit. Or maybe she'd get so brave to question her brothers about what I was doing here. Although I doubted they'd tell her anything. They always protected her and sheltered her from everything.

"Time to wear some color," I remarked, then passed by her, inhaling her sweet perfume.

Roses would be the death of me.

Five hours later, I sat in my own library behind my own desk with a cigar in hand, studying my twin brother.

This city home belonged to both of us, but I found it peculiar that he found himself here. He hated this place and hadn't stepped foot in this home since our father died.

Silence held steady in the room, my eyes on him. He was thinner and paler, dark shadows under his eyes. My muscles tightened and aggravation lit my chest. The thought swept through me that maybe, just maybe, I had fucked up by protecting my brother for all those years. Maybe I had made him weaker.

"So, you're going to join our bloodline with the Nikolaev bitch?" he spat out, the name like a disease on his tongue.

"Watch it, Maxim," I warned in a cold voice. He might be my brother but Tatiana was so much more. Something visceral and violent swept through me every time I thought about that woman. I wanted... no, *needed* her naked underneath me, her nails on my skin, and her round ass under my palms.

But even more, I wanted her protected. Marriage to me would render her untouchable.

"I thought you hated blondes?" Maxim asked casually, referring to our mother. When I didn't answer, he continued, "Illias... the name of my papa and brother. Both of you, the same person. Killers."

My gaze could kill a lesser man. Maxim was lucky to be my brother, or I would have killed him right here on the spot.

After what our mother had pulled off, Papa couldn't stomach blondes. Maxim was too high to realize he was mixing up the facts. Unless he thought he was talking to our father. We shared a name but we weren't the same person.

"You're just as fucked up as Papa," he said. "You'll chase a woman to death, just like he did. Will you pull the trigger and execute her like *he* did?"

My expression darkened, telling him one more word and he'd find himself dead. He opened his mouth, then seeing my hardened gaze, he closed his mouth, proving he still had some self-preservation left in him.

"Why are you in Russia, Maxim?"

His dilated pupils met my gaze, but I knew even before he opened his mouth he wouldn't answer truthfully.

"Vacation."

He stood up and left, leaving an unsettling feeling behind him, just as my cell signaled an incoming message.

Unknown number.

Motherfucking shit. I was so sick and tired of these videos.

Another incoming message. Marchetti.

I sent him to voicemail as I dialed up another number. Nico Morrelli.

"Hello?"

"Morrelli, this is Illias Konstantin."

A heartbeat of silence. "Fuck, I didn't believe it when I saw the number. I was certain it was a prank."

A sardonic breath left me. "Aren't we a bit too old for pranks?"

"Maybe, but I have daughters who broke into my safe as a prank. So there's that." A smile touched my lips. I could only imagine it driving him crazy. "What can I do for you?"

Amusement instantly left me as I thought about what I needed. I fucking hated asking for favors. But so far tracing the digital footprint had proven unsuccessful. Maybe Nico with all his resources would be able to pinpoint the general area that these videos are coming from.

"I need a trace," I said, the words bitter on my tongue. I should be able to depend on my twin for all technology matters but Maxim's brain was so fucking fried with drugs, he had become unreliable.

"Sure, although I thought you kept it all in-house," Nico remarked, knowing full well I did.

"This one is different," I told him. "It is more personal, and it's aimed at me."

Fuck, it was aimed at all of us - Marchetti, Romero, Agosti, Leone, even the Callahans since they joined in our organization. That night at the parking lot when my old man killed Adrian's father and my mother started this shit. The boy grew up and came for his revenge. Just as my father warned. Adrian's old man sought help from the Thorns of Omertà. He didn't get it. Instead Marchetti's father slipped the tip to my father of my mother's plans. It was how my father intercepted their rendezvous.

And now, Adrian wanted his revenge.

"What are we dealing with?" he asked.

"An untraceable recording," I said, leaning back into my chair. "The moment it finishes playing, it disappears." I let the words sink in. "The videos could be used as evidence."

"Well, shit."

That was putting it mildly. While I knew my connections could handle evidence and make it disappear if it ever made it to the legal system, it wouldn't help me with Tatiana.

Especially if she remembered who killed Adrian.

THIRTY-FOUR
TATIANA

Illias Konstantin.

On Nikolaev turf. Well, technically all of Russia was his turf but home was sacred ground and this one belonged to us. Not him.

I waited for my three brothers to end their back and forth about who's staying or going. Of course, Vasili and Alexei would stay. They brought their families. It was a given. Sasha should know that.

As two of my brothers dispersed, leaving me with Sasha, I finally opened my mouth to ask the only question that mattered.

"Why was he here?"

Sasha's gaze shifted to me, studying me. "Who?"

I narrowed my eyes, not in the mood for his games. "Don't 'who' me, Sasha? I'm not an owl. Why was Illias here?"

I realized my mistake the moment his name slipped through my lips. I should have referred to him by his last name. It was more impersonal.

"Why do you think he was here?" he replied with his own question.

I shrugged. "If I knew, I wouldn't be asking you. Would I?"

Sasha let out a sardonic breath. "Any of your friends ever tell you that you're a pain?"

"Nope." My lips twitched with amusement. "Nobody ever dared because they were scared of you and–" My voice faltered. I swallowed the tiny lump in my throat. Any boys in high school feared seeing my brother or my bodyguard. It meant someone was getting an ass-whooping. "You're the only one that dared to ever say it to my face."

He smiled, that cool, smug smile as he watched me with that ever-knowing look.

To the outside world, Sasha was a psychotic, cold blooded killer. To me, he was the brother who showed the most affection and understanding. Although still significantly older, he was closer in age to me than Vasili. And he was more playful. There were certain games Vasili would never dare to play with me. Sasha didn't give two shits. If I wanted him to hold a Barbie and play with me, he would.

"You look really good," he remarked.

"Don't I always," I joked, rolling my eyes.

The worry in his expression didn't wane. "You do, but the past year was hard. I was worried."

I waved my hand, hoping he'd stop worrying about me. He'd have a wife soon. He and Branka would be making their way to the altar in no time. I'd bet on it.

"We, the Nikolaevs, always come out on top," I remarked dryly. "You know that."

His expression told me that we didn't. Mother didn't come out on top. Father didn't come out on top. Alexei had a shitty life. Vasili almost lost the love of his life thanks to the web of lies Mother left behind. Okay, so maybe we didn't come out winners. Whatever.

"What's the deal with Konstantin and you?" Sasha asked as he leaned back in the chair. He hoped to catch me off guard, but he taught me too well. I'd never spill. Not until I was ready.

"No deal at all."

"Then why does he want to marry you?" My chest flared from hot to a full blown volcano. My pulse raced. My blood rushed through my veins like I had gotten an injection of a powerful drug.

"Say what?" My lips moved. I said those words. But I couldn't hear them, my ears buzzed so loud.

"He demands your hand in marriage, my lady," Sasha repeated dryly. Fucker!

When I was a little girl, I made him play pretend with me where I was a princess and he was a knight in shining armor. Then I made him mimic phrases I'd heard in a historical play but he always ruined it with his constant eye rolling every time he would say the phrases. Then he mockingly called me 'My Lady' and 'Your Highness' for months.

"The all mighty, powerful Pakhan wants you to be his bride. What say you, oh my lovely lady? Or should I say Your Highness?"

He even made that rolling motion with his hand in front of him as he bowed, like those men on the show. Although he seemed a bit rusty at it. The fact that he was sitting while doing it killed his suave.

"You're a dick," I snapped, getting to my feet. "And I won't marry him."

The fucker should be asking *me*, not my brothers. I wouldn't be a pawn shuffled around the board like I was nothing. Illias Konstantin needed a reminder of who the most powerful piece on the chess board was. The queen.

So he better get down on his knees and beg for my hand.

"Vasili wants peace," he remarked, letting out an amused breath. "But not to worry, I told them all as much. My sister knows what she wants and the Pakhan is not *it*."

The conviction in my brother's voice made me feel like a fraud. It was true I didn't want to marry him, but I wouldn't exactly say I didn't want Illias. My body seemed to have a mind of its own when it came to that villain.

Yeah, that villain couldn't be my king. I'd eat him for breakfast.

My mind immediately took over flashing images of me down on my knees, sucking him for breakfast. Goddamn my imagination. It was the last thing I needed. It was hard to deny the chemistry I felt when that man was around. Aside from that gazebo experience with Adrian, I had never felt such a strong attraction to another man. Just the thought of it made my thighs quiver.

Fuck, lust was the thorn that would be my downfall. I'd better get my head screwed on right before the thorns of lust struck again.

My steps felt as heavy as lead as I made my way to the door. Just as my fingers gripped the handle, Sasha's voice stopped me.

"Tatiana, you're playing with fire." Sasha knew me too well. It was the downfall of being close to your family.

I glanced at my brother over my shoulder, our gazes clashing. "My dear brother, we were born in fire. We might as well make just as dramatic of an exit."

"I'll kill him for you. Just say the word," he vowed and I knew he meant it. "But you know it won't end there. We'll have to put a plan in place. Hide." His lips twitched. "Somewhere warm if I know you."

The world must be off its axis if my craziest brother was being cautious.

Sasha's warning rang in my ears all the way back to my bedroom.

The Nikolaev Siberian family home.

So many memories. So many freeze-your-ass-off winters. But it felt good being surrounded by family. Sasha and his woman were the center of attention, leaving me to dig through my memory for the next clue.

The key that would open this box.

It was probably back in New Orleans. Somewhere. But I couldn't wait that long to open this box. So I resorted to lock picking using my hair pin. My brother Sasha would be proud. After all, he was the one who taught me the skill, allowing me to sneak out without being caught.

I bent the bobby pin to a 90-degree angle. Then I inserted it into the lock. I wiggled the hairpin. Up and down. Left and right. I pushed it in, applying pressure inside the lock barrel. I kept trying. One position. Then another.

Until I felt it. *Click.*

The lid popped open and I eagerly opened it. I stared at the discolored photos. I dumped them all out all over the floor of my bedroom that I hadn't occupied since I was a little girl. I studied each photo, but I had no idea what they meant. Or who they were.

A woman with beautiful blonde hair held a baby in her arms, leaning against a man who almost looked like... Adrian. Maybe they were Adrian's parents. It would make sense. I turned the photo around and found a year written in neat handwriting.

"That was the year Adrian was born," I muttered to myself.

I moved on to the next photo, showing a little house with a white picket fence around it and the man working in the garden and a six or seven-month-old baby sitting in a chair next to him, holding a tiny shovel. Whoever snapped the photograph caught the exact moment when the man looked at the camera and his smile was blinding.

I had *never* seen Adrian smile like that. It was the same smile but so fucking different that my chest cracked. A knowledge that I never wanted to admit to myself. A question I never wanted to ask.

Did he ever love me?

I didn't know. Or maybe I didn't want to know.

It was slowly becoming clear to me that I hadn't known Adrian well at all. I didn't understand the dark edges of what made him. The deep, dark secrets he harbored. Now that he was gone, I might never know him.

I go on. Standing in the shadows.

Was that what his message meant? That he'd haunt me forever. Or that he'd give me answers while he lingered in my heart like a ghost. I let out a heavy sigh.

Damn it. I wished he'd just left a notebook behind explaining what the fuck he was doing, instead of these cryptic photographs that told me absolutely nothing. Shuffling them all, I wondered why my late husband sent me on this errand.

Just to retrieve photographs.

Studying every single one of them, I searched for clues, anything that would tell me what was important about them. Aside from the sentimentality.

Thirty minutes of staring at the old photographs, and I was no closer to understanding them than I was when I first opened the box so I stashed them all in my bag.

The answer would eventually come. It seemed to be the case with all these clues.

Leaving my bedroom, I roamed the hallways of our Russian home. I was packed and ready to leave. I'd have to go back to our penthouse and search every damn inch of that place. I was eager to solve the riddle and put all this behind me.

Although it was a mystery as to what exactly it was that I'd be putting behind me. Adrian?

I was so deep in my thoughts, I hadn't noticed Isabella until she was right in front of my face, the look in her eyes frantic. I glanced around her for Nikola but he was nowhere.

"What happened?" I asked, alarmed. "Is it the kids?"

She shook her head. "No, the meeting–"

Her voice failed her, but the panic in her eyes spoke volumes. Alexei and Vasili went with Sasha to meet Branka's brother. It couldn't have turned into a full blown war. Could it?

"Branka has been shot," she breathed.

"How?" She was fucking meeting her brother. Killian wouldn't have lost his shit and shot her. Right? I should have tagged along. Goddamn it! Why in the fucking hell did I ever listen to men?

"Maxim Konstantin shot her."

I gasped in shock. It was the last thing I expected.

"What? Why?"

"He aimed for Sasha. I don't know."

None of this made any sense. Did the Konstantins start a war with the Nikolaevs on purpose? Was this the result of my brothers rejecting Illias? Shit, maybe I should have told them all I'd marry him. After all, the sex was great, at least.

I immediately mentally slapped myself. Focus on the present. Branka was shot.

Holy fuck, Sasha would go ballistic. If Vasili wanted peace, he wouldn't anymore. He'd support Sasha going to war against the Konstantins. Even Alexei would be fully on board now.

Doubt sprung in my mind and made its way into my heart.

Was that Illias intention all along with me? Getting close to me so he'd strike my family? Maybe it was the purpose behind his interest all along. Doubt was like poison slithering through my veins and my mind.

"You think the Konstantins started the war on purpose?" I asked Isabella. Not that she would know.

She shrugged. "Why would they do that?"

That was a good question. It wasn't as if Illias needed the excuse to start a war. He could have gone after us all along.

I shook my head, focusing on the problem at hand. We had to make sure Branka pulled through. "Tell me what you need me to do," I demanded. I couldn't help her with medical stuff, but I was certain I could help with *something*.

"Aurora is staying with the kids," she continued. "Can you help her with them? I'm going to go to the hospital."

I nodded, staring after her in shock.

Strangely, the man with dark eyes and even darker soul rolled through my mind. I wanted to make sure he was alright and that alone made me a traitor to my family.

THIRTY-FIVE
TATIANA

Three weeks since this whole ordeal began.

Branka spent two weeks in a Russian hospital. Then she and Sasha went back to our home there, while I returned with Vasili and Alexei to New Orleans.

Now that we knew she'd pull through, we all breathed easier. I feared the state of our family, namely Sasha, if she hadn't. Thankfully, we'd never find out how that would look.

Although we now had a different problem on our hands.

As anticipated, Sasha declared war on Illias. Vasili and Alexei, my other idiot brothers, backed him. The worst part, they both knew they couldn't win against him.

Our family was a different level of stupid and fucked up.

I must have been a different brand of idiot myself because I worried about Illias. Maxim was his twin brother. Yes, he was an enemy and tried to hurt my family. If he wasn't dead, I might have killed him myself for being crazy enough to attempt hurting my family. If he would have succeeded, I'd have declared war on the Konstantins myself, but I still didn't like the idea of the dark devil mourning.

Yes, I needed a sanity check.

The Russian Pakhan was a big boy and certainly didn't need me checking up on him. Yet, after two weeks of worrying about him, I finally caved in and typed up a text message to him.

For the first time ever.

My condolences.

I stared at the message. It was too cold. Too short. Too something.

Deleting the letters, I tried a different approach and typed up, **If you need to talk or whatever, let me know.**

Ugh, that wasn't very compassionate either. So I deleted the message again. Oh my gosh. When did I turn into a stupid, insecure woman? This wasn't me. I knew what I wanted and I went after it. I didn't dwell on writing a text message.

So I typed again. **Want a drink?**

I clicked send, then inwardly groaned. That was a dumb-ass message too. Shit.

Illias' reply was almost instant. **My place.**

My lips curved and something in my chest crackled and sparked, like sparklers going off on New Year's Eve. This must be what a young crush looked like. I never had that swooning, stalk your boyfriend stage. Yet, now it was catching up to me. I was tempted to Google him and ask my brother for every single detail about him. Luckily, I hadn't lost my smarts.

So I typed a message back, pretending to be cool. **You want me now?**

The reply was curt. **I always want you.** Swoon moment. My chest warmed and the vulnerability of my reaction to him was alarming.

My cell buzzed again. **Wait for me at my place. French Quarter. I'm at a funeral. St. Louis Cemetery.**

Shit, today was Maxim's funeral. He had to be at his gravesite. But here in New Orleans? I started to think maybe Illias Konstantin was up for a war with Vasili. Otherwise, he would have buried his brother in California. Or Russia. After all, he was the Pakhan of those territories.

None of it made any sense. I'd have to ask him about it.

Despite it all, I didn't regret Maxim's death. It was either him or my family. But I regretted the pain Illias probably had to endure.

Inhaling deeply, I typed a short response. **Ok.**

It was dumb, but I trusted Illias not to hurt me. Call it an instinct. Or being just plain dumb.

He had plenty of opportunities to hurt me or end me and he didn't.

And for the first time in my entire life, I felt the need to be someone's comfort.

I grabbed my purse and hopped into my car, then rushed to the cemetery.

THIRTY-SIX
KONSTANTIN

Maxim's tombstone rested right next to my mother's.

It was where he was meant to be. I had always known it'd end this way. Everything Maxim had ever done led to this. It still pained me to see him gone. My sister and I had a quiet service in Russia for our brother. It gave her a chance to say goodbye. It was safer that way, and it kept her protected.

Maxim had been unhinged ever since his woman died. I had tried to show him it was best to move on, but he refused. He pushed the old Russo when he broke the arrangement with his daughter. Though it was only an excuse. That old fucker Russo was a greedy bastard.

He had been gone for three weeks. It was her brother's bullet that finally ended him, and I couldn't get the blonde woman off my mind. She hadn't left my thoughts since the last time I saw her.

New Orleans wasn't my city. I never cared for it, but now it housed two of my family members in its cemetery. My father's body remained in Russia. It seemed cruel to my mother to have him buried next to her.

Humid summer weather filled the air. Sunlight glimmered through the old stones and threw shadows onto the century old cemetery grounds. Images of my twin brother played through my mind.

The addict. The heartbroken man. The geek during school years. The scared little boy.

After Mama's death he turned into a terrified little boy. Depression plagued him. Love drowned him. Then bitterness swallowed him whole.

The cruelty of our world didn't agree with him.

Somehow, I knew we'd end up here. No amount of protection could have kept him safe once he started losing himself in the white powder.

Marchetti, Agosti, Leone, Romero, Callahans.

They all stood behind me as the local priest gave his last blessing to Maxim's eternal soul. It was all fucking bullshit. None of us earned it. None of us would get it.

I stared at both tombstones, the engravings identical. They weren't far from Adrian Morozov. It still boggled my mind that his mausoleum was so close to my family's.

With the final blessing, the priest came forward and offered his condolences. I shook his hand, not bothering to make small talk.

My phone beeped and despite the priest talking about the eternal life he'd secure for Maxim, I ignored his babbling and retrieved my cell.

Surprise washed over me to see it was a message from Tatiana. **Want a drink?**

I wasted no time replying. **My place.**

Bubbles appeared, then a reply back. **You want me now?**

A sardonic breath left me. Now, yesterday, ten years ago. Tomorrow. Ten years from now.

Forever.

I wanted her forever.

I'd never truly lived until Tatiana came into my life. My brother was dead, but it was no fault of hers. His life slowly started ending the day we saw our mother die.

I typed a message back. **I always want you.** Then to ensure she knew where to go, I expanded. **Wait for me at my place. French Quarter. I'm at a funeral. St. Louis Cemetery.**

A short reply. **Ok.**

Satisfied she'd be waiting for me and tucking the phone back into my pocket, I returned my attention to the row of mourners. Some honest; many not. Maxim managed to line up a lot of enemies during his years of drug abuse. His hacking skills worked against him during those years because he wanted to fuck with people - for one reason or another.

Dante Leone approached offering his condolences and a handshake. I didn't bother replying, just offered a terse nod.

Marchetti was next, his eyes flickering around. "Just you?"

The question was odd but my mind was elsewhere, back in my place with the blonde angel who'd be waiting for me.

"Yes. Who else do you think would be here?" I asked sarcastically. "I just buried my brother."

Not that he was there for me much in the past years. As for my sister, I'd never bring Isla around these men. The two of us said goodbye to Maxim together, back in Russia. Neither one of us had been close to Maxim for years, his rage pulling him away from us.

Nonetheless it was a loss.

"Let me know if there is anything you need," Marchetti offered. I nodded. "Will the Nikolaevs cause further trouble?"

A sardonic breath left me. "Probably." But I was about to cause even bigger trouble for them. "I'll handle them though. They now cost me my brother and his woman. Adrian's fuck up could be perceived as partly their fault too. So it's their turn to pay up."

And I knew exactly how, or rather who, would settle that debt.

A commotion sounded somewhere behind me, but I ignored it as Amon Takahashi Leone approached. We shook hands, neither one of us speaking. He didn't bother with niceties. It was the reason I liked him. It was the reason I'd support him whole-heartedly against his cousin who ran the Yakuza. After all, it was his birthright. All he had to do was claim it.

"Thanks for coming."

"Of course." Amon's dark eyes flickered behind me to the source of the commotion and amusement passed his expression. I turned around to find Tatiana standing there arguing with her bodyguards.

She wore a black Gucci dress with white polka dots, the dress clinging to her curves. It fit her like a glove, but I'd have to seriously refresh her wardrobe with other colors. Fuck, anything, but the black. That had to go.

I headed towards her, not sparing anyone else a glance and my eyes locked on her angelic features. She might appear soft and innocent but Tatiana Nikolaev was a force to be reckoned with.

A queen in her own right. Protective. Fierce. Loyal.

It was what we all craved but not many found.

"Illias…" she murmured.

"I thought I said to wait for me at my place." My tone was low and firm. Maybe a tad bit too sharp.

"Tatiana–" Yan started, putting his body between her and me as a shield.

Tatiana let out an exasperated breath. "Yan, move or I swear, I'm going to kick your ass."

When he refused to move, she put both her hands on his back and shoved him out of our way.

"Unless you want poor Yan dead," I warned dangerously low, my eyes flashing angrily at Yan. "I suggest you remove your hands from his body."

Tatiana immediately raised them up in the air.

"Not touching. See, not touching." She shook her head. "You're mental, you know that."

"Maybe."

"You're both mental," Yan muttered. "At this point, I'm losing my job sooner rather than later."

"No, you're not," Tatiana said firmly, then met my gaze. "I know this is odd considering the circumstance of your brother's death." She cleared her throat, her eyes flickering behind me to where Maxim's tombstone lay. And so did Adrian's. "I thought I could give you a ride home."

I raised my eyebrow but remained quiet and waited. Watching. Her delicate neck moved as she swallowed, but her gaze never wavered from me. It burned into mine, blue flames stroking something inside of me.

Something foreign. Something wild. Something only she could tame.

THIRTY-SEVEN
TATIANA

My brothers would blow a gasket if they knew I was here. They declared war on the Pakhan, and here I was in front of him, the day of his brother's funeral, offering comfort. But I knew the raw pain of loss. I wanted to offer him comfort.

Sasha found his love match. He was happy; I could see it in his eyes. I used to have the same look in my eyes. Not anymore. Now all I saw was emptiness. Envy. I hated it. I hated this loneliness that clawed at my chest, stealing my breath away. But around Illias, I didn't feel any of those ugly feelings. I felt hope and something warm, like the comfort of a baby blanket.

So I'd follow this feeling. It seemed to always lead me to Illias. I didn't want to die alone, surrounded by cats. I owed it to myself to see where this thing with him ended. Even if it was temporary. If I didn't open myself up, I'd end up alone.

The men who were clearly part of the underworld drifted through the hundreds year old cemetery and watched us tensely. My gaze traveled over them. Every single one of them was extremely well dressed like models in a magazine. But all their eyes spoke of the darkness that only members of the underworld exhibited.

My eyes roamed over them until they stopped at the tombstone.

SON.

BROTHER.

MAY YOU FIND PEACE ALONGSIDE THE ROSES AND THORNS.

Maxim's tombstone was right next to Adrian's. A shudder rolled down my spine as my gaze locked on my late husband's resting place. *An empty tomb*, I thought to myself wondering if his ashes, wherever they were, found peace.

"Thorns and vows," I whispered.

My voice cracked. The emotion shot through me, wracking my soul. My eyes burned from tears I no longer had. I thought I was better, but all it took was a glimpse of Adrian's crypt, and I took two steps back in my healing process. Tiny trembles rippled through my body and oxygen thinned in my lungs. Illias took my hand into his and his fingers tightened around mine.

"Do you want to leave?" he asked, his words like the warm caress of a summer breeze against heated skin. "I want you to be okay."

I came to comfort Illias for his loss and here he was comforting me. That showed what kind of man he was. Right?

Easing a deep breath past my tight airway and into my lungs, I forced a smile to my face.

"I'm okay," I assured him. I couldn't smile but something in my eyes must have convinced him, because he nodded silently and turned to look at the next person that came over to offer him condolences.

Illias' composure was rock solid and I envied him. The same set of words, "My condolences," were murmured over and over as I stood next to him and slowly my composure came too. A few curious glances were thrown my way, but Illias refused to entertain them.

Until *him*.

Illias' body vibrated with tension that coiled under his skin. I could feel it seeping into me. So I followed his gaze to my left to the stranger with dark hair and even darker eyes. He was in his mid-forties if I had to guess. Earth-shatteringly and breathtakingly handsome.

I'd seen him before. I knew I had.

"Who's that?" I questioned Illias, interest lacing my voice. When Illias didn't answer, I flicked him a glance. Illias' eyes were narrowed on me as if he was trying to decipher something.

Just when I thought he wouldn't answer, he did. "Enrico Marchetti."

"Marchetti," I muttered, surprise washing over me.

Enrico Marchetti was the enigmatic CEO of the Marchetti luxury product empire. His face was never shown in public. A mystery behind one of the biggest companies in Europe. He was considered one of the wealthiest men in the world.

Thick dark hair grazed with silver at his temple. Olive skin. Broad shoulders. Tall frame in a perfect suit. Hardness behind that dark gaze.

Something in the back of my mind flickered. My blood cooled, fighting against the memory that tried to push to the forefront of my mind. I stiffened, as a mix of unease twisted my stomach.

I have to remember. I need to remember.

In my gut, I could feel its importance.

Marchetti slowly approached us, his hand in his pocket and his eyes zeroed in on me. With each step bringing him closer to me, the throbbing in my temples intensified. A frown touched my brow while an unidentifiable emotion flashed through Marchetti's dark gaze.

But as he came to stand in front of me, the expression vanished beneath the darkness of his gaze.

"Tatiana Nikolaev, I presume," he greeted me.

I hadn't realized I'd moved closer to Illias until his hand wrapped around my waist and squeezed. Fucking pathetic. I came to offer comfort and the roles had reversed.

"That's right, this is Tatiana," Illias answered. It seemed I'd lost my voice. But I quickly found it.

"And you're the infamous Enrico Marchetti," I retorted mildly. "Luxury empire king. At least that's what they call you."

"I see you keep up with me." Wryness touched his words.

"Well, not *you* per se." I had never seen a picture attached to his name. Yet, why did he look so familiar? "I do like your products, though. Besides, when you bought out all the other famous Italian designers, it was hard not to notice the Marchetti brand."

He stared at me, his face the picture of a polite mask but underneath it, I could sense a storm brewing.

My eyes darted to Illias to find his jaw had tightened, his tall frame focused on Marchetti, along with his sharp gaze.

"I see we're having a graveside meeting." A calm, deep voice came from the side, and I followed it to find the familiar beautiful face. His amused gaze lingered on me.

"Hey, you again," I exclaimed then realized how ridiculous that sounded. By his bemused expression he thought so too. "I kind of know you."

God, he wasn't that good looking to get me tongue tied.

"Nice to see you again. Although circumstances could have been better last time." Wryness touched his last sentence as he flicked a look at Marchetti and Illias, his face the picture of polite impassiveness.

Why did it feel like there was more at play here?

"Just in case you forgot, I'm Amon," he introduced himself. "Amon Leone."

As if I could forget his name or that face. Lordy. I could stare at him day and night, and never tire of his face. But Amon's handsome face wasn't the important thing here. It was distinguishing who was who here.

My brain cataloged through names I'd heard in the underworld. Leone wasn't one of them. Nor was Marchetti. Yet, that darkness and ruthlessness that marked every mafia man I knew was clearly part of their DNA.

In slow motion, or maybe it was just my slow brain, I turned to Illias to find a muscle ticking in his jaw. His dark, unforgiving gaze full of something terrifying was on the two men. His eyes were a dark, violent storm and his face etched with lines of anger.

"Marchetti. Leone."

Without a second look their way, he led me to the car and out of the cemetery. I couldn't help but notice his body vibrated with tension.

Yet his embrace was so strong and reassuring it eased the warning signs of the storm to come deep inside me.

I should have known it would implode.

THIRTY-EIGHT
TATIANA

The ride to Konstantin's place in the heart of the New Orleans' French Quarter was silent. The city still slept after the late night parties.

It didn't matter what time of year it was, parties always went on in this city.

I wasn't born here, but I loved it. Warmth. Jazz. Beignets. Jambalaya. Even the stupid drunks.

As soon as I parked and hit the cracked sidewalk of a familiar block of the French Quarter, I inhaled a deep breath, then slowly released it. There was something about this city that always appealed to me.

"Thanks for the ride home." Illias finally broke the silence as he came around my little red Audi R8, then slid his hand down to my lower back. The heat of his touch seared through the thin material of my designer dress, wishing I'd feel him on my skin.

Yan was already behind us as we entered the large courtyard of Konstantin's residence.

"How is it that you own this place?"

"It's been in my family for centuries." My eyebrow shot up in

319

surprise. "My father let your father take over this territory. My mother's family ran it before the Nikolaevs."

How did I not know that?

"I thought your family prefers the 'freeze your ass off' motherland," I remarked quietly.

His step halted and tension dampened the air for a second, an unidentifiable emotion passing over his face. He turned to face me, his gaze burning into me.

"What?" I asked when he gave me a strange look.

"I spend most of my time in California." Surprise washed over me, immediately followed by a memory. *Jesus Christ.*

"I remember where I've seen you before," I murmured, my brows scrunching. It was a very brief moment. At the Constantinople restaurant. "I met you at the restaurant there. How could I forget?"

"You tell me," he answered. "It certainly wounds my ego that I'm so unmemorable."

My eyes lingered on him and my lips curved into a smile. "Your ego seems intact."

The corners of his lips lifted and butterflies took flight in my stomach.

"You can go now," Konstantin ordered Yan who stood firmly at the gate. "I'll keep her safe in my own home."

Yan didn't move until I flickered my eyes his way. "I'll call you, Yan. Go spend the day with your family."

"Your brothers–"

"Leave my brothers to me." Then I smiled to soften my demand. "Go ahead. I'm fine here." I waited until he was gone before I continued, "Tour of your ancestral home then?"

I didn't think either one of us wanted to talk about our brothers. He wrapped his hand around mine and pulled me into his home. Then to my astonishment, a secret door opened and he led me into a dark hallway.

"Am I safe here?" I joked, glancing around as the door shut behind me. "Or is this the tour of secret passages?"

"I want you to know all the ins and out of this place," he explained. "Besides, this is the quickest way to the bedroom."

A flame filled my stomach with flutters and my heart stumbled over itself. Illias' gaze filled with darkness, thrilling and consuming. The heat in his gaze matched the fire burning through my veins.

I had been playing with fire. We both knew it, but the stubborn part of me wanted to see how long I could play without getting burned.

The truth was, I wanted to be here for him. Intentionally or not, Illias was there for me when I was hurting. He pulled me through. So maybe I could make him feel good now while he's hurting. I took his hand into mine and squeezed as he resumed walking down the secret passage until we reached the hidden bedroom entrance.

He pulled me against his chest, his grip tight, but I didn't mind it. I loved his hard body pressed against mine. The platform spun us, up and up, but all I could focus on was his hard, beautiful face.

The moment it stopped, we were inside the room and I reluctantly took a step back, already missing the heat of his body. My eyes traveled over the massive space.

A black double door stood closed on the other side, which would be our normal way in here. The room was dominated by a large bed. The largest I'd ever seen. The decor was masculine with black and gold tones everywhere. Black molding against the white walls. A mirror against the black ceiling. An enormous black leather sectional sofa that took up the sitting room connected to the bedroom and faced a massive flat-screen tv that looked like it receded into the wall.

Then a black lacquer cabinet bar that held more booze than some local bars.

Tantalizing. Tempting.

Developing a habit was easy. It wasn't as easy to quit it as it was to pick up the habit. Just a whiff of it and my mouth would water.

But then it hit me. I hadn't had a drop of alcohol since Russia. I savored the revelation and the hope that bloomed with it. Maybe I hadn't fallen so low to turn into an alcoholic. Truthfully, I hadn't felt a craving for it. More likely, they were replaced with the taste of Illias.

One addiction replaced with another.

I shook my head. No, it wasn't true. It was just healing.

"What is in that pretty head of yours?" Illias' voice called out to me. I slowly turned around to find him leaning against the white column, his hands in the pockets of his impeccable, expensive suit.

I let my eyes take him in for the first time with a clear mind. I really took him in, and for the first time ever, I see the similarities between Adrian and Illias.

Not in their physical appearances. Adrian's green eyes and dark hair were a far cry from Illias' dark eyes and even darker hair. But it was in their cheekbones. Their mouths. The way they both frowned. Even some mannerisms.

"That couldn't be," I rasped, whether to him or myself, I didn't know. "It'd be insane."

"What's insane?" he demanded to know.

I shook my head, unwilling to tell him these thoughts that refused to vacate my brain.

"Nothing," I muttered. "I'm just sorry you have to go through this." I chewed on my bottom lip nervously. It'd do neither one of us any favors if we avoided talking about Maxim. "Losing your brother."

Maxim might have been a lunatic, but he was still his brother. I loved my brothers for all their faults, just as they loved me.

"You want to know something, Tatiana?" I wasn't sure that I did but I nodded nonetheless.

The thread that formed between us wasn't normal. Nor regular. I kept telling myself we were just two souls comforting each other. He pulled me out of my grief. I'd return the favor. But the thread somehow pulled on my strings and became as strong as chains.

Yet I didn't feel like a captive.

"I would have killed my brother myself if it meant you'd come to me willingly." The cold tenor of his voice didn't match the inferno in his eyes. It made his words more impactful. It made my panic flare.

"T-this is temporary. A h-hook-up," I stuttered. Oh my God, I never fucking stuttered. I shouldn't be playing with fire. Illias wanted - demanded - a marriage. After all, he went to my brothers for it. It still pissed me off to think he didn't bother asking me what I wanted. It was my life, nobody else's.

It didn't escape me that the uttered words made me a hypocrite. I wanted permanency. My own family. My own children. It turned out, I was a weak woman, caving into lust and desire. Yet, the intensity of his gaze sent fear rushing through me. Why? I didn't know. Or maybe I didn't want to know.

"Just temporary?" Illias' voice dropped to a dangerous level. "What the fuck does that mean?"

"It means exactly what it sounds like. This is just…temporary." My words faltered at the storm gathering in his eyes. Goosebumps erupted over my skin. I ignored it. "Understand one thing. My brothers don't determine my fate or what I will or will not do. So yes, this is temporary, until I decide otherwise."

His jaw ticked. His eyes darkened to coals.

"Temporary," he ground out, repeating.

The cords of his neck visibly strained against his skin. The tension was so thick I could taste it on my tongue.

"Yes," I breathed. *You're such a liar and a coward,* my mind mocked, but I immediately shut it up. Besides, I wanted to bring the point across to Illias. If he wanted something from me, he'd have to discuss it with me.

"Nothing about us is temporary!" The force of his reply stunned me into silence. His granite mask cracked, revealing the torment underneath. "Nobody else is allowed to ever touch you again." Every word was accented by another step, and it brought him closer until we stood toe-to-toe. "Nobody else is allowed to make you laugh." The heat of his body enveloped mine. "Nobody else but me."

His voice dropped, turning ragged. It fed my own ragged breathing and thundering heart. My blood drummed in my ears. Our gazes locked. This close, I could see the hints of gold in his eyes. It reminded me of flickering light in the darkness.

It resembled hope. His or mine, it remained to be seen.

"Nobody can have you." He lowered his head and warmth brushed my lips. The darkness edged out the light and the gold disappeared, leaving pools of midnight in its wake.

My heartbeat slowed. My body burned. Our breaths intermingled. And time slowed.

For an agonizing moment, we stood, drowning in each other's gazes. In the next moment, he crashed his mouth down on mine and his hands wrapped tightly around my waist. Our bodies flush, I threaded my fingers through his hair and succumbed to my desire.

My body molded into his hard one, all muscle and heat, as his hand pressed my body firmly into his and his other gripped the back of my neck. His lips expertly kissed, exploring every corner of my mouth. Devouring me.

His mouth moved over mine, hot and demanding. The taste of him was intoxicating. Bold. Rich. Hard and primal. Completely addictive.

My body curved into his, grinding against him for friction. He kissed me like I was his salvation. His water after being stranded in the desert. A soft gasp escaped me. In one swift move, Illias hooked my legs around his waist and carried me across the room, our mouths never parting.

He set me down, our breathing ragged. His mouth descended on mine again as I pushed his jacket off his shoulders while he unzipped my dress. Our movements were frantic and desperate, as we tore our clothes off.

His jacket. His shirt. My bra. His pants. My panties.

All our clothing pooled at our feet, leaving us in bare skin. Our kiss broke apart and we stared at each other. He was beautiful. A sculpted body. Broad shoulders. Muscled chest. Mouthwatering chiseled abs with a faint dusting of black hair that tapered down to his hard shaft.

My mouth dried.

His cock grew in size under my scrutiny with every second that passed and a tinge of anticipation rolled through me. The mere thought of having him inside me again was enough to send me over the edge.

I finally dragged my gaze back up to his. His eyes were already on me, dark and smoldering. The heat in them was a molten flame.

He spun me around, his chest pressed against my back and his erection dug into my lower back. Hard. Ready. A full-length mirror hung on the wall, reflecting both of us. Illias' hands on my breasts, palming them. Pinching my nipples until they hardened into full buds, craving more of his attention. My skin was flushed and bright against his tanned skin. My eyes shimmered like the lightest sapphires.

"Look at us, moya luna," he rasped against my ear. Lust exploded through me hearing the gravel of his voice. The thickness of his Russian accent that was non-existent in other times. "*Nothing* about this is temporary."

He pinched my sensitive nipples. Hard. Pain and pleasure mixed. I craved it. I needed it.

"Why do you call me that?" I questioned in a raspy voice. "Moya luna."

Lazily, his hand explored every curve and every inch of my body, his strong fingers trailing down my ribs until they disappeared between my thighs.

His gaze met mine in the reflection, dark as sin. Light as possible salvation. "Because your hair glows like the moon in the darkness. Because you're the light in my darkness, Tatiana."

"Maybe I don't like it?" I challenged. I lied. I secretly loved hearing that endearment. After that first night at the gazebo, Adrian refused to call me by it. He said it was a silly nickname. He did call me a rose sometimes.

"You like it," Illias claimed. "You know why?"

I didn't answer, my breathing shallow as his gaze trailed over me like he was memorizing every inch of me.

"Because you're *mine*." He growled the last word as I watched his touch, possessive, intimate and sure, explore my entrance. My insides clenched with the need to feel him inside me, desire burning in my lower belly. Reading me like an open book, his fingers brushed against my clit and a breathy moan slipped through my lips. "Now say it."

His command was soft, promising pleasure but also pain. And as fucked up as it sounded, my body needed it.

"I… I-" My reply melted as he dipped a finger into my entrance, then lazily smeared my arousal over my clit. He pressed his thumb against my clit. A shudder rolled down my body and shivers broke on my skin. My hips bucked under his expert touch, the orgasm already nearing its peak.

It was embarrassing how fast it approached.

"I still have to punish you for taking out that butt plug without my permission," he purred into my ear, then his mouth trailed down my neck. His palm slid to my hip, his fingers digging into my pale skin. And I knew it was because he wanted to see his marks on me.

He wanted to mark me.

"Do you want to be punished?"

Yes. "No."

He pinched the sensitive peaks again. Harder. I instinctively jerked at the jolt of pain and pleasure, while a moan traveled through the air.

His dark chuckle vibrated against my back. "I think you do," he claimed, his teeth scraping against the skin of my neck.

Then without a warning, he slammed into me, filling me to the hilt. A cry tore from my lips as my pussy clenched around him.

"Look at my little slut so fucking wet. You're dripping," he hissed. "That's right. Strangle my cock. I know you want to be full. Both your pussy and your ass."

Another shudder rolled through me. He was right. I wanted him everywhere. Around me. Inside me. His hand closed around my neck as he pulled out and pushed back in.

"Look at us, Tatiana," he growled. "You might own me, but I fucking own you too."

My brain was too hazy to process those words. His thrusts were faster and deeper, his rhythm making my knees buckle. All thoughts and reason faded as he hammered into me so deep he hit all the right spots. The ones I didn't even know existed before him.

His hand around my neck squeezed. "You see it?" he grunted. "You see who you belong to? Look in the mirror and tell me who's fucking you."

"Y-you," I breathed.

Every inch of my skin was flushed. My eyes were glassy with lust and pleasure. My mouth was parted, moans and whimpers pouring from my lips. My breasts bounced with each thrust. The image staring back at me was a wanton and needy woman getting fucked. He wrung every ounce of pleasure from me and that wasn't enough.

He wants to own every fiber of me, I realized. And that thought terrified me, but losing this feeling when I was with him terrified me even more.

My gaze locked with Illias' in the mirror.

"Look at your pussy making a mess all over my cock," he taunted in a harsh voice. "You know why?" I shook my head watching him fuck me. Looking at us in the mirror forever changed me. I'd forever see him in the mirror. "Because I own your pussy." My lungs couldn't get enough oxygen. My brain was fuzzy. My pleasure kept building.

"You." Thrust. "Are." Thrust. "Mine." Thrust.

My heart thundered. He drove into me with increased force until his last plunge sent me forward. I would have collapsed if not for his hold. And still he continued fucking me, his grip around my throat tightening.

"Mine until my dying breath," he said darkly, the rawness of his voice matching the rawness of my heart. He dragged his cock out slowly, letting me feel every inch of him. "I'm never giving you up again."

Then he slammed back into me, turning my body into a live wire. His own instrument to use as he liked. As long as he kept doing it. The power of each thrust claimed me viciously and thoroughly.

The desire in his eyes matched my own, filling my soul with light that was about to explode. "Give me everything, moya luna," he rasped. "Because I'm going to give you the moon, stars, and the sun. We're just getting started."

With a last punishing thrust and our eyes locked in the mirror, he tipped me over the edge. I came with a sharp cry, my body shuddering and my pussy clenching around his cock. He followed me over the cliff, spilling inside me, his cock pulsing while we both gasped for air.

As we slowly came down from our highs, we stared at our reflections, his cheek pressed against mine. Our bodies slick with sweat, our eyes dazed with an emotion I couldn't name, he leaned over and whispered into my ear.

"We aren't temporary, Tatiana." His voice was rough, a thick Russian accent lacing it. "We were never temporary."

Fatigue pulled me into the dreams fast.

I dreamt of strong hands on my body, twisting my nipples and fingers slipping into my pussy. The familiar scent wrapped around me and I clung to it, scaring off my nightmares.

My back arched off the bed as a moan slipped through my lips. Warm skin was under my palms and I held on to it like a lifeline. Fingers angled inside me, hitting the spot and pleasure coiled deep in my belly. I writhed under the expert hands, needing more. Needing everything.

"You need me." The deep rough voice vibrated through me. "Just like I need you."

My eyes snapped open to find Illias watching me as he finger fucked me. The darkness of his gaze swallowed me whole, pulling me into his trap.

I was falling. I knew it. He knew it.

His fingers expertly traced my areola - slow and taunting. My nipples ached with need. I wanted his mouth on them. As if he read my thoughts, he took one nipple between his teeth. First he scraped the sensitive peaks, dragging a breathy moan out of me. Then he sucked the sting away while his other hand hovered over my pussy, teasing my wet entrance.

"Illias, please," I breathed.

"Please what?" His voice was husky with lust as he thrust two fingers inside me and tugged on my nipple with his teeth.

I arched against him, my breath catching as a moan ripped from my throat.

"More," I moaned, my body arching off the bed into his touch. "I need more."

He curled his fingers inside me, triggering an intense throbbing at the bottom of my stomach. Releasing my sensitive nipple, his mouth trailed up to the hollow of my neck, sucking my sensitive skin. Everywhere he touched, he left a wet, hot trail and then he bit the skin on my throat.

A zap of pleasure shot through me and straight between my legs. And all the while, his fingers leisurely slid in and out of me while slick, wet sounds filled the air. I clenched around his fingers as he slid them out.

"Please, no," I pleaded once he pulled out his fingers, the throbbing unbearable. "I want you."

The words slipped out. They couldn't be retracted. I wasn't even sure that I wanted to take them back.

First step towards recovery. Or maybe towards him. I didn't know.

For a moment, we stared at each other in silence, but my heart thundered louder and faster, cracking my ribcage with each drum.

Placing a hand on his cheek, our gazes held. Our breaths intermingled, our hearts beat as one. At least it felt like they did at that moment.

His hard cock nestled at the bottom of my stomach and I arched my hips.

"I want you," I whispered.

I'd be scared of pain and loss tomorrow. Tonight, I'd just surrender to this. Magic or whatever this was.

He gripped me by the hip and pulled me against his groin.

I brushed my lips against his, then murmured against them, "Please, Illias."

One moment changes lives.

This moment changed mine. He grabbed me by the throat, my legs parted and he thrust deep inside me, like he needed to possess me. And somehow he did.

My eyes rolled to the back of my head, my slickness welcoming him home.

He fucked me with so much power and pent-up animalistic need, matching my own. As if he waited for this his entire life. My legs wrapped around his waist, my fingers clutching his forearms for balance and strength.

He pulled out almost completely when a breathy protest left my lips, and he rammed back in. His pounding consumed us both, each thrust hitting that sweet spot inside me. Stars swam in my vision. The world turned upside down. Sweat covered our bodies.

"You're mine!"

"Y-yes!"

"Good, now scream my name."

He thrust deep and hard. Faster and faster. His hand squeezed tighter around my throat and a loud moan filled the air as I shattered around him, the waves of pleasure crashing through me.

My insides clenched around his shaft and Illias grunted as he spilled inside me, his seed warming my womb.

He kissed my forehead and murmured soft words that sounded like, "I've waited a lifetime for you."

THIRTY-NINE
KONSTANTIN

A shriek pierced the air.

My eyes snapped open and I immediately reached for my gun. Nobody should get past my security but nothing was ever foolproof. My heart was beating wildly as I took in my surroundings.

There was nobody around. Just Tatiana.

She was thrashing in her sleep. Her forehead was slick with sweat. Her hands fisted the sheets so tightly that her knuckles turned white I could spot them in the dark against the black sheets.

"Tatiana!"

She didn't respond, her thrashing continued. Her red lips trembled, her cheeks smeared with tears as she continued shaking and thrashing in my arms.

"Wake up, moya luna," I demanded softly as I held her against my chest. "Stay with me."

Her eyes shot open, those palest blue skies meeting my gaze and clashing with mine. The sorrow in them hit me hard in the chest. I knew I was running out of time. The moment she remembered the whole accident, it'd be game over.

She bolted upright, the terror in her eyes vivid as she stared at me with a horrified expression. Another scoot backwards and she pulled her knees to her chest, her hands wrapping around her knees while her skin appeared almost luminescent in the darkness.

Did she remember?

"You're safe." I kept my voice calm, clenching my fists while fighting the urge to touch her. My jaw tightened and my heart hardened recognizing the panic in my own heart. It was so foreign, I took longer than usual to recognize it.

It was the first time since my mother's death that I felt fear. An honest to God true fear that rattled me to my bones.

I feared losing her.

"Are you okay?" I asked her, hell wrecking through my soul seeing pain in her eyes. Those big blue eyes that have the power to destroy me and she didn't even realize it.

The delicate line of her neck moved as she swallowed, then nodded once.

I reached out for her and a relieved breath left me realizing she didn't pull away. I tucked her under the covers and she scooted into me, her body small compared to mine.

She closed her eyes and whispered, "I'm scared of dying."

My lips brushed against her forehead. "You're not dying anytime soon." She didn't seem convinced. "I'll always save you," I vowed. "Even when you don't want to be saved."

Her lips tugged up and I wrapped my arms around her, pulling her to my chest. Right under the heart that beat only for her, knowing that the moment she remembers it all, I might lose her.

A dark obsession took hold of me and roamed through my chest. I had kept it under reins for years but now, the beast was out.

This time she'd be mine. This time the beast refused to let her go.

FORTY
TATIANA

The early morning light cast shadows over the bedroom.

I lay still, staring at the ceiling and aware of the warm, strong arms that held me. I listened to Illias' strong breaths, the rise and fall of his chest against my back. The ache still pulled on my bones. Illias wrenched so many orgasms out of me last night that I lost count.

The fear that maybe I'd traded one addiction for another crept under my skin.

A strange rush of emotions overwhelmed me until it stole my breath. I didn't know what those emotions were. I had never felt them like this.

Maybe Illias literally fucked my brains out.

My skin flamed remembering all the times he'd made me come. After he'd fucked me into oblivion, he ran a shower and washed me, taking special care of my hair. Then he patted me dry, fed me in bed, only to start ravishing my body all over again.

I shifted my body slowly, turning my head to watch Illias' sleeping face.

He struck me differently like this. Less intense. Less overwhelming. But not any less handsome.

My fingers slowly reached for his lips but stopped right above them. I wanted to trace them, kiss them but a ding of his cell phone stopped me.

I froze, my finger lingering in the air, waiting for his eyes to snap open. They didn't.

Maybe last night's activities exhausted him too, I thought slightly amused.

Another ding of the phone. But this time a voice came through it.

My brows furrowed, hearing the recording coming from it, and I reached for his phone, wanting to silence it. It was never my intent to snoop, but drawn by invisible need, my eyes latched on to the screen and the world as I've known it ceased to exist.

I held my breath as the video played.

A young woman with vibrant red hair and dull green eyes sat on her knees. Her stare was blank. Her face was pale. Something about her expression hit home.

Hopelessness. Despair.

Like she no longer wanted to live. But that wasn't the worst part. It was Illias, standing next to her and his gun pointed at her skull. My heart drummed with fear for her. I held my breath, praying and hoping he wouldn't.

He wouldn't pull that trigger, right?

My brothers were part of the underworld, but they'd never hurt a woman. Women and children were off limits.

A dull '*bang*' sounded off. It wasn't loud, but it might as well have been. It echoed through my brain and I dropped the phone. I shifted backwards inch by inch, away from it and *him*.

The man who'd touched every inch of my body. The man whose hands were drenched with blood - innocent and guilty.

A tremble crept up my spine.

"Tatiana." The rough, sleepy rumble of Illias' voice touched me. His eyes flickered to the phone, video still playing. It restarted and surprise flashed in his expression.

As he watched the video, I inched my way off the mattress and slid off the bed, my feet touching the cold hardwood. The cool air swept over my naked body, goosebumps breaking over my skin. I pulled the sheet and gripped it to my chest, my knuckles protesting with an ache.

"Tatiana-" he started but I shook my head.

The video started playing again. *Bang.* I jumped out of my skin as if I heard the sound for the first time. My eyes darted to the screen. The woman's dead eyes stared blankly. Blood seeped from her skull and onto the white rug, red spreading like obscene ink.

The same scene played on repeat, over and over again, but he no longer watched it. His eyes were on me, studying.

I blinked back the tears, taking another step backwards, never taking my eyes off his face. When the back of my knees hit the coffee table, I collapsed into the sitting position, the lacquer cool against my ass. I wrapped my other arm around my middle, while the other was still gripping the black sheet to my chest.

Illias sat up against the headboard, the black covers rumpled around his waist and looking like a god. Smooth, tanned skin stretched over the naked, sculpted planes of his shoulders and abs. Even just seeing that video, my thighs clenched and heat spread down my body.

The stupid butterflies took flight. But thankfully, my brain was still intact. Mostly.

He swung his long, muscular legs over the side of the bed and pulled on black sweatpants. When he stood to his full height, they hung low on his hips. There wasn't a man on this Earth who wore sweats better.

Stop it, I scolded myself. *Murderer. He's a murderer.*

"I have to go." My voice shook.

"No." His dark eyes burned and his chest heaved. "You're not even going to ask?"'

My eyes flashed and my hands curled into fists. "I don't want to know. I don't want anything to do with you." A sardonic breath left him. His expression shattered, before it changed into a hardened mask.

"That's too bad," he said in a dangerously calm voice. "Because you have me." His forehead lowered toward mine, his unique and addictive scent filling my lungs. "I swear to God, Tatiana, there is no going back. You're my end game."

I swallowed. "Temporary," I rasped. "This was just temporary."

His palms cupped my cheeks, his darkness dominating me.

"I told you once, moya luna, we were never temporary."

FORTY-ONE
KONSTANTIN

Tatiana wasn't a fragile rose.

She held onto her thorns, like they were her life shield. But she didn't know how determined I could get when I wanted something.

Tatiana opened her mouth, then closed it. Her expression widened and she stiffened at my touch. But she kept her mouth shut, although I knew she had plenty to say.

She remained still, her ice blue gaze on me. But her calmness didn't fool me. Under her blue ice, the stubbornness stared back at me. Challenged me.

"I'm going to explain what you just saw there," I grumbled, unused to explaining myself to anyone. But she wasn't just anyone. "First, I have to make a call."

Her lips pressed into a thin line, but her eyes blazed with sure determination. The question was what was going on in her head.

Bang.

That damning recording kept playing. Over and over again. When I got my hands on whoever was sending those recordings, I'd strangle them. I needed to contact Nico Morrelli immediately and he might be able to trace the digital IP address of the recording.

"Can I use the restroom?" Her voice was measured. Controlled. Soft.

But there was no meekness in it. My gut warned she was up to something, but as I studied her, she kept her expression blank.

I nodded.

She grabbed her discarded clothes and disappeared into the bathroom. The door clicked and I wasted no time dialing up Nico Morrelli.

"You got another one?" Nico went straight to business.

"Yes, but this one keeps playing on repeat." The worst fucking one to show Tatiana. Or God forbid, Isla. "It's never done that before."

"Okay, I'm going to need you to lower your firewalls." I got to work straight away, lowering the firewall only to my phone, while keeping the firewall securities in place on all my other files.

"You should be clear to enter."

I could see Nico get right to work. Several minutes of silence, his typing on his keyboard fast and furious.

"Damn it," he cursed, the same time that the video recording disappeared. "Fucking shit."

I slammed my fist against the table, causing a reverberation through my arm.

"I'm assuming that means you weren't successful," I gritted out.

"How many times did the recording play out?" he asked.

"Way too many."

"The moment I started tracing it, its digital footprint was erased." The footage must have had embedded code in it that had it erasing the moment the footage stopped playing.

I stood up and strode to the window, releasing a heavy breath as I stared at the courtyard. My fingers tapped against the windowsill, over and over again when a shimmer of gold caught the corner of my eyes.

"Son of a bitch."

I watched Tatiana swing her long, slim legs over the green decorative rail that characterized French Quarter homes.

"What's the matter?"

"Thanks for trying." I ended the call with a click, just as Tatiana jumped off the balcony and landed on her bare feet.

She turned around, lifted her face to the window and our eyes connected.

Then she flipped me off and ran.

Jesus Christ, that woman would age me and have me keel over before I could put a ring on her finger.

"You can run, but you cannot hide," I murmured, coming up with all the creative punishments for my future bride.

FORTY-TWO
TATIANA

It'd been six weeks since I jumped off Konstantin's balcony. Six weeks since I saw a recording of the Pakhan executing a woman. Six weeks to do the right thing.

I still hadn't.

I'd like to say it was to protect my family. But it'd be a lie. There was no point in burying my head in the sand.

It was the first time I'd been out of my house since I escaped Illias by jumping off the balcony. Judging by the number of guards that Vasili assigned to me, shit with Pakhan wasn't going as well as my brothers hoped.

My brother's mansion, or better yet compound, was massive. It was a large piece of land that surrounded the house, along with high walls. Cameras and guards roamed every corner of the property.

The moment Yan pulled over in front of my brother's home, he turned around to face me.

"Your brother has been asking about your daily activity."

I met his gaze, light brown against his blonde crewcut. "Well, there isn't much to tell, is there? I haven't been out of the house."

He shook his head in disapproval, but he said nothing else.

Ever since Yan caught me leaving Illias' house the unconventional way, he kept watching me with worry in his expression. I should have known he wouldn't follow my orders and leave me unguarded. Yan fully expected to be fired any day now, so he acted more like my brother than my bodyguard. I allowed it.

And strangely enough, Konstantin kept his distance. Although somehow it felt more like the calm before the storm, rather than him giving up. I should be happy about it. I should celebrate.

Yet, I couldn't help but think about him all the damn time.

The door to my car opened and one of my brother's guards held it open. I exited the car and headed through the familiar home and to the gathering room.

With each step, the music and laughter's volume increased. I smoothed my hand over my dress. Isabella said to dress up like it was a black tie event. I didn't question it. I picked out a black Valentino gown that was tight around my breasts and waist, but fell loose to the ground with a white train attached to the back of my dress that fell from my shoulders to the floor. My hair was styled in a classy bun, and I opted for minimum make up and discreet diamond earrings.

Yan trailed behind me, his weapon peeking from under his jacket and my steps faltered right before entering the room.

"You can go home," I told him. "Vasili has plenty of men. One of them can take me home."

He shook his head. "No, I'm taking you home."

I sighed. It turned out Yan was just as stubborn as I was. "Then at least go and relax. You don't need to trail behind me."

A terse nod and he went ahead, towards the gardens while I still lingered in the doorway.

Lights shimmered. Music played.

Dinners at Vasili's were usually casual and hectic. Hence this came as a surprise. It would be only my eldest brother, Isabella, some of Vasili's associates, and me. Sasha and Branka were still in Russia, and Alexei was in Portugal with Aurora.

The gathering seemed to be in full swing already. Men and women dressed up elegantly and chatted among each other. It seemed to be a pleasant evening, everyone smiling. My eyes searched out my eldest brother. He made me promise him that I'd come. It was my first party since Adrian's death, but Vasili emphasized he needed me.

So here I was in my full glory.

I finally spotted him, speaking to a man with thick, dark hair and his back to me. My heart recognized him before my brain. Vasili's eyes flickered to me and he smiled, but my gaze was locked on the tall dark form speaking with him.

I stood frozen, watching as his companion turned around and our eyes met.

Darkness. Dominance. Secrets.

Vasili waved me over and I longingly glanced over my shoulder, regretting my promise now. I didn't want to be here. Why in the fuck was Illias Konstantin here? We were supposed to be enemies.

You didn't mind sleeping with the enemy, my mind whispered, but I promptly shut it up.

My heart thundered against my ribcage with each step that brought me closer to my brother and the enemy. I could feel Illias' smirk on me more than see it, his eyes watching my every move like a hungry wolf.

My heels clicked against the hardwood in sync with my wild heartbeats.

"Tatiana." Vasili seemed oblivious to my tension and smiled warmly as he hugged me. "You look beautiful."

"Thank you," I answered with a forced smile, keeping my eyes on my brother. The man who wasn't just a brother but also mother and father. The man who'd always been there for me, even when our own parents abandoned us. I barely remembered Papa. He was never around. And my mother hated me so much she jumped to her death almost with me in her arms.

"Big party," I remarked tightly.

"Isabella wasn't happy, but we were overdue." I nodded, still keeping my eyes on Vasili. "This is Illias Konstantin," he continued when I said nothing. "I believe you may have met him briefly in Russia in passing."

"Drinks, ma'am?"

A waiter showed up at that moment, offering drinks. Flutes of champagne and stronger drinks in shorter glasses. Tension surrounded our small circle. I could practically see Vasili's glare on the poor waiter.

I swallowed. I hadn't had a drop of alcohol in almost three months now. It wasn't the road I wanted to go down again. I met the waiter's eyes and smiled.

"Thank you, nothing for me." Tension evaporated like the air in the inflated balloon. I returned my attention to my brother and Illias. "Frankly, the meeting was so brief, I don't remember him."

Game. Set. Match. Motherfucker.

"I'll be happy to refresh your memory." Illias response was smooth and deep. Seductive.

I narrowed my eyes on him. "I sincerely doubt it. Obviously our meeting was *very* unmemorable."

The corners of his lips tugged up even more, as if I amused him. Or maybe he accepted the challenge. "Well, I'll have to try harder next time."

"Doubtful you'll succeed." The words fell from my lips, knowing very well it'd sound insulting. I didn't care.

"Tatiana!"

I shrugged my slim shoulders. "Lovely party, Brother."

Vasili turned to the Pakhan and swiftly changed the subject. Absent-mindedly, I listened as they discussed the latest revelation. Namely, the self-proclaimed Pakhan of Russia. Sofia Catalano Volkov.

Apparently the woman was slightly mad and coincidentally related to Wynter DiLustro, Sasha's little protégé. So many lunatics roaming around, it wasn't even funny.

Although crazy doesn't even scratch the surface on the Nikolaev portfolio, I thought, scoffing and my brother's and Illias' eyes shifted my way, studying me. The look in Vasili's eyes told me not to do something stupid.

Like starting another war. My poor brother. First he had to play a diplomat with Branka Russo's brother after Sasha kidnapped her. Now, he had to neutralize this shit with the Pakhan.

"You okay?" Vasili asked, furrowing his brows. I just waved my hand, indicating it was nothing so he returned his attention to Konstantin.

"What is her end game?" Vasili questioned, deciding to ignore my peculiar behavior. Good call for sure!

Illias shrugged one shoulder. "Ruling the East Coast, I'd assume."

"Do you deal with her?" Vasili questioned.

"No."

It was obvious to Vasili and I that Konstantin wouldn't reveal anything. I discreetly peeked at him. I'd never admit it out loud but Illias looked gorgeous wearing a tailored black tuxedo. He seemed even taller, larger than life. Sharper. You could even forget he was Pakhan and think of him as a businessman.

Until you looked into his eyes.

Then you saw the criminal. The murderer. The pillar of the Russian mafia who ran the criminal organization of Russia and the West Coast in the States.

"Tatiana, I was hoping you, Illias, and I could go into my office and–"

I started to shake my head. The way Konstantin was watching me wouldn't bode well. "No."

He watched me with a dark, half-lidded stare, and suddenly it felt like I stood in his domain. Not my brothers. His large frame threw shadows over my frame and soaked up all the oxygen in the room.

Illias' eyes dropped to coast the length of the slit, exposing my bare leg. My heart raced with an edgy beat and my blood warmed. I squeezed my thighs together, my skin buzzing like a live wire.

"No, what?" Vasili questioned, watching me too closely.

I took a deep breath in and released it.

"Umm... I haven't had a chance to see Isabella," I muttered. "I'll see you around."

Tilting my head, I whirled around and left both men standing there. One set of dark eyes burning a hole in my back.

I found Isabella in the kitchen. She looked beautiful in a red gown, holding her baby girl and soothing her.

"Hey," I greeted her. "Is everything okay?"

My best friend's brown eyes met mine. I brushed my fingers over my little niece's dark hair. She'd be the first child in our family with dark hair.

"Yes, she's cranky," Isabella murmured. "This party came at the worst time. Or Marietta's tantrums come at the worst time."

I extended my hands and Marietta immediately reached for me. "Are you giving Mommy a hard time, Marietta?"

Holding her close to my chest, my niece gave me a grin, melting my heart. She'd be a beauty one day, melting men's hearts.

"You have such a way with kids," Isabella remarked. I smiled, keeping my eyes on my niece. "You look gorgeous, Tatiana."

"You said black-tie event," I answered dryly. "I listened." My eyes darted back in the direction where I left my brother with Illias, but I couldn't see them from here. "Why is the Konstantin scum here?"

Okay, maybe that was a bit too bitchy. I was ready to follow through these feelings he stirred inside me but there were certain things I couldn't get over. The killing of an innocent woman was one of them. I had to draw a line somewhere.

"Tatiana!" she scolded on a hush, her eyes darting around us to ensure nobody heard that. The kitchen staff hired for this occasion paid us no mind. "Vasili wants a truce with him."

I snorted. "Why?"

Isabella let out a heavy sigh. "Well, apparently he's a worthy opponent and Illias threatened a turf war. Taking back the territories that used to belong to Konstantin's mother. Of course, Vasili wouldn't allow that but he doesn't want anyone in the family getting caught in the crossfire."

"So what?" I growled softly. "How is Vasili going to settle the score? Let the dark devil kill one of our brothers?" A guilty wince crossed Isabella's face. "You know something," I accused.

She shook her head. "Not really. Vasili said the only way to come to terms with Konstantin was to let him kill one of his brothers... or by marriage."

Illias had another thing coming if he thought I'd agree to any damn agreement that he'd negotiate with my brother. I made it clear to him it would be a conversation he'd have to have with me. Nobody else. I'd be nobody's pawn.

I snickered. "Well, good luck to anyone trying to take out my brothers. They'll be dead by morning. And there is nobody to wed. Alexei and Vasili are wed and Sasha is on his way to the altar any day now. So there's that."

Isabella's eyes lowered, the unspoken meaning lingering in the air. Marietta's head slumped to my shoulder and her face pressed against mine. She was falling asleep as I rocked her back and forth.

"Vasili promised me a long time ago he'd never arrange a marriage for me," I clarified when Isabella kept looking at me like I had forgotten I was no longer married. Or that Illias tried to arrange for my hand. "Nobody on this planet will make me marry anyone. I'll be nobody's puppet."

We couldn't trust Illias as far as we could throw him. You'd have to be stupid not to see it. The man wouldn't be the Pakhan for so long and from an early age because he was easily fooled. I'd have to hope that Vasili knew that even better than me.

Isabella was about to answer when her eyes darted past me. I followed her gaze to the back of the hallway where Konstantin and my brother entered Vasili's office.

Konstantin's eyes found mine and held my gaze with a knowing smile as he shut the door.

For the first time in my life, I doubted whether my big brother would keep his promise.

But I'd keep mine. I would never agree to an arranged marriage.

FORTY-THREE
KONSTANTIN

I shut the door to Vasili's office to Tatiana's glare and Isabella's worried eyes.

Heading towards the desk, I sat down in a chair in front of Vasili's desk, leaning back with one elbow on the armrest and studying him. He kept his expression masked but he was worried.

About many things... but most of all war with me... and Tatiana.

He'd be an idiot not to pick up on the sizzling tension traveling through the air when Tatiana stood next to me. And Vasili wasn't an idiot. But the bottom line was that Tatiana was my woman and, therefore, my responsibility.

I tapped my finger lightly against my thigh. Vasili asked for this meeting, to find a way to come to a mutual agreement for peace. Fuck if I planned to make it easy on him.

A clock ticked. Noise from the guests buzzed from the other rooms. Tension built until we could both taste it in the air. It pulled like a rubber band, ready to snap at any moment.

"Tatiana is not the arranged marriage kind of woman." His words cut the silence like a knife. My gaze found Vasili's. The statement wasn't a surprise. That woman did what she wanted, whenever she wanted. "And she seems on some path to revenge now." I cocked my eyebrow. I thought she kept her search for the chip a secret. "She thinks I don't know, but she's been searching for clues. I don't think she's ready for the next step."

Ready or not, here I come.

For the last few weeks, I'd had to deal with Omertà business. Sofia Volkov was on the move again. Except, every time my men got close to her, she disappeared. It was almost as if she was toying with us. Or waiting for something to happen. She was spotted in Moscow, in Paris, then Rome, even Japan. The psycho bitch was as slippery as an eel. She was wanted by the Kingpins of the Syndicate, by Cassio and his gang, by the Omertà, yet none of us could fucking find her.

But now I was back in New Orleans.

There'd be no more delays. I wanted Tatiana. I'd have her. I'd waited long enough.

Vasili sat in his chair behind his desk, seemingly calm but he was pissed. He knew I wanted her. He didn't want me to have her.

When I didn't speak, because I love seeing people squirm and I thrived on tense, awkward silence, Vasili continued. "Why her?"

My jaw ticked. *Because she's a queen. Because she makes me forget who I am. Because despite all the fucked up shit, we fit.*

But I said none of it. I wouldn't show Nikolaev how much leverage he had over me with his sister.

Let the Nikolaev family sweat a bit. It was about time they were put in their place.

"Seems like an appropriate way to settle the debt," I remarked coldly, reminding him what his family cost me.

"Even if I told her to marry you, she'd never do it. Not unless she wanted to."

I watched him with indifference while my chest twisted. I believed him that much. I could ask Tatiana for her hand, but the minx would refuse me. She wasn't ready to put my ring on her finger, but we were running out of time. The Yakuza were closing in. Sofia Volkov was up to something. Too many enemies knew that chip was connected to Tatiana somehow.

Tatiana was a force. I'd wager she had to be to grow up with two older brothers or she'd never be heard. Unfortunately for her, she was my vice. She had been since that night I touched her in that fucking gazebo. I'd like to think that if I knew the impact she'd have on me, I would have been smarter, but it'd be a lie.

The moment I spotted her, the Queen had put the King in the position that couldn't avoid capture. Checkmate. She won and she didn't even know it.

"I can be convincing." There was always the method his own brother resorted to - kidnapping.

"Pick the territory you want," Vasili retorted dryly. "You already started making yourself home in New Orleans. You want the city?"

I could get a lot out of Nikolaev for killing my brother. New Orleans. Louisiana. Ports. Luckily for him, I only wanted his sister. I had wanted it for so long, there'd be nothing that he could offer that would convince me to give her up.

And if he tried to keep her from me, I'd resort to war.

"No."

His gaze narrowed. A single word, but it told him everything. We stared at each other as animosity slithered through my veins.

I got up, buttoned my jacket, and turned to leave.

"If you can convince her to marry you and she does it willingly, I'll support it," he said. "I'll talk to her, but I won't force her to marry you."

I opened the door then replied, "I'm certain Tatiana will see things my way."

"And you'll keep her protected?" he asked. Vasili took care of Tatiana like she was his kid. Kind of like I had taken care of my own sister. "Adrian put her in danger. I don't want that repeated."

A sardonic breath left me. "Rest assured, I'll keep her protected."

After all, I'd been doing it for almost a year now.

When we left Vasili's office, I found Tatiana speaking to two men. Her smile was relaxed, but it was her body that betrayed her. She was tense and her eyes darted to her eldest brother, searching for answers.

I knew she'd fight an arranged marriage. I didn't need her brother's warning to know it.

Her laugh rang through the room, and I fantasized about killing the fuckers who dared to hear her laugh. Those should be reserved for me and only for me.

At the dining table, she attempted to find a different spot, but before she could seat herself, I took her arm and smiled.

"It's assigned seating," I said, unable to keep smugness from my voice.

Rolling her eyes, she followed reluctantly. "Considering this is my brother's home, I can sit wherever I'd like. Even in the kitchen."

"That's a great idea," I agreed. "Just you and me, eating in the kitchen. I love it. Shall we?"

She let out a frustrated breath. "Not with you," she hissed, taking a seat. "You'll spoil my appetite here or in the kitchen, so I might as well make my brother happy."

"Marry me if you want to make him happy."

Her head whirled around, her eyes flashing like pale blue sapphires.

"I will *never* marry you, Illias Konstantin," she warned, her voice low. *We shall see about that,* I thought silently.

"Why not?" It didn't matter what her answer was, she'd marry me. Willingly or not. She'd come around eventually. She knew we were good together and once I could trust her, I'd explain that video. I'd wager she'd understand why I did what I did - considering her own brother saved her from her own mother.

"Because I'm busy for the foreseeable future," she retorted dryly.

"Then get unbusy because we are getting married."

She shrugged her slim shoulders. "Sorry, can't do it." She leaned closer as she reached for the glass of water, then brought it to her lips. "I don't marry killers of innocents." Narrowing her eyes on me, she added, "Besides you should look up the definition of 'hookup,' Konstantin. It's just sex."

Taking her glass from her slim, graceful fingers, I leaned over and whispered in her ear.

"You're mine, Tatiana. Your tits, your ass, your pussy, your soul, your heart. It was never just sex."

I llias' hot breath against my skin and his vehement claim sent a shiver down my spine.

I schooled my features, aware that Vasili was watching us. I should have known messing around with Illias would come back to bite me in the butt at the end. Only fools played with men in our world.

It seemed I was one of those fools.

I focused on the waiters that quickly approached with food. As it was served, the scent of it drifted through the air. Seafood and chicken. My favorite. Except something smelled off with this food. Maybe it was bad. Rotten. I wrinkled my nose. Saliva gathered in my mouth and I swallowed. My body temperature heated, making my nausea worse. It was a hot flash, coming like a storm surge.

"What's the matter?" Illias must have picked up on my discomfort.

I stood up abruptly and headed towards the bathroom. The world spun and my nausea worsened. I clutched my stomach from the force of it. I had no idea how or when Illias found himself by my side, grabbing me by the arm.

"Tatiana, what's the matter?"

"I'm going to puke," I gritted, rushing towards the nearest bathroom but my legs weren't fast enough.

Illias scooped me up in his arms and hurried to the bathroom, then helped me lower myself, just in time. Violent heaves rocked my body as I wretched and emptied everything I had eaten today into the toilet.

Strong hands stroked my back in soothing circles as disgusting sounds left my mouth.

"What's the matter?" Vasili's voice came from behind me just as another round of violent heaves wracked my body.

"She needs a doctor," Illias said with utter calm, crouching by my side and never ceased stroking my back. Like it was normal for the Pakhan to sit on the tiled floor next to a woman throwing up her guts.

Kneeling over the toilet, I wiped my mouth with the back of my hand.

"Don't need a doctor," I muttered firmly, suspicion booming in my chest. "I just ate something bad, that's all."

"You haven't even started eating," Illias remarked. The way he watched me had a flicker of panic bloom in my chest. Like he had already known that I was pregnant and decided what he'd do to me.

I ignored the nudging feeling and got to my unsteady feet, then headed to the sink, while two sets of eyes watched me. I rinsed out my mouth and then slowly turned around.

Ignoring Konstantin's dark eyes on me, I locked gazes with Vasili. "Brother, do you mind if I skip dinner? Just in case I caught something."

Like a baby.

No, I couldn't jump to conclusions. No to hoping. No to dreams. It made reality too great to handle.

It could be something I ate. This morning. Or maybe a stomach bug. I chewed my lip waiting for his answer but Vasili remained quiet, watching me.

"Umm... I held Marietta earlier. Keep an eye on her in case she catches it." This should convince him that I was truly worried about this stomach bug. My niece could never catch a case of pregnancy. So yeah, I was a master schemer here.

I shifted my weight from one foot to the other nervously, scared my brother or even worse, Konstantin, would read my suspicion on my face.

The door swung open and Isabella came in. "Are you okay?"

Her gaze flickered over Illias and there was a strange look in her eyes. As if she came to a revelation that she wasn't certain she liked.

My tongue darted, sweeping across my bottom lip.

"Yes, a bug or something," I said, keeping my voice even while my heart raced with possibilities. *Hope.* Hope was for fools, yet it was impossible to extinguish it.

"Let me check you out," she offered, then her eyes turned to the men.

Vasili stiffened, the words I had uttered to him all those months ago still hanging between us. They were bitter and wrong. I should have never told him I hated seeing what he had, his happiness. Jealousy was an ugly thing and my brothers more than deserved their happily-ever-after.

Vasili didn't know how many times I'd regretted those words; how I wished I'd never uttered them.

"That would be great. Thanks, Bella."

The air shifted and relaxed. Vasili's eyes softened, an understanding passing through them. For all these months, an uneasiness lingered between us. It wasn't until this very moment that those bitter words I had spoken to him before he took me to the hospital to get stitches rather than my best friend eased the pain I caused him.

"I got her," Isabella assured him with a smile. "You two better go back to dinner."

Vasili lowered his tall frame and kissed her cheek. "Thank you, malyshka."

And all the while, Illias watched me with an unsettling conviction in his eyes, while my heart raged war inside my chest. But shadows lurked in his eyes and in my mind. Somewhere deep in my soul.

He knows.

The knowledgeable glint in Illias' dark gaze told me he must have come to the same conclusion I had.

"I'd like to be present," he declared, confirming my suspicion.

"I don't think so," I hissed. "You're a mere stranger."

I glared at Illias, who stood just as tall next to my brother, like a dark angel. His face was a mask of utter calm, not a single emotion on his face. But it was his eyes that betrayed him.

They weren't quite as cold. Or dark. The look grabbed hold and hung on, promising more long nights, rough hands and sweaty bodies between his black satin sheets.

"Tatiana, is there something you want to tell me?" Vasili's voice was quiet, but I knew it well. It was the voice he used when I'd done something to jeopardize the family. It rarely happened, but it took only one time for me to learn that tone.

"No." We both knew I was lying, but I held his gaze. "You and your guest return to your dinner." My eyes flickered to Illias, then back to my brother. "Please," I rasped, pleading with him silently.

My eyes must have conveyed my desperation, possibly my suspicions that he was right and I was indeed pregnant, because his gaze burned.

The irony of life didn't escape me.

Twelve months ago I prayed for a little miracle. And now, I was worried what a little miracle would mean for my future.

FORTY-FIVE
TATIANA

"**Y**ou're pregnant."

I stared at the ultrasound monitor, watching the small dot in amazement. The words that I craved to hear for so long. Yet, now it brought anxiety. Shock mixed with another feeling I hadn't felt in such a long time. *Happiness.*

My hand reached to the monitor where the dot moved around, my fingers tracing it.

"A baby." A hoarse whisper.

Something inside me shifted. Or reset. Things inside my soul have been shredded to pieces with Adrian's death, but slowly pieces started to come together. Until now.

This revelation clicked it all into place.

Isabella printed out the ultrasound pictures and handed them to me, her eyes watching me with worry. I took them with trembling fingers.

Putting one hand on my belly, over the cool liquid that Isabella put on there prior to the ultrasound.

"Is everything okay with the baby?"

Isabella smiled, checking the information. "Yes. We'll have to draw blood but so far everything looks right. You're between five and six weeks."

"Six," I muttered.

Isabella's eyes snapped to mine with surprise. God, he must have knocked me up right after his brother's funeral. I couldn't decide whether that was morbid or inspirational.

One life ended; another started.

"Please don't say anything to Vasili," I croaked, meeting her soft brown eyes. We have been through so much. Our college years. Her heartbreak. Mine. Our fucked up family history. "Not yet."

Isabella gave me a curt nod. "You kept my secrets," she murmured softly. "This is the least I could do. Besides, doctor-patient confidentiality forbids me from sharing anyhow, so I'm safe from Vasili and so are you."

Taking her hand into mine, I squeezed it tightly. "You don't owe me anything," I rasped. "We were friends first, then more. Family."

Isabella smiled, then hugged me. "Nikola and Marietta love you. You will be a wonderful mother. God I can already see it. Nikola will be protective of his cousin. He'll drive us nuts."

"He will," I mused. "He'll drive his sister and younger cousins crazy even more."

She helped me off the table and then handed me a change of clothes. A pair of jeans and a loose pink Valentino blouse with sheer sleeves.

"This doesn't look like your style," I commented as I put it on.

She chuckled. "It's not. It's yours. One of those deliveries that came here while you were in Russia with–"

With Adrian. When we eloped.

Rather than commenting on it, I switched subjects. "Any chance it came with matching shoes?"

Isabella shook her head, laughing. "As a matter of fact, they did. They are in your old room."

"Thank you, Bella. You better go back to Vasili. I'm going to grab those shoes and go back home."

Once Isabella left, I headed for my old room. My heart tripped as I marched down the hallway, then opened the door. Everything was still just the way it was when I left for college.

The bed was the same, the king size canopy with all the white ruffled sheets. Pink plush rug at my feet. White dresser and nightstand. The box with my pink shoes sat at the foot of the bed, like I had only stayed here last week when in fact it had been a long time.

I sank onto the bed, still gripping the ultrasound pictures. Black and white, showing the new life we created.

It wasn't how I imagined creating a life.

The tightness spread from my throat to my chest. Marriage to Illias was out of the question. Not after that video I witnessed. Frustration welled through my veins. I had nobody to blame but myself for my current predicament.

I was thrilled about the baby. The baby's father… not so much.

Slipping my feet into the shoes, I headed out of the room and down the stairs. Music and the clinking of silverware echoed through the luxury hallway. I headed to the nearest exit, hoping to find Yan by the car. Vasili would surely tell him to be ready.

My feet came to a halt at a voice calling my name. I realized too late whose voice it was. I was just about to resume walking when he called me again. I stopped, then slowly turned around to come face-to-face with my baby daddy.

Jesus Christ.

"Leaving without saying goodbye again?" he taunted.

My spine snapped upright, and I glared at him.

"Any more murders of innocent women or children you want to share?" I snapped back.

His eyes flashed with a terrifying darkness and his jaw clenched.

"You could have asked for an explanation," he said in a low tone. I was about to keep walking when he wrapped his fingers around my wrist. He pinned me in place with his eyes darkening like storms in the night. "You're pregnant with my child."

The words left him with such ease, as if finding out a mere stranger to him was pregnant with his child was an everyday occurrence. Maybe it was. God, what did I get myself into?

Konstantin and madness went hand in hand.

"What do you want, Konstantin?"

"You."

I gulped, a strange feeling twisted in my chest. It bled into my veins and spread. And all the while an awareness tickled the back of my mind.

"I already told you, we were temporary." He didn't respond, just stared me down. Probably trying to intimidate me. "I-I was honest from the start."

"We're getting married."

"For the hundredth time, no."

His eyes darkened with a warning. "You're pregnant with *my* child."

"You're assuming. It's a stomach bug." *Sort of.*

His calm façade cracked, anger and callousness in his eyes. For the first time since I'd met him, menace crossed Konstantin's expression. It was more terrifying than anything I had ever experienced. Was this the man that executed a woman on her knees? Were those his true colors?

His jaw clenched and he took a step forward, towering over me. "I let you go once so I could protect you," he said roughly. I frowned, wondering what he meant. "I never forgot you." His voice grew harder with each word. "But you, Tatiana, you forgot me."

Was he talking about the fucking restaurant? We met for a fleeting moment only. I didn't have patience for this bullshit today.

"I have no fucking clue what you're talking about," I hissed as I turned to leave.

"My child will *not* be born outside of wedlock." Illias took my hand into his and squeezed it. "Do you fucking understand me?"

"You're a monster," I breathed out. "A killer."

"And what do you think your family is?"

I jerked my hand out of his grip.

"My brothers don't execute women on their knees, Illias. They are a different kind of monster. It's your kind that I won't tolerate."

My breathing shallowed. My heart raced. My ears buzzed.

"Push me, moya luna, and I'll snuff out that pretty blue inferno in your eyes," he said in a calm tone.

"Shall I get on my knees now so you can put a gun to my head and pull the trigger? It'll save you time," I answered just as calmly while my heart raced in my chest, hammering against my ribs.

Something in his gaze flashed, almost as if the thought excited him. "Oh, Tatiana. I'll have you on your knees. But you'll enjoy every minute of it." Then he left me, staring after him and with his warning ringing in my ears. I knew full well this wasn't the end.

Only the beginning.

WHAT'S NEXT?

*Thank you so much for reading **Thorns of Lust**! If you liked it, please leave a review. Your support means the world to me.*

*If you're thirsty for more discussions with other readers of the series, you can join the Facebook group, Eva's Soulmates group (*https://bit.ly/3gHEe0e*).*

If you're looking for what to read next, jump into Thorns of Love (https://amzn.to/3Jf52We), the epic conclusion of Tatiana & Illias' story.

ABOUT THE AUTHOR

Curious about Eva's other books? You can check them out here. Eva Winners' Books https://bit.ly/3SMMsrN

Eva Winners writes anything and everything romance, from enemies to lovers to books with all the feels. Her heroes are sometimes villains because they need love too. Right? Her books are sprinkled with a touch of suspense, mystery, a healthy dose of angst, a hint of violence and darkness, and lots of steamy passion.

When she's not working and writing, she spends her days either in Croatia or Maryland daydreaming about the next story.

Find Eva below:
Visit www.evawinners.com and subscribe to my newsletter.
FB group: https://bit.ly/3gHEe0e
FB page: https://bit.ly/30DzP8Q
Insta: http://Instagram.com/evawinners
BookBub: https://www.bookbub.com/authors/eva-winners
Amazon: http://amazon.com/author/evawinners
Goodreads: http://goodreads.com/evawinners
Tiktok: https://vm.tiktok.com/ZMeETK7pq/

Printed in Great Britain
by Amazon

29909549R00216